Acknowledgements

My special thanks go to my editor, Louise Moore, whose support and patience during this book's long gestation were beyond the call of duty. I owe similar debts to my agents, the inestimable Mark Lucas and Nicki Kennedy.

I was also lucky enough to receive advice or help from many others and I thank them all for their generosity. They include Tom Lourie, Cheryl Everett, Lucinda Pilbrow, Annie Lee, Felicity Cave, Hugh Miller, Juozas A. Kazlas, Carl Swanson, Annick Deslandes, Sally Osmond, David Miller, Helen Meeson, Philip Meeson, Caroline Simpson, Alison Wheatcroft and Stephen Wheatcroft.

I

My mother told my sister and me this story many times. How it took days for the train to cross Russia and how, by the time they reached the border, it was clear that the baby was dead.

The father had known for some time. His three daughters, one by one, understood. The other passengers told each other with silent, shocked looks. Only the mother seemed incapable of comprehending what had happened to the child locked into her arms.

From the moment they boarded the train it cried. Not the babbling, gasping repetition of a newborn but the full, insistent cry of a six-month-old. When the Andreyev family arrived with their extensive baggage, their surly father and their screaming baby, everyone already in the car checked their tickets, hoping that they were in the wrong seats. When they found that they were indeed destined to travel west with the Andreyevs, they told themselves that the baby would soon stop crying and, anyway, the three girls took up little space. Each car was oversubscribed and each passenger wore a thick coat, hat, scarf and gloves. And the baggage! Bags, boxes, baskets, suitcases, piled high over the heads of the travellers, on the floor, on laps.

When, far later than expected and after an alarming series of shudders, the train finally pulled out of the station, the other passengers confidently awaited the silence that must come as soon as the child felt the lulling rhythm of great metal wheels on great metal rails.

But the silence did not come.

The train cut its way out of the city in a straight line like mighty scissors, past factories and apartment blocks and squares of snow and mud where children played. The passengers sat unhappily listening to the endless circle of cries. Those tiny gaps of silence when the baby drew breath were all too slender and each was followed by a roar of such misery that it seemed the child was voicing the sadness and regrets of everyone present. In other cars, passengers tried to lift their mood by introducing themselves, sharing bread and occasionally pork-fat, producing bottles, telling stories. But in the Andreyev car all relationships were stunted by the baby's screams.

As Moscow retreated behind the train the travellers were at first glad to see the countryside. It was good to peer, through the human bulk, the baggage and the dirt which obscured the window, at the snowy landscape. They soon tired of it. Mile upon mile – and for the travellers that meant hour upon hour – of dark pine forest, hour upon hour of flat land, unbroken by trees or roads or hedges, any variation in its colour or crop or camber obscured by the cover of snow. When forests came they were disappointing, dark slabs of uniform conifers. It was like travelling through a giant black and white jigsaw. And still, as night gathered outside the train and wrapped itself around the massive, endless expanse of snow that is Russia, the baby cried.

'Can't you stop it, for God's sake?' someone yelled at last. The speaker was a man, young, with cold blue eyes and red cheeks. But his exasperation was masked by the baby's yells and all the mother could do was shrug and shake her head.

The father ignored the child and his wife but sat still, thin-faced, hard-mouthed, his eyes busily running over the faces of the passengers in a way that suggested a certain professionalism. Four, yes four children, and the family well-dressed too, with each of the girls carrying a small leather travelling-case on her lap. It was clear to all that Andreyev had done well. His menacing air of officialdom prevented many a protest at the baby's cries.

After the first few hours the train stopped. There was no station, no light, no apparent reason. Some of the train's own staff, perhaps including the driver, were seen standing down by the rails smoking and a few brave passengers jumped out of the train and then a few more. The Andreyev car was soon empty except for the mother, the three girls and the shrieking baby.

Only when the first pearly light fell on the grey faces of the travellers did the train shudder into motion. And still the baby cried.

But then, hours after everyone had given up any hope that the noise would stop, ever, the gaps between the baby's cries grew gradually longer and the angry edge to the child's roars began to disintegrate. Passengers exchanged hopeful looks. Several prayed. They peered at the scarlet-faced bundle in the mother's arms. It was scarcely whimpering now. The monster seemed to be shrinking before them. The baby was falling asleep.

When at last silence fell, satisfaction stole around each passenger as though some special gas had seeped under the door. Everyone, except the mother, who still held her baby, fell asleep. Some slept a long time. The cramped conditions brought others this relief only in snatches. From time to time those who were awake glanced at the baby and a suspicion gradually became a conviction. It was white now, very white. And no matter for how long people watched it, they detected no movement at all. The baby was dead. The three girls watched horror register on the faces of the passengers. No one spoke of it, no one spoke at all. The woman continued to cradle the unmoving bundle in her arms, holding it to her as though to warm it.

As soon as he opened the door of the Andreyev car, the guard detected that something was wrong. It was too silent for a start. Then the way everyone looked up at him was wrong too. They seemed to be waiting for him to notice something. Only one person did not watch him, a tired woman with a sleeping baby.

He looked at the woman and at the bundle lying across her lap. He reached out to the child's small, white face. Cold. Colder than metal, colder than stone, cold as the grave. He lifted the baby's hand and tried to bend the fingers but they would not move. The baby had been dead for hours, more than a few.

The guard said: 'You will have to give the baby to me. It is dead and can travel no further.'

'No!' cried the mother. 'No, no, he's asleep.'

The woman was sobbing now.

'No! No!'

The father stood up suddenly.

'Give him to me,' he ordered, and the woman allowed the stiff bundle to be removed at once from her arms. Watched by the large eyes of his three daughters, he handed the baby to the waiting guard who took it gingerly.

The woman clutched at the guard's shabby uniform. 'Please, please, please, promise me that my child will be given a proper burial!'

The man looked at her. He could give no such assurance, indeed, he was even now wondering how to dispose of this unwanted, inanimate baby in as swift and trouble-free a manner as he could and the possibilities did not include hours of pickaxing at the frozen ground.

He left the car carrying the baby and was heard descending from the train. The mother cried silently and ceaselessly for the rest of the journey.

My mother knew this story well because she was the youngest of the three daughters on the train and the sobbing woman was my grandmother. It was a story I heard all through my childhood but when, in my teens, my mother moved into a clinic for the mentally ill, it slid from my mind along with her other stories like a shoal of small fish sliding through a crack in the rocks. Only when I gave birth to a son myself did the fish dart back again, flashing silver at me when, almost elastic with love, I held my baby in my arms. When he died and was taken away by a thickset woman in dark clothes that might have been a uniform, I sat in our house in California and it seemed that the woman who had sobbed in the train in the snow in eastern Europe more than sixty years ago was me and I was her.

2

It's a spring day, cold, but each time I cross a street the sun appears at the end of it like some advertising gimmick which glimmers from every billboard. I cut through the park. I watch the babies sitting inside their buggies, their bodies passive, their faces uninhabited like people on the subway. It's a full three years since I held a baby. It's almost exactly three years.

Click, clack. Click, clack. My new shoes on the sidewalk, scraping a little against my heel. Occasionally, when there's one of those strange gaps in the noise of Manhattan, when there are no sirens and the traffic hushes unexpectedly, it seems to me that my left foot hits the pavement harder than my right. I try to balance my weight but your walk's like your mother or some other relative you didn't choose and can't change. Click, clack.

The lobby of our building embraces you. It is a towering, glassy atrium and the bushes grow here as though in some hot, outdoor place. Some of them are like the trees my father grows in his yard back in California, only here their shape is more perfect, their flowers bigger, brighter, sweeter smelling. The elevator doors close and there is that light-headed feeling as it ascends. When Daddy stayed with me in New York, just that once, I brought him into the office on a Saturday morning. It was before the atrium, when we had the dark lobby with the wine red carpet. It must have been more than two years ago. As soon as the elevator started to catapult us up the building, Daddy was so shocked by its suddenness and power that he staggered backwards. I reached out to steady him but by then he had turned his face into the caricature of a grimace and pinned his body to the wall in a comic shape of mock-horror. I smiled, maybe a little relieved. We don't acknowledge Daddy's age and if he shows signs of frailty we ignore them. He isn't allowed to grow old or get ill.

I move fast along the hallway, checking for that click clack but the rug's too thick here.

'Hi.' 'Hi.' 'Hi.'

I'm usually first in but today there are a couple of other heads bobbing around the screens in our office. They register my presence with a deference which acknowledges that it's a big deal day and the deal's mine. It's only three months since Gregory Hifeld appeared at my desk fingering the lapels on a suit which was made of some fabric so solid, from Scotland probably, or Ireland, that he might have worn it for the last forty years without it creasing or fraying. He told me about his son. George has three divorces, a drink problem and no known business sense. A man unlikely to take over Thinking Toys from his father, not now or ever.

'You're sixty-eight, that's not so old. And you look strong and fit to me,' I told Gregory. Not so strong and fit as Daddy but then, nobody is. 'Why do you need to do anything about the business right now?'

He bowed his head and for a moment I thought he was going to cry. I looked away. 'I'm tired and my wife is ill. We'd like to enjoy the time we have left together.'

Soon, there was George Hifeld sitting across my desk right where his father had sat, yellow fingers and the tremor of a guy who needs a cigarette but thinks it might start all the fire alarms and a panic on eighty-three storeys. And finally, Mittex. Keen to buy Thinking Toys but trying not to

7

show it. Dark suits, nodding white heads like vultures. Their CEO-in-waiting, Jay Kent, asking questions, slicing through figures and long-range projections as professional and precise as a chef slicing onions. Today, they'll all sit at the boardroom table together for the first time and maybe, just maybe, by the end of the day, we'll know whether Mittex will buy Thinking Toys.

When the boss arrives, I have my fingers wrapped around my second cup of coffee. The cups are paper but they feel sort of good to touch, soft, like petting a dog.

Jim Finnigan is bald. He's obese. When I first started working here he was just fat but he takes the train in and a guy sells hot cinnamon buns, dripping with butter, right there at the station. Jim has three every morning. He tells his wife, June, that he only has one. He feels badly about lying to her and telling the truth to me but in our job, with its long hours in a room high in the sky, your family back home can seem sort of unreal. So if you're going to lie to someone it's going to be them. We're mostly truthful with each other.

'Jeez,' says Jim, pulling up a chair and putting his feet on my desk. 'Jeez, you're going to have a tough time in the boardroom this afternoon. I was thinking about it at the station and I had to have an extra cinnamon.'

The total has been creeping up over the years.

'The first time you ate four?' I ask.

He shuffles his feet on my desktop.

'Well . . . actually five.'

'Ji-im. You've been eating four every day?'

He nods miserably.

'Only for a month or two. Or three.'

He's sheepish. He's really apologizing to June.

'It started when I was so damn cold one morning and the train was late . . . the guy gets them ready as soon as he sees

8

me coming. And he says: "Delay today, sir, take another cinnamon bun to keep you from losing too much heat." And I let him put another one in a napkin for me. I mean, for Chrissake, to keep me from losing too much heat, for Chrissake. But I stand and watch while he does it. Then I pay him, then I take it. Oh, and then I eat it.'

'Oh, Jim.'

'Don't let me eat anything more today. Nothing. Okay? Nothing.'

'Okay.'

'And don't tell June.'

'Of course not.'

Jim looks at me twinkly-eyed. He says: 'So how you planning to handle Kent up in the boardroom?'

'He isn't my client, Jim. The Hifelds are my clients.'

'Precisely. So how are you going to handle Kent?'

Jay Kent, not tall but with the slimness and quickness of some metallic weapon.

'He wants you, Lucy,' says Jim and his words make me start a little because they're just the words Jay Kent used, sitting straight-backed in the Michigan restaurant.

Jim lifts his immense, ankleless legs off the desk, an operation which requires two hands, and manoeuvres his feet carefully into their favourite place on the garbage bin.

'Has anything happened between you two?' he asks. I can hear the exertion in his voice. 'And don't you try foolin' Uncle Jim.'

'Of course not.'

'Nothing?' asks Jim, searching my face.

'Nothing physical, is that what you mean?'

Jim pulls his face in two different directions at the same time so it looks like a face in a distorting mirror. 'Lucy, you know what I mean.'

'We talk a lot. On the phone.'

'Like, pillow talk without the pillows?'

'Friend talk.' Mostly Kent talks and I listen. He doesn't know a lot about me and I like that.

Jim studies me for signs of insincerity then he says: 'June thinks . . .' June, a dark bulk misshapen by clinging children, leaves romantic novels damp at the bathside and is reliably tearful when TV comedies dissolve into syrup. 'June thinks you only get yourself into relationships where you can't have a real relationship, for example with a guy like Kent who's married and has a small kid.'

I imagine Kent's kid, a wriggling blade of a baby, surrounded by plastic, blaring Mittex toys.

'The kind of relationship I have with Kent is limited for professional reasons.' I sound brisk because I wish June would stop talking like the studio audience in an afternoon show.

Jim doesn't seem to hear me. As he gets up he asks: 'What did you do this weekend?'

'Oh, just visited friends.'

'Uh huh. Why aren't you wearing any shoes?'

'They're right under my desk, Jim. They're new and they hurt a little.'

'Uh huh.' He shambles off and there's something dissatisfied in the hunch of his shoulders. When he turns he looks as though he's going to say something which hurts but he says: 'Lucy, I'm hungry. I want you to know I'm hungry but I'm not eating anything.'

My sister calls. It's not seven o'clock yet in California. She's due to leave for the hospital any minute and she sounds clinical, hurried.

'We've been trying to get you all weekend, Luce.'

'I was away . . .'

'Good! I hope you were having a good time somewhere and not moping about.'

'I moped a bit.'

Her voice softens suddenly. 'Oh, Luce, are you okay?'

'Yeah.'

'I took Daddy up to Stevie's grave. We left some flowers from Daddy's yard, spring flowers.'

'Thanks, Jane.'

It should have been me driving Daddy up to the children's section of the big cemetery. Supporting him as we walked to the place which marks Stevie's brief sojourn in this world. That's how I like to think of my son: someone who stayed a short while and then moved on.

'It doesn't seem like three years,' she says. 'Sometimes it seems like yesterday.'

If I let myself think about it, Stevie's death seems like now to me. That moment when I found my son's body lying white and motionless in his blue crib like something small floating on the surface of the ocean. That moment of simultaneous information and disbelief. That synthesis of the awful new reality and the reality which existed before. That hideous synthesis which can only be comprehended in stages, the first of which is shock. Most of all, I wish I could erase that moment but all I can do is turn away from it.

I say: 'I did call Daddy a few times on the weekend but I guess he was out. Is he okay?'

She hesitates. When she speaks her voice is kind. 'Of course he was low on Saturday, but who's going to be ecstatic visiting their grandson's grave? Afterwards we drove up to the beach house for lunch with Scott and we thought Scott seems a little better this year than he was last and Daddy was real pleased with that. Larry says you should use anniversaries to accept the alleviation in your grief. I mean, celebrate the fact that you're getting better, not feel guilty about it. Daddy agrees with him and I guess he should know.'

Daddy never talks about it directly, but he also lost a son. My brother. I don't even remember him. He died in some kind of accident when he was a small baby. When Stevie died Daddy still didn't talk about it but he understood. He knew, and he knew better than anyone.

'I hope . . .' Jane is cautious, so it's half a question, 'that there's been some alleviation in your grief.'

I don't want to talk about grief. I say: 'How's Daddy's hip?'

Lately there have been references to Daddy's hips, specifically the right hip. The references fall unguardedly and then are left rapidly behind like some piece of litter you didn't mean to drop but don't want to pick up.

That hesitation again, then Jane's voice, reassuring. 'I think it hurts sometimes but it doesn't seem to slow him down. For heaven's sake, Lucy, he's seventy-two and he's fitter than a lot of people half his age. As for his memory, well, we were remembering some field trip we took years ago and he said he could recall practically every rock we found.'

'Which field trip?' Each field trip is a discrete memory. There was always something which happened, something we found, someone we met. Only the rocks seemed the same.

Quietly, Jane says: 'Arizona.'

I remember that trip. I can feel its heat now. 'Arizona,' I echo.

I hear Jane's voice in my ear, treading carefully, speaking softly, anxious not to wake scorpions, disturb a snake. 'Daddy never says so, but I'm absolutely sure that what he'd really like . . .'

I wait.

'. . . well, he'd really like to see you, Luce. I know he was half looking forward to this weekend, although it's sad one, because he thought maybe you'd come home. He even said that he thought Mother might benefit from seeing you. Since I doubt she'd even recognize you, that may have been Daddy's way of saying he'd benefit from seeing you himself.'

'I have some big negotiations happening, Jane, I wouldn't want to leave town right now. But when it's all over, maybe I'll come.'

Jane takes my concession for confirmation. She says how pleased she is. I remind her: 'I only said maybe.'

3

In the early afternoon, when I've completed my preparations for the big meeting, I take my coat and go down on to the street. People are still eating in sidewalk cafés, standing up like horses. I go into a glassy diner and eat a bagel which has cream cheese bulging out of the edges.

Suddenly, I glimpse Daddy. He is peering at me through the window. In an instant I realize that the face belongs to a young woman who looks like Daddy and in another instant I understand that the sky outside has blackened and my own reflection is looking back at me. Dark hair, dark eyes, actually green but not in this strange snapshot, prominent bones. I never understood before now how people could say I resembled my father.

'Most beautiful women,' Jay Kent told me, 'have uninteresting faces. Your beauty is intriguing.' He was making a statement. His tone was dispassionate.

The coffee the diner serves is so strong and bitter that it makes my mouth curl just the way Kent's mouth curled that cold morning in Michigan. Day two of the Mittex trip to Thinking Toys in Michigan and it was still snowing. Jay Kent stood on the edge of the parking lot on the edge of the pine forest sniffing. He was cold but that wasn't why he was sniffing. The workers were arriving in their cars. Cheerful workers, their voices ringing in the frosty air as they greeted one another across the parking lot. Most were overweight, some were obese, but they had an unmistakable aura of rural contentment as they waddled in for their shift. Half-curious

14

looks at the still, slick little group on the edge of the lot. If our presence caused disquiet they didn't show it.

'Santa's elves.' Kent's cheeks and eye sockets were hollow with cold. His eyes were blue glass. 'Santa's happy little elves, plodding into the grotto.' There was nothing affectionate in the way he said it.

'Not even a small part of you would want to live out here and be one of them?' I asked him. I thought everyone had a rural dream buried somewhere inside them. Kent pulled his lips back over his teeth. I didn't know if his lips were thin with cold or if they were always that thin.

Then, later, wrapped in wood and warmth at the restaurant, his lips full now, he said: 'Neither could you be one of those guys, don't kid yourself, Lucy.'

'Actually I used to be sort of like them, Kent.' No one calls him Jay. Except possibly his wife.

He raised his eyebrows at me. He's learned to keep his face and his body still in a way which makes small gestures significant and movement threatening.

I said: 'When I worked in private banking in California I used to plod across the parking lot into work just like one of Santa's elves.'

'Private banking? In California?' The lips turned down.

I was defensive. 'I had some very big clients, mostly Pacific Rim.'

'You were wasted there. I assume this is back when you first started out?'

No, it was right up until I moved to New York, devastating my husband, disappointing my family, upsetting my father. It was just three years ago. But I wasn't going to tell Kent that. He watched me, waiting for my reply. I studied the menu. Finally I said: 'Well, it all sounds like roadkill to me.'

That's when he straightened his back and said: 'I want you, Lucy. I don't know what to do about it.'

I knew I should look at him. It took a moment and when I did his eyes were waiting for me, gunmetal blue now, invulnerable despite his words.

I hoped he meant that, when the old CEO retired from Mittex and Kent was steering the company, he wanted me to be his investment banker. Jim's been hoping that from the beginning. Thinking Toys–Mittex is a good deal but if Mittex are so impressed that they trade their bulge bracket bankers for us then it's a very big deal. So when Kent said he wanted me it was possible he meant professionally and that's how I chose to interpret his words. Slowly at first, then fast, very fast, I gave him my own analysis of the toy market and where Mittex might consider leading it and he listened to me without moving at all except possibly his eyebrows.

Jay Kent's body still did not move while he explained that his interest in me was not restricted to his company's possible acquisition of my client or even my analysis of the toy market.

Before I answered I tried to be as still as he was but I must have moved my head, maybe shaken it, because I felt my hair banging softly against my cheeks. I watched my fingers trace the grain of the wooden table.

I said: 'We have to respect professional boundaries. We're working across the table from each other in some delicate negotiations.'

Fast, too fast to think, he said: 'You can have a professional boundary and a personal relationship at the same time. If that's what you both want.'

I looked down at his wedding ring and then involuntarily at my own. Occasionally I think of taking it off but something stops me, perhaps the thought of Scott still wearing his. I said: 'Maybe.'

As I leave the diner, glancing conspiratorially at the woman in the window, I wonder how it will be today, negotiating with a man who knows me the way Kent does.

On the way home to the office I pass by the flower shop. I stop, go back and send June Finnigan flowers – spring flowers, mostly tulips but some spiky irises too. I sign the card from Jim.

Back at my desk on the eighty-third floor, I finger my heel. There's the sponginess of a blister there now. I look out of the window but I cannot see the ground and, because the glass is tinted, I can only sense the presence of the sun outside. Swinging around in the Manhattan sky at an impossible altitude, the temperature monitored and the air controlled, we barely perceive the weather. We experience the world as reptiles. We have thick skins and primitive nervous systems.

Gregory and George Hifeld arrive with briefcases and toys. They wait in our office, father and son, side by side. People come over to shake hands and pick up the toys. Gregory explains them stiffly. I sniff George's breath for liquor as we talk about airplanes, George's passion. He has two antique airplanes and a landing strip outside his father's house.

'These divorces,' he says, 'they're going to cost me the goddam Stearman.' He chews the end of one of his fingers. 'Maybe the Mustang too.'

'You can smoke on the stairs. I mean, you're not supposed to but there aren't many smoke detectors and people do,' I say. He looks grateful and then glances at his father for permission. He's forty-two.

When Fatima announces that Mittex are in the boardroom, we get in the elevator. No one looks at anyone else. I wonder if I've done the right thing, keeping Jay Kent and the Hifelds apart and negotiations so loose until now. After all this work, everything could be over today when they hear the sound of each other's voices. I remember how, on the phone to my sister this morning, I almost agreed to go home for a while when these negotiations are over. I promise myself that this is a deal which is going to work and not founder today on personalities. And I only told Jane maybe.

As I walk into the boardroom I know that Kent has been waiting for me. He's talking to someone and he doesn't move but, barely perceptibly, when he hears my voice his back straightens. When he turns to greet me his eyes have a fullness, a shine, which shouldn't be there right now in this meeting. He looks at me a moment too long before he looks at the Hifelds. He wants you, Jim said.

I greet Kent's adviser from the big investment bank I'd like us to replace. There are colleagues, too, members of the team Kent's gathering around him for the day when he takes over from the old CEO at Mittex. I know from the late-night calls Kent makes when he's away from home, relaxed, intimate, slightly drunk, that he wants that day to come soon.

I introduce our analyst and the Hifelds. I see Gregory as Kent must see him. Correct. Tall. His back is erect but his face tired and his brown eyes sad. He doesn't want to be here, talking to young men who are fast and incomprehensible like technology, talking to them about selling his company. He's spent his life building it, supporting the community which depends on it, and, with George's help, he was supposed to grow old there. George sits next to him, smelling of nicotine, grinning too broadly, dishevelled despite the new suit.

When the meeting feels ready to start I am irritated to see the Hifelds with heads bowed submissively as though they're inviting Mittex to swallow up Thinking Toys together with their whole factory in one mouthful.

'So, George,' says Kent abruptly. I jump a little. George,

who has been leaning too close to the Mittex woman on his right, jumps too.

'Tell me, George. What can you do? What place could we find for you in the new Thinking Toys?'

George smiles. He brushes hair across his forehead and out of his eyes in a sweeping gesture he probably established in boyhood, only now there isn't any hair.

'Um, well, I don't want to run it,' he says unnecessarily. Kent smiles back at him but his eyes glitter and I know he's going to be merciless.

Gregory coughs. 'I probably should have given George more responsibility,' he says. 'Who knows what he could have done?'

We do. We all know.

George's eyes stare right ahead of him.

'Oh boy,' says Kent slowly. He's stroking his chin. 'Oh boy,' he says, 'I wonder, George, how you'll deal with the changes we have in mind for Thinking Toys . . .'

'Well,' proposes the bulge bracket banker. 'I'd like to suggest we take a look at some of those changes.'

Kent explains that Mittex think Hifeld productivity is too low and wages too high. That one thousand employees is too many employees, too many by one thousand. Gregory's face is frozen.

I clench both fists but feel the deal slipping irrevocably away from me.

Gregory looks at Kent. 'Your world,' he says, and his voice trembles a little, 'is plastic. Maybe you don't understand that high-quality wooden products are labour intensive. Our labour is second to none. Their loyalty, and the quality of their work.'

Kent gives Gregory a sudden smile but only for a moment, like a weapon which has caught a second's sunlight in the course of its deadly arc. 'Mr Hifeld, Gregory, I know the welfare of your workforce has been a priority for you and I admire the ingenious way you've been able to maintain the high-wages low-productivity situation in the woods back there with your value-added educational products. Make no mistake, I admire everything you've done. But at Mittex we don't have the same allegiances. We believe we can make your products to as high or higher a standard in the Far East. We see no reason to manufacture in Fullton, Michigan, for twice the price.'

'The Far East?' echoes Gregory. 'The Far East?'

'That's where most of our manufacturing facilities are located.' Swish, swish. Kent's a scimitar. 'We're concentrating resources in Malaysia right now.'

'The Far East . . .' Gregory Hifeld echoes. 'It would make your figures look good but the price in human terms would be incalculable for Fullton.' I know how much he must hate Kent. At this moment, I hate him too.

There is a knock on the boardroom door. An interruption. This wasn't supposed to happen and I assumed everyone knew that. The door opens and Fatima inches in. She looks thinner than usual. How can she have lost weight in just one hour? I realize it's the way she's moving. Her face, when she turns from an over-elaborate refastening of the door, is a caricature of her normal features. I give her a mean look and the whole room watches her in silence although she's trying to edge towards me as if no one's noticed. When she reaches me her face is red as she hands over a piece of paper. On it is Jim's big, sloppy writing.

'Emergency. Come now. Sorry. J.'

I stare at the paper. There is no emergency which is enough of an emergency to pull me out of this meeting. Anything could happen with me out of the room.

20

'Please, now, Lucy,' Fatima whispers. Everyone can hear her. She might as well have yelled it.

I look around. I don't mean to look at Kent but I do.

'Excuse me,' I say, turning to Gregory and back to Kent. 'Could we take a break for five minutes?' I make no attempt to hide my irritation. 'I can't imagine what this is about.'

From Fatima's face it's easy to see this is no negotiating ploy and Kent nods at me.

'Sure,' he says, 'we'll take a break.' The Hifelds nod, George too vigorously.

Everyone watches me leave, Kent most intently. I give an apologetic shrug as I edge out of the door.

In the hallway I look at Fatima for an explanation but she says: 'Can you go into Jim's office? Right now?'

'What's happening?'

She looks away from me. 'I don't know what it's about. Jim's waiting for you. Oh Lucy, I think it's bad news, I'm sorry, I'm so sorry.'

We walk to the elevator and go down nine floors and get out together and we don't speak. My mind doesn't even begin to examine the possibilities. There's a numbness where fear or panic should be. I don't think anything at all. I'm waiting. I'm a reptile.

4

Jim, behind his desk, his feet propped on the edge of the garbage can, is expressionless. When I walk in he struggles up, circumnavigates his desk and puts his arms around me. His immense sponginess makes me want to giggle, or maybe that's embarrassment. Jim and I have never been this close before. When he looks up I see to my amazement that he's crying.

'Jim?' I say.

'Sorry . . .' His voice is strangled. 'I'm crying because this shouldn't happen to you, Lucy.'

I still don't ask any questions. I like not knowing.

'You want to sit down?'

'No. I want to get back to the meeting.'

'Lucy, it's your father. He's dead.'

I am silent. I wait for some rush of pain or emotion but none comes. I feel nothing.

I say: 'But he can't be. Jane saw him on the weekend . . .'

'He's dead, Lucy.'

Stevie's small body, lifeless in his blue crib. The five of us standing around him, gaping in disbelief. Daddy, me, Scott, Larry and Jane. I am the first to reach for Stevie. I lift him from the crib and he feels heavier than usual, a dead weight. His face, apart from the tiny line of blood, is white and perfect. His eyes are closed. One hand has been raised a little, as if to ward off death, but as I lift him it rolls lifelessly downwards. Jane said: 'He's dead, Lucy.'

'The details . . .' says Jim. 'I don't know the details. But it's not straightforward. Your sister wants you on a plane as soon as possible. Lucy . . . as I understand it . . . it appears your father may have drowned. In the ocean.'

I look at Jim and I am brisk. I say: 'Are you sure about this?'

Jim says: 'The police need to interview you. You want to call your sister so she can explain?'

'No, Jim, not right now.'

'Fatima's already booked you on to a flight west. Seven p.m. You should get home and pack. You can't go alone —'

I hear a voice in the distance. Some woman dressed as me. She says: 'You're sure he's dead? Daddy's not just hurt, he's really dead?'

Jim's head seems to tumble downwards on to his chest like a ball that's been dropped. 'Aw Lucy. Lucy, he's dead. I'm real sorry.'

'I don't understand the hurry, Jim. If Daddy's dead then there's no point rushing.'

Jim moans a little. His face creases up until it's an unmade bed. 'It hasn't hit you yet. When it hits, it's going to hurt.'

'Okay, I'll fly tonight,' says the woman, 'but book me a much later flight. Or early in the morning. I want to see this deal through before I go.'

She starts to leave the office. She knows every face is turned in her direction. Each one of them is distorted. A lengthening or a deepening. Back in the elevator she is surprised by the ghost of a man, a big man but a man who is growing old, who is so shocked by the elevator's velocity that he staggers back against the walls.

'Daddy's dead,' the woman says as she walks down the hallway but the words don't mean anything and she doesn't break her stride.

The boardroom feels warm. Most people are standing. There's a residue of some desultory chatter. Our analyst is over by the window holding a boardroom coffee cup in one hand and the saucer in the other. The light out there is pale now and beyond him, floating eerily in the late afternoon sky, are the lights of other offices.

Silence when they realize the woman's back. People are quick to return to their seats. They stare at her and it's obvious they've all read the note.

'Is everything all right, Lucy?' asks Gregory. Kent is frozen to his chair.

'Well . . .' For the first time, she hesitates, this woman. Then she says: 'My father just died in unusual circumstances. I'll be flying out to California tonight, so I'd appreciate the concentration and cooperation of everyone in this meeting right now.'

'Don't tell me what you agreed,' says Jim when we're out on the night street looking for a cab to take us to my apartment. 'I don't want to know. You should not repeat not have been in there, you should have been talking to your sister on the telephone. She's distraught. She called three times and she would have called more if she hadn't just been leaving to break the news to your mother.'

'My sister's a doctor, she's never distraught.'

'Well, she's very worried about you. And your brother-in-law, Lennie, he phoned too.'

'Larry.'

'Larry. Larry phoned and he's distraught too.'

'He's a shrink, he's never distraught. Did Scott call too? I'll bet all three of them called, right?'

'Yes, Scott called and he sounds like a real nice sort of husband. Very concerned about you. Lucy, stop denying it. You want to know what happened out there on the ocean to your daddy, you really do.'

In the street lights I see a few flakes of snow are falling.

'I'll soon know. And once I know I can't unknow it.'

Jim is impatient. He waves his short arms at cabs which already have passengers. He stamps his feet when there is a pause in the traffic. Then the lights change and a line of cars bounds up like a fierce, too-big dog. A tow truck passes so close that it seems to breathe on me.

'Hey,' says Jim, taking my arm protectively. He gazes into my face. 'You scared of those big fellas?'

I nod. I'm scared of them but I say: 'You don't have to take me home, Jim.' Daddy's death still doesn't feel real. Right now it feels like a ploy to get me back to California, back to my past.

'I do too. You're flying from Newark and I can drive you over there.'

He's never been to my apartment before. When I unlock the door he lingers by it, blinking.

'I don't believe you're really this tidy,' he says. 'No one is. You must have been expecting company tonight, possibly Jay Kent.'

'Oh Jim, I never expect company and Kent's never been here.'

'Will you please call Jane with your flight details so she can meet you?'

'I don't want her to meet me.'

'Call Scott, then.'

'I'll be fine alone.'

'I'm not letting you get on a plane unless someone's meeting you off it. And don't try to argue, I'm your boss.'

I sigh.

'Who's it going to be?' he asks, handing me the phone. 'Jane or Scott?'

'I don't want to stay with either of them.'

'Just let them take care of you. Jane wants to do that, I can tell.' Jane has always taken care of me. She was my doctor long before she was anyone else's. When I was a kid I had the kind of ill-health which needed managing and it was my big sister who managed it. Less exercise. More exercise. Less excitement. More food. Less food. It's three years since anyone's cared about me as much as Jane and my throat tightens when I think about the way her long, swift fingers folded me a sling, examined my cuts, bathed my wounds. But I don't say that to Jim. I say: 'I've escaped from all that now, Jim.'

He looks upset. Jim loves his family. He only escapes from them during office hours.

'When did you last speak to your sister?' he asks.

'This morning and before that on her birthday. No, more recently. Maybe a few weeks ago. We call each other sometimes and it's very civilized but she just can't forgive me for going away and neither can Larry and neither can Scott.'

Jim swallows. 'They'll forgive you when you tell them you're coming home.'

I say: 'I'm calling Sasha.'

'Who's she?'

'He. Alexander.'

I search for Sasha's office number. Probably it's changed since I last spoke with him but I start dialling anyway. Jim takes the receiver from me.

'Hold it. Who is this guy?'

'My mother has four sisters and the nicest is Aunt Zina and Sasha's her son. He's almost exactly the same age as me. There are lots of cousins but he's my favourite. They live their Russian lives in the Russian quarter of town and it's just like Moscow only warmer.'

'What does he do, this Sasha?'

'Works for some big aid organization. I think it promotes indigenous culture. He more or less oversees the whole of Eastern Europe, right across eleven time zones.'

'You mean, like Stalin?'

'You'd get along with Sasha. He's a cinnamon bun kind of a guy.'

Jim looks at me suspiciously. 'Could he eat five?'

'I'll bet he could.'

'Disgusting. Sounds like a greedy pig.'

This time he lets me dial. Almost immediately, a thick Russian accent answers, without enthusiasm.

'Is Alexander there?'

'No,' says the woman. Her tone reveals that she is already bored with our conversation.

'When will he be back?'

'I don't know.'

'Is he in the office today?'

'He was here before.'

'Is he coming back?'

'Probably.'

The voice is young and I know its rudeness and indifference can be licensed only by its owner's beauty.

I ask: 'Are you Sasha's secretary?'

'I am Alexander Pavlevitch's personal assistant.'

I think of my mother, young, beautiful, Russian, working as personal assistant, no, secretary, to my father at the university. Did she answer Daddy's phone this way, hostile with indifference, her tone implying some intimacy of her own with the man to whom she obstructed access?

'Maybe,' I suggest, 'if I call in ten minutes?'

'If you want,' she says, hanging up.

Jim is ambling around looking at the pictures and the rugs.

'What are all these rocks, for God's sake?'

'They're Daddy's. He's a geologist and he's always giving people rocks.'

'I thought he was a professor or something.'

'A professor of geology.'

Jim strokes the rocks. 'They're sort of beautiful. If you like rocks.'

'I collected those stripy ones myself. I used to go with him on field trips.'

'Where did you get them?' Jim cups his palm around one of the striped rocks and rolls another in his fingers. The feel of the rocks, smooth but unyielding, pleases him. He passes one to me and it is warm and hard. I run the pads of my fingers over its stripes.

'Arizona.'

'So, how come they have this pattern all over? Did your dad ever explain that?'

Daddy explained everything, using his hands to illustrate whole geological eras, raising his eyebrows until they met his shock of black hair, humanizing the rocks he held up to us. I was so enraptured by his performances that I didn't listen to a word he said. Even in repose he had the kind of face you wanted to see in motion. Sharp-boned, his chin forceful, his nose large, he looked like a guy who had something to tell you. I slip the stone into my pocket.

'If he did, I've forgotten. I don't think those rocks impressed him too much.'

'Why don't you put the phone down, Lucy?' asks Jim. I'm still cradling it against my shoulder.

'It just told me there are messages.'

I already knew that. They piled up over the weekend, five of them. I assumed they were from my family, marking Stevie's anniversary, expressing concern, questioning my whereabouts. I didn't listen to them. And now, when I realize that one of the messages might be from Daddy I feel my stomach shrink inside itself like a sea anemone.

Jim's thinking the same thing. He says softly: 'You'd better retrieve them, kid.'

Two from Jane. One from Scott. And two from Daddy. The first, on Saturday morning, just registers his attempt to contact me. The second is different.

'Lucy, I've tried calling you already. Now it's Saturday night and this has been a hard day for you. I know that. If you're there and you're sad and you're just not answering the phone I want you to pick up right now.' His voice is so powerful, so demanding, that I will myself to pick up. After a moment's silence, Daddy is insistent. 'C'mon, Lucy! For me.' I think: Lucy, for God's sake, pick up the phone. As the silence grows longer my heart aches at my own absence, at my silence.

'Okay, then, I'll just say this.' He cradles the receiver in his large, veiny hands, holding it close to his face. His voice is big. My big, blustering Daddy. 'I know how much you're suffering. I know how much you've suffered. But don't lock up your grief like some scary wild beast. It's time to open the cage door and let it run right out, why, you might even find it turns into a little dog, a little dog you can pet. It will never go away but it won't be so fierce again. And now let's use this anniversary to take stock. You've been away almost three years, Lucy. I never argued with you for going. And I'm not arguing if you want to stay. You can even marry some unsuspecting fool in New York but, whether you do or not, just release Scott because he's a good guy and he's still waiting for you here. That's my advice. And, by the way . . .' A hesitation. A note, a small one, of vulnerability. 'Don't worry about me. I'll be all right.' His hip. His age. The possibility of failing health, the inevitability of his death.

All the things we don't allow and never talk about, it's as though he used a moment's silence to shout about them. I swallow.

Daddy's voice drops, or maybe he moves the receiver away from his face. 'I don't want you to be sad, Lucy. Please don't be too sad.' It seems the call's over. A long pause. And then his voice again, thick with emotion now: 'Take care of yourself, my little Lucy. Please take care.'

I save the message and play it again. It makes my body prickle all over, as though a cloud of small insects just landed on me.

'Are you okay?' asks Jim. He's watching me. He's not even pretending to examine rocks or look out of the window. 'Lucy?'

'I'm okay.'

He states: 'So, there's a message from your father.'

'Yes.'

'A nice one?'

I think for a moment. 'He intended it to be nice,' I say at last.

I save the message and play it once more. It's true that Daddy didn't argue with me for leaving. He was the only member of the family who didn't say he felt angry or hurt or betrayed by my departure for New York. He was the only one who didn't expect me back next week. And it's true Scott's still waiting for me. He still lives in the little beach house where the pine trees stop and the sand starts and when I think of Scott I think of his huge body sprawled across two chairs on the porch, cradling a cup of coffee, his eyes grey blue like troubled sky, scanning the ocean for me as though I'm going to arrive by boat.

'When did he leave it?' Jim asks sharply.

'Saturday. I didn't have time to listen to it before.'

I save the message again and then find a bag and open it on the bed. For a while we say nothing as I pack and Jim sits in the adjacent room. He starts to tell me about his own father's death. Jim's dad had the decency to do things the slow way. Weight loss, hand-holding, apologies, farewells. Sometimes Jim's voice breaks and I know he's crying.

While he weeps softly I dial Sasha's number again. I wait for the voice of the beautiful young woman who sounds the way Mother sounded an impossibly long time ago. A man answers.

'Planning and Development, Eastern European section.' The voice makes planning, development and the whole of Eastern Europe sound beyond tedium.

'Sashinka, is that you?'

At once his voice changes.

'Good God, who can be calling me Sashinka and speaking English to me at the same time?' When I do not immediately supply an answer he starts to guess my identity. 'Hmmm, let me think. Someone from far back, obviously . . .'

Sasha always liked games. He liked to win them. On rare occasions, many years ago, when we got together with large numbers of Mother's relatives, Daddy would take all the kids aside and attempt to impose American baseball on the Russian mind. The result was always shambolic but Sasha was guaranteed to rise from the mess pointing out that his team had most certainly won.

I say: 'Correct. Very far back.'

'But someone with an American accent of absolute purity. Curious. Because Americans have always called me Alex.'

'Not this one, Sashinka.'

'Ooooooooooh. Nu tak . . .' Sasha begins to mutter to himself in Russian. Although his English is, of course, perfect, his cadences are not wholly American and when he

31

lapses into Russian he does so with the ease and grace of a seal diving gratefully into the water.

'Aha. Aha. I have the answer. You're family but you're American. My American cousins, Jane and Lucy. You're Jane or Lucy, indeed, you are probably Lucy, no, certainly Lucy. Am I right, Lucia?'

'Yes, Sashinka, you're right.'

'How delightful. How very delightful to hear from you.'

'But I'm calling you because . . . I'm calling with bad news, Sasha.'

I am aware of Jim, motionless on the chair.

'Oh,' says Sasha. 'Oh, oh.' And that oh, oh is thick with the knowledge that our lives are built on the shaky foundation of our own mortality and that of our loved ones. Oh, oh. Sasha is preparing to peer down through the cracks in the rock to that abyss beneath.

'A death,' he says. 'A death in the family, I fear.'

'Yes, Sasha, a death. In the family.'

'Oh Lucia, is it your poor mother . . . ?'

Fleetingly, bitterly, I wish I was calling to announce Mother's death.

'It's Daddy. He drowned today. There was some kind of accident in the ocean. I don't know more than that, don't ask me more.'

'Oh God. Oh God. I offer you many heartfelt condolences. But where are you now?'

'I'm in New York and flying west tonight. I know this is short notice. I know I haven't seen you for a few years. I know I'm taking ruthless advantage of my favourite cousin. But would you meet me at the airport?'

There is a pause for his surprise. I add: 'Please?'

'Well of course, there's no question about it. Will I take you to your sister's? Or Scott's?'

My turn to pause. 'Actually, I can stay at Daddy's house. Probably it shouldn't be left empty.'

But Sasha is quick. 'No, Lucia, that would be too melancholy and, besides, it would please me very much if you would stay with us. And my mother, of course, would be delighted.'

'Are you living with Aunt Zina again?'

'Certainly.'

'Aren't you still married to Marina?'

'She informs me that I am not. But this is no time to talk of such things. Please stay with us, it would make us very happy.'

I try to protest but he continues: 'My dear Lucia, although it is some years since I have seen your father, I have many warm memories of him. He was a good man, the best of men, and I am quite overcome with sadness for you. I take it your mother has been informed?'

'Apparently. But I don't know if she could comprehend it.'

His voice is salty. 'Such a great loss for all who loved him.'

Everyone seems to feel Daddy's death more acutely than I do. 'Thank you Sashinka.' I give him details of my flight.

'Sashinka will be there,' he assures me. 'Despite the fact that he is almost pathologically late, on such an occasion his punctuality can be relied upon.'

'All arranged?' asks Jim as I put the receiver down.

'Yup.' Back into the bedroom. 'Can I tell you what happened with Thinking Toys now?' I open the closet and pull out some old but comfortable shoes. I am relieved at the way they close gently around my battered feet. I throw the new ones into the bag and start to fold a nightdress. Jim's curious. He'd like to stare openly at the bedroom, at the clothes I'm packing, but he doesn't want to be intrusive and so he sits in the armchair in the next room with his back to me and the door wide open.

'Did you tell the meeting about your father?' he asks. 'Or did you actually pretend everything was normal?'

'I told them. It strengthened my position.'

Jim grimaces with his back.

'They all turned into lambs, even Kent, and acquiesced to virtually all my suggestions.'

'Which were?'

I summarize the problems that arose and the solutions I proposed and Jim looks impressed.

'Good. You did good.'

'It's kind of peculiar when someone congratulates you with their back to you.'

Jim twists around. He looks into my face.

'You did real good.'

He twists away again.

'And there's more. George is going to fly a company jet.'

'What?'

'Well, maybe. He sat there saying he couldn't run a toy company, couldn't participate in concept, development, management, research, marketing . . . Kent was getting more and more scathing. Then someone, okay, hell, it must have been me, asked about the Mittex jets. Whaddya know, there are three of them. Three jets and George Air Force trained. The answer's obvious, so long as he can stay off the liquor.'

Jim turns around. He checks anxiously that I'm not packing anything too personal. He says: 'Except one thing makes that kind of expensive.'

'What?'

'No one's going to travel in a jet George Hifeld's flying, I mean, not without their own parachute.'

I giggle.

'Okay, I'm all packed.'

He stands up and looks right at me.

'Lucy. Your father's dead,' he says.

And this time I let the truck roll its big wheels right over me. My heart is crushed in my chest, my breath is short. I gasp at the pain. I feel the heat of my tears. My sobs are a mechanism which has seized control of my body. He's dead and no one else will ever love me so much. He's dead and the lifetime of knowledge and wisdom inside his head counts for nothing any more. He's dead and now there are empty spaces which his big body and firm voice used to fill. He's dead and the house he lived in and all his things and the people he knew and the places he went are all still there, but there without him. And when enough tides have washed in and out then all evidence of his life will have vanished too. I sob time after time into his void. But he's dead, and he can't answer my sobs.

5

At Jim's house, June is waiting. She ushers me in from the cold night and puts her arms around me and walks me through the hall and into the living-room, over toys, past small children, around a big bunch of flowers.

'Darling,' she says, 'don't even try to dry your tears. When my daddy died I swear I cried every day for a year. That's the only way to make it better. You've just got to cry and cry and cry.'

June is lonely, the only woman in her block, perhaps in ten blocks, who stays at home reproducing. Every year another baby. Jim is bashful as he announces each forth-coming birth.

'That wife of mine,' he says, 'I just can't stop her having babies. She wants a whole goddam football team.'

He is half proud, half awkward now in his own home, reminded by my presence that all day he has been someone big in investment banking but here he is only Daddy, caught up in a whirlwind of demands, small children and domestic details which he relies on June to control. He stands, submiss-ive, Chaplinesque, with his feet turned out and his shoulders bowed as children crawl up his legs.

June keeps her arms around me and continues her incanta-tions. 'Oh darling Lucy, I wish you came here more often,' she says. 'You've got some crying to do, you know you can come here to June to do it. Just you hear me, you just hear me now.'

And, in the warmth of their living-room, a baby calling somewhere else in the house and the flowers June thinks are from Jim misty inside their cellophane, I do cry, over and over, my sobs as repetitive as some tried but reliable machine. When, later, it's time to go, Jim takes me out to the car. The windshield and all the windows are frozen.

'Shit!' says Jim, getting back out. 'Who would have thought it was cold enough to freeze in that time? Should've put her in the garage.'

He reappears, pursued by June with a steaming pan and various small children, some in pyjamas. He jumps into the car and starts the engine. June pours hot water across the windshield and the icy fog cracks and dissolves and behind it are the kind, plump faces of June and the children, smiling into the dark car. As Jim drives off the image of their faces seems imprinted on the windshield despite the street lights and the garish colours of the restaurants and stores we pass.

After a long silence, Jim coughs.

'Your dad got much family?'

'None at all. All our relatives are on my mother's side.'

'Nobody?'

'His family lived in a religious community and when he gave up the faith he had to give them up too. He hasn't been in touch since he was sixteen.'

'That's drastic,' says Jim. He blows his cheeks out. 'That's very drastic. Leaving them all at sixteen. Boy, it must have been hard. Hard to do it, hard afterwards when he was all alone. How old was he when he met your mother?'

'That was much later. He was already teaching at the U and she was a secretary there. They met and married within three weeks.'

'A whirlwind romance, huh?'

She was beautiful and mysterious and foreign and exciting. I think that's how she used to be. I'm not sure if I imagined her that way or if I really remember it.

37

'Didn't he meet anyone else? After she . . .' Jim falters.

'After her first acute psychotic break?' I offer. 'No, he's been devoted to her all these years.'

Jim coughs again. 'How you take a death depends . . . it sort of depends how far down the line you are to accepting your own. How far down that line are you, Lucy?'

My own voice comes back, filtered by a great distance.

'After Stevie I didn't care if I lived or died any more. It's been pretty much that way since.'

'You're right down the line? Total acceptance?'

'Yes. It's good. It means you can ride on an airplane or with a crazy cab driver and not feel frightened. You can walk home at night. You can unlock your apartment without thinking that someone might be in there.'

'I don't believe you, Lucy.'

'Jim, I'm ready for my own death and I always have been. It astonishes me when the plane doesn't fall out of the sky. There have been a few occasions in my life when I thought I was almost dying – falling in a canyon, nearly drowning in a pool, a car crash – and the only thing that shocked me was to find myself alive.'

'No. No. I don't believe that. You think your bucket went right to the bottom of the grief well when your baby died but there's still a lot left in there. When there's nothing else in the well, that's when you're ready to die. In my opinion. Because we grieve for ourselves, not for our dead.'

'We miss the dead, Jim. That's grief.'

'No, that's missing them.'

We continue in silence to the airport. Jim insists on parking the car. When I leave him to go to the gate, refusing his offer to accompany me, I glance back once and see him standing there, still in the hurrying crowd, his stance humorous with feet turned outwards and hands dropped helplessly by his sides, his body swollen. He does not wave but he watches me. I cannot control my urge to cry. I can barely make my legs keep walking towards the airplane. I'm going home.

On the flight it seems to me that Daddy's death and Stevie's death and the death of my brother, name unknown, features forgotten, all roll up into one huge ball of sadness and grief which sits in the adjacent seat crushing me like an obese passenger. I'm thinking of you and I don't want you to be sad. Please don't be sad, my little Lucy.

I turn the rock from Arizona in my pocket over and over until it is warm again. Daddy said that the stripy stones were worthless, globally abundant, geologically uninteresting, but I liked them so much that I took them anyway. They were my only souvenir from that terrible trip.

It began right after my brother died. I guess Daddy thought it would be good to get mother away from the house. Of course it was a subdued vacation, Mother mostly silent, but after a while something in the primitive landscape touched us and we submitted to its timelessness.

Daddy liked clambering through the red canyons in Arizona until the rock dust had turned his dark hair red. Jane was seven and she followed him: I was only four and I followed Jane. We followed on one white-hot day I will never forget. Mother refused to come, choosing to sit in the car, a strange, upright silhouette in the rear window, sizzling, despite the open doors and windows, on the lonely blacktop.

Daddy had a way of moving fast through the desert. He slipped between obstacles like a ghost, climbed dried riverbeds with firm steps that defied the small rocks to slide from under him, and sometimes he jumped, without hesitation, across cracks or between big rocks. Jane and I soon fell behind. I carried my own small rock hammer. I seldom chipped at rocks but told Jane I intended to use it to protect us against rattlesnakes and scorpions. Then, when we felt too hot for falsehood, when the sun was so fierce it seemed to hinge us to the ground, Jane and I admitted to each other that the rock hammer was probably not a useful weapon against deadly snakes. It was no more than a lucky charm. We advanced through the desert cautiously, looking at the ground. Way ahead of us we could hear the ringing of Daddy's hammer or his voice, 'C'mon, c'mon girls,' echoing from around some vast, rocky corner. Then, when we reached the corner, he would already be distant. We never seemed to catch up with him.

After the fall, when my arm had become one vast, throbbing temple of pain and the rest of my body, thought, feeling, everything, had disappeared inside it, Jane emptied the rocks we had found from our canvas bag in a way which indicated their unimportance. With concentration stitching her mouth into a small, straight line, she turned the bag into a sling. Then she left me and went to find Daddy, my arm against my heart throbbing its pledge of allegiance to the rock cliff. I watched her scramble along the bone-white trail of some absent river, growing tiny beneath a massive eyebrow of rock until she disappeared behind a pillar and didn't reappear.

Alone in the canyon with the ridiculous rock hammer, I understood why Mother had chosen to fry in a car. In the car you could look in front of you and see the blacktop rolling so far ahead that the distance and sun seemed eventually to melt it while here in the canyon the rocks and cliffs pressed in on you like a crowd. A silent crowd. I looked all around me and the silence was so intense that it was a presence here. It seemed to come tumbling down the canyon sides like great boulders, crushing the life right out of me. It was unbearable. My leg was reluctant to walk since some vicious fingernail of rock had scored the skin right off but I knew I had to move.

I stumbled when I left the shade as though the sun had just slapped me. Its light and heat were viscous, impeding my progress, dragging at my slow, swelling leg, plucking at the canvas sling. I limped gradually, stopping frequently, learning not to lean on rocks that would burn me. When the silence was broken I thought at first that it was by the shriek of some shrill, angry bird and instinctively looked up. I searched the sky standing so still that I barely breathed. When the sound came again I recognized it. A woman's voice. A woman's voice so forceful and high-pitched that it eventually collapsed but within seconds it had recurred, this time with even greater strength. Its pitch was higher and louder than anything natural. And in this heat, which magnified even thought, I recognized the voice's craziness and hysteria and I shivered. I had thought we were alone in this wild country and now it seemed some other, crazy person had joined us.

The woman's words, long forgotten now, echoed around the canyon. I watched a lizard scuttle up a vertical rock, pause, and then disappear into a crevice. And then, my legs weakened by fear, I stumbled towards the source of the noise.

I emerge, suddenly, from between the canyon's rocky teeth to find myself by the road. The canyon is a semicircle and a fourth of a mile away, standing on a blacktop faded by the sun and splintered by cold nights, the car seems to waver in the heat. Standing next to it, also wavering, as though this isn't the parched desert but some underwater place, are Daddy, Mother and Jane. No crazy stranger, just my family, their faces turned to me in silence.

I found the stripy stones in my pocket later, when I was waiting for X-rays at the hospital. They pleased me because they looked as though someone sloppy like me had painted them. I kept them on the floor of the car and when we drove home, suddenly, violently, soon after the red canyon, the rocks slid from side to side every time Daddy turned to the right or the left. And, although it had been set and plastered at the hospital, each time he flung us around another bend and the rocks slid, my arm throbbed with pain. We were fleeing Arizona and Daddy's face and knuckles were white. Maybe he guessed that the woman he found when he walked out of the canyon was not the same woman, would not ever be the same woman, we'd left behind on the blacktop in the hot car.

We seldom spoke on that journey, except for Mother of course. When she lapsed into long silences we sank inside the silences with her, relieved, wanting them to last for ever, to last all the way back to California, and Daddy would accelerate still more, as though speed would put more ground between the last gas station and the next, between Mother's last outburst and the next. Jane and I assured Daddy that we didn't want lunch, we didn't need the bathroom, we didn't want to stop for anything because most of all we didn't want Mother to get out of the car. And maybe we thought that when we finally got her home she might be the same Mother she was before, as though she'd stayed at home all along.

It is some years since I last saw Sasha and I have an irrational fear that I won't recognize him. But his wide face, his mouth stretched right across it, is first in the group of faces clustered at the gate. He is smaller and broader than I remember him, perhaps smaller and certainly broader than me. His face has grown fleshy, his hair thin.

I put down my bag and at once he flings his arms around me, pushing his bristly cheek to mine. He smells of cigarettes, leather and chocolate.

'My dear Lucia, I don't know whether to be happy to see you or sad at your loss. I think I must allow myself to experience both emotions simultaneously.' He picks up my bag. 'Don't you have any more than this?'

'No.'

'How different from my wife for whom no trip is complete without an excess baggage fine.'

'Are you and Marina divorced?'

'Let us say that I regard her as my excess baggage fine in life's journey. Follow me, please.'

I am content to trail behind Sasha's round, leather-jacketed back into elevators and across the dim parking lot to his car. The last time I saw him was four, perhaps five years ago, at the clinic. A birthday celebration for Mother at which she behaved badly. I remember how angry I was that he seemed to find the whole event comical, and how my anger itself amused him.

When he pauses by the elevator he asks: 'How long since you were in California, Lucia?'

'Three years.'

'You haven't been back since you left? A brave exodus indeed.'

We reach his car and Sasha turns to me. I am able to examine his face for the first time. Its structure is lost in folds of flesh, his teeth are uneven, his hair is thinning at the centre and unkempt at the sides but his eyes have a piercing, frightening beauty. They are like Jane's, like my mother's, like my grandmother's.

He is looking at me too, about to speak, reluctant to do so. At last he asks: 'Lucia, what have you been told about your dear papa's death?'

'Nothing. I mean, just that he drowned in the Pacific. I don't even know where.'

'At Big Brim beach, as I understand it.'

'Big Brim?' A line of uninviting sand dunes by the coast road, the beach invisible.

Sasha is persisting hesitantly. 'You know nothing more? You are unaware, for example, of police involvement?'

'Oh, the police. I think someone mentioned the police.'

His face folds itself with concern. 'Lucia, you look so tired that I can hardly bear to tell you this . . .'

I feel no curiosity, no anticipation.

'Instead of driving you now to our apartment where Mama and Aunt Zoya have been cooking and preparing your room and looking forward to administering tender affection, I must take you at once to your father's house as you originally requested.'

I think of the old house, crouched on the hillside like an enormous, dark bird waiting to flap its wings and fly out across the valley beneath. It's been waiting for me and now, at last, I'm back.

Sasha continues: 'Your sister called us . . .'

'But I didn't tell her I was staying with you.'

'She was aware of it all the same. Sisters are like that, as our mothers will confirm. Jane called to say that you must go directly to Uncle Eric's house. Mama tried to argue but Jane explained that this is at the request of the police.'

Shaking my head with incomprehension I climb into the car. As we drive through the pay station, the lighting making the colours of the cars look like other, different colours, I remember how Jim said that Daddy's death was not straight-forward.

'I confess,' says Sasha, 'to some confusion about such police interest in your father. But no doubt all will be explained on our arrival. I think I remember the route. It will take us, perhaps, forty-five minutes?'

'Nearer an hour.'

We drive east. Until Sasha winds up his window I breathe the air in deeply. I recognize in it the balminess and saltiness of San Francisco.

Sasha says: 'Now Lucia, you will need a car and tomorrow we will hire one. There is a cheap company only a few blocks away.'

'Actually, Sasha, my colleague's having a hirecar sent over in the morning.'

'Good gracious. A hirecar delivered, actually delivered, to our house. It is possible your humble Russian relatives will find this, and your metropolitan clothes, somewhat intimidating.'

I redden and, since we are crossing the well-lit bridge, perhaps Sasha notices because he says: 'Forgive me. I must remember that you are no longer the little girl who could be relied upon to get lost on a rocky beach or somehow drop a shoe down the elevator shaft at Grandma's apartment.'

When I am silent he adds mischievously: 'Or perhaps that girl is still hiding in there somewhere.'

I say: 'How about you, Sash? I was surprised to contact you on the same number.'

He sighs: 'I, too, am surprised at this. But, whenever I think of leaving the foundation, my empire or my salary expands enough to keep me there. Perhaps you feel horrified that Sasha is living with Mama as he used to and driving to the same office he drove to fifteen years ago. But the ease with which one can resume the rhythms of one's past is astonishing, as perhaps you will find now that you are back.'

I shake my head. 'I'm not going to resume anything.'

'Beware, Lucia, sometimes the past is too strong for us.'

For an instant it seems to me that the car's momentum has nothing to do with its engine. We are being dragged back into the past, towed helplessly along by a powerful but invisible truck.

From the moment the freeway narrows and the dark shapes of trees congregate at the roadside like mourners I find myself reliving another journey along this route. Although I have travelled the road countless times since, I recall now my family's precipitate return from Arizona many summers ago and the smells and colours of my memory have the freshness of new paint. We could have taken the slower route through the valley but Daddy chose the freeways where he could go faster and the quantity of traffic made us unremarkable. On the freeways the other road-users were lost in their own dreams and we hoped they would hardly notice there was a crazy woman bouncing and yelling on the front seat of our car. As we crossed over the bridge Mother seemed to understand that we were close to home but this did not calm her. 'You murderer!' she shrieked at the surprised man in the toll cabin. Jane and I sank lower in the back seat until our heads were invisible from the cabin. 'God, yes,' she snarled, 'God, yes, I see it in your eyes that you also have killed! Oh, I know all about you.'

Daddy apologized and we took off rapidly like a boat blown on by some irresistible wind, the wind that had blown us swiftly away from gas stations and grocery stores and, on one awful occasion, a roadside motel. It had blown us all the way from Arizona.

When we turned into our bumpy, rocky drive Mother quietened suddenly. She stared up at the house with something like meekness and Jane and I exchanged grateful glances. We were home and Mother was better. Daddy stopped the car and we got out of it slowly. It was already a habit to do things slowly because we had learned that jolts and surprises triggered a corresponding response, many times magnified, in Mother. We stretched. We blinked with the astonishment of people who have thought of nothing but their destination and now have arrived there. We staggered a little with the knowledge that we were no longer in motion. We looked around us. We noted the way the grass and the trees seemed to have stretched themselves out a little to fill the spaces we left during our few weeks away. We glanced, cautiously, at Mother. She sat in the front seat of the car without moving. I saw that she still wore the white, contorted mask that had mysteriously covered her real self ever since I broke my arm in the canyon. Gently, Daddy opened her door. Mother still did not move. Daddy said, his voice so soft that I wanted to hug him: 'Tanya, let's go inside, you'll feel better now you're here.' We gathered around the car door, although not too close in case there was a sudden armwaving ambush of crazy recriminations. But Mother, her face flattened and snakelike, spoke quietly. She said: 'I am not getting out of the car. You treat me like some piece of cargo to be pulled across the world, a box, a bag, some battered old suitcase left at the quayside. Well now, simply, you cannot leave me anywhere because I do not intend to get out of the car.'

We stared at her. Ever since the canyon we had attempted to restrict and calm her movements, now she was volunteering to do this herself when it was least appropriate.

'Do you hear me?' she yelled so loudly that I jumped backwards off the drive and into some poison ivy. Jane and I looked at Daddy and saw his face, which had been set hard all through the long, miserable drive home, crumple like an old shirt. 'No, Tanya, you can't sit here forever . . .' he began but his gentle voice disappeared rapidly beneath her screams. 'I am not . . .' Her face was swallowed into a massive wet, black hole of mouth and tongue and teeth. 'I am not, not, getting out of the car.'

47

We waited and waited for her. We waited motionlessly. Then, reluctant to leave her alone, we went into the house. It got dark. Daddy brought her food which she ignored. He spoke to her with soft kindness. She closed the car door on him. From the kitchen window I saw his helplessness when she shut him right out. He was big enough to force open the door, lift her, drag her from the car into the house but he didn't try that. He didn't even shout.

She stayed there all night and most of the next day and Jane and I remained indoors. We looked at her from the kitchen window sometimes and it seemed to us she didn't move at all. Occasionally, oppressed by the strange silence and the curious impasse in our lives, we sat on the deck which looks out over the valley. It felt good to have the whole house between us and Mother. Then Daddy, apologetically, sadly, told us that he would have to call for help. His shoulders were bent and he looked smaller. Two men and a woman came. The one in a suit had a long, hushed conversation with Daddy in the kitchen while his colleagues tried to talk to Mother through the car window. She did not wind it down or reply or give any indication that she heard them. It was evening when they took her away. When I could bear her screams no longer I ran down through the yard. The heat of the day was thinning and night-time seemed to reach out at me as I ran in and out of the trees. I didn't stop when branches grabbed me or bushes scratched my legs. I sat in the furthest corner of the yard with my fingers in my ears where I wouldn't hear any more of her yelling ('So! You are murderers! He has sent you to kill me, now I understand it!'). Finally there was silence and when I crept back around the barn I found a new emptiness. The car and Mother were gone.

Sasha and I travel in silence. The roads curve around low

contours. The lights of the city behind us have dissolved in the darkness. Even the hum of the car's engine seems like a kind of silence. When we reach the undulating hills I am lulled by their rhythm and by my memories of their rhythm. My eyes close and fatigue sweeps over me.

6

'Are you falling asleep?' asks Sasha suddenly.

'I'm not sure if I'm asleep and dreaming or awake and remembering.'

'How close to the turning are we?'

'It's over the top of this hill and down a bit.'

Sasha slows. The car engine whines. He swings right.

We ride high along the valley's steep sides, bouncing in and out of the craters in the dirt road. I know that, over to the left, when the bushes clear, the valley can shock you like a vast eye, open and glaring. But now there is nothing out there but the dark.

We near Daddy's house. My heart speeds, my breath shortens.

'Don't I recognize this one?' asks Sasha, pausing before a break in the foliage. Our headlights fall across a drive, snaking mysteriously into the fold of the hill.

'No, that's the Holler house.'

'Friends of yours?'

'I used to play with Jim Bob Holler. I thought I was in love with him when I was nine and he was eleven.' I start a little at the sudden, sharp memory of Jim Bob, blond hair crewcut, his body nutbrown, in motion, running, at the edge of a pool, his stride breaking as a harsh voice, his father's, commands him to walk.

'Aha,' says Sasha, driving on slowly. 'Nine and eleven. Was there perhaps a juvenile undercurrent of sexual awareness?'

'I didn't know about that stuff when I was nine.'

'And later? When you did?'

'Jim Bob wasn't around by then.'

He is peering along the sides of the dirt road looking for the next break in the foliage. I haven't thought about Jim Bob Holler for years, or that Arizona trip. Shock and fatigue and my sudden return have brought the distant past up close.

'Now, I'm sure it's on that bend,' says Sasha, leaning towards the windshield as though this will help him see in the dark.

A distant mailbox glints in the headlights. 'No, before it. That's the Zacarro house up by the bend.'

'And were the Zacarros good neighbours?' murmurs Sasha, inching forward.

'Okay I guess. Mr Zacarro had polio when he was a kid and he limped a bit.' More than a bit. When he moved forward one half of his body seemed to want to stay right where it was. He had to drag that whole side, his left side, along with him, animating it like a ventriloquist animates his puppet. I used to imagine Mr Zacarro's side lying lifelessly in their porch on the days he decided not to take it with him to work.

Suddenly Daddy's drive seems to jump out from the foliage at me. I draw back.

'Well? Are we here?'

Daddy made the drive himself, embedding round-faced seawashed stones in the dirt in a labour that must have taken months. But Daddy liked physical work. The neighbours hired men with machines to dig or build or asphalt but Daddy made things himself and he fixed things himself. He was always meaning to fix the drive. It was a good drive but over the years it sank in places, so you had to throw the wheel to left and right to avoid the deepest holes. I have travelled around those holes many times. For real and, far away, in my sleep. On foot, to the school bus. In my corner of a car filled with family or suitcases or shopping. As a passenger in cars driven by young men, their fathers' cars, smelling of their fathers' cigarettes, with a father's newspaper thrown on to the back seat. And when I learned to drive, along with parallel parking, I learned where to swing the wheel to avoid the rises and falls of Daddy's rocky drive.

'This is it,' I say. But when Sasha turns to me for an answer I realize that I thought the words without saying them. 'Yes, here, we're here,' I tell him.

No sooner has Sasha turned the wheel than he must halt the car. There is bright red and yellow tape threaded between bushes so it hangs right across the drive. On it the words Police Do Not Cross Police Do Not Cross are repeated like a mantra. It is the words, not the flimsy tape, which prevent us from driving straight through.

Suddenly there is light bouncing off my face, off the windshield, pouring into all the car's dark crevices. We turn and the beam of a flashlight diverts a little to reveal a rectangle of uniform. Sasha winds down his window. A policeman leans towards us.

'I can't permit you to drive any further.'

I stare at him. 'I live here,' I hear a voice say. 'I mean, I used to.'

The officer looks across Sasha at me.

'Maybe . . .' he suggests, looking down suddenly. The light follows his eyes. 'I have your name right here on this list.'

I give him my name and he nods.

'Oh. Oh, okay. You're the other daughter? The one from back east?'

He looks at Sasha. I explain: 'This is my cousin who just met me at the airport.'

The man shines his light on the clipboard again. 'Okay,

well I'd like to ask you to leave your car this side of the barrier. It's getting pretty congested up there.'

Sasha reverses into the dirt road.

'You have a flashlight?' asks the man when we duck under the police tape.

'Only a cigarette-lighter,' Sasha admits apologetically.

'Be careful, those rocks are dangerous in the dark. We're lighting the top with gumballs but it's a while before you get to them.'

Sasha takes my arm and waves the cigarette lighter uselessly before us as we stumble towards the house, stubbing our toes, my heels slipping into the gaps between the stones. The policeman shines his light for us but as we step beyond its beam there are a few minutes of darkness when the stars seem to appear overhead and the fresh night air envelopes us. We inhale its damp woodiness.

I close my eyes. Despite the difficulties of negotiating the drive's incline and curve, despite the sound of Sasha puffing and cursing at my side, I experience the deep peace of my last moments of ignorance. Soon I'll know everything.

'I believe,' says Sasha, 'that Jane and Larry are here waiting for you.'

Up the incline and round to the right and I open my eyes. I stop at the sight of the big house. When I remember it, and that is often in my dreams, I remember it as it was when I was small, painted a pale egg-blue, surrounded by the slender trees and sparse bushes which Daddy planted. In the time I lived here it changed to its present state but I had forgotten how choked by growth it has become, how the trees now press against the windows, how creepers suffocate the porch.

'Lucia? Are you all right?'

I nod. The doors of the house and barn are flung open, and that feels like a violation, as though someone usually dignified just had their clothes ripped off. The scene, lit by a police car, flashes at me surreally in first red then blue then white. Alongside the flashing car are others, two of them police cars. In all the time I lived here there were seldom visitors and never police cars except possibly after someone poisoning coyotes poisoned Mother's dog instead. And now here are three police cars, parked randomly, abandoned with a gumball flashing, windows open and a radio talking inside one.

As I pull Sasha around the barn I feel as though I am reaching the end of some epic journey instead of a few hundred yards of rocky drive. My heart beats fast and suddenly I have no breath and can progress no further. I lean against a car, first sideways, and then I twist my body and prop myself against its roof with my elbows.

'Lucia?'

My voice is small: 'I'll be okay in a minute, Sasha. Give me a minute.'

I look up at the big, flashing house. Its gables have sinuous woodwork and the porch posts have candycane twists. It should be cute as a gingerbread house but it isn't. It looms right over you like a big bully. It mocks me and it mocks the beating of my heart. I remind myself that I was other people when I lived here. A baby, a kid who learned how to hammer rocks before she learned hopscotch, a girl who had to creep around the house in case she disturbed her crazy mother, a lovesick teenager. They were all other people and the house mocks them all.

Sasha waits for me by the car. He moves his weight awkwardly from foot to foot, stamping a little. Then he takes my arm and tugs me a little towards the house.

'I understand that extra lighting may be required,' he says irritably as we weave around the flashing trees to the porch, 'but do you think it is necessary to turn the place into Las Vegas?'

As I climb the steps, another police officer emerges from the house, faceless in his uniform and the artificial light. He wears a radio around his belt and a crackling female voice issues from it. She seems not to be speaking English.

'Uh-huh?' says the man.

The foliage is brushing against the back of my neck like spiders. I can hear Sasha behind me, breathing heavily.

The man prompts: 'Name or ID, please.'

On the other side of the house is the deck and when you lean over it you're leaning right over the valley. But whoever built the house must have understood that looking at the valley, flat and rolling on forever like an ocean, only dry, can drive you crazy. So he added this porch, nestled up to the barn and the yard, overshadowed by the hill and now overhung by foliage. The dark side of the house. As a child I'd spend hours here and the porch swing where I sat is still in the same spot by the door. For a moment I glimpse a small girl, in the very corner of the swing like a doll someone threw there, and my heart aches for her loneliness. I blink and she's gone.

The man puts his hands on his hips and eyes me closely.

'I can't allow you in here,' he says.

I reach for the swing and my fingers find a crust of rust. The seat does not move. Some flakes of rust fall like dandruff and there is a faint metallic smell. At first Mother sat next to me, telling stories, reorganizing my hair, smelling of sugar as we rocked back and forth. Then, after she stopped being that kind of mother, I sat here with Lindy, my giggling blonde-haired friend. Finally, I was the lonely doll hunched in the corner as though their absence was so massive it took up the whole of the rest of the swing.

'Ma'am, would you please identify yourself?' A new soft-ness in the officer's tone makes the back of my eyes sting. A moment later they drip with hot, salty tears. My legs feel weak and I sit on the top step of the porch and watch the tears fall on to my lap.

Sasha mutters something and the man leans over me. 'You have some connection with the decedent?'

I say: 'Daughter.' The word sounds odd, as though I've borrowed it from some other language. He disappears and there is a sound like gunshot. The screen door, slamming.

Sasha sits down next to me, one plump arm lying across my shoulders, his leg pressed next to mine. We sit together on the top step of the porch, lit garishly in red and blue and then white, while police officers, some in uniform, others in suits, shuffle past us silently up or down the steps.

And then a voice says: 'Luce?' and I jump up and there is Jane.

We stand facing one another. The wooden structure of the porch frames her so she looks like some photograph that someone took three years ago. My memory has made her taller. It has made her body more like a reed and her jaw sharper and her eyes bluer but now she steps right inside the image I've been carrying around in my head and the two merge imperceptibly. We stare and then she holds her hands out and I step towards her. She wraps her arms around me as though I am still a small child.

'You're too thin,' she chides me. I'm supposed to pull away from her now but I can't. I'm crying. I was okay until she used that big sister voice. Her hug tightens. I smell her perfume: it is faint, the aroma of crushed flowers. It smells good. At last I stand back, sniffing, rubbing the tears from my eyes with the inside of my arms.

'Oh, Luce,' she says softly. She takes my hand and strokes

it as though she's trying to dry it. 'Luce, you don't know how much I've missed you.'

There's no one in New York, not one person, who would ever speak to me so sweetly. I chose that. I chose to go. I think of the glassy blue of Kent's eyes as he told me he wanted me.

I experience again how it feels to be loved as Jane puts an arm around me and holds me close. She has never left me in doubt of her love. As a child, at school, she was always there to compensate for Mother's absences and inadequacies. She advised me on friends, teachers and math. Once, memorably, she saved me from drowning at the local swimming-pool. She stayed with me at the hospital, her face chiselled by anxiety, after the car crash with Robert Joseph in the valley. And it was Jane, after she'd left for med school, who could see at once that Mother's homestay was too much and urged Daddy to have her readmitted to the clinic. Then later, years later, when Stevie died, Jane sat with me for hours, maybe days, talking and in silence, somehow knowing what to do when everyone else, even Scott, was frightened or intimidated or upset by my grief.

She pulls back to look at me. 'If only you'd called us we would have met you at the airport . . .'

The gentlest of reproaches and from someone who is entitled to be angry. My departure from San Francisco was as painful as it was incomprehensible for Jane. And now I have hurt her again.

I flounder. 'It's been so long . . . I didn't know how you'd feel about me just arriving . . .'

'Pleased is how we would have felt. We've waited three years for you to just arrive.' Her generosity is simple and unquestioning. Astonishing quantities of water run down my face, over my cheeks, into my mouth, drip from my jaw.

Sasha steps forward. He does not kiss Jane but shakes hands with her. There is a formality in the condolences he offers and a formality in her acceptance.

'The time must now have come,' he says, 'to ask the precise manner of Uncle Eric's death.'

Suddenly Jane's older, more tired. 'The police think . . . the circumstances . . . I wish there was a way of saying this that didn't sound so awful.' She takes my hand. 'The police are working on a theory that Daddy's death wasn't accidental.'

I nod. I'm pretending to understand.

'They think . . .' asks Sasha carefully, 'that he intended to die?'

Suicide. It's the first time I've even allowed myself to think the word but now I think it I realize I've been avoiding it since the moment Jim told me about Daddy's death, since the moment he said the death was not straightforward. Suicide. An old dog, slinking around the house, which it is possible to ignore. Just. Until, that is, the dog demands to be fed.

Sasha holds out a hand to steady me.

'That's ridiculous,' I say. I hear myself. Weak, small, as though all the air has been squeezed out of me. 'Suicide. That's absurd.'

Jane says: 'Lucy, it does sort of look like maybe Daddy intended to . . .' Her voice fades. I barely listen to her words. I'm thinking that I've never heard Jane falter so helplessly. I've always admired the way that, when she starts a sentence, you can tell she knows how it's going to finish. I watch her, waiting, and when she speaks again her voice is strong. 'But,' she says carefully, 'the police are treating Daddy's death as homicide.'

Sasha echoes: 'Homicide . . .' and when I glance at him

his eyes have sunk a little deeper into his white face and he is chewing on an unlit cigarette. He says: 'Surely not. Surely not Uncle Eric.'

I speak again and my voice is stronger now. 'You mean the police think someone killed him?'

'They're waiting for a full autopsy report but apparently the initial examination indicates —'

'Killed him! They're saying someone killed Daddy!'

'Shhhh, Lucy.'

'Is that what all this is for? The tape across the drive and guys with uniforms and clipboards and flashlights? They're here because they think someone killed Daddy!'

Jane's voice is quiet. 'Luce, I know it's a shock but you have to remember that it may not have been violent or painful or —'

'But who would kill Daddy, for God's sake? No one would have any reason —'

'Shhhh. Stop shouting, Luce.'

'Daddy was a university professor, not some kind of thug. Good, decent people like Daddy from happy families like ours don't get murdered!'

I am yelling into the darkness, I hear my own voice crossing the porch but within an instant the thick night air seems to absorb my words as though I had not spoken.

7

Jane slips into the house, slim and sharp as a threaded needle. Sasha follows her, holding the screen door open for me, but on the threshold, my belly fluttering, I stop to inhale the old house, its special smell. Oil and rugs and wood and coffee. It seems for a moment that something sweet is missing, then I realize that time has played another trick on me this strange night and that I have remembered the house's smell as it was long ago, when I was small and Mother was well and the house aroma always included a little of her perfume and the scent of lemon furniture polish and soft, sugary cookies.

'They've asked us not to go anywhere but the hall and the kitchen,' Jane is telling us from down the hallway. She puts her head into the den. I hear her say: 'My sister's here.' The reply is indistinct.

All the lights in the house are on but there are still pools of darkness in the hallway. I start to walk. I walk in and out of the shadows. A man eases past me, apologizing as I crush my body against the wall.

'Please don't touch anything,' he murmurs.

When he has gone I go into the living-room and stare around me. Daddy's chairs, the arms and back of his favourite worn thin. Photographs. Books. And rocks. Rocks used as paperweights. Round, smooth rocks in a pile by the fire like an exhibit in a gallery. Specimen rocks on the shelves. Rocks of startling formation or the lurid colours nature sometimes throws up, rocks wedging open the door or placed lovingly on the bureau. Rocks as sculpture. Rocks as pictures.

'Has much changed?' asks Sasha from the doorway.

I do not turn around. 'No, nothing's really changed.'

I go to the big sliding doors and open them slowly. They growl back at me. Then I cross the deck and lean out over the valley below. It is a plate of darkness stretching on forever. Tiny sets of car lights, two, maybe three, glitter silently, far apart. They move slowly. Occasionally a cluster of lights indicates a house or a farm. I try to see any of the quadrangles formed by tracks and orchards but there is nothing out there but stillness and silence. I search, from some old habit, for the long, straight stretch of blacktop where the car I was riding in with Robert Joseph turned upside down. I look for the farm I walked to one day with my friend Lindy, the friend who used to swing with me on the porch. We were seven and we set off down the hillside and across the hot, flat valley floor and kept right on walking until we reached the farm. They gave us water and melon and then drove us home in the back of their pick-up. I'd always wanted to ride in the back of a pick-up like the farm kids. We bounced along the dirt road of the orchard watching the big clouds of dust bubble up behind us and pretended we were a storm blowing through. I strain now to see the farm and the dirt road but I see nothing at all, as though there's really nothing down there or maybe just a great, dark ocean which you can't cross.

Sasha is still waiting at the door but inside the room now are the man who edged past me in the hallway and a woman whose hands are covered in latex. The man speaks. 'Ma'am, we haven't completed our work in here yet.'

I look at him. 'What sort of work?'

'I must ask you to vacate this room until we can give you clearance to enter.'

I am about to leave when I notice that in one hand the

61

man carries a collection of small plastic bags. They remind me of the bags Daddy used for tiny rocks and rock dust. When NASA sent the geology department moon rocks, Daddy kept them in bags which looked just like this.

'Do you have rocks in there?' I ask the man.

'These are forensic samples,' he says. His face is immobile but he shifts his weight from foot to foot, waiting for me to go. The woman stares at me.

I lead Sasha past the den. It is a small, near-windowless room full of paper and rock. A uniformed woman and two men in suits peer at Daddy's blinking computer screen. They do not look up.

Larry is making us coffee in the kitchen. When I walk in his eyebrows shoot up and he smiles at me then embraces me. I can feel how his body has expanded and when he pulls back I can see it. Even his features have thickened so that his nose is less prominent and his tidy beard looks too small for his chin now.

'Lucy, it's good to see you,' he says. 'Despite the circumstances.'

He sounds as though he means it. His look is knowing, not searching, a look I remember well.

'It irritates me the way he stares at me like he knows more about me than I do,' I told Scott once. But Scott admires Larry and he shook his head. 'He's a shrink not a witch doctor, Luce. He only knows things about you which you know about yourself but refuse to acknowledge.' Scott was only half being humorous when he said that.

Larry greets Sasha and Jane passes us coffees. I look around. The kitchen didn't change in all the years we lived here and it never occurred to me then how shabby it was. I never noticed that the stove is too small for the space allotted it or that the sink is stained and battered or that the doors of some units don't fit or even close. It never bothered me that part of the work surface was still covered in lino.

I say: 'Jane, did you put sugar in this coffee?'

'Just a little.'

'I stopped taking sugar years ago.'

She smiles. 'I know. But you looked like you needed something.' And although I resent the sugar I also enjoy its sweetness, the sweetness of childhood.

The officer from the living-room appears noiselessly.

'Kirsty'll be with you in a minute. I have to take your prints,' he says.

I realize he is talking to me.

'My fingerprints?'

'I have to. You opened the door to the deck and held the deck railings . . . did you touch anything else?'

'No.'

The man has laid out a small attaché case on the table in front of me.

'Please remove your wrist watch and jewellery,' he says mechanically.

Larry and Jane and Sasha watch me as I submit my right hand to him. He lifts it by the wrist and my fingers dangle like dead fingers. He takes one, pressing it on to the paper, rolling it harshly. He does this with each finger in turn, and when he has completed my right hand he does the same with my left and when he has completed ten fingers he rolls each hand in ink and then on to the paper, the fingers and then palms, until by the time he finishes we have established a sort of rhythm as though we're making a painting together.

'Now you,' he tells Sasha.

'But I haven't touched anything.'

'I need to take your prints just in case.'

'I prefer not.'

The man sighs and shifts his weight.

'Maybe,' he suggests beadily, 'we already have them some place?'

Sasha is haughty. 'Certainly not. But I really prefer my fingerprints not to be lodged forever on some vast computer.'

'These are elimination prints and they'll be destroyed right after this case has been closed,' says the man.

'Unless,' adds Larry, grinning, 'you're found guilty of a crime.'

Sasha looks from Larry to the police officer with contempt. 'You do not need my fingerprints.'

Jane says: 'For heaven's sake, Alexander.' I look at her in surprise. Her use of his full name, her irritation, her coolness. She has never taken so little trouble to hide her feelings about our Russian relatives. Mother adored and disdained her family at the same time. Their very Russianness annoyed her, although, perhaps because, she shared it. Jane has inherited all Mother's disdain without its curious partner, love.

'They took my prints too, Alexander. They took Larry's. They took Scott's. They took them from everyone who's been in the house today.'

Sasha looks at her stubbornly. 'Allow me, Jane, to indulge my Russian paranoia.'

Jane's voice is taut with irritation now. 'You sound so Russian that it's easy to forget you were born here and you've lived here all your life. You didn't suffer under the Soviet system. Paranoia is for people who did.'

She thinks Sasha is acting Russian. Jane describes any dramatic behaviour as acting Russian. When I lost my temper, burst unnecessarily into tears, shouted or behaved otherwise demonstrably, I could be sure that Jane would say: 'Quit

64

acting Russian, Lucy.' Mother, of course, acted Russian to Academy Award level.

Sasha is wounded now. He and Jane stare at one another. They are wordless but there is a shared childhood behind that stare. Larry is about to intervene when we hear voices. The woman I saw in Daddy's den is right outside the kitchen. I can't see the man she is talking to, only his shadow, absurdly elongated by the light. Then he disappears and the woman turns to us, looking from face to face.

'What's the problem?'

She is about my age and about my height. I see now that she is wearing not a uniform but dark clothes which have the simplicity of a uniform.

'I need to take a set of elimination prints here,' snaps the officer. 'But this guy's refusing to allow me.'

Sasha shrugs. He looks clownish now, his mouth set in a wide, taut line, red circles appearing on both cheeks. 'The procedure is unnecessary. I have touched and will touch nothing outside this room.'

The woman says: 'Who are you?'

Larry and Jane introduce me and explain Sasha's presence and the woman nods. She looks like someone who used to have a trim figure but for some reason – work, children, ill-health – her body is amplified now. Her hair is short and dark but when she puts her hand to her neck I know she is fingering the hair which used to be there. She is a woman who, probably not so long ago, changed. Like me.

'I have not seen my late uncle for perhaps four years,' Sasha informs her frostily.

'Okay,' she says. 'So long as we can contact you if we need to, we'll leave your prints tonight.'

The fingerprint man closes his briefcase and melts out of the room. I wash my hands while the woman explains that she would like to interview me and asks Sasha and Jane and Larry to sit out on the porch while she does this. I dry my hands on Daddy's towel and see that, even though I scrubbed them, I have left more inky fingerprints here.

Jane pauses before she leaves the room. 'Kirsty,' she says. 'Could this interview wait until tomorrow or the next day? Lucy's not just tired but she's still very shocked. Her health has never been good and she really shouldn't get too stressed.'

These words touch and embarrass me. Touch me because I am unused these days to the loving concern of others. Embarrass me because, although I was sick a lot as a kid, I now thrive on stress.

The woman turns to me. Her look is scrutinizing.

'What do you think, Lucy?' she asks.

I say: 'Oh, thanks Jane, thanks very much, but you don't need to worry, I'll be fine.'

Sasha follows Larry and Jane out of the room. He gives me a long look but I don't understand what the look means.

When we are alone, the woman gestures me to sit down at the table with her.

'Just relax, Lucy.' It's true that I'm tense but I wonder how I have betrayed myself. I thought I'd managed to maintain a sort of stillness which might look like calm.

'At this stage I only have a few informal questions.' She places a notebook in front of her. 'I need some basic details like name, date of birth, address . . .'

I say: 'Can you tell me what's going on?'

The woman looks down at her notebook. 'After a preliminary view of your father's body, the medical examiner has some concerns. There's a full autopsy tomorrow but it's our job to respond, even at this stage, to the ME's first analysis.'

'And what is that analysis?'

Her eyes are brown. They meet mine. 'The decedent was

found by a fisherman at 11.30 a.m. floating off the coast at Retribution. At first he was assumed to have drowned but the medical examiner believes that in fact he was dead before his body entered the water.'

Her voice echoes inside my head. In fact he was dead before his body entered the water. Finally I say: 'How did he die?'

'Well . . .' Her brown eyes swivel away from me, over the ill-fitting stove and the battered sink. 'That's not clear yet. His clothes were found, folded in a pile, at Big Brim beach. His car is missing and we can't explain how he got to the coast. What we do know is that the killer attempted to make it seem like your father went for a swim and died in the water. We believe that this was a premeditated, carefully planned crime: only his lack of knowledge of forensic techniques let the killer down.'

'But . . .' I protest. 'No one would have a reason to kill Daddy.'

She is silent and her face does not move.

I say: 'It must have been some crazy person on the beach. The kind of maniac who stabs joggers for their radio and two dollars fifty hidden in their belt.'

The woman is watching me. Her look is not unkind but she says: 'No, Lucy. I don't see it that way. Only a tiny percentage of homicides are carried out by total strangers and, frankly, this doesn't look like that kind of death.'

'What kind of death does it look like?' I know my own voice is loud. I know this when I hear her quiet, even tone.

'The kind where the victim knew his killer. In fact, we may have reason to believe he knew his killer well.'

I wait for the reason but she doesn't offer it.

'You think it was someone close to him? A friend? Someone . . .' I swallow. There is a layer of salt around the inside of my mouth and it feels dry and crusty. 'Someone I might know?'

'It was probably someone known to you or your sister. But maybe not. Because your father may have had parts of his life you were unaware of.'

I shake my head. 'Not Daddy,' I say.

She waits, watching me. I ask: 'Isn't there some other explanation for all this? I mean, maybe he had a heart attack on the beach and the tide washed him out to sea. Or, he hit his head on a rock and sort of fell into the water . . .'

She is quiet but firm and she never takes her eyes off me. 'I realize you must find those theories comforting. But nothing in the preliminary autopsy can confirm either of them.'

I blink at her. There is fatigue standing between me and comprehension. I notice that there are stains on her dark clothes, just below the shoulder. That's where babies leave their stains, when they press their faces up against you. So now I know why she changed shape, cut her hair.

I ask: 'When did he die?'

'We're waiting for more information on that. Probably he died early on Monday. Lucy, I have to ask you where you were on Sunday night.'

'At home.'

'Monday morning?'

'I got to work before eight . . . I had a big meeting which I needed to prepare for.'

'I have to confirm that. Please give me the name, address and telephone number of your employer.'

She writes down these details.

'Now, your sister already explained that you were staying with friends on the weekend. Where was that?'

I feel my cheeks begin to burn. 'That's what I told Jane . . .'

She raises her eyebrows.

'You weren't staying with friends?'

'Well, no.'

'So where were you?'

'At home. In my apartment. I barely left it after I got home on Friday evening.'

There is a silence before she speaks again. 'Did you talk to anyone? Visit anyone? Call anyone?'

'No.'

'Not all weekend?'

'I was working. I had a lot of preparation for Monday . . .'

'You can't provide one single person to verify your whereabouts this weekend?'

'No.'

She is persistent but her even tone does not vary. 'No one? Are you sure no one saw you? Not a doorman or a sales clerk or a neighbour?'

I shake my head. 'New York's not that kind of place.'

'So no one saw you all weekend,' she states quietly. She looks away from me. She runs her eye over the battered sink, the ill-fitting stove, the lino.

I say: 'That doesn't mean I wasn't there.'

Her eyes are back again, swift, shrewd.

'Why did you lie to your sister, Lucy?'

'Because I didn't answer the phone. I didn't want her to know that I wasn't picking up on her. I didn't want to hurt her.'

'I see. When were you last in California?'

'Almost three years ago.'

'Was that the last time you saw Dr Schaffer?'

'No, he visited me six, nine months later in New York.'

'So you hadn't seen him for more than two years?'

'No.'

69

'And you didn't return to California at all in the last three years?'

'No.'

'When did you last speak with him?'

I tell her about the messages Daddy left on my phone on Saturday.

'Did your sister call also?'

'Yes.'

Her eyes are large, dark. 'But why didn't you answer these calls? You were there all weekend . . .'

'When I work at home I don't pick up, it's the only way to get anything done. Probably I would have if I'd known Daddy or Jane was calling.'

She looks all over the room as though she's following a fly.

'Did you save the messages?' she asks at last.

'Yes.'

'I'd like to hear them.'

I falter. 'I'll have to find out the long distance access code . . .'

'Let me know as soon as you have it. As soon as possible.' She stands up. I jump up too as though she just unhandcuffed me.

'You look tired, it's extremely late now in New York. I certainly have further questions for you but they can wait until tomorrow morning. I assume you're staying with your sister?'

My cheeks were just cooling and now they're hot again.

'Now I'm here I figured I could maybe just stay . . .'

'In this house?' She hasn't raised her voice but there is a note of alarm. 'Forensic won't finish for a while,' she says. 'But even when they do, you'd be unwise to stay here alone.'

'But I'll be fine . . .'

'Lucy, until we know what happened to your father and why, we can't be sure of your safety. His keys weren't found on the beach. We don't know who has them.'

As she leads me down the hallway she pauses.

'We're having difficulty accessing some documents on your father's computer. You don't, by any chance, know his password?'

I shake my head.

'Any guesses?'

'Hmmmm. Probably a rock name . . . obsidian, jade, quartz, pyrites . . .'

She smiles. 'I'll look in a rock book. Lucy, I'd like to see you back here tomorrow morning. Is nine-thirty okay?'

'Sure.'

'Keep this in case you ever need to contact me.' She hands me a card. Her name is Kirsty MacFarlane. She is a senior detective in the police department's homicide division.

I say: 'You see homicide everywhere because it's your job. It's your life. But there are some places it just doesn't occur. In an ordinary family like ours, for example.'

The woman doesn't reply. She opens the screen door. From the hallway I could hear the voices of Larry, Jane and Sasha chatting in cordial, late night tones. Now I see Larry on a porch seat and Jane, her coat wound tightly around her, on the swing. A smoke ring wafts between us. Sasha, on the steps, at the edge of the porch's circle of light, watches me as he exhales.

Jane turns to me. She looks cold and tired. 'Are you okay?'

I nod.

Sasha says: 'Come, Lucy, let me take you home at once. Mama will be waiting for you.'

Jane and Larry exchange concerned looks and then Larry speaks. 'There's a bed ready in our apartment.'

71

I think of Jane and Larry's city apartment, of its white chairs and white surfaces and white rugs.

'Mama has already prepared a bed for you,' insists Sasha, 'and she will be most disappointed if you don't sleep in it tonight.'

I look at Jane and she nods her permission but when she hugs me farewell she says, without confidence: 'Will you come to the beach house tomorrow? Larry and I are going at lunchtime and Scott would sure like to see you. Or . . .' She looks away, ready for rejection. 'Or maybe you don't want to go to Needle Bay? Or see Scott? Or any of us? I don't understand what's going on with you, Lucy. If you really don't want to be with us, we'll try to understand.'

I am reproached by her kindness. I say: 'Jane, I want to see you all more than anything.' And as I say this I know it's true.

Her body relaxes and she smiles at me.

'Including Scott?'

Foolishly, secretly, in the dark city, I've imagined my reunion with Scott many times, and always as a joyful occasion at the beach house on a day warm enough to thicken the air with the scent of ocean and pines. In my dreams, we smile at one another. We notice the small insignias of ageing (a colourless hair, a deepening line). We welcome them for the wisdom which comes with them, because wisdom allows us to forgive.

I say: 'I'm looking forward to seeing Scott.'

Sasha drives us back to the city. He offers me chocolate and, when I refuse, eats it himself. He tells me to try to sleep and then is silent but my eyes don't want to close and I stare at the road ahead as it rolls ceaselessly under our headlights until it seems that we are still and only the road is moving.

As we approach Aunt Zina's dingy apartment building I

am overtaken by emotions for which I am unprepared. Since Grandma's death her apartment has been occupied by Aunt Zina and for years I visited here regularly with my mother. Now that part of my childhood, like a dog which has been waiting patiently all this time, leaps up to greet me, knocking me over with its weight. The squat, shabby building, its bare and underlit lobby, the elevator, daubed with graffiti in Russian, the smell of cabbage, the unexplained insistence that the stairs here are not negotiable although the building is just four storeys high: the unchanged patina of my relatives' lives combines now with my grief to overwhelm me. As we wait for the juddering elevator I peer down the shaft, the way I peered down it on every childhood visit and, just for a moment before the car descends, believe that I have located the small, dirty shoe of a child almost buried beneath other garbage.

When the elevator doors slide open on the third storey to reveal my aunts, I am too tearful to speak. Aunt Zoya, a large, thin broom of a woman, and the smaller, bustling Aunt Zina engulf me at once in a tide of love. They bear me across the hallway to the apartment where the air is dense with the smell of Russian cooking.

'But your poor papa,' they say as the door closes behind us. 'Why did he drown? What do the police say about such a thing?'

I tell them all I know and the aunts cluck and shake their heads, exchanging troubled looks.

'Surely this is not possible,' they say miserably. 'Surely no one would harm your dear papa.'

'He was a kind man,' Aunt Zina informs me. 'He was more than generous because he had an instinct to give. He would give his time, his attention, his money . . . many husbands would have turned their back on Tanya but Eric continued to give. Lucia, your papa was a man with a sense of right and wrong. He adhered to what was right.'

I feel pleased. Yes, Daddy always tried to do the right thing.

'As well as his heart I admired his mind,' adds Aunt Zoya, whom I now remember, many years ago, in animated discussion on the beach with Daddy, fingers pulling the hair from their faces, the wind blowing it right back. What did Daddy talk about with his wife's homely, clever, elder sister, a woman I had noticed others acknowledge then ignore? I wish now I had listened to their intelligent conversation instead of digging holes in the sand.

'His mind,' she continues, 'was never quiet. He did not cease to gather information and inside his head he organized it, redirected it. And, of course, he shared his thoughts freely.'

Their words warm me. The way the detective spoke about Daddy dehumanized him. He was reduced to a homicide case, renamed The Decedent, probably given a number. Now my aunts are giving me back the man.

'No one could wish to kill such a one as your papa,' they assure me. 'It's impossible and the police will find they have made a mistake.'

I look to Sasha for agreement but he is busy pouring a pale liquid into small glasses to celebrate my arrival and does not catch my eye.

'And your husband,' they ask. 'Is he still at the university?'

'Yes. And his book's been published.' Scott didn't tell me that. I know it because, late one night, I turned on the TV and the small, still New York apartment was suddenly filled by Scott's voice. The men behind the transcontinental railroad: industrial heroes or just corrupt speculators? I crouched right in front of the TV, staring as Scott stroked his chin the way Larry strokes his beard sometimes, watching him thinking, hearing his voice without listening to his answer. When the programme finished I switched off but remained in front of the TV and the silence in the apartment was acute.

'But,' ask my aunts, 'are you still married to him?'

'We haven't lived together for a few years. But we haven't discussed divorce either . . .'

They brush aside these formalities. 'Does he love you?' they cry. 'Do you still love him?'

'I think so. But . . .' I flounder and Sasha rescues me.

'Mama, Aunt Zoya, if you were so cruel to a dog you would be arrested. For heaven's sake, let us toast Lucia instead of grilling her.' And he clinks his glass against mine.

I am purred over, stroked, fed and watered. Little contribution is demanded from me. I listen to stories of relatives until I am confused by the half-remembered names of the spouses of second cousins. Finally, inevitably, they speak of Mother.

'We visit weekly,' Aunt Zina assures me. 'And even Sasha comes sometimes.'

Sasha, relaxed now in an armchair, balancing a glass on his knee, raises it in confirmation.

No dereliction of duty by me is implied but I am nevertheless stung. I telephoned Mother at the clinic a few times when I first left California but the conversations were at best difficult and I gradually allowed them to peter out. At Christmas or on her birthday and sometimes in between I send her small, colourful cards. I spend a long time selecting them. A picture of a brown dog like the one she used to own. Something abstract in which her colour, blue, is dominant. Cards from a Russian exhibition showing innumerable birch trees or peasants in felt boots pulling sledges through the snow. These small, thin colourful pieces of card are strong enough to bear our whole relationship these days.

As if sensing my feelings, Aunt Zoya throws up her long arms. 'Such beautiful pictures you send her!'

Aunt Zina darts. 'Yes, yes, she saves them all and speaks of you often. Your return will bring her great pleasure.'

I know my face is crimson. I wish they wouldn't talk about her as though she were sane.

Sasha looks at Aunt Zina. 'For God's sake, Mama,' he says. 'Do you know what time it is in New York? It is five in the morning and Lucia only learned hours ago of her father's death. Do you think it is fair to talk to her when she should certainly be sleeping?' And he adds something in Russian.

Aunts Zoya and Zina agree quickly and lead me to the room which was once Grandma's and is now to be mine. It is little altered and it seems to me that even Grandma's scents of candy and medicine linger here. The room is fleetingly half-lit each time a car passes. I lie cocooned in her bed, glimpsing by occasional carlight, as though in a series of photos, the accumulation of mementos, pictures and souvenirs which, at the close of each day, furnished Grandma's world. In the living-room I can hear my relatives quietly murmuring the music of the Russian language, so that they seem to be half speaking and half singing. It is Daddy's death, I reflect, which has brought me, in the space of one day, from an eighty-third storey in New York back into the heart of my family's past.

8

In my dreams I am terrified by the roar of a big truck. I hide until a telephone rings, then a doorbell. There are distant voices. I am finally awoken by a strange quality to the light. A yolky yellow bathing my eyelids, wrapping itself around me as though I'm inside an egg. Or maybe I'm at home and I left the lamp on all night. Then I remember that Daddy is dead and I'm back in California. Once again, shock, sadness and grief, all physical sensations, as violent as the cartoon books I read as a kid. Bang! Bif! Bam! Phoof! First my belly, then my chest, then more blows somewhere around my temples. I open my eyes and there is sun in them.

I wander through the living-room. The walls are thick with shelves and each shelf sags beneath its contents. Books, boxes, bags, stacks of papers and letters, ornaments, some of them with pieces broken off but placed alongside. One, a long-necked swan, has, I'm sure, awaited repair since my childhood. There are also a few pretty rocks, certainly donated by Daddy.

In the kitchen, Aunt Zina is busy. I watch her flitting from fridge to oven and back like a humming bird. Then she stands before the stove with a frying pan in her hand. As she twists her wrist to right and left the pan tilts and batter runs evenly across its hot surface. She frowns with concentration. I am struck by her similarity to my mother. So this is how Mother might have looked one day if she were sane. The movements swift and precise, the eyes bright, the hair sensibly bobbed and scarcely grey.

'Aaaah,' she cries when she sees me, a cry of pleasure. She produces coffee, toast, kasha, jelly, blinis, juice, and as soon as one sample is consumed, begs me to try another.

'Sasha left early, too early, for work this morning. And he had a meeting so late last night that he was obliged to leave it directly to find his dear cousin at the airport. They work him like a slave at that place. A slave.' She speaks with passion and shakes her head energetically.

I smile. 'You haven't changed a bit,' I tell her.

She hands me a large photograph in a new frame.

'Since when? Since then?' She giggles. I recognize the three sisters, Zoya, Zina and Mother, seated shyly with their parents. The father, bones standing high in his face, his mouth proportioned without generosity. Grandma, eerily young, younger than I am now, unsmiling but beautiful, her eyes penetrating.

'Sasha will find a place to hang this,' Aunt Zina informs me, looking doubtfully around the room for wallspace. 'Zoya discovered this old picture and had it made big for my birthday, perhaps because it particularly flatters her.'

I study Aunt Zoya, the least attractive, even now, of the sisters, and it is true that youth loaned angles to the curious roundness of her face.

'It was taken soon after we arrived in America and Papa took his first job with the building company. Before Katya and Olya were born. Except Mama looks a little bit pregnant, don't you agree?'

'Maybe. So it must have been . . . 1941?'

'Or '42. Zoya is perhaps fourteen, I am twelve. Your mother is nine, no, ten years old. Even then she was beautiful.'

I stare at the smallest of the girls. She is not smiling but receptive to the camera's stare, her blonde hair curving around her cheeks, the bones of her face already prominent

78

like her father's, her eyes dazzling although in the photograph they are grey. The girl who grew up to be Mother.

'We were poor but still Papa paid for this picture. He understood how the ordinary is fascinating when time has left it behind.'

'You weren't so ordinary, none of you,' I tell her but I am still staring at Mother.

When Mother and Daddy decided to marry, only Zina offered no opposition to their hasty, passionate union. Grandma and Grandpa presented alternative candidates from the Russian community. Aunt Zoya pleaded for longer consideration. The giggly teenaged Katya and Olya begged Mother to find someone younger. It was true that he was almost ten years Mother's senior and already a professor in the university's geology department. Mother worked in the Russian department. She was a secretary. Like many women of her generation, it did not occur to her to study there. One summer her boss went on vacation and she had nothing to do, so, when the geology department advertised for people on campus to help them move premises, she volunteered. She worked for Daddy for three weeks and at the end of it the geology department was rehoused and they were married.

I like that story, I've liked it since I was a small child. Mother told it well. She described how she helped Daddy catalogue rocks. Not one roomful, not two but . . . and here she waved her arms in a vast, expansive gesture, three, yes three rooms full of rocks! She leaned forward and closed her eyes a little when she told us how she watched Daddy run his fingers around the bubbles of malachite and stroke the rings of haematite. How he labelled each rock gently and handled them with care while she listed them.

She said: 'I knew then that for Daddy rocks are not lifeless the way they are for most people. And I knew that a man who had enough love even for rocks must have a little to spare for me!' She beamed and her face, which could look unhappy in repose, was another face, the face of the beautiful woman who reorganized the filing system, who catalogued the rocks, who married the professor. She straightened her hair and then her body. 'And the geology department held a party for us. They made a cake . . .' She giggled girlishly. 'They made a cake in the shape of a mountain with all the geological layers! They asked me for a joke to identify them but, you see, I had already learned a lot and to their astonishment I was able to do so!' That laugh again, happy, loud. The laugh of an intelligent, high-spirited woman. 'Pre-Cambrian, Palaeozoic, Cambrian, Odovician, Silurian . . . !' She joyfully threw out each name like a beacon flashing its light across the water.

'God!' I exclaim involuntarily. 'God, where did that woman go?' The woman who married Daddy. The woman who told us the story of how she married Daddy. The woman with thick fair hair that seemed to spill out of her head. The woman with the blue eyes who laughed loudly, delightedly, who looked as though a light had just clicked on inside her whenever she smiled. One day I walked into a canyon and when I came out she had become another woman completely.

'Sometimes,' Aunt Zina informs me, somehow understanding my thoughts, 'it is possible to find a little of the old Tanya, even today.'

But it is many years since I stopped looking for my mother amid the human wreckage at Redbush clinic. Silently I hand back the picture. In exchange, Aunt Zina passes me a key.

'For your shining new hirecar.' Her eyes glitter. 'It was delivered this morning by a young man. A young man in a uniform. These old apartments have a lack of parking places.

Naturally the young man did not know that. It happens he has taken a space Dimitri Sergeyevich downstairs considers his own and this unpleasant person and bad neighbour has telephoned twice about the problem. Sasha finally explained the circumstances and he agreed to allow it to remain but for today only.'

'When I come back tonight I'll park in the lot where Mother used to leave the car.'

'No, Lucia, it is two blocks away. Sasha can park there, you must use his space.'

I have no intention of taking Sasha's parking space but it is eight fifteen and there is no time to argue. I explain why I must leave at once and Aunt Zina snorts.

'Why should the police interview you so urgently? It is impossible that you can be of any assistance to them. They are simply wasting their own time and yours.'

It is easy to guess which car in the lot is mine. It gleams with newness. As I climb in I am surveyed by a silver-haired man, bent almost double. It is not clear whether his hands are on his hips to express outrage or to hold himself up. He says something gruffly to me in Russian.

When I arrive at Daddy's house I find the uniformed officers and the tape at the end of the drive gone. As I swing up the hill something shines at me through the trees, sharp as a knife, bright as chrome, so that when I turn the corner my heart is thumping. I expect to see a big truck but I find only litter, a can top which the police must have left behind. There would never have been litter when Daddy was alive.

The day's early warmth embraces me. I stand in the shadow of the house and, except for the occasional ticking of the hot car, I feel the completeness of the silence. Nothing moves. Even the leaves are still as though the old place has been waiting for me. Inexplicably, I recall a detail from the story Mother used to tell us about Grandma's baby boy dying on the train when the family was escaping from Russia. I recall how, when the border guard opened the door of the car, he knew at once from the motionless passengers that something was wrong and that they were waiting for him to notice it. How their very stillness drew his attention to the woman with the dead baby on her lap.

I swing round, convinced that something is wrong, sure that there is something here in the stillness I should notice. But the leaves hang limply as handkerchiefs, the branches are motionless, the house and the barn ring with their own silence, the stones of the drive shine where the sun cuts across their surfaces. The only thing amiss is the can top. I pick it up.

I still have a key to Daddy's house. In the three years I was away I didn't take it off my key-ring. I place it in my palm now where it lies flat as a fish. I walk beneath branches to the porch and I like the noise of my walk. The dead bark and knife-sharp leaves of the eucalyptus trees are so dry that they crackle and rustle beneath my feet and overhead the foliage releases a medicinal aroma.

At the threshold of the house I pause to accustom myself to its smell, its coolness, its darkness. Its absences. Impossible to believe that Daddy has entirely vacated this space which was his for so many years. Impossible to believe I won't find him here.

'Hi!' calls a voice. The detective. She is advancing towards me, briefcase in hand, dark under the dark trees. My fingers wind themselves around the can top.

'What a beautiful day. It's only March but it sure feels like summer's here,' she says cheerfully. Together we go into the house. We stand at the door to Daddy's den and she tells me that she has taken Daddy's computer.

'We're still having trouble getting into some documents. You haven't remembered his password?'

'I'm sure I never knew it.'

She wants me to sign for this and the other paperwork she removed from the den.

'What paperwork?' I ask curiously.

'Oh, financial stuff.'

'Like . . . bank statements?'

'Exactly that. We need a full picture of your father's finances.'

I wonder why, but I sign the documents she gives me without asking the question.

'I've copied it, but you still need to sign for it,' she tells me, putting piles of papers on Daddy's desk. 'Scott's going to need these originals.'

'Scott?'

'He's your father's personal representative.'

'His what?'

'His executor. That's what executors are called these days.'

'Scott?' I echo incredulously. 'Daddy appointed Scott executor?'

She looks at me.

'Is that so surprising?'

'Yes. Scott's a real smart guy but math isn't his strong suit. He nearly flunked it in high school and even with a calculator he never gets the same answer twice . . .'

Her look is keen. 'You think Professor Schaffer should have asked you instead?'

'Well . . .' Of course he should have asked me.

'After all, you're the banker around here,' she adds, watching me closely. She's wondering why Daddy didn't trust me to carry out his wishes. I'm wondering too, but I shrug. I don't want her to know that Daddy has hurt me.

'I guess he had his reasons,' she says at last. I wish she'd stop looking at me. I am grateful when she suggests that she interview me out on the deck and I can turn my back as I lead us across the living-room.

'At least you're the beneficiary,' she says. 'You and Jane. Did you know that?'

'I sort of assumed it.'

I pull back the sliding doors. I prepare myself for the shock that is the valley but even so I have to pause a moment to absorb its immensity and flatness, its tidy productivity. It is laid out beneath us like a huge table, groaning with food.

We sit down. The day had seemed still but as soon as the detective draws her notebook from her briefcase the pages flutter.

'I'm hoping,' she says, cradling the papers to her like an infant, 'that by now you've thought of someone who can confirm you were home all last weekend.'

I shake my head. 'There isn't anyone.'

'You worked the whole time?'

'I didn't see anyone who can confirm I was in New York.'

'You didn't leave the apartment?'

'I took some short breaks for food.'

'Is work what you usually do on the weekends?'

I hesitate. 'It's what I do all the time,' I say at last.

The detective raises her eyebrows. I look out across the valley. It stretches as far as you can see. On the other side are hills and sometimes on cool, sunny winter mornings you get an intimation of them, the way, when you're at sea, you sometimes think you can spy land.

'Do you know anything about your father's movements over the weekend?' the detective asks me. 'Did he talk about any plans?'

I omit mentioning Daddy's visit to Stevie's grave. I say

that I knew he intended to spend Saturday with Jane and Larry and Scott.

'Sunday?'

I shrug.

'I have good reason to be interested in how your father spent Sunday afternoon. I want you to think hard and tell me whether you recall him mentioning that he expected company? Or was there someone who visited him most Sundays?'

I think hard and then shake my head so the valley seems to jump from side to side. Then it is still again and its lines are straight. It is neatly divided into big quadrangles by roads and smaller quadrangles by blocks of fruit trees.

She says: 'His car's still missing. Do you have any idea of somewhere he might have driven it early on Monday? Did he like to go into town Mondays? Or was there some friend he met for breakfast?'

'Well, he might have intended to take some kind of exercise with his friend Seymour. They sometimes did fitness things together.'

The woman does not respond and I see that Jane's already made this suggestion and Seymour has already been contacted. She asks me more questions about Daddy, about his habits and his friends and his character. Detailed questions, which I find hard to answer. I've never analysed what sort of a man he was. I hear myself stumbling and then I fall on the small tributes my aunts paid him last night and offer these to the detective.

'He always tried to do what he thought was right.' I sound lame. The detective seems to sense that she is hearing someone else's words.

'When you were small, when you went to other kids' houses . . .' she persists. I tense. We didn't much go to other kids' houses because it meant the kids would sooner or later demand to visit our house and that was not okay, at least not until later when Mother was in the clinic. 'Did you meet their fathers? Do you remember thinking that your father was similar or different?'

I nod. 'Oh yes. Other people's fathers were sort of scary. They had loud voices and they were too big.'

She smiles. 'Too big?'

'I mean, they got in the way. They sometimes wanted to play with their kids but I guess that back then most fathers didn't really know how. They'd organize a ballgame and then get mad because we made up our own rules. And they'd shout a lot ... I mean, if you just went down to the store with them you could be sure someone would get shouted at for something dumb like, say, messing with the bubblegum machine.'

'Your father didn't shout?'

I shake my head. Daddy was always kind. He didn't try to organize games unless we asked him and then he didn't make some creaking and inappropriate attempt at participation. He expected us to amuse ourselves. Other fathers, hoarse-voiced, frantic after ballgames turned chaotic and toys broke, handed mothers the kids back with obvious relief just as soon as they walked in through the door from shopping or visiting. Daddy didn't have anyone to hand us to and he gave no sign he wanted to. He never seemed sad when summer camp ended or relieved when school started. I wonder now at how even and unchanging he was. Did he ever feel mad at us and not show it? I try to recall Daddy getting upset or emotional or acting Russian, even a tiny bit. I can't. I can't even recall him laughing the way other people sometimes laugh, red-faced, shaking, with their heads thrown back.

The detective says thoughtfully: 'Jane's told me about your

mother's problems. I guess Professor Schaffer had to play both mother and father to you. That must have been hard when he had a job as well. Did he leave you alone a lot?'

It seems to me that, once Mother was trapped on her private, hellish treadmill of psychosis, I was always alone. Standing in the canyon, Mother's shrieks bouncing off its walls, I felt an acute loneliness which didn't go away, not ever, not yet.

'Well, there was my big sister,' I remind her. 'She did a lot of the stuff Mother should have done.'

'You and Jane were close as kids?'

I look out across the valley. 'I don't know what would have happened to me if it hadn't been for Jane,' I confess. 'I mean, I was her first patient. I was always sick and she took care of me.'

'Maybe that's why she went into medicine,' suggests the woman.

'Because of me being sick? Well, maybe. There was this car crash in the valley when I was just out of high school and she helped me a lot then, too.'

I look down at Sunnyfruit Orchards, to that long, straight stretch of road where the car I was riding in with Robert Joseph turned right over, remembered now as a series of snapshots: the road, vertical instead of horizontal, a fruit tree too close and then another upside down, the grainy proximity of the orchard's dirt. The first person I remember being there was Mrs Joseph, with a friend who happened to be in the house. The friend told me not to move and held my hand, talking to me kindly. Someone must have called the house because Jane, just home for the summer, arrived soon afterwards. She stayed by me and Mrs Joseph's friend seemed to evaporate. Then the ambulances came. Robert was badly hurt. Jane said I had to stay right where I was while they lifted his body very slowly through the open doors, the stretcher moulded around his shape. She said: 'No, Luce, he isn't dead, he really isn't.' In the hospital I learned that he was crushed along one side and that maybe they would remove a leg. They released me that same day with a couple of minor fractures in one foot and when I came home I could see Robert's father's car still down in the valley. It lay crooked at the side of the road, roof down, like a big insect dead on its back. It was another whole day before the Josephs had it moved. And now, all these years later, I'm staring out across the valley and searching for the car again as if I just graduated from high school and am in love with Robert Joseph. In my left foot, a dull, persistent ache.

'Lucy?'

I look back at the detective. She's asked me something but her voice got lost years back. She repeats the question, maybe louder this time. She wants to know whether there were any arguments within the family, what Daddy's relationship was like with Scott and Larry, whether he had enemies. Mostly I shrug in answer.

'We're nothing out of the ordinary,' I say. 'Everyone gets along. Nobody hates anyone. Daddy didn't have enemies, he wasn't that kind of a man.'

Her voice is sharp. 'Lucy, why did you leave California?'

'Career reasons,' I tell her quickly.

'There wasn't some kind of a rift in the family? An argument?'

'Oh no, no. I was a personal banker but I really wanted to move into investment banking. The only opportunities here are in Silicon Valley. Otherwise you have to go to New York.'

She looks at me, waiting to hear more, as though she already knows there is. She waits so long that finally the words come stumbling out of me.

'We had a baby but he died.' A statement. Flat like the valley. Unemotional. There's a twist in my voice but it's too distant for anyone to perceive. It comes from across the valley, beyond the horizon.

The woman does not react.

I add: 'Sudden Infant Death Syndrome.' The twist moves closer. It could be a tornado.

'Your baby's death played a significant part in your decision to leave?'

'Yes. I left soon afterwards. It was exactly three years ago. That's why I stayed home all weekend. That's why I didn't answer the phone.'

She nods and closes her notebook.

'That's all I have for you right now. Thanks for your help.' She tries it both ways but the notebook won't fit back into her briefcase. It has grown fat on my grief.

'I was expecting my colleague, Detective Michael Rougemont, to join us this morning,' Kirsty says, 'but I guess he's been detained elsewhere. He'll want to talk to you soon.'

I rise but she is still re-organizing the contents of her bag. After a moment, I realize the movements she makes aren't necessary. She takes out a small notebook and puts it back twice. She's stalling while she thinks about something else, something else she wants to say, wondering what words, what tone to use. She's so distracted that I can watch her openly. The dark-clothed detective has her own quiet beauty. I see that now for the first time and for the first time I notice the thin, criss-cross lines around her eyes. Shadows beneath them. She gets home and she's tired. When she's asleep her children call for her in the night. She goes to them like a sleepwalker. Then she lies awake thinking. She thinks about her homicide cases. She thinks about people who kill other people.

She stands up suddenly and her eyes are exactly level with mine. We're the same height. We're probably about the same age, too. She says carefully: 'The death of a parent can bring the past right up close. Have you already felt that?'

I nod, acknowledging the past's new clarity.

'Maybe when you went to New York you thought you could leave everything here behind,' she adds. 'But now you're back you could just decide that it's time for you to stop running. I have a feeling that you're going to turn around and look at whatever it is that's been chasing you. You're going to look it right in the eyes.'

The woman waits for me to say something.

I ask: 'Where is Daddy's body now?'

It's not what she was expecting to hear. She pauses a moment before she replies. 'In a police mortuary.'

'I'd like to see him.'

'That's really not necessary. Your brother-in-law has already identified the body for us.'

'I'd still like to see him.'

She looks kind. 'I don't advise that.'

'I must.'

She flicks back her ghost hair and smiles sadly. 'I'm supposed to encourage idents so I won't argue with you.'

In Daddy's den she makes a call and after a brief discussion we agree that I will go this afternoon to the police mortuary at Bellamy, a coastal town to the north of the city which must be the nearest mortuary to Big Brim and Retribution.

I watch her car bounce down the rocky drive and then I do not return indoors. I walk right around the house until my body is aslant on the steep hillside. One leg long and the other bent, I edge along the base of the deck. The tree trunks are big enough to hold on to now, big enough for a treehouse. I remember how much I wanted a treehouse when I was a kid, my disappointment when Daddy examined all the trees and said we didn't have one strong enough. I guess his house will be sold now and whoever buys it can build a treehouse if they want to. I am arrested by jealousy for the family which lives here next. I cling to a tree, the valley glimmering through the foliage behind me. I close my eyes and try to imagine the faceless people who will replace us. But the house, the barn and the yard are already fully inhabited by my own family's past.

I skirt the sunken garden, overgrown now, and at the Holler orchard I cut back up through the trees towards the barn. Thorny branches catch at my clothes, bushes emit herbal aromas. I'm watching the ground. Not so far from the Holler orchard, I find a rock. Its shape is familiar. I pick it up. It is not a rock but a shoe heel. I examine the heel and then pocket it but before I can move on up the hill I hear a sound. Crack. It lasts only a moment but within that moment I am seized by a new knowledge. I am not alone. Crack. The snap of a dry, fallen branch underfoot. I recognize it like my sister's voice, like the slam of the screen door, the squeak of the swing.

I reel rapidly around. The branches, the leaves, the grass seem to stare back at me, as though surprised into motionlessness. I swing to the right and left, quickly, anxiously, and then more systematically turn through a hundred and eighty degrees, staring through the trees, up into trees, around the trunks of trees. A few are thick enough to hide a human figure. I stand so still that I don't breathe. The hillside seems to hold its breath too. There is no sound and nothing moves but way back, through the Holler orchard, a shadow flickers which could be a man moving fast or it could be a tree shuddering in the far breeze.

Reluctantly I go back up to the house. I turn around twice

more before I get there but see nothing. When the screen door has slammed behind me, I find my purse and tuck the shoe heel into one of its small compartments. I snap it shut. The snap echoes into the silence like the twig which snapped out in the yard, snapped beneath someone, face unknown, intent unknown.

Out on the deck the silence persists. I lean on the railings and keep a constant vigil across the yard. I'm looking for movement but, apart from the occasional, startling bird, there is none. Gradually the valley claims my attention. My eye meanders over the usual landmarks. The place the car turned over. The intersection. The farm where I arrived with Lindy after so long and hot a walk that it seemed like the orchard was inside our mouths. The dirt roads along which they drove us home, bouncing in the back of the farm pick-up, Lindy's blonde hair flattened by the heat, the pair of us grinning as the pick-up weaved and we were thrown to right and left. Lindy Zacarro. When I think of her I feel a small circle of pain inside my belly. Lindy Zacarro, the girl who sat on the porch swing giggling with me. My best friend, for a while.

I feel the small hairs on my arm and my neck stand up. At first I don't know why. Then I see that, far below me, cutting slowly across the valley floor, glinting like a silver fish, fin uppermost, is a tow truck. From here it is no bigger than a toy and its progress is silent. When it reaches the intersection it turns north. I watch until it has disappeared in the mist, which is never mist when you're down there but just the edge of your vision.

9

As I drive away from the house, heading for the coast and my family, I recall, involuntarily, Lindy Zacarro's face. I haven't thought about her for years and then yesterday I remembered her presence on the creaking swing and today fragments of her keep surfacing in my memory, as though there's some mad filing clerk who's determined to put everything we have on Lindy Zacarro right on the desk in front of me. I recall her face. Round, very pretty, blonde, and a lot of pink. Pink tongue, pink lips, invariably pink clothes. The prettiest, pinkest girl in the class.

When the farmer, the back of his neck brown and creased like thick leather, brought Lindy and me home, Lindy gave him directions to the Zacarro house. She didn't even have to look at me to know this was the right answer. Once Mother came out of the clinic, we didn't play at my house any more. I had hoped when Mother was finally discharged that she might be the way she used to be, before she went crazy in the canyon. But after Daddy took us to visit her in hospital a few times, I knew this was impossible. Mother sat in her small room and regarded the three of us in distasteful silence, as though we were hitchhikers who had ambushed her car and were demanding a ride. I waited for her to recognize me and put her arms around me. I wanted her perfume and that smell of sugary cookies to envelope me. I thought if I could touch her maybe this strange new shell would shatter and Mother would break out from inside it and start to make cookies and tell stories. But when I advanced across the room towards her, she looked shocked and Jane immediately pulled me back. As we filed silently out, Mother began to cry. Daddy gestured for us to wait in the hallway but I lingered a few minutes, watching him crouch as close to her as she would allow, talking softly, reassuring her. I hoped his words would coax Mother out from inside this stranger.

When at last she came home I could see that she was trying to resume her old self, her old life. She tried hard but now this was a mask. When she laughed it was too loud and when she told stories they were strange, jumbled narratives which collapsed before she had reached any satisfying conclusion. When she attempted physical affection she either clutched me to her, suffocating me, or her touch was so light it felt like insects and sent me scuttling irritably across the room. She found small practicalities, like cooking, almost impossible. Cookies emerged hot from the stove, smelling right but with the consistency of rocks. We pretended to eat them while we hid them in our pockets. We pretended, to Mother and to each other, that she was normal.

'Luce, maybe it's not a good idea for friends to come home with you right now . . .' Jane warned me sagely. Her hair ran down her back in one neat braid and I admired her for doing this braid all by herself. If I wanted to braid my hair I'd try for ten minutes and finally ask Jane to do it.

'But Mother's better,' I insisted. I was playing real hard at normal.

'Sure. We know she is . . . but other people may not see it,' she warned me, her voice kind like Daddy's.

'Sure they will,' I insisted. What she meant was, other people couldn't be trusted to join in our make-believe, but I didn't understand that. 'I mean, maybe just Lindy can come here,' I added, cajoling, not pleading.

Jane's face wrinkled. 'Not even Lindy,' she told me quietly. 'I'm saying this to protect you. I know what could happen.'

I was mad at her. I was often mad at her, and I see now that this was the sort of anger children feel for their parents whenever their parents prevent them from doing something which jeopardizes their safety. The parent seems unreasonable to the uncomprehending child. The parent appears to be using their authority arbitrarily to prevent the child from growing up or away, to be issuing prohibitions in their own interests and not the child's. So I sulked. I sulked all the way over to the Zacarro house and it was some while before I could bring myself to tell Lindy that Jane said she couldn't come over to our house any more and, when I did, she sulked too.

About twenty minutes south of Scott's house, I stop at a place where you can pull off the road and park right by the edge of the cliff with only a thin safety barrier between you and the sea. This place is called Seal Wash but there are no seals visible today. I switch off the car's engine and I can hear the sea hammering against the rocks below as though it's trying to break down the cliff and my car along with it.

I take the shoe heel from my purse. I get out and stand close enough to the cliff to look down on the massive body of water pressing against the land like a threatening crowd. Watching the water hit the rocks and swing, hissing, in all directions makes me dizzy. I look up at the coast road, winding along the land's edge. When there is no car in sight, I fling the shoe heel as far out to sea as I can. Either the throw is feeble or the wind catches the heel but it bounces back against the cliff face beneath me, slowly as though weightless, before it disappears into the water.

After Seal Wash there are a couple of sandy bays, then Big Brim. My heart beats fast and I try to slow down but the other traffic, seeing the sudden straight stretch of blacktop, accelerates. There is a parking lot alongside the road on the right and, on the left, high sand dunes mask the sea. In a moment I am through, the coastline is rocky again and the road winds around it once more.

When I reach Needle Bay and see the gentle curve of the beach where I lived with Scott, I am almost overwhelmed by emotion. Instead of swinging down the track which leads through the pines to the beach house, I stop at the hilltop parking lot. Soundlessly I visit again that inner landscape of loss, quiet and empty after Stevie's death.

The little wooden cottage is invisible among the tree tops but the beach screams white and beyond it the sea stretches away forever, its colour darkening with its depth. I have been here many times in my dreams and now that I am back at last I feel a sort of relief. There is even nostalgia for that brief period when we moved here, right after Stevie died, when my grief was as fresh and spongy as new-made bread. Life was straightforward then. It consisted of grief. There was nothing else to feel and nothing else to do but relive, tirelessly, relentlessly, the night of Stevie's death. Since then that night has been so often recalled that, like some over-used toy, the colours have washed out of it. It has been laundered, ironed and allocated its place in some deep closet. And now I am back at Needle Bay the closet door swings suddenly open.

I spent the last day of Stevie's life working. Most people had already started their Easter vacation but an important Pacific Rim client was in town and before meeting the client at his hotel I thought I should go into the office to study his portfolio. I'd tried doing that kind of work at home but somehow Stevie, although he was so small, took up the whole house.

He was asleep when I showered and dressed, probably because he had awoken many times in the night. Then, just before I was due to leave, he woke. I fed him and changed him and Scott held him but it was no good. He started to cry with that tenacity, that dogged determination, which meant he had no intention of stopping.

'Go,' Scott said. 'Just go. He'll be fine.'

As I drove down the pretty street where we lived, I could hear Stevie's protests echoing inside my head and mostly what I felt was relief. I was going to a job which I was good at and leaving behind a situation which was completely outside my control.

I spent the day with the client. He was demanding but at the end of the afternoon he congratulated me on my work. I hadn't thought about Stevie all morning but during the afternoon I had experienced sudden flashes of longing and by the time I returned to the house I just wanted to smell him and feel his small, soft body in my arms. Larry's car was in the drive and so was Daddy's Oldsmobile. I parked on the street and, the moment I switched off the engine, I heard the sound which had followed me down the road that morning. Stevie was crying again. I sat in the car listening and my body reacted involuntarily. Each repetition penetrated a little deeper until my muscles were stiff.

Inside, the house was filled by Stevie's misery. Scott appeared from the kitchen with an avocado and gestured helplessly with it up the stairs.

'We fed him, we changed him, we distracted him but he won't stop. Jane's up there with him now.'

'Has he been crying all day?'

'Nope, he saves it up for you.'

It was hard not to take Stevie's tears personally.

I didn't go straight upstairs. First I looked into the living-room where Larry and Daddy were playing chess before dinner, apparently oblivious to the sound overhead.

97

'Hi, Lucy,' Daddy said to me. 'Check,' he told Larry.

Larry turned and gave me a conspiratorial nod, trying to suggest he was letting the old man win. But I knew that the hunch of Larry's shoulders was probably the hunch of defeat. I never beat Daddy at chess, although perhaps that was because I didn't want to.

I climbed the stairs and the noise increased with every step. Jane was sitting by the window holding the baby against her shoulder. The slim late afternon light fell on to the book she was reading while Stevie's wails were directed behind her. As she read, Jane stroked the baby's back.

'I tried everything,' she said when she saw me. 'And in the end I just gave up and let him cry.'

I took Stevie from her, very gently. He turned his wet face to me and, for a moment, it unscrewed itself. The skin whitened and his eyes widened and it seemed the noise would cease. But the silence was fragile and when I placed his body against mine his back arched and he lifted his head and roared with renewed vigour.

'Thought you'd done it for a moment there,' said Jane. I shook my head. Stevie seemed to be drawing on some well of human misery and it was a deep well.

'He was crying when I left. He's crying when I get home. And yet they say in daycare he's quiet as a mouse. What am I doing wrong?'

'Nothing. He just needs to cry, some babies do.' Jane's tone was professional.

'Why am I such an incompetent mother?'

Jane was even firmer. 'You're not.'

The noise was increasing in intensity. The meal was ready. Jane and Scott tried to persuade me to leave Stevie in his crib.

'Holding him isn't helping and you need to eat,' Jane said.

'He's sure to fall asleep soon,' Scott assured me but I knew that he didn't like leaving our baby alone either, shrieking in anguish.

When they had gone downstairs I shut the door and incarcerated myself with Stevie's noise. I sang and opened the window and closed it again and shook rattly toys in his face. But still he cried. Finally I sat where Jane had sat and waited as Jane had waited and eventually, many thoughts later, there was silence. I looked at Stevie's tiny face, battered with the effort of his protests. His warm body was inert but pliable. He was once more that creamy, peaceful baby he was supposed to be. He was lovable again. I laid him gently as china in his blue crib, and the voile, which was looped and swaggered in a fantastical canopy high over his head, danced a little. I pulled the blanket up and then gazed at his perfection for a few moments before joining the others downstairs.

When, after the meal, I went upstairs to check on him, I knew the moment I opened the door that something was wrong. The room had a special silence, the silence of death, and my skin recognized that silence and bristled before I recognized death itself. I switched on the light and ran to the crib. I pulled back the blanket.

I held my own breath as I waited for his. I looked for breath, I listened for breath, I pushed at one shoulder to shake a breath out of him. I scanned his chest, hands, face for movement. I pulled at his hand so it would curl back. But there was no movement in the stiff, cold fingers and I knew that here was a lifeless effigy of my Stevie and that he would not breathe again.

The silence which had been hanging over the room descended, weighty and stifling. My throat constricted and then stretched, my voice emitted a long, high noise. But the density of the silence suffocated all sound and I could hear nothing.

When the others came in, breathless, their faces hollow and their eyes big, nobody spoke. They pressed against the crib and their movements caused the swaggering blue voile around it to flutter in a mocking imitation of life.

Faces around the blue crib, contorted with horror. Scott, his lips blanched and his skin translucent. Jane, next to me, eyes burning in a white mask of a face. And Daddy. Daddy's mouth open, like a swimmer who has just surfaced after too long, gasping for air, his eyes full with the weight of the shock, looking up from Stevie's body into my eyes and then slowly sliding off me as if the weight was too much to bear.

When I lifted Stevie out and held him to me and he failed to curl his body against mine, press his head into my shoulder, it seemed to me that the silence in the room was deafening.

'Sit down, Lucy,' said Larry firmly.

'Calm down. Calm down now.' Jane this time. But I did not understand their tone or their words. I thought I was already calm in the face of a vast inevitability but Larry seemed to arrest me, trapping my arms against my body, then holding his hand up as though he was going to slap me. Jane took the baby in a rapid, authoritative movement.

'Stop, Lucy,' said Larry. And the silence, which I now realized I had been covering with a blanket of screams, thinned.

Jane and Larry laid Stevie's body on the changing table and began to pull at his clothes. Stevie was yielding but unhelpful. Larry felt for a pulse, Jane listened at his chest and they looked at each other and no words were necessary. Then Jane shifted her weight over Stevie and drew her elbows up and laid her hands on his heart, one on top of the other, and flapped over him like a long, slim, angular bird.

'No point,' said Larry. His voice was gruff. 'Too cold.'

'We should try,' Jane insisted but when Larry only shrugged she dropped her elbows and I moved in to pick Stevie up and make him warm again, to stop the last heat from leaking out of him.

Larry said: 'I'll call the police.' His voice was already professional, the voice he would use in the phone call.

There was a roar, so loud that I instinctively covered Stevie's head, his ears, with a protective hand.

'The police! What do the goddamn police have to do with anything?'

'Shhhhh, Daddy,' said Jane, but Daddy looked at her and his old arms began to flail. His movements were jerky and unaccustomed. His mouth was stretched into gaping shapes I did not recognize. Tears ran down his cheeks and dammed in the crevices they found there as he looked at Jane for the support we all rely on. It was the first time I saw him cry and I turned now, placing my back between Daddy's wet face and my small, dead baby.

'Daddy, it's routine,' Jane said in her hospital tone. 'A baby's died and the police have to come.'

I saw Scott flinch at these words. He was still frozen by Stevie's crib. He hadn't moved at all since he first came in.

When the police officers arrived, Scott was holding Stevie, wrapped in a blanket. He carried Stevie upstairs and the officers followed him. Others arrived, some went. I was interviewed by a white-haired man. I said: 'It's my fault.'

The man, who had thought the interview concluded and was leaving the room, paused and looked down at me and his whole body weight was behind that look.

'Pardon me, ma'am?'

'It's all my fault. I'm to blame.'

He sat again, nearer to me this time.

'Now,' he asked. 'Now, how is this your fault?' His eyes were large with something more than compassion. Suspicion.

'The blanket must have been too heavy. Last night was so cold, I put the big blanket on him but it was warmer tonight, I should have fetched a lighter blanket, maybe just a sheet . . .'

I could hear my words tumbling out on to the detective who opened his notebook and wrote something laboriously in it. When he looked up at me he said: 'We'll find out if there's a cause of death. But with SIDS there's usually no cause at all. Mothers always blame themselves, especially working mothers. They try to find something they did wrong just to explain it. But there usually isn't any reason.'

'It's all my fault,' I said.

The white-haired detective said: 'I'll send my colleague in to sit with you a while.'

He left the room and I could hear Larry talking to someone in the living-room.

'Hysterical,' he was saying. 'Rushed down the stairs shrieking and then back up them and when we got to Stevie's room she was running all around it, yelling.'

I wondered who they could be talking about. Certainly not me. I had been icy calm throughout.

The detective's colleague arrived. He was young and his hair was neatly parted. He closed the door, sat down and watched me for a moment in silence before he leaned towards me. He leaned so close that he hissed. He said: 'Have you heard the word of the Lord? Open your heart to the Lord and He will help you in your misery. I can give you a number to call for a female counsellor from my church. Please don't tell my colleague I said this.' I stared back into his bright eyes with incomprehension but without hostility. He was a part of the madness of that night.

Soon, Jane came in and sat down beside me. She took my hand but did not speak and the young detective left.

Much later, Scott brought our dead baby in. He lay in Scott's arms, the blanket folded back to reveal the small, still face.

'They're going to take him,' Scott said. His voice cracked and broke into a thousand pieces. Tears gushed down his cheeks as he handed me the unyielding doll who used to be Stevie.

A man and a woman stood in the doorway, the light behind them. They wore neat, loose uniforms of dark blue, almost black. Like vultures, they awaited my son's body. I turned from them with hostility.

'Take your time, sweetheart,' said the woman.

I grasped Stevie for this leavetaking, holding his inelastic body against mine, studying him greedily. When I turned back, the woman moved forward and held out her arms to receive him. The emptiness of the place where Stevie had been felt like an emptiness which penetrated deeper than my heart and into my soul. As the couple left with my son I felt a loneliness beyond anything I had ever known, an eternity of loneliness, the loneliness of the grave. I covered my ears so I could not hear them drive away.

When I looked up, I saw Daddy. His face secreted misery. For a moment our eyes met in acknowledgement of each other's wound and his filled with tears. He did not look away from me.

'There is . . .' He tried to speak. His voice was husky. He restarted his sentence several times before he was able to complete it. 'Lucy, there is no escaping the immense pain which lies ahead.'

I nodded. I opened my mouth to speak but my own voice had a peculiar, unused quality like a blunt knife which could not slice the words. I had wanted to tell Daddy that, in some buried, primeval part of the brain which does not think, which cannot be controlled and which does not deal in the rational or the everyday, I had recognized my pain and found I was able to greet it not as a stranger but as an old family friend.

10

The tide at Needle Bay is going out. While I have been sitting here at the hilltop it has left a perfect fingernail of damp sand along the edge of the beach. The sun, where it catches the ocean, blanches the blue water. Waves peak, sparkle and disappear.

I start the car and begin my descent through the aromatic pines. I hear the car tyres squishing against the track, still damp after the winter. Soon the sun will have pulverized it to dust. Then, a clearing in the trees, a carport, a car, and beneath me the little wooden cottage appears, squatting on the beach, sand lapping against the porch. It was newly painted when we moved here, yellow as the sun, but its brightness has already faded.

I get out and pine needles roll beneath my feet. I am halted by their intense scent and by the vast brightness of the sea only a few hundred yards away.

The back of the cottage lies low, as though someone planted it in the sand and it didn't grow. Down the dangerous steps and around to the doors and windows and porch at the front. My feet hit the thick, dry sand and my body works to walk in it so that when I reach the wooden steps it feels, as when I reached Daddy's house last night, like the end of some epic journey.

Scott is on the porch, sitting looking at the sea, just the way I've always imagined him waiting for me. There are two books open on the table in front of him and he fingers a coffee cup. When he sees me, dragging my heavy feet through the sand, my shoes in my hand, his face rearranges itself. All his features momentarily fly outwards and then are recomposed but not in exactly their right places and I know that he, too, has dreamed of this reunion many times.

When I reach the top step Scott stands up and puts a hand on the railings. We stare. There is three years pressing between us and a sort of shyness. And then I walk right through those years and right up to him and he puts his arms right around me and it feels like slipping into old clothes which long ago moulded themselves to your shape. He holds me hard against him and then harder and then he shudders and I know that he's crying. I stay wrapped in the warmth of his body and the bigness of his frame and the security of his arms.

Finally, and it's a complicated manoeuvre, we sit down at the table together and I hold his hand and stroke his big, shaggy head while he cries. It's like stroking a lion. I move one of the books so it doesn't get wet. I whisper that I'm sorry and it makes him cry harder.

'Are you apologizing for going away?' he asks at last, his voice strangled by tears, not like his real voice.

'I'm not sure.'

'Then why are you sorry?'

'I feel as though it's all my fault.'

He turns to me and looks right at me, his grey eyes red now and his face swollen.

'What? Stevie? Your dad?'

'Everything. Everything which makes you cry.'

He sits up and puts his arm around me and we both look out to sea like the couple who moved in here together, four years after meeting, three years after marrying, two weeks after Stevie died.

I say: 'Are you angry? Are you real mad at me?'

He says: 'I've been mad at you for three goddamn years, Luce. In my head I've yelled and yelled at you. And now you're here . . . I don't want to yell, I just want to cry.'

When he's cried some more he says: 'I can't believe Eric's dead. He was sitting right here on Saturday. I loved that guy more than my own father.' His voice cracks and breaks and to comfort him I move still closer so that I'm right under his shoulder. I'd forgotten how well we fit together.

'How was Daddy on Saturday?' I ask.

'Oh, quiet. Because it was Stevie's day, I guess. Quiet and sad. I've been thinking all day about how much sadness there was in his life.'

'No!' I protest. It's an instinct. I don't want Daddy's life to have been sad although only yesterday I failed to recall him ever laughing.

'Sure it was sad. He married this breathtakingly beautiful woman and it turns out she's not fascinating because she's Russian, she's fascinating because she's crazy. That's sad. And his baby son died. Then his grandson. Then you went away. That's all goddamn sad, except that it brought me closer to him because we both missed you so much and because he could understand about Stevie. I've found that I can only completely relate to people who understand about Stevie.'

It occurs to me now I'm home where I'm loved that all the time I was in New York I didn't relate to people at all.

'The police interviewed me yesterday,' Scott is telling me. 'Just like I was a goddamn suspect. I tried to explain how much I loved Eric but she ignored it, like I was saying something embarrassing.'

'Who interviewed you?'

'A woman detective. There was a man there too, an older guy. He didn't say anything but he nodded a lot and I think he understood. The woman asked all the questions. I kept thinking I'd seen her before. Then this morning I remembered. At our old house on Lalupa. I think she came the night Stevie died.'

I stare at him. I stare at him so hard my eyes feel bulbous as glass which might crack.

'What do you mean, Scott?'

'There were so many of them, going in and out. It seemed like the entire police precinct was there. But I'm certain she was one of them.'

'No,' I say. 'No, no, I didn't recognize her at all. I don't even remember any woman that night.'

Scott asks: 'Have you been to Stevie's grave yet?'

I shake my head. 'I know you sent me that picture of the headstone but I still remember it as a little mound covered with flowers.'

'Want me to go with you?'

'Yes.'

I haven't heard a car so when two figures round the house I am unprepared. Jane embraces me as warmly as she did yesterday. When I am close to her I sniff her summery perfume and when I look into her face I see her intelligence. It is indicated in her fine bone structure, the way her fair hair falls to her shoulders without complication.

'Hi, Lucy,' says Larry, standing behind her, puffing after his walk through the sand. Scott delivers cold drinks and we sprawl around the porch talking, just the way we used to. I look away from my family to the sea. It shifts restlessly in its great bowl. I hear their voices without listening to their words and gradually a distance seems to grow between me and them until the sea thunders as though I'm sitting right on the shoreline and their voices are far away.

'I mean, did he actually mean to go to the beach to swim? Or was he coerced into going?'

'He and Seymour were doing some new fitness programme. It did involve a lot of swimming.'

'Listen, Big Brim is renowned for its cross-currents.'

'True, but –'

'But nothing. If he wanted to swim he wouldn't have
chosen that God-forsaken place, he'd have gone somewhere
safe, like here. Eric was lured to Big Brim, or forced there
against his will.'

I look away from them down the beach. I can define my
whole life in beaches. As an adult, before Stevie, after Stevie.
Before Scott, after Scott. As a teenager, one of a pack, playing
volleyball, in love with Robert Joseph. As a daughter, with
Mother and Jane and maybe Aunt Zina and Sasha. Holding
picnic bowls with both hands and screwing them down into
the sand, scraping sand from the cooler, dusting it from
between my toes, feeling it ooze wet beneath my fingers or
run hot beneath my feet. Conversations counterpointed by
the slosh of the sea, informed by the direction of the tide,
interrupted by the call of gulls and the shriek of children. It
seems now that I have never left the beach.

'The point is that he could have died anywhere.'

'What do you mean?'

'Well, they didn't have to kill him on the beach.'

'You're saying someone . . . it could have happened right
at his own home?'

'Maybe.'

'But then why is his car missing?'

'I'll tell you. It didn't happen at his home. He drove it
somewhere and then died there. Maybe he happened to
witness something he shouldn't have seen. They killed him
on the spot and hauled him to the beach. Something like
that. When they find the car –'

'If they find it.'

'If they find it, then it'll probably be right where he died.'

'Jane, do the police know how much time there was between death and immersion?'

'I guess they'll have to wait for the full autopsy report before they can know that, maybe not even then.'

'So you're really suggesting he died somewhere miles away and then his body was driven to Big Brim and he hit the water right there?'

'Sure.'

'C'mon, Larry, have you ever been to Big Brim?'

'Well, no.'

'You have to cross two, no, I think three, sand dunes, no one's going to do that carrying a body.'

'But Scott, who's going to do any of it? I mean, who would want to kill Eric?'

There is a silence into which a wave crashes. A gull screeches. A child cries. A phone rings.

Scott's feet thud on the wooden porch as he gets up and goes inside. We listen to his tone as he answers the call, guarded at first. When he asks: 'Where?' there is anxiety in his voice. We look at each other, then at the doorway of the beach house. In a moment, Scott's big frame fills it.

He says: 'The police have found Eric's car.'

His words make me jump a little, so that my elbow flaps at an empty coffee cup and it flies suddenly into the air. Larry almost catches it but misses and it falls on to the warped planks at our feet. Jane goes inside to take the call while Scott bends to pick up the pieces. I stare at them lying in his hand, three pieces, cleanly broken.

When Jane emerges again, her face is pale. She sits down and Larry lifts her hand on to his lap and strokes it there.

'They found Daddy's car about five miles away. A place called Lowis. It's south of here . . .'

'I know it,' says Scott. 'It's not far from Bellamy, right where you come off the freeway to go into the San Strana valley. So how come . . . ?'

Jane is already shrugging. 'The police don't know how come yet. They've done all the forensic tests they need to do on the Oldsmobile. They asked me where they should take it. They thought the cheapest option was to tow it back to Daddy's house so I said okay . . . now I'm wondering if I shouldn't have just told them to tow it to a scrapyard.'

We look at each other.

'I'm glad it's going right back where it belongs,' I say. There's something pleasing about the idea of Daddy's house, restored to order after the police presence, with his own car right outside. But Larry is already shaking his head at me.

'This is a time of change, Lucy. Nothing's going to be back the way it was, ever. You should understand that.'

I look out across the beach's bands of colour. Light brown where the sand is dry, a strip of dark sand at the water's edge, then a band of light blue, dark blue and finally an impenetrable black as the bottomless water stretches on to infinity.

11

Bellamy is a pretty coastal town. Back behind the artists' shops and the cafés and the fishing boats that the tourists see is the police precinct and a small courthouse. Jane and Larry and Scott tried to dissuade me from going to the mortuary there to see Daddy's body. Finally, Scott insisted on accompanying me.

I said: 'It'll only upset you.' But he fixed his jaw in a way I don't remember and told me he was coming anyway.

We scan the address and the street but the building to which it leads us seems not to exist. We walk up and down looking for a sign which says Mortuary.

'Let's ask in the library,' Scott suggests. We go into the nondescript rectangle of a building and as soon as the doors swing closed behind us we know that this must be the mortuary. We know it from the smell, which we recognize, at some animal level, as the smell of death.

We ring a bell and a white-coated man slides back a glass panel in the wall.

'Do you have an appointment?' he asks, looking us up and down.

'Lucy Schaffer, three-thirty.' Suddenly I want to giggle and the man seems to detect this. He looks at me petulantly. He says: 'You're late.' He is wearing white boots and a badge with his picture in one corner which says: 'David Davis, Morbid Anatomy Assistant.'

'I mean, how did you expect the mortuary to look?' he asks as if we've been arguing with him. We don't reply.

He leads us through a side door into a large, floodlit room. The smell is stronger now, it is very strong. Scott wrinkles his nose at me. It is the smell of burnt rubber. It is the smell of sadness. It is a smell which strips human beings of any hope or nobility. It is the smell of putrefaction.

'Okay, now this is a bad air day,' the assistant tells us. 'I mean, we've had a few brought in from the streets this week so the smell is particularly strong right now. Usually I can't pick it up at all because I'm so used to it but today even I can smell it, so I guess it must be choking you guys.'

He is leading us through the airless, windowless room. It is lined by big metal drawers. The assistant leads us half-way down the room and checks his notes and checks the name on the drawer. It says: Professor Eric Schaffer. I stare.

Scott turns to me suddenly. His face looks blue in these floodlights, as though bruised.

'You can change your mind now, Luce. It's not too late.'

The assistant has his hand on the drawer. He raises his eyebrows at me. He is a young man and his features are even. Then he slides back the drawer. Inside is a sheet and beneath it is Daddy, just the way Stevie's body lay beneath his blanket.

'Luce . . .' Scott hisses at me. 'Luce, don't do this. Don't look.' He is so close to me that I can feel his warm breath on my hair.

But I nod at the mortuary assistant and he pulls back the sheet to reveal to me once more death's strange mask. A mask modelled on Daddy's face. White, thin, puckered, like a toy which someone has left out in the rain.

At the base of the neck, where the doll has been stitched, roughly like a baseball mitt and with string, are purple pimples.

'Oh!' I say softly.

Scott has turned away, his hand to his mouth.

'Oh,' I say, 'but he looks so cold!'

David Davis laughs with unnatural vigour. He says heartily: 'They're all cold in here. For them, it's Alaska.'

Scott has started to heave. Great tremors pass through his muscles. He keeps a hand locked across his mouth. I say: 'Could I be alone here with my father for a few minutes?'

David Davis looks displeased. He works with the dead and they are undemanding. He is unpractised at helpfulness. 'Our regulations don't allow that.'

I look anxiously at Scott and then back to the mortuary assistant.

'Please. Just for a very short time.'

The man looks at Scott's white face and heaving body and sighs. 'Come with me,' he tells Scott, leading him back up the room, and for a moment I watch them go, walking past the shiny steel drawers of the dead as though they're making their way through some enormous kitchen.

I turn back to Daddy but suddenly the room goes dark. Daddy's body, the whole world, disappears into some black hole where the darkness is of an unnatural, enveloping density. My heart bangs violently, its protests fill my ears, tiny nerves in my fingers and toes sting me. Everything I fear most, everything I don't think about, ever, but which sometimes roars at me in my dreams, suddenly it is all here, surrounding me. I open my mouth to scream but I have no breath. My own formless fears, the smell and the darkness all suffocate me. And then the lights blink back on.

'Whoops, sorry!' calls David Davis from the door. 'I just switch off automatically when I leave the mortuary. I hope I didn't frighten you!' The door bangs behind him.

Daddy lies on his metal bed, impervious to my beating heart and shaking fingers. Impervious to everything. I lean closer to him and am quieted by his stillness. I want to say something I never could have said while he was alive because we aren't that kind of family.

'I love you, Daddy.'

But Daddy isn't here, behind this cold mask. He can't hear me.

He's still big. Death can't take that away from him. And he still has that strength in his face which drew people to him. His bones jut inside his cheeks, his chin is strong, his forehead high. Even when he rots, and now that he is dead his body will rot, it will be clear from his skeleton that he was big and strong and special.

'I mean, I don't love you less because you're dead.'

Along the left side of his face there are swellings, an unnatural blue, sometimes with cuts at their nucleus. I lean across him to examine them. I don't like them. I try to see Daddy's face without looking at them and I learn that he had aged since I last saw him. Lines have been etched not by time but by worry. There is no worry in his face now but this is its patina. I touch his hair, whiter and thinner than three years ago but still leonine in its magnificence. I study the network of lines running down his cheeks, the small scars, the mole, the freckles, the little blister below one ear. Marks accumulated over more than seventy years. Life's hieroglyphics telling Daddy's story to anyone who can decipher them in death.

I whisper: 'Daddy, what worried you so much? Was it me? I hope it wasn't me.'

Carefully, I pull the sheet at his side up a little until one hand is revealed. It retains something of the ocean in the faint blueness of its veins. Neat fingernails, bulging knuckles. Big, square, practical. I loved to watch Daddy work with these hands. Making things. Fixing things. Chipping at rocks with sharp, precise movements until they yielded with a powdery shudder.

Very gently I touch one finger. It is not a human finger but a cold, cunning model of a finger. I examine the lines on his palm, his wrist. His left wrist. I see that it is circled by a bracelet of white flesh, thin as a needle. I touch this but it is barely perceptible to the pads of my fingers.

Footsteps. Not the soft prowl of David Davis but the clicking of high heels walking purposefully. I replace Daddy's hand as though it were made of glass and when I look up a woman is standing before me in a blue silk suit, exquisite and understated jewellery and expensive hair. There is a curious clash of scents, perfume and death. Does she wear all this for the dead?

'Do you have permission to be here?' she demands.

'Yes. My husband . . .' The strangeness of these words, after all this time, jolts me. '. . . My husband felt nauseous and David Davis just took him outside.'

She looks mollified.

'I'll have to stay with you or you should leave until he gets back. We can't allow unsupervised visits.'

'Are you a medical examiner?'

'Yes.'

'Did you examine my father's body?'

She sighs. I wonder how old she is. Her clothes and hair and make-up are like a disguise. Have I also been wearing a disguise for the last three years?

'Actually yes. But I can't discuss his case with you in detail.'

'Can you tell me what this is?'

I point to the thin, white line around Daddy's wrist. She glances at it but moves no closer to me or Daddy. She doesn't need to. She's familiar with the scar. She hesitates.

'Please tell me,' I say.

At length she says: 'It's an attempted suicide.'

My breath catches and I am motionless.

'Many years ago. When Professor Schaffer was a young man.'

I shake my head. 'No. No. He never would have done that.'

'He was right-handed and he tried to cut the artery on his left wrist.'

'But I've never noticed this scar before.'

'It shows the classic signs of a self-inflicted wound: it's noticeably deeper on the left side than the right. He managed quite a deep cut before he gave up. He would have bent back his hand so that the vessels withdraw behind the cartilage and bone and the pain would have gotten too much before he could do an effective job.'

'When? When did he do this?'

'All I can tell you is that it happened a very long time ago.'

I stare at Daddy's wrist.

She says: 'You didn't see it because you didn't expect it to be there. Plus he probably wore his wristwatch low.'

'These blue marks down the left side of his face . . . what are they?'

'Bruises.'

I am quick with anxiety. 'Bruises? There was a fight?'

I am determined not to cry. If I do, this woman won't answer my questions. She'll call for someone to come and she'll click back through the mortuary on her stilettos.

'I can't ascertain whether there was a fight but the bruising is certainly non-fatal. It may have occurred immediately prior to death or soon afterwards but it wasn't so extensive as it looks now because bruising continues to spread across the body after death for some days. By the time you bury Professor Schaffer, he'll be a lot darker.'

My voice is too strained to emulate the detached, clinical tone with which the ME would be comfortable.

'What about the cuts?'

'Also non-fatal. The puncture marks are not deep and there's no major artery or vein involved. They're caused by impact with some hard, sharp object, probably rock, it's hard to tell. Unfortunately, bruising does not reproduce the shape of the injuring object.'

I forget to be clinical. 'You think he hit Daddy's face? With rocks?'

The ME sighs and her jewellery rattles crossly.

'A few of the injuries are consistent with attack by a right-handed assailant but I'd say it's more likely that the Pacific Ocean inflicted these wounds shortly after death.'

'But . . . isn't Big Brim a sandy beach?'

She shrugs. 'You've crossed the line now, between my work and Detective MacFarlane's.'

'Can you tell . . . do you know if he suffered when he died?'

She pauses. I have risked a brisk reply and now I wait for it. But she says: 'I believe he didn't suffer. When the decedent has fought death or been in great distress there are a number of indicators. Not only is distress very clearly visible on the face but other muscles can be so contracted that the body is almost curled. It's not unusual to find the fingernails are damaged or have become embedded in the palms during the struggle for life.'

I turn my head away. I am thinking not of Daddy but of Stevie. He looked peaceful, as though sleeping, but the way he lay in his crib, one arm raised a little, suggested some instinctive, ineffectual struggle against death.

Her tone doesn't soften but there is a new, distant note in it, kindness or some poorer relative. 'None of these indicators was present in the case of Professor Schaffer.'

I look right at her. 'Are you sure my father was a homicide

victim? Are you certain? Nobody who really knew him can believe that he was killed.'

The discreet laughter of gold jewellery. The ME doesn't like her judgement to be questioned.

'Then,' she says sharply, 'maybe nobody really knew him.'

Silence in the mortuary. She relents a little. 'In cases of drowning,' she explains, 'we find diatoms, which are the microscopic algae present in water, all around the body. The heart pumps them there during immersion. If the body is dead prior to immersion then the diatoms don't reach any organ beyond the lungs. In the case of your father I did not find them anywhere else but the lungs.'

'But how did he die?'

There is a small, involuntary reaction from behind the make-up. 'I'm not completely sure yet. We're going to take another look. But we'll be through by Friday and can release the body to you any time next week for the funeral.'

A door opens. David Davis, Morbid Anatomy Assistant, alone now. The ME take the opportunity to leave but after a step or two she pauses and turns.

'Miss Schaffer?'

I nod.

'I offer you my sympathy on the loss of your father.'

'Thank you.'

'I should have said that before. In my job it's too easy to forget the complex, interesting individual the decedent used to be.'

She resumes her departure. The mortuary assistant calls to her: 'I'm sorry, Dr Ball.' His voice carries effortlessly in the still room. His tone is respectful. I bet he never turns the lights out on her. 'I had to be absent for a short time, her husband started barfing.'

Dr Ball excuses him with a wave and disappears.

I take a last look at the shape in the drawer, the shape which Daddy used to inhabit.

'Goodbye,' I say.

David Davis covers Daddy's hand and pulls the sheet back over his face. The drawer runners rumble as they transport Daddy's body back into its metal box.

Scott is sitting, white-faced, in the lobby where the smell is fainter. He stands up when I come in. Wordlessly we head for the doors. When we walk through them we will be completely free of that smell.

'Thank you for your help,' we say. David Davis smiles.

'Oh, my pleasure,' he assures us. 'It's always nice to see some living tissue in here.' He grins broadly. He has enjoyed his power over us.

As we leave the mortuary, the sunshine of late afternoon warms us. We walk across the asphalt and the air bulges with a youthful energy. A group of uniformed police officers leaves the courthouse, walking a slow, sinewy walk as though it feels good. Out on the street, people wear colourful clothes. They mostly move in the same direction like participants in a bright dance. This is life and we return to the car enjoying its embrace.

'That weirdo turned the lights out on you deliberately,' Scott tells me on the way back up to Needle Bay.

'He sure seemed to enjoy it.'

'I'll bet he's done it before. When we got outside he said that most women scream.'

'If you're really frightened you don't scream.'

'Were you really frightened?'

'Yes. It was like a weekend break in the underworld.'

Driving back to Needle Bay, Scott sighs. 'Jeez, Luce, it's hard to believe anyone could have killed Eric, especially not anyone who knew him. I've been racking my brains all night . . .' Scott, wrapped in a sweater, maybe two, sitting out on the wooden porch, the tide crashing in the dark. He is thinking, remembering every friend Daddy ever mentioned, looking for names, explanations. 'I mean, he didn't have any enemies. Sure, he could be irritating, it was impossible to budge him in argument, he kept his emotions so much in check that sometimes I felt mad at him. But no one would have killed him. Unless there was someone way back, from his childhood.'

'He left all that behind him, Scott. He had no contact with his family and they had no way of finding him.'

'Later, then. When he was a young man.'

When Daddy was a young man, he tried to saw through the artery on his left wrist.

I sigh. 'Do people really settle old scores fifty years too late?'

We drive in silence. We pull up to some traffic lights and a man, his hair bushy and shoulder-length, stands at the intersection holding a sign scrawled on cardboard: 'I am a Vietnam Vet. I fought for my country but now I have no home and no job. I feel betrayed. Please help me.'

Scott reaches for his wallet and waves a bill out of the window and the guy walks over and takes it from him.

'Thank you sir. And thank God you have so much god-damn money you can afford to throw a little at me like I'm some common beggar.'

The lights change and we drive on rapidly.

'Shit,' Scott says. 'That's the last time I hand anything to those guys.'

I glance at him. He looks crushed by the man's aggression. His face is still white and his limbs are hunched as though his shirt is too small. I say: 'That's what Daddy would have done. Daddy was always giving people on the street money.

And if they spoke to him that way he would have shrugged and understood how hard it was for the guy to take it.'

'Yeah,' agrees Scott morosely.

When we get back to Needle Bay the beach is almost empty and the sun has started its descent. We sit on the porch and gradually Scott's face and body resume their normal roundness and his cheeks start to reflect the pink of the late afternoon sun.

He asks: 'Could you tell how much Eric had changed since you last saw him?'

'Well, he did look a little older. Mostly he looked sort of worried.'

Scott nods. 'Yeah.'

I feel my voice crack as though I just threw it up against some rocky wall. 'What was he worrying about?'

'I don't know. But if you looked at him without him realizing then you could see he was a man with burdens. I mean, burdens which he felt compelled to pick up whenever a moment arose. I think that describes it, Luce. He was burdened. Oh, for Chrissake, I didn't mean to make you cry.'

I sob: 'I should have been here. I should have been here for him.'

He puts an arm around me but his words continue. 'It seems right that he died around the anniversary of Stevie's death. It seems right because Eric was devastated when Stevie died and I'm not sure he's been exactly the same guy since then. Like, it was one burden too many for him.'

Stevie's small body lying in the blue crib as though it was floating helplessly in the sea. Causing not tiny ripples but a tsunami. I sob again and again.

Scott wraps himself around me and the porch envelopes us both like an elderly parent. The paint and former smoothness of its wooden uprights is weathered to a rough boniness.

The beach is deserted except for two swimmers, far away, walking slowly into the sea. They hesitate when they feel how cold the water is and then continue. Soon they are two tiny heads on the ocean's surface. I watch the way the great body of water lifts and then lowers them like a big cat playing with its prey.

I ask: 'Do you ever think of moving from here? Maybe buying somewhere again?'

'There soon won't be a choice.'

'Does the owner want it back?'

'The ocean wants it back. Next month the tides are going to be exceptionally high and if the weather's bad too . . . well, I should probably get out for a few days.'

I imagine a big wave tipping its burden of water right into the cottage, smashing it to pieces. The little house, nothing more now than disjointed pipes and yellow lumber and the seats from the porch and a few rusty kitchen pans, would whirl and eddy as its components were carried away in different directions to be scattered on faraway shores. Islanders would wander along the tide-line gathering pieces of roof.

'At the highest tides last year,' says Scott, 'a window got smashed.'

I stare at him.

'Were you here?'

'Yes.'

'Oh Scott. Were you alone?'

'No. It was scary but it was only spray. Next time, it might not be.'

'Was it at night?'

'In the middle of the night. When we went to sleep the ocean had seemed pretty quiet.'

It was the middle of the night and someone else was here

asleep with Scott. I feel something in my stomach contract inside itself like a sea anemone.

'Who was here sleeping in the middle of the night?' I ask, too quickly, then regret it. Scott does not look at me. His face is pinker than the sea now, pink as the sun itself. He turns to me and his tone is the mixture of aggression and mockery used by the Vietnam Vet who fought for his country but now has no home or job and feels betrayed.

'Why do you care?'

'I'm sorry I asked. I have no right to care.'

He glares at me. His shoulders are square suddenly so that his soft frame is all right angles. He says: 'I have a girlfriend. She teaches French on campus. She lived in France for many years. She has a son who lives in France with her ex-husband. Right now she is spending a semester with her son.'

'That would be in France?'

'In France.'

'In the house of the ex-husband?'

His face clouds. 'You can stop right there, Luce. I'm not discussing this any more.'

'I only asked if —'

'Just stop.'

He's angry. I've seen him mad a lot of times, but never with me before.

'How about you, Luce? Do you have some guy who matters in New York?'

I get up to go. Scott gets up too. He stands right in front of me. 'No,' I say, walking around him. 'I don't.'

'So. So now you know about Brigitte you're leaving.'

'I'm leaving because I want to get to Big Brim beach before it's dark.'

He looks troubled. 'Don't go there alone, Luce.'

'I want to.'

'It will make you feel lousy.'

'My father's died and I already feel lousy.'

He sighs and his eyes search mine. 'Then,' he says at last, 'I guess you should hurry before it gets dark. Wait . . . I have something for you.'

We go inside the cottage and the little living-room seems to jump at me. In my dreams and memories there was never this damp saltiness, shoes never banged on the floor with such a clatter, the faded red furnishings were never so vibrant.

'Here!' Scott yells from the bedroom. He wants me to go in. 'You can't keep wearing those city clothes. I still have your old ones.'

He is bent into the closet. Inside it, I see a few women's clothes hanging with Scott's shirts. They could be Brigitte's but no, I recognize them as my own, my California clothes, not the kind I wear now. There aren't many. When we came here right after Stevie died I threw out most of my clothes and I recognize that now as the beginning of my absence.

'I'm not sure I want to wear that old stuff . . .'

Scott puts them in a bag, a swimsuit on top.

'Take them. It's getting too warm for city suits now and they're forecasting a heatwave.'

'In March?'

'That's what they say.'

He walks me around the cottage to my car and stands watching me until there are so many pine trees between us that they seem like one enormous tree. When I reach the coast road I can see him far below on the beach, his hands in his pockets, walking towards the sea. I wish he would look up but his eyes are fixed on the ocean. Brigitte. I wish he hadn't told me about her.

12

I pull in at Big Brim's exposed parking lot. It lies at sea level and runs right alongside the highway. There are no trees. There is no shelter of any kind. Although I know from the intensity of the light that the sea is nearby, it is masked by the mountain of sand which runs alongside the road. Traffic zooms past, rocking the car. When I open the door the trucks feel too fast and too close. I cross the blacktop as soon as I can and start to walk up the dune.

At the top I can see the red sun but the ocean is still invisible behind two more dunes and only when I have climbed these, sweating now, does the flat beach sprawl beneath me. I sit down, breathing heavily. I try to imagine Daddy walking these dunes. He was fit but not so fit he could climb them without stopping frequently for breath. Did he choose to swim at this beach or did he stumble here against his will? Did he walk this way with someone he believed to be a friend? Or behind him, next to him, was there someone he was powerless to resist?

The sun burns low now, throwing a massive red search-light towards the shore. Far out to sea I locate a couple of fishing boats. They are up the coast a little towards Retribution. The boats look immobile. The sea looks immobile. How did it carry Daddy's body so swiftly, in just three hours, from this beach to those boats?

The beach stretches for maybe a mile, unbroken by anything more substantial than driftwood and seaweed. There are long, curved sand spits at each end which, someone must once have thought, shaped the ocean like the brim of a hat. I can see no rocks to bruise or scrape against Daddy's body, although some may hide beneath the water's surface.

I run down the last dune towards the sea until I feel the damp sand by the water's edge firm beneath my feet. The sea is the colour of blood, stained by the swollen sun. I feel the water biting at my toes. I stand ankle deep, lifting the hem of my skirt. The ocean is icy. It is deceptive here. It rocks quietly. It invites you to swim because there are no big rollers rising up and smashing themselves against the sand. It beckons you to walk out into its calm depths but Scott says its cross-currents make it the most treacherous place to swim in this whole stretch of coast.

The beach is empty now except for a couple of people and one of them is heading back to the road. The other, a large man, is marching, almost running, along the tideline towards me, a small white dog trotting a few feet behind him. When I turn my back on the Pacific and follow my footprints up the beach I see that the man and his dog have halted nearby, collecting something, driftwood, perhaps, or clams, although there is little of either to break the monotony of the sand.

I reach dry sand and sit down. Only half a sun remains but it is powerful, its colour running across the sky and the water so there seems no difference between them. I feel my face, turned towards it as though in worship, shining red back at it.

I think of next month's high tides and how they could demolish Scott's flimsy cottage and any trace of our brief life there together. Except that, even when it's gone, the beach house will still be there. It will remain until everyone who goes to Needle Bay sees the pine trees without thinking: wasn't there once some kind of a hut here? Sort of small and square, squatting by the trees? When no one's left who imagines for a moment they can see a house beneath the pines, only then will the house be gone for good.

The sun is disappearing. The sky still glows where it used to hang and the water remains bloodstained. I stare at the place the sun was a moment ago, silent as I think of all the ghost houses and landmarks which once were, and then which existed in people's memories and were gone for ever when the people died.

Maybe it's the same with humans. Maybe they still exist until there's no one alive to recall them. It feels good to think that. It makes Daddy seem not so dead and involuntarily I look up the beach as though, if I'm quick, I'll glimpse him walking here. And in the evening light, which isn't failing yet but which is already thickening, there is a figure. It has appeared over the dunes and is heading towards the sea. It gets closer and I see that it is the tall, thin figure of a man, incongruous here in a suit and necktie. He must have stopped on his way home from some city office. The driftwood collector straightens up and stares. The little dog dances.

The man heads towards the ocean. He carries his shoes and walks purposefully. It occurs to me that maybe, just maybe, he is not going to stop when he gets to the sea. He is going to walk right into the water until he disappears in his suit and necktie beneath the waves. Involuntarily, I jump up. The driftwood collector jumps too. I hear the puff of his breath, the slap of his dog's feet on the wet sand. But before they can reach him, when the ocean is almost touching him, the newcomer turns suddenly and walks back up the beach. I sit down. The man with the dog diverts.

The tall figure is framed by the fiery sky. It seems he is walking towards me. Soon I can see his face. It is cadaverous. Hollow cheeks, prominent nose, immense mouth which is pulled clownishly but not humorously downwards.

'Hi,' he says in a reedy voice. 'Forgive me for disturbing you. Is it Lucy? Lucy Schaffer?'

I stare at him and my astonishment answers his question. The mouth splits his face in two. He is smiling.

'I'm Detective Michael Rougemont. I'm involved in the police department's investigation into your father's death. I live not so far from Professor Schaffer's house and I knew him a little. I'd like to express my condolences.'

I nod my thanks. I remember the thin, elongated figure I took for a shadow which stood talking to the woman detective in the kitchen doorway. And this morning she named some colleague who had questions for me. He flashes some kind of an ID which I ignore because my surprise has changed to anger at this intrusion. He has cornered me on this vast stretch of beach. And the way he walked right up to me, without looking at me first, suggests that he knew I would be here. With an intensity which is physical, which emanates from somewhere inside my belly, I dislike him. I look away from him out to the darkening sea.

'Take it,' he advises, waving the ID a little. 'Look at it. You should check these things, Lucy, to make sure they're real.'

'I think you're real,' I say. He smiles again and holds out his hand. Gingerly, I shake it. My hand feels as though it is inside a bag of bones. He sits down next to me and I turn away from him again.

'I hope you don't mind me talking to you right now. But I was passing and I thought that, in the circumstances, I'd like to take a look at this place again.'

'You've been here before?'

'Many years ago now, more than thirty.'

I am flippant. 'And has it changed much, Mr . . . ?'

'Rougemont. But call me Michael.' He is looking along

the beach to the right and then the left. He puts his huge head on one side.

'Well, I don't remember that guy being here before,' he says at last, gesturing to the pear-shaped man, who now strolls back along the beach, one arm pressing driftwood to his side, his dog behind him. I look at Michael Rougemont and his face has cracked into the broad smile again. He likes his own jokes. He has yellow teeth. I do not smile back at him.

He looks suddenly serious. 'Your father was a rare man, the kind people listen to and trust. It seemed to me that he placed his family at the centre of his life. A lot of men don't do that, can't do that, or won't, and we lose something, sometimes our whole family. So we admire men like your father. I'd like to hear you talk about him, Lucy, and not his recent history. I'd like to know about him right from the beginning.'

'You're investigating the end of his life, not the beginning, Mr Rougemont.' I have no intention of calling him Michael.

That awful smile again. 'Oh!' he says, and it is an exclamation of pleasure. 'Oh. Well, it happens that the two are often connected.' I survey his smile with disgust. I see that he likes connections. 'It reminds me of a toy I played with as a kid. I used to line up little tin soldiers. If you pushed the first they'd all fall down one by one. You knew it was inevitable but it was fascinating anyway, it was probably the inevitability which was the fascination. Oh hell, Lucy, but you never had any little tin soldiers. You had soft toys which you hugged a lot, furry things, like a dog.'

I stare at him in surprise but he isn't looking at me. He's watching the sea. I don't want to give him the satisfaction of knowing that he's right. I did like soft toys and I remember now that my special favourite, my friend, was a brown dog

130

with winsome eyes and floppy ears. His name was Hodges, I don't recall why.

'What do you want to know about my father?'

'Anything you can remember. Stories about himself, his family, his youth . . .'

'Stories were my mother's speciality.' Head thrown back, eyes widening and narrowing, voice rising and falling, hands gesturing. Mother could sure tell stories.

'He must have said something about his past. You must have asked him.'

I look at the detective and recognize his odd, sad expression as one of habitual pain. Some distant suffering has left its tyre tracks across his face. He's already talked about loss, about men losing their families. For a moment, I feel curiosity, even compassion. But I say: 'There's no way of knowing about Daddy's past. He left it all behind a long time ago.'

Rougemont chuckles, an odd animal sound.

'Oh, Lucy, forgive me. But you can't lose your past any more than you can lose your shadow.'

I shrug. 'Then he dissociated himself from it.'

There is a silence. We both look out to sea as he waits for me to speak. And to my surprise, I do speak. At first my words come fast and low so that the gentle sloshing of the waveless ocean competes with my voice and Michael Rougemont has to lean one large ear towards me. Then, gradually, my voice gains strength as though it is stiffened by the ocean's saltiness.

I tell him about Daddy's strange beginnings in a small religious community high in the mountains in Utah. The hours of the day and the days of the week were regulated by prayer and worship and communal diligence. The community was closed to outsiders and dominated by its religious elders, one of whom was Daddy's own father. Daddy hated it. Too smart for open rebellion, when he was just a teenager he worked as a carpenter and mechanic. He learned to fix almost any machine. He looked like he was praying a lot but mostly he was planning. He was planning his escape.

A man with a truck came once a week in summer to buy the fish which the community caught in the mountain lakes. One visit, the truck broke down, Daddy spent most of the evening fixing it. He was excused prayers to do this: the community didn't want the driver spending the night with them, dreaming about doing who knew what to their daughters. When the truck drove away, Daddy was in back with the fish. He had three dollars and a hunk of bread and, although the driver let him into the cab when they were half-way down the mountain, Daddy already smelled awful. When they got to Salt Lake City, the driver took Daddy to a hostel. He lived here and found a day job and enrolled in night school. His native community gave him a lifelong aversion to organized religion and the lifelong love of mountains and rocks which became his career.

'Uh-huh,' says Michael Rougemont, grimacing, nodding his big head. 'Uh-huh. That's very interesting. Who told you all that?'

'Daddy.'

'Did he tell you he ever went back?'

'It wasn't that kind of place. If you left, you never could go back.'

He rearranges his black-suited legs so they stretch towards the sea, knees bent like a gigantic spider's. 'Did he have siblings?'

'Seven. He was the youngest of eight.'

'Utah, huh? Eight of them. Were they LDS?'

'I'm not sure if they were members of the official Mormon

church. I think their community may have been some sort of splinter group.'

Rougemont is still nodding as though his head's a toy on the end of a piece of elastic. A cheap, clownish toy, definitely Mittex, not the sort Gregory Hifeld makes. 'Uh-huh, uh-huh,' he says rhythmically. His mouth meanders all over his face. Old man river. 'And he never, to your knowledge, tried to contact them?'

Pig ignorant, dirt poor, God fearing and God awful. Daddy described his family that way when, years ago, I was foolish enough to ask about them. His words frightened me. There was an angry harshness about them that sounded more like Mother than Daddy. I never asked again.

'He didn't want to. He started a completely new life without them.'

But for the first time I realize the enormity of what Daddy did when he was only sixteen and that the probability was he loved some of the seven siblings or one or both of his parents and that he must have lain awake at night in the hostel in Salt Lake City aching for his family's love and missing them and even wanting to go back up the mountains to them. When I think of the young man's loneliness, it makes my heart slide and my mouth taste salty. I remember the tiny white scar that I saw today ringing Daddy's wrist and my heart is suddenly struggling like a fish which has flipped out of the stream, leaping and dipping.

'When did he come to California?' asks Rougemont.

'Well, I don't exactly know. He was certainly here by the time he was in college but I'm not sure how old he was . . . I think he funded his studies by working in an auto repair shop at some time.'

'He told you that?'

'Not exactly. But in Utah he sure learned how to fix things.

133

He carried on fixing things right to the end of his life. He fixed old cars, tractors, jeeps, anything.'

'When did he meet your mother?'

The chasms in my knowledge gape at me. Years and years, Daddy's years, between high school and meeting Mother. They must have passed slowly enough at the time, the people and events probably seemed then to have their own importance, but now Daddy is dead those years are lost. No friendship survived it, there were no stories about this period, they have occupied no place in my imagination, they have yielded no landmarks. Ten, no, fifteen years have disappeared completely and can never be re-found.

I tell him how Mother and Daddy met and how she named all the geological layers in the wedding cake and how she liked to tell me the story.

Michael Rougemont somehow, without me noticing, seems to have moved closer and is watching me through the dim light which hangs between us.

'Was she a good mother?' he asks.

I eye him in the half-darkness. He must already know the answer to this. 'My mother's schizophrenic.'

'She's always been that way?'

'Eventually she was diagnosed as an episodic schizophrenic. That means she has periods between psychotic breaks but they get shorter and shorter. By the time I was fourteen she pretty well lived at the clinic.'

'When she wasn't psychotic, she was at home looking after you?'

I swallow. 'Well, she was at home. I wouldn't say she looked after us. Her behaviour was unusual and it got worse. By the time I was in second or third grade I hated her leaving the house because she was guaranteed to do something embarrassing.' Like, laughing uncontrollably during the

134

Pledge of Allegiance at school open day. Then staring at the Principal in ashen, unsmiling horror when he told a funny story. Or stopping the car to accuse some shocked pedestrian of following her.

'But Lucy, your mother wasn't always sick. Not when your father married her and she named all the geological layers. Not when you were small. Was there anything that triggered it, I mean the first time it happened?'

I don't tell Rougemont about the trip to Arizona we took right after my baby brother died. I don't tell him how Mother's misery exploded right there on the burning black-top as though the Arizona sun had heated her grief to boiling point. I don't tell him how hard I've tried to recall the words I heard her yelling from inside the canyon. I say: 'I was just a small kid. I don't remember. It took years for them to diagnose her as schizophrenic but when they did we under-stood a lot more. It's a chemical imbalance of the brain, it doesn't need an emotional trigger.'

'It was all pretty tough on you, Lucy,' remarks Rougemont. The sand, which was dry when I sat down on it, has absorbed some of the ocean's dampness now and the night air is thick with moisture. I stand up.

'Luckily, I had Jane. Why don't you talk to her about all this?' I shift one foot from side to side so that the sand bursts up between my toes as though animated.

'I already did. But no one knew Eric Schaffer the way you did. No one. Not even Jane.'

He's right. I wouldn't say this out loud to anyone, least of all Jane, but I've always believed, guiltily, secretly, that I was Daddy's favourite. Or maybe he had the knack of making each of us think we were favoured.

I say: 'I'm staying with my aunt. I should go back there now.'

135

Rougemont nods. Between sitting and standing there is a moment of stiffness and of pain, then his face clears. We collect our shoes and without speaking make our way across the reluctant sand. At every step it seems to rearrange itself around our feet with a small sigh. The constant fretting of the ocean grows fainter. As we cross the dunes, our legs and arms working hard as though in deep snow, Rougemont puffs and his breath heaves. He falls behind me. When we reach our cars, his parked too close to mine, the traffic which swishes past us illuminates Rougemont's face and I see it is wet with sweat and the lines across his forehead and around his mouth look long and deep. I realize for the first time that he is old, not so old as Daddy, but not so very much younger.

I unlock my car. When I turn back to Rougemont I see his hands are shaking. He can't slot his key into the lock. He tries to put his body between me and his failure but I stand right by him, watching his efforts, staring at his big hands. I recognize old man's hands. Daddy's. Gregory Hifeld's. The bigness of the knuckles, the prominence of the veins. I step forward and gently remove the key from his fingers. It hangs on a ring with just one other key, a door key. Rougemont's house. Rougemont's car. Twin axes of his existence bound by a small circle of metal. Most people, by the time their hands shake, have accumulated a weightier key-ring. They carry keys to friends' or relatives' houses, back door keys, summer house keys, office keys, the key to a spouse's car, a secret box, a filing drawer. But Rougemont travels light. I remember that he talked of men who lost their family, how it was the price you paid if you couldn't, or wouldn't, put them at the centre of your life. I slip the key into the lock and turn it for him.

'Thank you, Lucy,' he wheezes. 'I appreciate the help you've given me. I'll be seeing you real soon.'

'Goodbye, Mr Rougemont.'

I reverse the car and swing south. In the headlights I capture a large sign by the side of the road. It reads: 'Big Brim Beach. Danger, swimmers! Cross-currents!'

The apartment is thick with the smell of cooking. Aunt Zina urges me to kick off my shoes in the living-room and relax while she makes the evening meal.

'Oh.' She has seen the small piles of sand which spill from my shoe. 'You have surely been to Big Brim beach. Did it bring you closer to your papa?'

'No,' I admit, easing off the other shoe.

'There was a telephone call for you,' she tells me. 'A man. I think he was calling from New York where people so often speak like machine-guns. I was unable to understand a word, not even his name. No doubt he will call again.'

'Jay Kent?' No one sounds more like a machine-gun than Kent.

'Possibly,' she says, going back to the kitchen. 'Yes, it might have been that name.'

A little later, Sasha comes home. He offers me a whisky.

'I'm very glad, Lucia.' Sasha smiles benignly when I accept. 'Whisky is the perfect relaxant.'

He hands me a drink and watches as my face curls when I sip it.

'Your quality of life would greatly improve if you could acquire a taste for whisky.'

'It sort of burns my mouth.'

'Then I shall make it more palatable.' He disappears and returns with ice in the glass, clinking like money.

Settling himself in his own chair, his leather jacket and the chair both creaking, he asks: 'Lucia, when is the funeral?'

'I don't know. I saw Jane and Larry and Scott today at the beach but we agreed to talk about all the business stuff at Daddy's house tomorrow.'

'I can guarantee a good turn-out of aunts, uncles and assorted cousins. But my question is this: will Aunt Tanya be there?'

The usual guilt at the mention of Mother. I confess: 'To be honest, Sash, I hope not. In case she does something awful.'

'Lucia, Aunt Tanya should certainly be at her husband's funeral. I offer, for myself and for my mother, to undertake all necessary care on that day. We can pick her up, look after her, take her back to Redbush.'

'But supposing she . . . ?'

'She has great physical frailty these days. However, to please you, I will walk with her arm in mine. I can assure you that I have an iron grip.'

'She used to scream and shout sometimes.'

'Also unlikely these days, but at the first hint of such behaviour I will remove her from the room.'

'Well, thanks. I'll ask Jane . . .'

'No, no,' Sasha insists. 'I want you to make the decision. The way you make decisions in New York.'

I hesitate. Then I accept his offer.

'I believe that to be the right decision.'

'Thanks, Sash.'

'A fascinating and pleasing relation, the cousin,' he says. 'More than a friend but perhaps less than a sibling. Now what happened today?'

I look back over my day. The valley gaping at us as the detective and I played at reconstructing Daddy's life. The shoe heel curved in the palm of my hand, the snap of the undergrowth, the toy tow truck silently traversing the valley floor. The waves at Seal Wash banging against the cliff. Scott sobbing at the beach house, Daddy's bruised face at the mortuary, Rougemont's line of tin soldiers.

I say: 'I broke a coffee cup.'

Sasha's eyes glint. 'Nu tak. Did it shatter symbolically as we might expect of a falling cup in a play by, shall we say, Chekhov? Or was it merely chipped?'

'It broke into three pieces.'

Sasha sips his whisky and licks his lips.

'Not so satisfying as a thousand tiny splinters but, all the same, let us see what symbolism we can read into the three tidy pieces . . . perhaps they represent the perfect circle of Larry, Scott and Jane which is now in danger of breaking, breaking from within.'

I muse on this. 'With Daddy they made a perfect circle. It seems the four of them saw each other almost every week, mostly at the beach house, sometimes at Daddy's house or at Jane and Larry's apartment.'

'Aha. Yes, I see that with Uncle Eric gone the balance of relationships will change and the circle is certainly under threat. So you see, our cup may have a symbolism.'

I look at him with admiration. He shrugs modestly. 'Two degrees, a doctorate and God knows how many years with a cultural foundation must surely enhance one's interpretative skills if nothing else.'

Aunt Zina arrives with a tray of small, salty delicacies.

'Eat these, please, while you wait for your meal,' she insists. 'It will not be cooked for at least a half hour and no meal can be truly appreciated by the excessively hungry. I know for a fact that Sasha was too busy in a meeting to eat his lunch. And, as for you, Lucia, melancholy can stimulate the appetite.'

She returns to the kitchen and we reach for the tray.

'What was the meeting at lunchtime?' I ask.

He rolls his eyes towards me.

'Lucia, there was no meeting. Simply Mama called the office and my assistant had been instructed to disseminate this misinformation. I was doing a crossword in a small café one block away.'

'But why can't you admit that you take a lunch hour?'

He sighs. He selects a nut-sized appetizer from the tray. He describes his tyrannical boss and other colleagues in unflattering terms and this makes him cheerful. He pours more whisky. I laugh at his caricatures. He dissolves into the high pitched giggle I remember. It feels good to sit here and talk with my cousin. My whole body relaxes into the chair until it feels as though the chair is a part of me.

'How about that woman who answers the phone?' I ask.

'Natasha.' The change in his voice is barely perceptible.

I say: 'When I called from New York we had the briefest of conversations. It just couldn't be brief enough for her.'

'Her conversation, like her skirts, is very brief.'

'Oh-oh. I get it, Sashinka.'

Sasha's broad face grows pink.

'Get what?'

'That's why you're not married to Marina any more. Am I right?'

The pink is deepening to red. He glances rapidly at the kitchen.

'Lucy, Lucia, how could I forget about that formidable perception of yours? But, how did you know?'

'From your voice when you said her name.'

'God, women. I mean to say, women.' He leans towards me and speaks in a whisper. 'Listen, Lucia, she's twenty-one and she has legs which stretch all the way to the second storey. And perhaps I should inform you that our office is on the eighth. She's straight out of some Pedagogical Institute in Moscow, sensational body, and I do mean sensational, lonely in California and thinks, I'd like to believe with certain justification, that I'm wonderful. What's a hot-blooded guy to do?'

'All these meetings Aunt Zina says you have to attend after work . . . are they meetings with Natasha?'

'Indeed, you have correctly detected that Natasha is often the other participant in my meetings. How grateful I am to you for staying in our apartment and amusing Mama while Natasha and I are working so very hard together. Previously many meetings had been confined to early mornings, a time of day most people find too unromantic to alert suspicion.'

'Does Aunt Zina disapprove of Natasha?'

'There is no need to inform her of the relationship to gauge her reaction. It is entirely predictable.'

'I certainly won't be informing her.'

'Thank you, dearest Lucia.' Sasha pours himself another drink as Aunt Zina appears, laden with food. 'Thank you, I love you.'

The next morning I drive out to Daddy's house wearing a blue dress which I found among the clothes Scott gave me. I remembered it as soon as I pulled it from the bag and when I slipped it over my head it seemed to slide against my body with a small shudder of recognition. It is slighter than the clothes I wear now, sleeveless and with a looseness that feels as though it's following me instead of encircling me. Aunt Zina threw up her hands with approval when she saw it. 'Beautiful, and, you know, you look very like your mama in it. She also wore blue dresses.'

I said: 'She's crazy, Aunt Zina, I don't want to look like her.'

Aunt Zina slipped an arm around my shoulders.

'Before Tanya was crazy, she was beautiful, and often still is,' she said, pulling me close. 'You do not share your mother's illness, Lucia, but her great capacity to love. Such capacity has high value. Many lack it.'

I pulled back and looked into Aunt Zina's watery blue eyes. 'Love?'

'This surprises you? Her illness certainly took her away from you but in your early years she loved you as fiercely as any woman ever loved her child. And you her. Indeed, you were inseparable.'

I tried to remember my mother's love. I tried to remember a time when loving her didn't lead to disappointment.

'Lucia,' said Aunt Zina softly, 'only to you she spoke Russian.'

I shook my head because, outside her Russian family, Mother never spoke her native language to anyone and certainly not to Jane and me. When she was in a relatively stable condition we sometimes asked her how to say hallo, how are you? but she refused to respond and, when I announced that I was taking Mr O'Sullivan's Russian Stage One in junior high, Mother became so restless and tormented that I switched to German.

But Aunt Zina was insistent. 'She spoke to you often in Russian and you responded. You learned rhymes, songs. Don't you remember singing with her?' She shakily murmured a few bars of nursery music, miming something with her hands, perhaps a bird. I was sure I had never heard the song before.

'Will you visit her today?' asked Aunt Zina and, blushing, I explained that I had arranged to meet the others at Daddy's house, to organize the funeral and other formalities.

'Maybe tomorrow,' I said.

Driving now towards Daddy's house, up and down the low hills, I try to remember that other mother, not the one I dread visiting at Redbush clinic but the engaging, exciting mother from whom I was inseparable. But I can no longer catch her. She is the hem of a departing dress, perfume in motion, a warm, rapid touch and a low voice. She cannot be reached.

I bump up the drive and there, parked right in front of the barn where Daddy used to leave it, is his old grey Oldsmobile. It is rusted in places and there is a noticeable dent in its front fender but I warm to its familiarity. Since I am first to arrive, I take the space right next to it.

Heat swells the air here and when I get out of my car the blue dress seems to float around me. I finger the Oldsmobile's faded paintwork. The car is battered. Daddy liked its oldness, the constant need to replenish its oil and analyse each new squeak. He fixed worn machines compulsively and if he was ever happy it was when he was absorbed in an engine. In the barn is a tractor he was fixing for years; before that there was an ancient printing press, a pick-up, a motorbike, a generator.

I try the driver's door. I am not expecting it to open so I almost fall into the car when it does. It is empty. Not a newspaper or a sticker from a parking lot or even the rag Daddy usually kept here for wiping windows. I sink into the driver's seat and close the door. It seems to me that, very faintly, I can smell him in here. That sweet, soft, oily smell which clung to his overalls or his torn plaid shirt when he worked in the yard, fixed the car, changed one piece of metalwork for another on his old tractor. For a moment, Daddy is right in the car with me, a pencil behind his ear, his square fingers oily, thinking hard about some machine, concentrating in a way that involves his whole body.

When I unlock the house the heat inside it bounces out at me like an excitable dog. I lay a hand on the wall as though to steady it. The surface feels warm. I pin back the door and walk right in and the first thing I notice is that there is light where there should be shade. The hall light is on. The light in Daddy's den is on. I shrink back into the dark edges of the hallway, suspicion an instinct. Who has been here since I locked the house yesterday and left for the coast? I conclude that the police must have come inside to leave Daddy's car keys, and I am looking for them when I hear a voice.

'Morning, Lucy,' says Kirsty MacFarlane. 'I came to check that the car came home all right.'

'I think someone's been inside,' I tell her. 'There are lights on. Here and in the den.'

'Maybe Jane?' she suggests, but we are passing the living-room now and I have halted in the doorway.

'The sliding doors! They're open!'

She looks at me and then walks purposefully across the room. She moves silently, like a big cat. A space about two feet wide gapes between the doors. Through it, I can feel a breeze, very slight, from the deck. The drapes tremble.

'Are you sure you didn't leave them open yesterday?' she asks, examining the catch. 'There's no sign that this has been forced.'

I watch the drapes drift slowly like something helpless in water.

'Well, pretty sure . . .' It seems a while since I've been sure about anything. I remember unlocking the sliding doors and crossing the deck when the detective arrived. I try to recall locking them before I left but all I remember is the prickling sensation in my neck when I felt someone was watching me out in the yard and how, as I sat on the deck later, a tow truck crawled across the valley beneath me.

The detective checks the front door too but there is no sign that this has been forced either.

'Daddy's keys . . . is it possible that whoever . . .' I look around the dark hallway for other, better words. 'Whoever was with him at the end . . .'

She nods.

'Yes, that's a possibility. I suggested to your sister that she change the locks as soon as she could. Have you taken a look around to see if anything's missing?' she asks.

'I just arrived.'

'Let's do it.'

First we glance into the den. It looks just how it looked yesterday but the detective pauses.

'I don't think I left things exactly this way,' she says, going in and surveying the piles of papers on Daddy's desk. She rearranges one of them. 'But maybe you or your sister have taken a look at this stuff? Or Scott, since he's executor?'

'I didn't look at it. And no one else said they were coming here.'

She is speaking quickly now, frowning. 'I'm almost sure I left the will and the insurance policy right on the top here. I thought they'd be the first things you guys would need to see, when you felt ready to deal with things.'

'Have they gone?' I ask, staring at her.

'No, but they're underneath the bank statements and some letters from your father's mutual fund.'

Downstairs everything seems normal. The kitchen is tidy. The coffee cups which the detective and I drank from yesterday are where I left them by the kitchen sink.

She goes upstairs. Like the rest of the place, it is a repository of the past. The rooms are mostly used as closets. There are boxes stacked everywhere, in rooms and hallways. So now that Daddy is dead the closets must be cleared and the boxes opened and it will be like unleashing smells from bottles which have been closed tightly for years.

Kirsty says: 'You sure have a lot to sort out here.'

I agree with her. Looking in boxes and drawers and closets. Throwing things out. Giving them away. Making decisions. Selling the house. Dispersing Daddy's life. Our family's past will be scattered across thrift shops and junkyards and rock shops like a meteor shower. Someone else will drive Daddy's car, his clothes will be worn by strangers and his books will be read by other people, perhaps even people who turn down the corners of pages or break the spines.

At the top of the stairs, she opens the nearest door. The bathroom. Daddy's soap in an onyx holder. His razor. His toothbrushes, two of them. Toothpaste sticking to the handles, bristles bent outwards or falling inwards like a crowd of drunks.

At the bedroom door I try to say something, some routine pleasantry, but my words disappear. They give way as suddenly as ice cracks. Kirsty watches me. Her eyes look black in the dark hallway. Finally she says: 'Want me to go first?'

'No.'

But my hand still does not move. All my life, I was taught to knock on my parents' door before entering. Have the old rules changed now that Daddy's dead and Mother never leaves the clinic? All the rules, all of them? Don't I need to scrape my feet on the hall rug when it's raining or take a shower in the morning or say please pass the salt instead of reaching for it or ask: 'Can I help you?' if someone frail, blind or confused is trying to cross a street? I close my eyes and walk right in.

14

Behind me, I can sense the woman's movement, involuntary and sudden as the shying of a horse. She suppresses it with professional rapidity. That's the effect the bed has, even when you've seen it before. It's an impossible fairytale concoction of swaggers and loops and bows. It hangs over the whole room like a big blue castle dominating the landscape.

'My mother made this bed,' I explain. 'Like her, it's completely crazy.'

Kirsty nods and I guess that she has already tried to interview Mother. I ask: 'Did you get any sense out of her?'

'Well, she did speak back. In Russian.'

'In Russian! That's a new one.'

I look around the bedroom. It is unchanged in even the smallest detail. The same ornaments and photos on the vanity. The same swaggering blue curtains at the windows. The same big blue picture on the walls. It was Mother's room: Daddy did nothing to make it his own, as if he expected her to get better one day and come home. Even though he must have known she wouldn't.

On the bureau are photos of relatives, unrecognizably youthful. There is a wedding picture of Mother and Daddy looking happy, not stiff the way most people look at their weddings. Another shows the four of us on the beach. I am perhaps two years old and Mother, laughing, holds me up to the camera while Jane leans against Daddy. Daddy is laughing too, in that way I don't ever remember him laughing, with his head thrown back and all his teeth showing. I pick up the picture and examine it closely. It seems impossible that we were ever those people.

The detective says: 'You know what this bed reminds me of?'

I turn back to her. Her tone is conversational but my body goes taut like a rubber band.

She says: 'Your baby's crib.'

I do not move at all, except that after a moment's silence I realize my mouth is open a little. I close it.

'Oh, I forgot to tell you – but maybe you already realized. We've met before.'

She waits for me to speak. Finally she says: 'It was three years ago. I mean three years on Saturday.'

The back of my neck feels cold.

'I was in the early stage of pregnancy myself,' she continues. 'Maybe that's why I remember it all so well.'

I ask quietly: 'How's your baby?'

She smiles and her face softens. 'Fine.' Then immediately her muscles tighten and her face resumes its characteristic lack of expression.

I cross the blue rug and sit on the bed, right on the edge, politely, as though I'm visiting someone who's sick. I look up at the canopy and see a deep blue sky, layer after layer arching into infinity. I wonder at the confidence and ambition of the woman who made such a bed and such a room. That other Mother, who holds me, laughing, to the camera and who loved me as fiercely as any mother ever loved a child. And, said Aunt Zina, you her. Indeed, you were inseparable.

The detective says: 'Of course, I met your whole family that night, including your father. Isn't that something? There aren't many homicide victims I've met when they were alive. Professor Schaffer was pretty shocked by your son's death. You all were, but I do recall his grief in particular. When we were doing, you know, all the things we had to do, your father was sitting alone there, down in the corner of your living-room, crying quietly to himself.'

I didn't know this. The world contracted to my own shock and grief that night. I don't like to think of Daddy crying quietly in the living-room like an animal which has dragged its wounded body to safety. I wish I'd found him and put my arms around him.

'I've seen a lot of tears, enough to fill a swimming-pool, probably, or a small lake,' Kirsty is saying. 'There are wailers and shriekers and big sobbers and gaspers but your daddy sitting crying so quietly was one of the worst.'

Scalded by her words, I jump to my feet. Then I am awkward. Suddenly I have too much body and I don't know what to do with it all.

'Did you buy that beautiful crib for your baby because it reminded you of this bed?' asks the woman, watching me.

I am surprised to hear my own voice, rusty like something which has lain unused in a barn a long time. I say: 'I never thought about it . . .'

'Maybe you decorated the crib that way yourself?' Her eyes never leave me.

I cough. 'No. Jane and I bought it.'

She is wandering around the room, studying the furniture, gazing at the blue pictures. 'You two sisters bought the crib together? That's fascinating. And you never noticed the similarity to your parents' bed?'

'Well no, I don't think so.'

'Except the baby's crib was a lighter blue, wouldn't you say?'

'Yes, probably.'

When I was round and still with the sense of anticipation of late pregnancy that dulls the present, Jane told me she wanted to buy the baby's crib. Her voice was steady when she admitted that she had just about given up all hope of having children of her own now and that she wanted to be a good aunt, a special aunt, to my baby. We went to all the big stores and the expensive little ones and the more stores we visited the more elaborate our ideas became. When we saw the blue crib with all those ruffles and frills and the voile drapes we just had to have it. I looked at the price tag and hid my face. But Jane insisted. When they delivered it, I couldn't believe we'd got caught up in such a crazy notion. All those flounces and fussy details. It just wasn't the kind of thing either of us would buy. I wasn't sure I even liked it. I thought of sending it back to the store but I couldn't hurt Jane's feelings and it became Stevie's crib and, when everyone who saw it admired it, I came to admire it too. Then Stevie died in it and I hated it. I told them to take it away when we moved to the beach house. I never even asked where it went.

'If somebody broke in last night, they certainly would have taken those silver boxes,' says the woman, gesturing to the vanity. 'Were there any other items of value in this room?'

I shrug. 'I don't think so.'

She holds open the door. We resume our tour of the dusty house. The detective wants to know which room was mine and which Jane's. Both are full of old boxes now. And there is the room where Grandma slept on her occasional visits, or Daddy did when Mother was ill and needed the big bedroom all to herself.

'Whose was this?' asks the detective when, at the end of the hallway, we open the door on to a small room, painted in pale, pale blue like distant sky. It smells musty.

'Daddy used it as a study before he moved his desk to the den. There are probably rocks in the boxes.'

'And before that? Could it have been your brother's room?' she asks and for the second time this morning her words halt me and I am speechless. She adds: 'You did have a brother, right?'

I nod. 'But he died when he was just a baby.'

'Was this his room?'

'I don't know.'

'You don't remember him?'

'I don't remember anything about him.'

'That's surprising,' she says, turning and leading me away. 'You were just about old enough to remember something so dramatic.'

I don't ask her how she knows this. I don't say anything. The death of my baby brother is something seldom, if ever, mentioned. When Stevie died there were references to Daddy's loss but he made it clear that this was not a loss he wished to discuss. I hope that my silence will tell the detective all this.

Going downstairs, she says: 'Well, the dust up here hasn't been disturbed for a while. If there was an intruder anywhere, he was probably in the den. But since nothing's gone let's just hope that you left the lights on and the doors open last night.'

I nod despondently. Let's just hope that. She looks at me. She's despondent too. 'Do you have any idea how many keys your father carried around with him? I assume the house and car keys were on the same ring?'

I remember Rougemont's big hands slipping around the lock of his car. His car key, his house key. How this seemed such a meagre accumulation.

'Oh, Daddy clanged when he walked. I mean, car key, house key, barn key, desk key, key to the old tractor, key to Jane's apartment, maybe the key to Scott's house or Seymour's house . . .' I swallow. 'And now whoever drove away with Daddy in his car last Monday morning can get into all those places.'

We are silent. We don't look at each other.

Then the detective asks quietly. 'Aren't you glad you didn't stay here last night?'

'We've really got to get the locks changed soon,' I say.

She nods. She turns and starts to walk out to the porch. Through the screen door, beyond the porch and beyond the trees which embrace the porch, a small section of the day glimmers brightly.

'Have you taken a look at your father's car yet?' she asks, when the screen door has slammed behind us.

'Well . . . I sat in it earlier. I sort of smelled him in there.'

She raises her eyebrows.

'You smelled . . . who?'

'Daddy. Oh, not a bad smell. A sweet sort of smell like oil and soap. When someone dies it's hard to believe they're gone, completely gone. You feel as if they're still there, only they're being elusive. You swing around quickly to catch them out of the corner of your eye and sometimes you can smell them. I opened the car and it had Daddy's own special smell. I got right in and for a moment I felt as though he was sitting there next to me.'

The woman watches me closely. I wait for a rapid, dismissive remark but she says: 'I wonder . . . when we leave our own personal scent behind us, I wonder how long it hangs around. I mean, maybe there ought to be some scientific way of using smell to analyse when your father last sat in that car.'

'Oh, he's been in there within about forty-eight hours.' I say this without thinking, without stopping to wonder whether a smell can linger for a day or a week or a month.

Her look is curious. 'What makes you so sure?'

'I don't know. If you try to get scientific about it then the whole thing sort of dissolves.'

'Wait.'

She gets into the Oldsmobile on the passenger side and gestures for me to climb into the driver's seat. We slam the doors shut. At first I fold my hands on my lap like a well-behaved first-grader, then I hold the wheel as though I'm driving. We sit there, the detective and I, driving nowhere, mute, breathing silently. I close my eyes and a moment later I smell it again. The aroma is so distant that I can detect it only occasionally.

'Well?' says the woman at last. 'What do you smell?'

'It's real faint but I do smell Daddy.'

I look at her profile. It is aquiline, sharp. She's watching the road ahead intently although there is no road. She says: 'I smell fingerprint powder. It's sort of metallic.'

I breathe silently again. 'No, I'm not getting that at all.'

She says: 'So your sense of smell seems to be saying that the decedent . . .' She pauses and corrects herself. 'That Professor Schaffer drove this car somewhere himself on Monday morning.'

I nod.

'The car was found at a place called Lowis. Do you know it?'

'Not really. I've seen it from the freeway.'

'Often?'

'You pass it on the way to the San Strana valley and Scott and I used to eat at San Strana when I was pregnant.' I craved the eggs Benedict served by a white, wooden restaurant in the heart of the valley. We'd go there for Sunday brunch and watch the river meander by as we ate. The river carved the valley and San Strana is a fertile place, its narrow sides dotted with old houses and farmsteads, artists' colonies, restaurants and health farms.

'But you never stopped in Lowis?'

I shake my head.

'It's just about the only place they've allowed any recent construction around there. The Oldsmobile was in a housing area. Big homes, pleasant, quiet. A lot of kids. Most of them never saw so many patrol cars before.'

I imagine the fingerprint man trying to do his job inside the Oldsmobile with a dozen small faces pushed against the windows.

'Did your father ever mention Lowis? Maybe he ate there or visited a friend there?'

'No . . . We could look in his address book . . .' I suggest.

'I have that copied and I already looked. He didn't seem to have any connection with Lowis and no one there remembered seeing the car before. It sort of stands out among all those new SUVs.'

We both smile without looking at each other.

She says: 'Local folk differ in their opinions but most of them think that the car had been there since Monday afternoon, probably since Monday morning, and a few are claiming it was there all weekend.'

'Didn't anyone see him leave it?'

'No, Lucy. No one saw a damn thing.' Her tone is resigned. She's a homicide detective. No one ever sees a damn thing.

'But were there any fingerprints?'

She sighs. 'Someone took a lot of trouble to wipe the car completely clean. We managed to pick up a few old prints, a few stray fibres, but they were pretty much all your father's. Some from Jane but you'd expect that because he drove her to your son's grave on Saturday.'

'Can I have the address where it was found?'

'Okay, if you think it might help you remember something useful, I'll check in my notebook and tell you the exact address,' she says.

When she gets out she stoops to examine the big dent on the Oldsmobile's front right fender. She crouches, running her fingers again and again over the chipped paintwork with the deftness of a woman running her fingers over a lover.

'Did your father ever mention this?'

'No.'

'It looks pretty fresh,' she comments. 'But forensic didn't have anything interesting to say about it.' She straightens. The sun feels oppressive today. The weight of its heat seems to pin me to the drive. The leaves around the porch hang helplessly. When I duck into shade it brings little relief.

'I sure wish we had more information, Lucy,' the woman says. 'There are so many questions about this case. Over the next few days I'll be interviewing everyone who knew your father well. I'm hoping people will start remembering things they've forgotten. You and Jane especially.'

I don't know why I blush at her words. In order to hide this, I squint up at the sun, which has just stalked me through a gap in the trees.

'I mean,' she continues, 'for example, my colleague Michael Rougemont has this amazing memory. He can recall small details from cases over thirty years ago. So it really frustrates him when other people forget everything.'

I know my face is red. It feels as though it is swelling in the sun.

'For instance, Lucy, you and Jane both say you can't remember a thing about your brother's death.'

I swallow. 'I was very young . . .'

'Sure, but the loss of a sibling has a huge impact on a

family. I'd expect one or two images to have survived. And I'd expect considerably more than that from Jane.'

'Larry would say we've buried the trauma.'

'Sure he would. Sure. And that would explain why you don't remember anything, not one thing, why you don't even remember your brother when he was alive.'

I say, slowly, shakily: 'I remember that I loved him. That's all.'

Her voice is gentle now. 'Didn't anybody ever talk about it in your family?'

'Never.'

'I mean, when your son died, didn't your father talk about it then?'

'Not directly. It was referred to as a loss and Scott and I always knew he had a special understanding. But Daddy never discussed it.'

'And you never asked him?'

'Oh no, I couldn't possibly have asked him.'

'Did you ever ask Jane?'

'We just never have talked about it.'

She sighs. 'Do you even know how the child died?'

'Oh yes.' I am prompt. 'I know that. In an accident.'

She waits for me to say more and then sighs again.

'Do you have any idea where that accident took place?'

I shake my head.

'At Big Brim beach. He drowned there. You really didn't know that?'

I stare at her.

'Oh, Lucy,' she murmurs and her tone is at once intimate and despairing.

15

Scott arrives before Larry and Jane. He's pleased to see the Oldsmobile back in its usual place.

'You're here, the old car's here, I can kid myself that things are going back the way they used to be,' he says when we're sitting out on the deck. The view glimmers at us but we only half absorb it, as though it's a flickering TV with the sound turned down.

'Larry doesn't approve of that,' I remind him.

'Of course, things haven't been the same since you went and now they can't ever be the same because Eric's gone. But is it so bad to make-believe for a few moments?'

I smile at him.

He tells me how his book went into a new edition, how he was even interviewed about it on TV.

'I saw you,' I say.

'You saw me on TV?'

I nod but he is quick. 'So you switched right off.'

I look at him until he finally lifts his big head and looks back at me. I say: 'No, Scott, I didn't switch off.'

When we hear an engine we go around the house to the barn. Larry and Jane have arrived and Larry is first out of the car. He wears a shirt the colour of shallow water which is stretched tight over his body, emphasizing his swelling waist. Above it, around his ribs and arms, there is the pinched look of an old man. When Daddy went swimming I didn't like to look at the hollows in his torso or his thin arms or the ring of extra flesh which hung limply around his belly.

And now I see Larry climbing out of the car and I'm mad at him for reminding me of Daddy and of ageing. He's just about old enough to be my father but when he married Jane he opted into our generation and now this body, age hollowing and plucking at it, belly bulging, is a betrayal.

'Sorry we're so late,' he says. 'We've been visiting your mother.' I feel colour creeping up my neck and head like a fast-moving shadow and Larry seems to watch this with amusement.

'How was she?' Scott asks.

To answer, Larry and Jane wrinkle their faces as though the sun is shining in their eyes although they are standing in the kitchen lifting packages from a big brown deli bag. Of the four of us, only Larry and Jane have remembered lunch. Or maybe Scott and I just assumed they would organize it.

'Well, she was subdued,' says Jane at last.

'Does she understand about Daddy?'

They look at each other and then Larry answers. 'She seems to comprehend that something sad has happened. She may not know what that is.'

'She fluttered a lot,' adds Jane. 'You remember how she sort of flutters when she gets upset?' She waves her arms and wiggles her fingers in a half-comical gesture which I recognize at once.

I say: 'It's when she feels helpless.'

'And distressed,' Jane agrees.

'The most she ever fluttered was when I nearly drowned at the pool that day. It was because she wanted to do something but she couldn't, or she didn't know how, and she just had to stand there while you saved me.'

We were at the local swimming-pool and I was learning to snorkel when I breathed water instead of air. My eyes and nose and mouth were full of water and the warm, damp passages which link them were swamped by water too. Above me the sky was more deep blue water. As I looked up I saw its infinity for the first time. I saw that blue is the colour of depth, and the depths of the sky stretch on forever and on and on. I stopped struggling. I stopped swimming. My head sagged and I submitted to the beauty of the blue pool's infinity of water. Then, suddenly, a powerful mixture of flesh and muscle gripped me under the chin and I felt the rhythmic strength of the swimmer's stroke as I was pulled, floating helplessly, to the edge. When I opened my eyes I was on the pool's hard paving, kids crowded around me, Jane standing over me, pumping me, banging at me, until I threw up all the liquid and my body became solid again. I remember Jane's serious face, wrapped in concentration, and beyond it, Mother, her blue dress flapping, her fingers flying, and beyond them both, the sky.

Larry stops taking interesting food out of the deli bag and puts an arm around Jane. He knows the story of how she saved me. He has always liked it and it pleases him again today. 'And she's still saving lives,' he says. His voice is both proud and foolish.

I look at them both, standing side by side, and wonder, fleetingly, irreverently, what sort of parents they would have made. And I see Scott staring at them, at their linked arms. He is wondering why they have stayed together and why we haven't. They are the couple who couldn't have a baby. We are the couple who couldn't keep a baby longer than six months.

After that the day is businesslike. We look at the will first. Daddy left everything divided equally between Jane and me. That is no surprise. Only his appointment of Scott as personal representative causes a ripple, with Scott first disbelieving and then shocked and then pleading for my help.

'I haven't done personal finance in a long while . . .' I protest but he yelps like a dog someone just stepped on.

'You have to do it for me, Luce. You just have to.'

'How long are you staying, Lucy?' asks Larry, pointing his beard at me.

'I have to get back right after the funeral.' I feel a movement of disapproval, a raised hand or an arm flexed, ripple around the the group. I add: 'Well, I certainly can't stay past the end of next week. I have a big deal which might collapse if I'm not around.'

For a moment, I cannot look at them, then, when I realize they can't look at me either, I steal glances at their averted faces. Finally Larry speaks, his tone serious. 'Lucy, there's a lot to do after a death. A lot of decisions, a lot to sort out . . . you can't run off to New York and leave it all to Jane.'

I hope Jane will contradict him but she is silent.

'Will you have time to sort out the executor stuff for me before the funeral?' asks Scott helplessly.

'Probably,' I tell him. 'If I work hard enough.'

'When do we want the funeral?' asks Jane. 'How about next Tuesday? And have we informed everyone we need to inform? C'mon, let's get things sorted out.' She reaches for a notebook and pen. I watch her affectionately. Jane is retreating into the detached efficiency of the clinician where she feels safest. She learned to do that in childhood when Mother made life impossible and now she uses the same professionalism every day. Dealing with bereaved relatives, or those who face bereavement, is a routine part of her work. The extraordinary is routine for Jane. Routinely she has to tell patients that they are going to die. I know that she never stalls or stands shuffling her notes or her feet at the patient's side or avoiding the terrible truths or forgetting to use the patient's name. She delivers the news with her usual unbending directness. She walks right into the patient's room and asks how they are feeling and then says: 'I'm sorry, Mr Smith. When we tried to operate we found that the cancer was far more widespread than we thought. We did what we could. But I'm sorry, very sorry, that I have to tell you this is not a fight we can possibly win. I hope you'll agree that it's more dignified now to give in to the disease and concentrate our efforts on maximizing your pain relief and comfort.'

Of course, different people react to this news in different ways. Some people are angry with the doctor or the disease or themselves or even with some relative who sits still with shock at the bedside. Some people don't want to admit that they have lost the fight, and continue to demand further treatment. They are pugnacious with the doctor because they know that there's no point being pugnacious with their illness. Some shake or cry like small, frightened children. Others display a sweetness of temperament or a quiet resignation which can anger their relatives. A few are relieved. With all these reactions, Jane is firm and commanding so when she leaves the room the patient has generally agreed to her proposed treatment. And, as she walks out, the patient always thanks her.

'Okay,' says Larry, adopting her businesslike tone. 'I suggest that next we look in Eric's diary and cancel any appointments he made. Then we need to discuss who else to inform.'

We fetch the diary. We look at each other, not wanting to make the first call. It seems Jane is about to offer when Scott surprises us. He says: 'I'll do it. Give me the numbers.'

We can hear him in the study, breaking the news to people. Some seem to know already but they have questions, about the police, about Daddy, about the circumstances. We hear Scott struggle to answer them, knowing that most are unanswerable.

Larry makes coffee the way he likes it, strong, so that the

smell insinuates itself all over the house, burnt like molasses. He produces some big, round peanut cookies.

'My new passion,' he explains sheepishly. 'I found them at this place on my way to work. I'm addicted.'

'You're going to have to find another route in the morning,' Jane tells him. I think of Jim and his cinnamon buns and smile. When I bite into the dry cookie tiny crumbs of flavour explode on my tongue and all around my mouth.

'It's the combination of sugar, salt and nut,' says Larry, watching me. 'It's irresistible.' He looks down at his developing paunch apologetically.

I point to an entry in Daddy's diary. 'Daddy saw Mr Zacarro on Sunday night,' I say. 'Isn't that peculiar? One of the last people to see him was Mr Zacarro.'

'Oh, he'd gotten real pally with Mr Zacarro and Mr Holler,' Jane tells me. She is thumbing through Daddy's address book, making lists of names, and she doesn't look up.

'Daddy? And Mr Zacarro? And Mr Holler?' They were neighbours, not friends. I haven't seen either of them for many years and Daddy certainly never mentioned them.

'I really didn't like it, but what can you do?' says Jane absently while she writes.

'You didn't like it?'

'They weren't good for Daddy. He'd stay over at the Zacarro house real late, talking and drinking beer.'

I want to question her further but right now Scott comes back in, red-eyed, red-faced.

'Joni Rimbaldi was real shocked,' he says. Joni was Daddy's secretary in the geology department for many years. 'She was just at her house by Tigertail Bay, getting her make-up on to meet Eric for lunch in town today, and I call to say, hey Joni, lunch is off, Eric's dead and he's not just dead he's murdered. My God. What a call.'

'Maybe we should phone in an hour or two. Make sure she's okay,' suggests Jane and we all nod. That is certainly the right thing to do.

Over lunch, Larry says: 'Lucy, I guess you must agree that the house should be cleared and sold?'

I look at him.

He explains: 'The choices are renting it or selling it. As I assume none of us is going to live in it.'

'Sell it,' says Jane rapidly.

'Either way,' Larry points out, 'it has to be cleared.' He speaks emphatically, as though he anticipates contradiction. Maybe Jane had warned him I might start acting Russian.

'I know that, Larry,' I say quietly. 'But it's going to be painful.'

'There's no alternative,' he insists.

'What will we do with it all?'

Jane and Larry look at each other.

'We take what we want, we sell anything worth selling, we give a lot away and we just have to grit our teeth and junk the rest,' says Larry. 'And, Lucy, it may seem heartless but I think we should start real soon.'

'No . . .'

'Lucy, it's going to take a long time and we need to use you while we have you here.'

'When do you want to start?'

'Tomorrow, today, immediately.'

'I'm not sure, Larry. It feels like a . . . sort of betrayal.'

'Why?'

'Daddy accumulated all this stuff over a lifetime . . . we can't just throw it away in a week . . .' My voice sounds small and childish.

Scott leans forward. He says kindly: 'It'll take months, Luce, that's why we have to start soon.'

'It'll take months,' I say, 'because there's a right person and a right place for everything . . . I mean, some old tractor enthusiast who'll want the old tractor. Some geologist who'll want the rocks and love the tools. A gardener who –'

'It would take years to dispose of everything that way,' Jane tells me. 'And a lot of the stuff here is junk.'

Larry nods. He is still a bull looking for a red rag. 'The whole place is stuffed high to the roofbeams with junk,' he insists. 'If we start to get picky about where it goes then it never will go anywhere.' Larry and Jane have a clean apartment which they keep free of clutter and its sister, dust. Jane doesn't like to receive beautiful ceramics or small knick-knacks as gifts. The white apartment is designed so she has nowhere to put them. I watch her as she discusses, with clinical seriousness, the disposal of our past. Waste and recycling department. Hostel for the homeless two blocks from the hospital always needs furniture. Vietnam Vets sometimes collect. Geology department to value the rocks. Later, as I negotiate the car around the holes in the drive, her words rattle around in my head like gravel in your shoe.

When I told Larry and Scott and Jane where I was going, Scott looked concerned, Jane shook her head but Larry only stroked his beard. 'I understand your curiosity,' he said.

'The police have asked everyone in that neighbourhood about the car already,' Jane pointed out.

'And they didn't find out a thing,' added Scott.

'Well, maybe Lucy will,' Larry told them. 'Let her go. She needs to feel she's doing something.'

I was surprised by his support. I had spent the day disliking him.

There are two ways to reach Lowis. I can take a fast road west towards town and then swing north on the coastal freeway or

I can drive right down into the valley and rumble across its floor, past orchards of identical fruit, feeling as though I'm going nowhere until I reach the intersection. That's where the tow truck turned yesterday. Eventually this route leads up to Sacramento but long before that it passes by the easternmost edge of San Strana. I could take a scenic drive right through San Strana and, when I come out the other side, I'll be in Lowis. I pause at the end of the dirt road, feeling the valley pulling me like gravity. Then I turn towards town.

It is late afternoon, a bad time to drive west. I wear sunglasses and pull down the car's visor but still I drive into the sun with my eyelids half lowered.

Lowis is easy to find: it is the first settlement in the valley and if you want to go further into San Strana you have to drive right through it. The town is less picturesque than Cooper and some of the older places in San Strana: the ancient trees and old habitations are still here but they have been smothered by a band of expensive modern housing. I drive around until I find the address the detective gave me, a long, curving street where leggy vegetation is already beginning to hide the new houses. Behind fences I can hear small children shrieking the way they do when there is water. Maybe sprinklers, probably swimming-pools.

The detective explained that the car was left on a curve by a cluster of trees where the occupants of two if not three houses might assume that it belonged to someone visiting their neighbours. I stop the hirecar in the spot she has described. I feel safe here. No house overlooks me. I could get out and walk back down the street and no one would notice the car and probably they wouldn't notice me either.

I drive up and down the street twice. Finally I park right where Daddy's car was parked. As I walk away I hear my own feet on the broad sidewalk. Click clack, click clack.

Immediately I am alert. I stalk my footfall and the imbalance disappears instantly, the way it always does as soon as I become aware of it.

At the end of the street there are trees. Three kids with skateboards linger beneath them, watching me. I walk right up to them and as I get closer I see three more kids, hanging from branches or leaning against dark trunks. I say hi. I am relieved when, after a pause, my greeting is returned.

'See where I parked my car right down there?' I ask, turning and pointing. They nod soundlessly. They are all boys. They have the fleshiness of early puberty.

'On Monday there was another car parked right there all day, maybe longer. A real old car, an Oldsmobile, with a dent on the front fender. Did any of you guys happen to see it?' I hear my own words and a curious cadence in my speech. I think that's how I talked when I was their age but maybe it's just the way I heard other kids talk, because my isolation was complete before I was eleven.

'Sure,' says one of them. Another agrees. Another says that he passed right by the car twice and a competitive voice insists he not only saw it but nearly crashed into it on his skateboard. Two of the boys slip into rivalry, claiming successively more intimate relationships with Daddy's Oldsmobile. I smile.

'Mrs Steadman in 3315 finally called the police,' another says helpfully.

'Do you have any idea how the car got there?' I ask and there is silence.

'Nope,' says one.

More silence, then a voice informs me: 'Someone got murdered in it.'

'But how did the car get here?' I persist. 'I mean, did someone park it and walk away? Park it and climb into some other car that was waiting? Or, how about this: a tow truck. Maybe it got towed here and dumped.'

They look at me. One kid puts his foot on his skateboard and wheels it backwards and forwards as though he's about to go somewhere.

'I saw a tow truck,' he offers. But he can't remember which day or whether it was the morning or the evening.

'Are you the police?' asks a boy who is sitting on his skateboard. 'You don't look like the police.'

'No,' I admit. 'I'm interested because the car belonged to my father.'

'Did your dad get murdered?' he demands, his voice high, half joky, unsure of himself.

'Well . . .' I hesitate. It's new territory for me, too. 'Yes.'

They are greedy for details. I tell them that Daddy seemed to have been killed at Big Brim beach but no one knows how or why anyone would want to kill him and no one understands how his car could have got here. They present me with a series of theories that are right out of a TV show. Daddy wouldn't pay his blackmail money. Daddy committed suicide and made it look like murder. Daddy had a long-lost son nobody knew about who appeared and wanted all his money. Daddy saw something bad, like a rape, and then got into a fight trying to save the victim. Daddy was a mafia boss. I look at their smooth faces and bright eyes. Whatever serious difficulties they have encountered have mostly been on screen, far removed from their quiet existence in Lowis. Maybe if they stay here in the San Strana valley for ever they will escape life's battering and stay smooth-cheeked.

'This is my father you're talking about,' I remind them, and they fall silent. 'He was a good man. A college professor. He wouldn't have been involved in any blackmail or long-lost son or mafia scenarios.'

'You don't seem too beat up over it,' observes a crewcut who is sitting on his skateboard. I stare down at him in surprise. The boy makes himself look back up at me but he shrinks a little inside his baggy short pants and massive T-shirt.

'Sure she does, Tony, for Chrissake. It's only little guys like you who cry when they're sad,' says a much deeper voice, and Tony reddens.

'My mom didn't cry when her dad died but she needed anti-depressants anyway,' announces a child from the branches of a tree.

'So, did you cry?' Tony persists. His face is red now and he is glaring up at me as though he's angry. 'Did you cry when they told you?'

'At first I was too shocked. I've cried a lot of times since then.'

'You don't look like you've been crying. Didn't you like your dad?' he insists. His ears are crimson, and, beneath the crewcut, his scalp. He scoots his body backwards and forwards without moving his feet.

'I loved him,' I say. 'I loved him very much and right now I feel as though I'll never be the same person I was before this happened.' I feel my face crease up and I know I'm going to cry. At least that should please Tony. I turn away from the boys and walk back down the street. Behind me is silence.

'Thanks for your help,' I say over my shoulder when I can speak but my throat has thickened and the words can barely escape. There is silence behind me.

'Hope they catch the guy who killed him,' calls a small voice eventually.

16

I am walking over to the Zacarro house to ask Mr Zacarro about the Sunday evening he spent with Daddy when I am ambushed by a memory so powerful that it halts me.

I have stumbled down Daddy's drive, stubbing my toe twice and once grabbing the low branches of a eucalyptus to prevent myself falling. I have walked along the dirt road, and noted that the potholes are in just the same places they were when I was a child, although the foliage has of course grown. The Zacarro house has a corner lot and when they first moved in, before it got draped in trees and bushes, the neighbourhood kids cut the corner, treading in the dry dirt between the plants and occasionally treading on the plants themselves. Mrs Zacarro was the gardener but she didn't seem to mind. It was Mr Zacarro, a man of renowned temper, who caught me once. He yelled furiously and finally switched on the sprinklers. When I arrived home, wet, dirty and tearful, Jane was irate: 'I'm going to call him right now! I'm going to tell him that you're sick and he shouldn't do that kind of thing to you!' I pleaded with her not to. As I turned into the steep Zacarro drive, I found myself, even now, hoping that she never did.

Over the years, storms have washed away much of the drive's surface. I remember when the asphalt was so new it was sticky and you could smell it from our house. Now the only smell is the smell of heat, beating against every surface, battering the face of the leaves until they hang in submission.

I trip in a pothole and brush against something at the edge

of the drive. A plant, insignificant in appearance, fighting for space with fleshy weeds. Its pink flowers are bowed and dusty. Its leaves are sticky. Within two steps I can feel its residue on my legs and within another two the air is thick with the perfume it has released and, almost before I finish inhaling it, my heart has stopped beating and become a stone, falling towards the earth. My chest heaves. I gasp for air. My eyes fill with tears. I hear a sob as the memory escapes from some deep, closed, quiet place inside me.

It was morning, early but not too early to feel the sun's touch on my shoulders and the backs of my legs as I walked up this drive to ask about Lindy. I had gone to bed anxious and woken anxious. I felt shy but I had to go because I had to know that everything was okay. I moved slowly. I walked right at the side of the drive knowing the touch of my leg would release a sticky sweet aroma from the pink flowers which Mrs Zacarro had planted alongside the asphalt. She had planted them from the bottom to the top and I walked with one leg trailing through them so that by the time I was within sight of the house I was dizzy, close to nausea, from the sun and the oppressive cloud of perfume. My leg was covered in a viscous film like flypaper. Some insect, maybe a bee, was droning too close to my hair but by now my head felt detached from my body and I did not even attempt to wave it away.

Drugged by the aroma, I didn't even feel astonishment when I looked up and saw Mother emerging, fingers fluttering like trapped birds, from the Zacarro house. Although I knew this was astonishing. At that time Mother seldom left our house and never alone. As she drew closer I saw horror on her face and an extra energy fuelled her walk which I knew to be dangerous. When she saw me she looked right at me and then away.

'You can't possibly go in there,' she said.

I didn't need to ask why. I knew they'd found Lindy.

Mother didn't pause but walked right on past me with the disconcerting, jerking gait of someone in an old newsreel.

The whole class went to the funeral. Lindy had been the prettiest girl and that was a reason for some people to dislike her when she was alive and for everyone to cry some extra when she died. Except for me. I couldn't cry at all. I tried but no tears would come.

Slowly, I stumble on up the broken asphalt towards the house, hungrily inhaling the plant's vanishing perfume as though it carries some encoded information about the past. When I'm more than half-way, when I've passed that place where Mother instructed me to turn back, I tell myself I'm finally completing the last journey I made here, so many years ago. I've thought about Lindy more in the last couple of days than in all the intervening years but I still excluded her death, as though I long ago pushed some kind of delete button. She died when we were eight. The next few years were informed by her death. Eventually I determined never to think about her at all. I was so successful that when we arrived here and Sasha, half-joking, asked me whether the Zacarros were good neighbours, all I could recall was Mr Zacarro's limp.

When I reach the top of the drive I see a car facing the garage. The trunk is towards me and I notice at once that it is closed with three metal padlocks, enormous padlocks which look like they came from a jail. The padlocks make the hairs on the back of my neck reorganize a little.

I ring the doorbell. I wonder how Mr Zacarro feels about old friends of his daughter. I wonder if he hates them for still being alive. I wonder if he yells at them and then turns on the sprinklers.

There is no responding sound from inside so I wander around the house the way I used to when I came to play with Lindy. I move slowly, as though the hot air is resisting me. At the side gate I see a pool. In the pool a large brown body floats motionlessly, back down, arms and legs splayed. There is no ripple or movement on the water's surface. Various flotation aids sit on the still water or around the edge, some in luminous oranges and yellows. A floating armchair is moored to one side.

I let myself in quietly through the gate but when it clicks softly behind me the brown body at once folds itself and raises a hand, breaking the water's smooth surface. As if joining in the greeting, the water toys begin to bob, jostling against Mr Zacarro's body and one another.

He bellows: 'Is it Jane or is it Lucy?'

'Lucy.'

'Good!' he yells disconcertingly.

I stand closer to him now but he continues to roar at me. 'I'm real glad you came. Real glad, Lucy. I want to say how sorry I am about your daddy and I want you to tell me what's been going on over there. I tried to get up the drive but they got some kind of dumbfool barrier and then I got stopped by some guy who thought he was real important because they gave him a uniform and a clipboard. Want some beer?'

'Well . . . thanks.'

I don't recognize Mr Zacarro. I remember him as a large man and when he heaves his body up into the floating armchair in a practised manoeuvre around the pool steps I see that he is still large. His head is almost hairless now.

He instructs me: 'Just on the porch there's a fridge and it's full of cold beers. Bring me one too, will you?'

The porch. When Lindy and I weren't on the swinging seat over at my house we were here in the porch playing with our

173

little toy horses. Lindy's favourite was a sweet-faced chestnut. Mostly they were made of plastic, a few were china and soon got chipped but Lindy's chestnut horse had a soft coat and legs you could bend. Trigger. His name comes bounding into my mind like a horse galloping up to a gate. His name was Trigger and Lindy used to say that when she was a little older she'd have a real horse which looked just like him.

I glance around the porch. I had a few of my own little horses over here when Lindy died and I never came back for them and now I half expect to find the cardboard stables we built, the ever-present Trigger, the toys I left behind. When I see that they are all gone I feel an absurd disappointment.

I take the beers outside and pass one to the floating man. He gestures for me to sit down at a poolside seat.

'So, Lucy Schaffer,' yells Mr Zacarro. 'I guess I've glimpsed you since you grew up but I remember you best playing out back with the kids.' His voice is without modulation. I swallow. I don't want to be the first to mention Lindy.

'How are Davis and Carter?' I yell back. By now I've worked out that he must be deaf and I should speak loudly.

'You don't have to shout. I'm not deaf. Davis started up Hooleran Software and now he's got a turnover of I don't know how many zillion dollars a year, and Carter's doing just great in real estate, four kids and counting. They're busy so I don't see them too often. But they call me.' He gestures to the telephone nearby. I look around for the first time and realize that the back yard is furnished. There are the usual poolside couches and chairs but there is also a dressing-table, a chest, a TV, two mirrors and a few photos hanging on the metal fence which nestles into the hillside. By the side of the pool, arranged neatly, is a small pile of rocks. Some are round and consist of interesting seams, others are crystalline.

Mr Zacarro watches me. 'Your daddy gave me those rocks. He often brought me rocks and I put them all right there.'

As he gestures, his flesh folds down his big stomach like ribbons of brown dough.

'What's that one?' I ask, pointing to a rock which lies behind the rest, larger and flat-faced. Words are inscribed on it.

He smiles. His smile is crooked.

'It's a headstone.'

The headstone is way down at the shallow end. I get up to take a closer look. I read: 'Remember death. Joe Zacarro always did.'

'There's a space underneath for my dates,' he explains helpfully. 'Do you like it?'

I nod, returning to the vast body, sprawled in its floating armchair.

'Did you see Daddy Sunday night, Mr Zacarro?'

'Joe. Yep, he came over here, so did Adam Holler.'

'You were one of the last to see him alive.'

'I know that, Lucy. It doesn't make me feel good.'

'How was he, Mr Zacarro?'

'Fine. And call me Joe.'

'Do you know whether he saw anyone else on Sunday?'

He shrugs a big shrug. 'Didn't say so.'

'What time did he go home?'

'I don't know. He was here an hour or two.'

I see small goose-pimples appear across his chest.

'Aren't you cold?' I ask. 'Can I get you a towel?' He smiles and I guess that my solicitous tone has pleased him. And then something sad flits across his face like a leaf scuttling along in the breeze and I know that he's just wished he still had a daughter to ask him if he's cold and needs a towel. He thinks about Lindy every day.

'Well, Lucy, I don't feel the cold these days,' he yells. 'At first it was hard, in the winter, but I just don't feel it any more.'

'You swim all year round?'

'The truth is that I don't do so much swimming now. I float a lot.'

He drinks some beer and then slips it into a can-shaped crevice in the arm of the chair. Whenever he speaks, the chair bounces in the water and tugs at its rope so that it seems Mr Zacarro will soon drift right away.

I look around again.

'You . . .' I hesitate '. . . you live out here? In the pool?'

'Oh, sometimes I go inside the house. But it hurts, see. When I'm up on land I lumber around like some kind of big old moose. I got one leg shorter than the other so I've always been a moose. Don't you remember that about me? I always thought it must be the one thing people noticed.'

Mr Zacarro limping. Mr Zacarro turning on the sprinkler because the water travelled faster down the hose than he ever could. Mr Zacarro chasing after Davis and Carter, shouting with fury and Davis and Carter laughing, laughing at their father, knowing he could never catch them. I experience again that mixture of acute pain at his humiliation and terror at his anger. For a moment I cannot look at him.

I say: 'When did you build the pool?'

'Boys were teenagers I guess. I got so I came home every night and had a swim, winter and summer. I'd always known I was a water creature. I can move how I want in the water, look real symmetrical. I guess I just spent more and more time here so now I hardly leave it.'

'But you'll come to Daddy's funeral?'

'Sure. I get dressed sometimes, I go to the store, fill the freezer. Since Gracie left I've pretty well eaten out of the freezer. I don't like to leave the water more than an hour or two. Lucy . . .' He paddles his chair around with his hands so that he is facing me. 'Did I already say I'm real sorry about your daddy? He was a great guy. So clever it made my brains hurt. Funny. Loved you two girls a lot. But, what the hell were the police doing over at your place? Adam Holler had it from Bernard Dimoto that he drowned at Big Brim beach. Did he drown or didn't he? I mean, will you tell me what's going on?'

I'd like to evade his question but can think of no way to do so.

'Daddy's death . . .' I flounder and then borrow the phrase Jim used back in New York. 'It wasn't straightforward. The police say it's homicide.'

There is a silence and then Mr Zacarro gives a long, low whistle.

'Homicide. For Chrissake! Homicide! Oh Lucy, Lucy, that's just garbage. Homicide's garbage.'

There's a long pause. I watch him. He is silent but his lips form the word homicide again and again.

'Can you think . . . is there anyone you can think of who might have some reason to kill Daddy?'

'Kill Eric!' he roars. 'No one would kill Eric! I mean, exactly what are the forensic geeks saying?'

I shrug. 'That he didn't drown. He died first and then his body somehow got into the water.'

'Oh shit, shit, this is awful.'

His lips form more silent words.

'Daddy's clothes were left at Big Brim beach. But no one knows how he got there because his car was found over at San Strana.'

He stares at me with big, liquid eyes so the wrinkles on his face look like ripples.

'The San Strana valley for heaven's sake!'

'Lowis, to be precise.'

He is bellowing. 'Lowis? Lowis!'

'Did he know anyone there? Did he have any reason to go to San Strana?'

'No, no, no, he never mentioned anyone up at Lowis.'

He shakes his head. His lips move in silent conversation with someone.

'Did he say on Sunday that he planned to swim the next day? Did he mention some new fitness programme he was following with his friend Seymour?'

'No, no, he didn't say anything about swimming. We talked about a lot of things, you know how old guys like to chew the fat, Lucy, hell, we talk a lot of garbage, probably we talked garbage on Sunday but he never mentioned fitness, or Seymour or swimming or Lowis or . . .' His voice falls away and he looks hard at the pool's glassy surface, trying to remember Sunday night, trying to remember everything Daddy said.

'Did he tell you he was meeting anyone?'

'No, no, no . . .'

'Did he give any indication what he planned to do on Monday?'

'No, no.'

'Did he say he was worried about anything in particular? Did he seem like a man who worried a lot?'

'Eric, nah. He wasn't worried.'

I watch him, a land mass in the shimmering pool. His mouth is turned down, his eyes droop. I'm sorry I've made him so unhappy today. He's had enough unhappiness.

I say softly: 'Joe, there's a big dent in the front of Daddy's car . . .'

'There is?'

'I thought the dent might already have been there.'

'Never mentioned it.'

'Did he have any car problems?'

'Yeah, one big problem called an Oldsmobile. He could afford a new car. But did he buy a new car? No. He liked to spend the whole time fixing the Oldsmobile, that's why.'

'Did it break down recently?'

'He never would have told me because he knew I'd have said: get rid of that heap of garbage.'

'Did anyone tow it recently?'

Joe shakes his head. He is not looking at me. Under his breath he mutters: 'Homicide.'

I get up to go.

'I guess the police will probably be interviewing you soon. Mr Holler too.'

His big, doughy face studies mine sadly. When I leave he calls after me: 'You come swimming here any time you like. D'you hear? Any time, whether I'm home or not, you swim here and not on some goddamn dangerous beach.'

I try not to look at the padlocked trunk of Mr Zacarro's car but now I've seen it I can't pass it without remembering Lindy, stroking that toy horse which she said would be just like her real horse one day. And as I walk down the crumbling drive, sliding a little on the loose asphalt, as small creatures scuttle in the bushes at my side and I notice that Mrs Zacarro's pink, perfumed flowers must nearly all have died after she left, replaced now by weeds, it seems to me that at one time there was a real horse and he was chestnut. Lindy cantered him, her blonde hair bouncing with his stride, her back straight, leaning forward briefly to run a hand down his neck. The horse's flanks shone in the sun and you could see his muscles working like shadows under his gleaming coat. I skirt carefully around the one remaining sticky-leaved plant.

179

I don't want to smell its drugging aroma again. Lindy on a horse. Was this a memory of an actual event? Or the memory of a daydream, and not even my own daydream but Lindy Zacarro's?

17

Larry and Jane suspect that someone visited Daddy's house again last night. I find them in his bedroom, removing anything that might be valuable.

'I'm furious that the locksmith didn't come yesterday like he promised,' Jane tells me, examining a small, silver box.

'Even with the locks changed we should take this stuff away,' Larry says.

I shut the closet door because I don't like the way it gapes at me. Some of the drawers in the dressing-table are open too and in the middle of the big blue bed is a tangle of silver objects and small, sparkling rocks.

Over on the bureau are the pictures I like of Mother and Daddy's wedding and the four of us on the beach. I place them carefully on the bed with the other items.

'Those frames aren't real silver,' Larry informs me.

I smile. 'It's the pictures which are valuable.' I show him the beach snapshot. 'I like to remember Daddy laughing that way.'

Jane pauses to look at the picture.

'Except, he hardly ever did,' she says.

Larry strokes his beard. He says: 'Lucy, will you check the den to see if it's just the way you left it?'

I spent several hours working in Daddy's den yesterday afternoon, sorting out files for Scott.

'You think someone was in there last night?'

'We think someone was in the house because Jane double-locked the door and this morning it was only single-locked. But we can't find any other place they've been.'

I am relieved to find that my tidy piles of paperwork are still arranged across the desk and floor just as I left them. But when I examine the files more closely I find small discrepancies in their organization. Inside the drawers, two files have been removed and replaced back to front. Jane was right. Someone has been here.

Jane and Larry see this from my face when I get back up to the blue bedroom. They look at one another and then back to me.

'They tried to put it back just the way it was but they didn't get it exactly right,' I say.

'Whoever it was doesn't want us to know they were here,' says Larry, sitting down on the bed.

'But they left the lights on and the doors open yesterday,' Jane reminds him.

'Maybe they were disturbed,' I suggest.

'By what?'

'By the guys bringing the car back?'

'Maybe,' concedes Jane. She picks up an ornate silver photo frame and puts it on the bed. I wonder who the mysterious, faded faces inside it can belong to.

Jane turns to me. 'What do we have in that den which someone could want? I mean, they're obviously looking for something. They could have taken any of this silver, but they didn't. There's some kind of a file or a document which is worth more to them. Are you sure nothing's missing down there?'

'Of course I'm not sure. But I looked at most of the files yesterday and, apart from a few I took back to Aunt Zina's with me, I can't immediately see any are missing.'

I continue working in the den. Two men arrive wearing red shirts on which are emblazened the words Buddy, you're safe with us. I can hear the hum of their voices and the rasp of their tools as they change the locks. Afterwards they walk around the house with Jane telling her how vulnerable it is to intruders.

'We can't possibly do everything they're suggesting,' says Jane when they've gone, sinking on to the chair in the den. I look up at her. I am working on the floor now, files all around me.

'Like what?'

'Oh, at best alarms and CCTV and automatic gates, at the very least window locks and some shrub clearance so the place is more exposed. Let's just empty the house and sell it fast and leave whoever buys it to worry about security.'

She gets up and picks her way across the floor through the files.

'You're sure making progress here.'

'Those are all closed,' I say, pointing to the big green files that she has just stepped over. 'That means I've informed anyone necessary of Daddy's death and finished all the paperwork. I should be able to close these by tomorrow. The files on the desk and in the drawers will take a little longer.'

'Is everything straightforward?' she asks.

I enjoy working with Daddy's files, finding notes in his small, intelligent writing, analysing his figures, checking his investments. It feels like an act of homage.

'Daddy had a good system here. There's just one minor anomaly so far, but I'm sure I can sort that out with a few telephone calls.'

'What is it?'

'Oil well stuff. Maybe I was too tired when I was working on it last night at Aunt Zina's. I'm going to take another look today.'

'Oil?' Jane asks.

I nod. Daddy did oil exploration work in the vacations sometimes. Before he married and then again many years later, when I was still home and Jane had gone to college. I used to go with him but, unlike rock specimens, oil seemed to be found in flat, dull places. The only thing to do was sit around by the motel pool all day reading and waiting for Daddy to come back.

'But he hasn't done any of that kind of work for years.'

'When he did he was smart enough to take a part of his payment in royalties. Which means he was entitled to his percentage as long as the wells he found were still producing. Believe it or not, a couple of those wells are still active.'

'He was still taking an income from the oil companies? Was it much?'

'I haven't checked the most recent statements but certainly until a few years ago it would have been about enough for him to live on, if he lived frugally.'

Jane whistles. 'And he never even mentioned it!'

I say: 'I guess I'm crossing too many t's and dotting too many i's here but I sort of like to check things until they work every which way...' Jane smiles affectionately. She used to laugh at me for doing my math homework twice, to make sure I got the same answers both times. 'So I've tried to work back from his bank and other statements to the oil revenues. And I can't find them.'

She looks at me in surprise.

'You can't find the money?'

'Not so far.'

'What did he do with it?'

'He collected the earliest payments, the ones that go way back to before we were born. Then, suddenly, after a few years, he stopped.'

'Were these regular payments?'

'Annual.'

'And every year it just sort of . . . disappears?'

'Well, I haven't found it yet.'

She looks thoughtful.

'I'll bet Seymour can help.'

Seymour was Daddy's closest friend, a retired petroleum geologist.

'I'm going to call him,' I agree. 'And he'll probably explain it right away.'

'Don't forget to tell him the funeral's on Tuesday,' she says over her shoulder.

I open the desk drawer to look for Daddy's address book so I can call Seymour. The address book isn't there, just a lot of the kind of junk you keep in your desk drawer. Pincers for removing staples and old airline boarding passes and bad photos of the ones you love. One picture shows Stevie and me. I am holding him loosely and my smile is uneasy. Stevie's face, as usual, is curled into a small, red ball and his mouth is open wide to scream. Behind us, a part of Scott's body is visible, hunched, hands stuffed helplessly into his jeans pockets.

I put back the picture and withdraw some browning newspaper cuttings. The typeface of the *Valley Gazette* is instantly recognizable. Incredible, It's Snow at Hollow Grove! How The City Sends Its Pollution To Our Valley. Wedding News.

Curiously, I unwrap Wedding News. It is so carefully folded that I rip it a little. I flatten it on the desk with the side of my hand. It reports the marriage of Robert Joseph to Karen Sylvester.

Although I haven't been in love with Robert Joseph for many years, the newspaper article seems to bubble and swell. I stare hard at the grey picture. His hair is clipped shorter and his face is thinner but the smiling groom is unmistakable.

I search for a date, do not find one, then read the report. The groom is a doctor. The bride is a banker. The groom's mother hosted a party at their beautiful home in the valley. The bride wore historic lace which a forebear worked while her husband was away fighting the Confederates. The bridesmaids wore yellow. There is a list of guests.

I go out to the deck and look down at the quiet order of the valley. I enjoy the symmetry between the fruit trees and their shadows. The tidy quadrangles please me, my eye rests on the right angles of the intersection.

The bridesmaids wore yellow. The bride is a banker, just like me. His mother hosted the party: maybe his father is dead, just like mine. And Robert, who wanted to be a movie director, became a doctor. Maybe the car crash altered him. Maybe spending so much time in hospital and nearly losing his leg changed his ambitions. Maybe he didn't like movies any more. For me he stopped being at eighteen but since then he grew and changed and married and probably had children and I am just a tiny grain of his history.

If I look south, I can fool myself that I see the Joseph farm, although I know it's only visible from further around the dirt road, a speck of bright green as vivid and surprising as spinach stuck in your teeth. You can easily fry down in the valley but the aqueduct runs right by the Joseph farmstead and their yard is an oasis, green and cool and shady. That summer I spent with Robert Joseph we lay locked together in a hammock swinging beneath two big, stout-trunked trees talking about everything and being in love. Teenage love. Easy to ridicule afterwards but it felt real enough at the time. And all that talking. Robert's mother said she liked to hear our voices buzzing away in the hammock. She was nice and she had nice friends. I sometimes wished she was my mother and then felt guilty about it. Once I mentioned Mother and

186

Mrs Joseph said, surprisingly: 'Oh yes, I remember her from Cornington.' Cornington was a grade school Robert and I both went to before they reorganized the county. Mrs Joseph said: 'We had the Cornington Country Cook-Out and your mother helped with the food.' And I knew from the way she said it, although her tone was even, that Mother had done something hideous: brought the wrong kind of frankfurters or no frankfurters at all or frankfurters that were glazed with green mould and that perhaps, when she had realized her mistake, she had cried pitifully in front of Mrs Joseph and the principal and all my teachers. I waited for Mrs Joseph to say something more about Mother and the Cornington Country Cook-Out. I was glad when she didn't.

Back in the den I find Seymour's number and he answers the phone right away, as though he's working at his desk.

'Lucy, hey Lucy, good to hear from you,' he says but his voice cracks suddenly. 'Boy, do I miss Eric. I miss him already and he's only been dead a few days, I don't know what it's going to be like in a month or a year. And I keep cutting items out of the newspaper for him. You know, this morning I tore something out of *The Rock Hammer* which I knew would make him real mad. I mean, apoplectic. I was chuckling to myself at how mad he'd get and I put it in an envelope and wrote his address on it! Can you believe that? Glad I realized before I bought a stamp.'

I smile. In Seymour I can capture a little of Daddy. It's like finding a photo of the beach house right after the ocean has washed it away. He and Daddy had an antagonistic relationship, mostly because Seymour became a Christian and Daddy liked to argue with him. At the end of a long day's disputing Seymour used to say: 'Well, Eric, I guess you have to fundamentally agree with someone before you can argue with them for all this time.'

'I don't agree with you!' protested Daddy. 'I don't agree with one word you say!'

I could tell they enjoyed this routine.

We talk a little about Tuesday's funeral. He approves when I say we've decided on a secular ceremony. Then I tell Seymour about Daddy's oil royalties.

'Simms-Roeder still producing, eh? Well, I'm jealous. What a great find that was for Eric.'

'But Seymour, I can't find any record of the money. Where it came in and where it went out. There's just the oil company's statement that it was paid. Did Daddy ever tell you what he did with it?'

'Nope. It must show on his bank statements, Lucy.'

'It doesn't. It doesn't show on any statements anywhere. I called the oil company and they were unhelpful . . . do you have any contacts there now?'

'Oh boy. Most of the people I knew there have retired. But I guess I could try . . . let me work at it for a day or so. Will you come by for the answer? Katherine would sure love to see you too.'

I promise to stop by at Seymour's on Friday evening.

Hours later, when I look up and see that the square of sky beyond the small overhead window has turned the inky blue of late afternoon, I wonder why Daddy cut out the article about Robert Joseph's wedding. Did he intend to give it to me, then forgot or did he change his mind?

The two detectives, Kirsty and Rougemont, arrive. Rougemont greets me as though we know each other well, smiling too broadly. Jane is friendly. She and Larry make coffee and she tells how we think the intruder came again last night.

'I really don't like it. I'm relieved the locksmith's been,' she says. 'Sometimes I get the feeling we're being watched.'

I look at her in surprise. It's hard to imagine anyone less inclined to paranoia than Jane.

'I've seen this guy outside our apartment,' adds Larry. 'He doesn't seem to be doing anything. Just sort of hanging around out there.'

'Uh-huh,' says Rougemont. He's sceptical but he's hiding it well. 'How many times have you seen him?'

'Well . . . just twice,' admits Larry.

Jane smiles as she passes around the coffees.

'We're getting nervous and it's making us imagine all sorts of things,' she says.

'Someone with a spare set of keys has been here,' Kirsty says. 'You didn't imagine that.'

'Hide a police officer here overnight,' suggests Larry, 'in case this guy tries to get in.' He sounds authoritative, as though he's running the investigation. Although the detectives show no sign of resentment, I flinch a little for them.

'He'll have what he wants by now,' says Rougemont. 'I doubt he'll come back.'

'He might,' insists Larry.

'Okay,' says Kirsty pleasantly. 'We'll put a couple of officers in the yard tonight and see what happens.'

Rougemont drinks some of his coffee in gulps, his Adam's apple bouncing in his throat. Then he says he'd like to wander around the house.

'What are you looking for?' I ask him.

'I'm an old dog who likes to sniff around houses,' he says, loping off. Mother had a brown dog when I was real small. He liked to sniff around. He liked to hide and then leap out, barking and scaring me.

Kirsty asks if Scott's here.

'He's teaching today,' I explain. 'Plus he doesn't need to be here so often since I'm doing all his executor stuff.'

'Why do you think your father didn't appoint you in the first place?' she asks and I recoil from the sharpness in her question.

'That's obvious,' says Jane quietly.

I look at her in surprise. She's pouring more coffee now and, although she is distracted and the task mundane, her movements are graceful.

'You've left California, right? Daddy respected that decision. He didn't want to give you responsibilities here which would drag you back, even though he knew you'd be the best person. It was a generous, loving gesture.'

I know at once that she is right. Jane has detected my pain and relieved it, the way she always does. I glimpse Larry, too, looking at her with admiration.

She asks the detective: 'Any news from the ME?'

'We're now sure the time of your father's death was pretty close to eight in the morning. Death occurred very shortly before immersion. That's all.'

We consider the significance of this.

'So,' says Larry cautiously, 'he didn't die anywhere near the place his car was found.'

'I guess not,' agrees the woman. She speaks with the weariness of someone who has had this information for a while and already considered all possibilities. 'Lowis is at least thirty, forty minutes from Big Brim.'

Jane asks: 'Did the ME get any closer to finding out how Daddy died?'

'She's consulting Charles Rossi. He's a high-profile professor of forensic pathology.'

Kirsty puts a hand into her bulging briefcase and pulls out her notebook. She flicks past pages thick with writing until she arrives at one half-filled. 'I have an unusual question to ask you . . .'

I wait for the unusual question, my body tense. I steal glances at Jane and Larry and they look tense too.

She says: 'It's about a tow truck.'

I stare at her.

'I realize that it seems impossible. But could your father have been driving one the night before he died?'

Jane and I look at one another and pull faces.

'Well, no,' we say.

The detective rearranges the long hair she used to have. 'We put out a request for any information which might help us locate your father on Sunday night/Monday morning and a highway patrolman contacted me. He says he spoke to the driver of a tow truck late on Sunday night on the big freeway into town about nine miles inland from Big Brim. He claims to have a good memory and he recalled your father's name and described him accurately.'

Jane sounds incredulous. 'He thinks that Daddy was driving a tow truck?'

'He's adamant about it. Does that make any sense to you at all?'

She looks at me.

I shake my head. 'I can't imagine it.'

Larry points his beard at the detective in a way which means he's about to speak. 'Was it towing anything?'

'No.'

'So why did the patrolman pull it over?'

'The truck had already stopped by some kind of a wreck at the side of the road. Officer Howie asked to see the driver's licence and now he thinks it had your father's name on and that the driver fitted the description we issued. Unfortunately, he didn't write any of this down at the time, not even the number of the truck.'

'Was the tow truck picking up the wreck?'

'It was evidently trying to but there was something wrong with the winch and the driver said that he was waiting for someone to come over and sort it out. Officer Howie is real convincing. He says he doesn't make mistakes.'

'We all make mistakes,' I say and the detective smiles at me in a way that reminds me of my mistakes.

She says: 'His real mistake was that he didn't write anything down. If only he had taken a number or some other details about the driver or the tow truck. He thinks it was an old truck, that's all he noticed.'

'Was the driver alone?'

'No. There was at least one other man with him, possibly two. Officer Howie admits he's not sure about that. Of course, it may have helped us to explain how your father got to Big Brim or how his car got to Lowis. So you can see why I'm kind of attached to the idea.'

Larry smiles at her. 'Scientists do that kind of thing too. It's so God-awful when the data doesn't fit your hypothesis that it makes you want to doubt the data.'

Rougemont comes in. I thought he'd been inside the house but he smells of eucalyptus. He sits down at the table, folding up his long legs, and picks up his coffee cup.

'Is that cold? Can I make you a fresh cup?' offers Jane. Her voice is kind. Probably a lot of people detect Rougemont's sadness and it makes some of them cruel and others kind.

He smiles. 'No, no, coffee's generally cold by the time I remember to drink it.' The woman detective tells him that Jane and Larry and I don't know of any reason Daddy should have been driving a tow truck on Sunday.

Larry says: 'He just wasn't that kind of guy.'

'Oh,' says Rougemont, putting his big head on one side. 'He sure used to be that kind of a guy.'

We all stare at him while he sips cold coffee.

'What do you mean?' Jane demands.

'Well, I think I told you that, many years ago, I used to know your father a little. And he certainly had a tow truck back then.'

'Daddy? Had a tow truck?' echoes Jane. 'No!'

'No,' I add. 'Not Daddy.'

'Sure.'

'Could you have made a mistake?' says Jane.

'No. He even kept his driver's certificate updated. Although that doesn't mean he drove one recently.'

I ask: 'When did he have this tow truck, Mr Rougemont?'

He sucks in his lips and narrows his eyes.

'Hmmmm . . . you were a small girl then, Lucy. You might not remember, I thought maybe Jane would.'

'Why would a geologist need a tow truck?' Larry asks sceptically. But I know the answer. The tow truck is already inside my head and it didn't just drive there. It has always been there, I just had to draw back the drapes and find it, standing right behind them, sparkling in the sunlight.

'He was fixing it,' I say. 'Like the tractor and the printing press and the Oldsmobile . . . He used to lie underneath it with spanners, fixing it. It seemed enormous. And it was chrome, I guess, because it was silver and shiny. In front there was a sort of face. I mean, headlamps for eyes and this big fender which looked like a monster mouth.'

'You remember!' says Rougemont with admiration. 'You were only four, Lucy, and you remember! Of course, I don't know when he got rid of it. You may have been five or six or seven by that time. However, since it sometimes seems no one in this family can remember anything, well, I'd say you've shown definite progress!'

Kirsty agrees enthusiastically and they both look congratulatory, as though I just won a game show. I glance at Jane. Her pale skin is glowing pink.

'Listen,' she says. You have to know her very, very well to know that when she speaks in that icy calm voice then she's real angry. Larry knows it and I know it and we both sit up a little straighter.

'Listen. When people can't remember, sometimes it's because their memories are so unpleasant or painful that they don't want to remember. You must be aware of that. You must have gathered that there are things in our childhood we decided long ago to forget.'

She means Mother. Always present even when you haven't seen her for three years. Flapping over our conversation now like a big white bird.

But Rougemont ignores or is unaware of Jane's anger. 'Sure, sure,' he agrees, nodding his head in his strange elastic way. He's still grinning like a game show host, like a guy who thinks the contestants are having big fun being humiliated. 'Oh, sure, but for heaven's sake, how can remembering a tow truck be so painful?'

His voice rises as though it's about to be crowned by canned laughter. Instead there is silence and then into the silence comes the unhappy voice of a very small girl close to tears.

She says: 'Because that's how they towed her away.'

Everyone swings around to face the girl. They are looking at me.

'When Mother wouldn't get out of the car . . .' I'm talking to Jane but now she's staring down at the table top as though something's written there but she's decided not to read it. 'You must remember when Mother wouldn't get out of the car?'

Jane says nothing. When she looks down that way it feels

as though she's closed her eyes and shut me right out. She thinks I'm acting Russian. She thinks this is a betrayal, but I can't stop now.

'When we got back from Arizona and Mother was psychotic but we didn't know that's what it was because it was the very first time, when we were still thinking this was some small temporary problem and normal service would be resumed . . . well, she wouldn't get out of the car. She stayed there all day and all night and most of the next day until you could smell urine from ten feet away. When they came for her, two men and a woman still couldn't get her out of the car. They just couldn't do it, they couldn't even restrain her. They tried to drive her away but she was too threatening for safety. She nearly defeated them. Except, there was a tow truck. It was parked right outside the barn, it must have been one of Daddy's old wrecks. So they used it to tow her away. I mean, the car. With Mother in it, isn't that right, Jane? Isn't that what they did? I didn't see but I sort of guessed when I saw they were gone and the car and the tow truck. I was hiding in the yard. I guess I heard it. I guess I remember it. The engine sounded like a big, ugly monster and the transmission made this grinding noise as they manoeuvred it which sounded like its teeth. The tow truck took Mother away. And, you know what? I think she found that unforgivable. She was just horrible when we visited her and I think that was because she was mad at us for having her towed away instead of leaving her to sit in the car the way she wanted.'

The silence that follows is painful like needles. The two police officers watch me keenly. Larry is startled, his air of detached observation temporarily abandoned. Jane's face is red and its shape has changed a little as though some of the muscles beneath it have rearranged themselves. When she

195

speaks, her voice is very quiet, scarcely more than a whisper.

'We couldn't leave her sitting there in the car for ever, messing in it like a dog.'

'We could have waited. Until she was ready to get out.'

'Then we might have waited for ever.'

I'm speaking softly too. In this kind of silence, which shouts every word, no more is necessary. 'I think she would have come when she was ready.'

Jane looks at me, her head thrown back a little as though I'm some very bright light which could dazzle her. 'She wasn't eating. And you were in tears the whole time. That's what really got to Daddy. It wasn't an easy decision for Daddy but he did it for you as well as Mother. Are you saying he did the wrong thing?'

And at this I shake my head, rapidly as a dog which has just run out of the water, because I know that, among his many qualities, Daddy always tried to do the right thing.

'No. I'm just saying it was horrible.' I turn to Rougemont. 'That's probably why we neither of us wanted to remember the tow truck. Well, now we have. We've remembered it from way back, just like you asked us to. So maybe you can explain what relevance it can have to last Sunday night or anything Officer Howie said.'

Rougemont sucks thoughtfully on his lower lip as though it's a cigarette.

'Oh,' he says at last. 'Probably none. I mean, I agree with Larry that Officer Howie must have made a mistake.'

18

I reach the highway patrol headquarters at Bellamy at eight-forty. When I called from Aunt Zina's last night, they told me that Officer Howie begins his shift at nine.

'Who wants him?' added the voice suspiciously.

'Well, it's sort of personal.'

'Uh-huh,' said the voice knowingly. His tone indicated that Officer Howie has a lot of personal life. 'Well, get here at fifteen minutes before nine and someone should be able to organize for you to see him.'

I find a uniformed officer in the lobby and persuade him to intercept Officer Howie before he leaves the precinct. His joky but resigned manner suggests that I am not the first woman to have him do this. A few minutes later the immaculately uniformed patrolman appears. He walks cautiously but his caution barely masks the strut of a handsome man. He looks at me doubtfully, scanning my hand before he shakes it, as if he fears I might use the opportunity to press a paternity suit on him.

'My name's Lucy Schaffer. My father died recently and I understand that you may have been one of the last people to see him alive . . .'

He stares at me.

'On Sunday night you inspected a tow truck he was driving. On Monday morning he was dead, not so far from the place you saw him. He was a homicide victim and it's possible he was killed by one of the other people who were in the truck with him.'

He looks over my head, remembering Sunday night, Daddy, the tow truck.

'Jeez. Oh jeez. I didn't really see who was in the cab with him . . . A detective already asked me that. Detective MacFarlane. She seemed real doubtful that it was the same guy but I recognized the picture. Plus I recalled the name. Yeah, Schaffer.'

'How sure are you?'

He has the unassailability of youth. 'Completely sure. And there were certainly some other guys with him. Maybe one. Probably two. Certainly no more. You couldn't get four in that cab, it wasn't such a big truck, it was a real old one.'

'Can you remember anything about them? Anything at all?'

'I didn't get a good look at them and they stayed quiet the whole time.'

'Did my father get out of the tow truck?'

'No, ma'am. He wound down the window and explained that he had a winch problem. See, he'd come to take this wreck away which was right by the side of the road, but he had a winch problem. He said someone was on their way to fix it.'

'Officer . . . did my father appear distressed in any way? Or anxious? Or worried?'

He smiles. His smile is white and symmetrical.

'Ma'am, most people are anxious and worried when they get pulled over by the California Highway Patrol.'

'I mean, was he especially unhappy? So ill at ease that it's possible he was being held in the tow truck against his will?'

The man pauses and thinks.

'Nah. He was nervous but not that nervous. There's nothing I could have ticketed him for but he sort of looked as if he thought I was going to anyway.'

'And the accident . . . what had happened?'

'Accident?'

'The wreck they were trying to tow away.'

'Oh, now. Now we're talking weird. I just came on duty and the wreck was right at one of our worst blackspots. I assumed there was a crash there earlier in the day. The car was completely burnt out. I mean, unidentifiable. But you know something? I just found out yesterday that there was no accident.'

I stare at him. His eyebrows are raised, his features seem to jump out of his face with surprise. 'Nothing. There were no reported incidents on that part of the coast road last Sunday.'

I am thinking but my thoughts lead nowhere. 'So . . .' I say slowly. 'So, how do you think the wreck got there?'

'I guess what must have happened was, they were towing it from somewhere else and they stopped and unhooked it because they were having trouble with the winch.'

'Did they get the winch fixed?'

'No, ma'am, they did not. That wreck stayed by the side of the coastal highway causing big traffic problems on Monday morning. I sure wished I'd taken your father's number.'

'It blocked the highway?'

'It doesn't have to block the highway to cause problems. People slow down to rubberneck and that delays everyone for miles back.'

He looks at his watch ostentatiously.

'Just a couple more questions,' I assure him. 'Can you describe the tow truck?'

He pulls a face. 'Hmmmm. Well. The lighting isn't great down there but I'd say it was real old, almost antique. I guess your father had it a long time.'

His statement is half a question, which I ignore.

'Did it have black numberplates?'

Another white smile flashes briefly. 'It was certainly old enough for that. But I didn't see. I didn't look too hard, I had no reason to.'

'Can you remember anything else? Anything at all that was said, anything about the other people in the cab? Anything that didn't seem to be right about it?'

'No, ma'am. It was just a routine check for me.' He has hardly looked at me all the time we've been talking but suddenly his eyes meet mine. 'Ma'am, I understand your father was a homicide victim, but why are you asking these questions?'

'When your father's killed it makes you ask questions.'

'Does Detective MacFarlane know that you're here?'

'No one knows I'm here.'

For a moment he looks at me with distress and, ridiculously, I want to cry because this stranger, however briefly, has shared my grief. He says: 'I'm sorry. There didn't seem anything too unusual out on the freeway that night. Your father didn't look like a guy in trouble. But if he was . . . then . . . gee, I'm sorry, real sorry.'

From Bellamy I drive down the coast a little way. The road follows all the twists and turns of the tortuous coastline but the traffic speeds up when it reaches the long, straight stretch by Big Brim. This must be the least popular beach in the area. The parking lot where Rougemont left his car right by mine is almost empty. Only two cars and a tow truck.

A tow truck. At Big Brim. Antique in appearance, chrome-covered, its silver arm pointing skywards like a shark's fin. I brake and swing around in a U-turn. The driver behind me honks and his passengers stare after me and so does the car behind and the car behind that.

I pull in by the tow truck and, rocked by the wind of each passing car, I walk around it twice. Far from monstrous, it seems to me small and battered with age. Its chrome sparkles playfully in the sunshine. The network of crane and winch piled on to its back has the solidity of another era. Its numberplates are yellow on black. The make of the truck is obscure because so many letters have fallen from its name. Diver or Divine, maybe. There is no garage name although the remnant of one is almost visible on the driver's door. The truck is so aged that I suspect it is still on the road only through good luck and constant tinkering and I am reminded, suddenly, forcibly, of Daddy and the Oldsmobile.

I find a map in the hirecar and on the back of it write the shadow names along with the truck's number and a few notes on its wheels and colours. I examine the tyres, running my fingers down one zigzag tread. The truck is harmless without its driver. The driver is powerless without his truck. I look across the road at the dunes. My heart beats with the speed of a hunter who is close to his quarry.

During a pause in the traffic I dart across the blacktop. I take off my shoes and my feet are rapidly submerged, almost to my ankles, in sand. It resists every step. It tells me to go back. I ignore its warnings and move on resolutely, my whole body leaning forward where my legs should be. Much slower than I want to, I drag each foot towards the sea. And all the time I am looking for him, looking for the driver of the tow truck, until when I reach the third dune it seems to me that there has always been a tow truck driver in my life, terrifying me, carrying away those I love most, evading me whenever I turn to confront him.

I look across the beach. The pear-shaped man and his little dog are here again. Two women, jogging slowly. A mother with a small gaggle of children surging around her.

A few dogs in the sea, their owners watching them. And then I see him. He is alone on the dunes and is perhaps a fourth of a mile away. A man, tall, dark, probably young. He is heading towards the road and almost certainly the tow truck but he has misjudged the beach's length and he is crossing the dunes a fourth of a mile too far north. I see him from the top of the third dune and he is already nearing the top of the first. I watch him. He is not humbled by the effort of walking here. He marches up the dune with resolution.

At the dune's pinnacle he pauses and something makes him turn. He turns right around until he has turned to me. He stops. We stare at one another across billions of grains of undulating sand. I know he knows I am looking for him. We stare, too far for eyes, too far for faces. Then he turns again. He has only to descend one dune and walk along the roadside for a fourth of a mile.

I run back down the dune I just climbed and start to ascend the second. My whole body works against the sand, my toes, my neck, my head. The sand seems to suck at my legs, my feet are weights, my arms saw at the air. When I reach the top of the dune nearest the road, my heart still thumping the hunter's thump, every cell in my body still focused on my quarry, I look at once at the parking lot. I am already too late. The dark figure had only to run along the road and he would have reached his truck before I was down the second dune. I imagine the monstrous growl of its old engine, the whine of the transmission, the roar as he accelerated into the traffic.

19

I sit down on the baking sand. I stare at the place the tow truck stood. It was an answer, an explanation, and now there is only a void.

When I retrace my route across the dunes I move slowly this time, slowly enough to feel the sand scorching the soles of my feet. I run down the last dune to the beach and, when the sand is firm and damp underfoot, I put down my shoes and walk right on to the sea. It is docile here, like a blue lagoon. I walk up to the water in a straight line and pause when I feel the ice of its touch at my toes.

'Hey!' shouts a voice. 'Hey, you, yes you!' I turn. A large, amorphous shape is walking, half running, towards me, his tiny dog racing alongside him. He carries some curiously shaped driftwood under his arm. As he gets closer I can see his cheeks bouncing on his face, his belly wobbling with his walk, the water-bottle secured around his waist leaping up and down. When he reaches me, he is too breathless to speak.

'Gee,' he wheezes. 'Gee, just wait a minute, will you?'

He pulls at the water-bottle, throws back his head and pours liquid into his open mouth.

'I want you to know that this is water. Not beer or bourbon or any of that kind of stuff,' he puffs. He rolls his eyes virtuously but his mouth is moulding itself into distressed shapes. I wonder what has upset him. Perhaps he is habitually upset.

'I want you to know something else as well. That mostly

when guys yell after you on beaches, they're crazy and you should run away. That's usually the case. But it's not the case with me.'

I stand with my hands on my hips. 'Good. What's the problem?'

'I have to tell you something. I need to warn you. Point A. The tide comes up real fast. When it comes. Right now it's going the other way. Point B. This looks like it might be a good place to swim. Gently shelving. Calm waters. But the reason it doesn't get the big waves is that there are these currents. They're unique. Very special. Caused by the sand spits at each end. Oceanographers come here to study the currents though all they have to do is ask a fisherman. Anyway, it means this beach is no good, I repeat, no good, not safe, bad news, for swimming. I just thought you should know that.'

He has been wagging his finger from side to side.

'Thanks. Actually, I already knew. I heard about a baby who drowned here a long time ago.'

'Ooooh, that's too bad. This is not a good beach for a kid to swim. It looks great, but it's not, it's the worst.'

'He was only a baby.'

The man looks at me uncertainly and then takes another gulp of water. 'How'd he drown then? His mom take him in the water?'

'I don't know.'

'Is that why you came here today, lady?'

I make shapes in the sand with my toes. They trail through the tiny grains making a pattern like a maze or some ancient hieroglyphic.

'Okay, okay, you don't have to answer. We can present ourselves with a series of choices at this point. Choice Number One. We can sit here and have a pleasant talk and you can tell me what's the problem. Choice Number Two. I can turn right around and go back to my house and you can do whatever you want to do when I am no longer around to see it but I should state here and now that I do not vote for choice number two. Choice Number Three. You can decide that you want to remove yourself, right now, from this beach to the parking lot, without talking to me at all. If you opt for choice number three I will no way take offence.'

The sea breeze ruffles my hair. The man's hair is thick and brown and the breeze blows it upright like cartoon hair.

The man says: 'Do you need me to run over those choices again?'

'No. You've made a mistake.'

He looks at me, wide-eyed. 'You know more choices?'

'You thought I intended to commit suicide. Right?'

He studies the sand bashfully. 'Well . . . it's the way you put your shoes right down and then walked towards the ocean in a straight line. That's what they generally do.' His eyes look back at me but he does not lift his head. He's shy now. 'I mean . . . weren't you?'

'No.'

'No?'

'My father was found dead in the water a little way down the coast one week ago. He left his clothes right here on the beach.'

The man grits his teeth and throws his head back as though he's been burnt.

'Oooooh, gee. Gee. That guy. The one they're saying was a homicide. That guy was your father?'

'Did you see him?'

His vast, rubbery features model and remodel themselves into contours of unhappiness. 'Nah. I didn't see anyone. That's how I know he wasn't here.'

'He died last Monday morning. The police think he died at eight.'

'Uh-huh. He didn't die here.'

I stare at the man. 'What do you mean?'

'I'm generally on patrol by seven,' he explains. 'No one was on the beach that morning. I already told the police.'

'But his clothes were found here.'

'No clothes here at eight o'clock. I mean, I didn't walk right down the beach but I'd have seen them. I live at the other end, I'm the only person who can get here without crossing three dunes.'

'Who found his clothes?'

'Me 'n' Cinnamon.' The dog, which has flopped on to the nearest dry sand, looks up when it hears its name and then flops back down. 'I went home at eight-thirty for a cup of coffee and I came out at nine-thirty just like today and that's when I saw the clothes. I called the police and they came. Boy, they sure hate coming over the dunes in their uniforms.'

The man walks up the beach a few paces and then sits down next to his dog, his legs sprawling towards the ocean. Cinnamon puts his head on the man's knee. I sit down too and my hand begins to trace more shapes in the sand. Complicated shapes. Mazes. Aztec mazes, Inca mazes.

'So someone put my father's clothes here after he died,' I say at last. It's more of a statement than a question but the man nods agreement.

'Correct. Or, the medical examiner got the time of death wrong. They can do that. If your father died on this beach while I was having my cup of coffee then . . . I'm sorry.' And when I look up his mouth is pulling in all directions, speaking some sad, silent language of its own.

'Who was on the beach when you came out of your

house at nine-thirty?' I ask. He gestures to the widely-spaced assortment of walkers, mostly with dogs.

'The same sort of people that are here today. No one suspicious or unusual. No one I could specifically describe.'

'There was a man here this morning. Tall, dark, alone, no dog. He must have left about ten minutes before you saw me . . .'

'Uh-huh.'

'Did you speak to him?'

'No.'

'What did he do?'

'Just what you did. Looked up the beach, looked down the beach. Walked right up to the sea and stood there like he was planning to go in. Saw me coming and went right away again.'

'Did you notice anything about him?'

'Tall, dark, like you said.'

'What sort of age?'

He lies back in the sand.

'I can't tell ages any more. He was about like you.'

'What was he wearing?'

'Jeans.'

'Did you notice anything else at all?'

The man sighs enormously. 'I moved right towards him just in case but he backed off. Probably he didn't mean to do anything. I've been patrolling this beach a few years now and I'm pretty good at judging these things.'

I ask: 'So, what happened to you?'

'Whaddya mean, lady?'

'How come you patrol this beach?'

He sighs.

'You're right, something did happen. See, I used to be a truck driver.' He offers this as though it's some kind of explanation. I look at him, stretched out in loose sweat pants over the sand, and I see how, over the long miles, his big soft body gradually moulded itself into the shape of his truck seat.

'Then I stopped being a driver and started in the truck hire business. Big risks, I learned to bite my nails. But I was successful when I was only forty-one, I mean, successful enough to have other people run the business for me so I can do this.'

He sits up. His back is rounded and his head hangs.

'I ran over this guy once. Cows, sheep, when you're driving through grasslands down in the foothills of the Rockies, that's normal, you get used to that. But a man . . .'

He scratches his head vigorously, like a child learning to write who's trying to scratch out some error. 'I can tell you, I thought I'd never get over it. Night after night I'd dream about what I saw in my windscreen.'

'I'm sorry,' I say.

'Well, this is a popular place for people to end their lives and I try to persuade them otherwise. I mean, maybe some of them go off and do it some other place but I feel like I'm still saving a few and making up a little for what I did. I sure wish I could have saved your father but I really don't think he died at Big Brim.'

'You don't?'

'Nah. He went in at Seal Wash. Just maybe Bellamy but there are restaurants along the facing cliff and someone would have seen. So my money's on Seal Wash.'

'Why?'

'An informed guess. Based on what I know about the currents. Based on what the fishermen say. Your dad was found off Retribution and there are currents from here but there are also some which go right there from Bellamy and

Seal Wash and it's easy to . . . well, the road runs real close to the water. 'Specially on the clifftop at Seal Wash.'

Daddy's body plummeting from the clifftop into the depths of the blue ocean beneath. A splash. A splash which would be loud enough in a swimming-pool but here in the ocean it would seem nothing more than the crash of a small wave on a small rock.

'Are you okay?' asks the man.

I nod.

'That's only a theory. Maybe I made myself that theory because I feel so bad to think I could've missed him. I only miss a few.'

I smile to reassure him. I know it's not a good smile, that I've just pulled my mouth into a straight line with maybe a wrinkle or two at the edges, but it's the best I can do right now. The small, wiry-haired dog has crawled over to me, his expression obsequious, and is nuzzling me now. I stroke his ears and he rolls on to his back for me to scratch his belly.

'Aw, Cinnamon. Cinnamon is a softee,' says the man affectionately.

I ask: 'Can you remember where his clothes were?'

The man sighs and looks up and down the beach. 'Just right around here, I guess, but back up towards the dunes. That's unusual, see, if he was a suicide. People generally leave their clothes nearer the water.'

I stand up and dust the sand off myself and the breeze picks it up and blows it a little way along the beach.

'Thanks,' I say. 'You've been very helpful.'

He looks up at me doubtfully.

'You okay now?' he asks.

'I didn't come here to kill myself. Really.'

'Oh sure,' he agrees but I can tell he still believes that I did.

20

At Seal Wash the sea today is restless as a hungry animal. The black rocks which jut from the ocean's depth look more menacing than they did on Tuesday and when water sloshes against the cliffs it throws spray high into the air.

You could park a car so that the passenger side was almost at the edge of the cliff and, with a little dragging and pulling, you could dump something inanimate, a bag of rocks, a human body, right into the ocean. Of course, it would get battered along the way but neither the splash nor the spray would be remarkable and the object, that is, the bag of rocks or the human body, would soon be lost in the vast, deep blueness.

There is the crash of an immense wave and a few moments later I feel the ocean's damp cloth on my face.

Or maybe Daddy got right out of the car, Daddy and his killer, someone known to him, with whom he was relaxed, talking. When Daddy was looking away, the killer acted. If you pushed someone off the cliff here, you couldn't be completely sure they would die. The sea looks fierce but a strong swimmer might get to the safety of a nearby rock. No, as the medical examiner said, Daddy was dead when the rocks bruised and scratched him, dead when his body toppled down the cliff. Did his killer watch the freefall of the body, listen for the splash? Or did he get right back into the car and drive rapidly away to Big Brim beach? Few people were around. He dumped Daddy's clothes near the dunes, further from the water than a swimmer might, but he wanted to minimize the risk of being seen. Then, sweating, his heart beating with exertion, did he return to his car and drive away?

'I know what you're thinking and I agree with you,' says a voice.

I spin right around and a long arm is extended to steady me. Michael Rougemont grasps me with his bony fingers.

'Don't get too close to the edge!' His eyes are so wide that they're staring and, even though I know he's serious, he looks comical.

'Are you following me?' I demand, stepping inland. His grip loosens and his arms drop. I see his car parked on the other side of the clifftop.

'I'm probably here for the same reason you are. You're thinking that your father died at Seal Wash and I agree with that. Maybe he didn't even go to Big Brim beach. So we wasted our time drinking in the atmosphere there at sunset on Tuesday.'

'Those cuts and bruises on his face —'

Rougemont looks down at the black rocks protruding like bad teeth from the sea.

'Probably nothing to do with his death and everything to do with the Pacific Ocean.'

The Pacific Ocean roars and spits at us. On my next breath, I inhale salt.

'Mr Rougemont, yesterday you said you knew Daddy way back when he had a tow truck. How did you know him?'

He pauses and when he speaks he speaks carefully.

'I met him when your brother died.'

I turn to look at his battered old face.

'When my brother died?'

'I was the investigating officer.'

The ocean's percussion crashes beneath us.

'Why were you investigating?'

'A baby dies, it's usual. For instance, when your baby died, Kirsty investigated.'

'It's an incredible coincidence,' I say, 'that you two are both working on Daddy's case too.' He doesn't reply and I realize that it isn't a coincidence.

'Of course, you have no memory of your brother's death,' he tells me.

'No.'

'Although it did seem to me yesterday that your memory was starting to work.'

'I don't remember anything at all about my brother. Except that he existed and I loved him.'

'I've been wondering if you can remember something much more recent. Can we get into your car?'

It feels good to shut out the breeze, the spray and the crash of the rocks. I sit behind the wheel. Rougemont adjusts the passenger seat for his long legs. He places his hands on his knees. Then he asks me when I last saw my father.

'Oh, your colleague already asked me that,' I say but he does not apologize or withdraw the question.

'I told her that he visited me once in New York, probably about two and a half years ago. But we spoke often.'

'When was the last time you saw him in California, Lucy?'

'Just before I left. Almost three years ago.'

I drove over to Daddy's house to tell him I was leaving. I didn't telephone first, I just arrived and that made my heart thud as I rattled up the drive. I sometimes wondered what Daddy did when I wasn't around. When I found him in oily overalls, his face red with sun and effort, happy under the old tractor, I felt relief scoop my whole body up like a warm hand. He wheeled himself out from under the machine, got up very slowly, and greeted me with pleasure. He had the relaxed detachment of someone who has been deep in concentration.

We took our coffee out to the deck and sat in silence, watching the view as though it might move, although the valley was still as a reptile. Even the trucks which crossed it on the straight road moved sluggishly. A sudden breeze made the leaves overhead busy. Daddy planted those trees and for some years he had been concerned that they were too close to the foundations of the house. Now he looked up as though he was surprised by them and hadn't seen them almost every day for more than thirty years. He said: 'When you put a little sapling in the ground you can't ever imagine it getting this big. It's sort of like kids. All the evidence is that kids grow up, it's a fact of biology and evolution, fossils tell us, history tells us, our eyes tell us that kids grow up. But when they're small, you just can't believe that your own are ever going to become adults. You're not bringing a kid into the world, you're bringing an adult. It's one hell of a responsibility.'

'You're thinking about your father now,' Michael Rougemont informs me. His voice makes me start. 'What are you thinking?'

So I tell him about planting the trees too close to the house and thinking your kids can never grow up.

'Is that what he said when you told him you were leaving California?'

'No . . . I told him a little later. He didn't challenge my decision. I didn't ask for his permission but he gave it to me anyway.'

Rougemont asks quietly: 'Was it hard saying goodbye?'

'Yes, it was hard.' I don't tell him how Daddy cried.

'But,' continues the detective, 'you said goodbye. And, except for that brief time in New York, you didn't want to go through the pain of saying it again. So when you came to California last weekend, maybe that's why you didn't tell anyone you were here.'

His words burn my ears. I hear him say: 'You were here in San Francisco last weekend. Right, Lucy? You flew out Sunday night. Shortly before your father died.'

I am hot. I wind down a window. Immediately the car is filled by the sound of the sea.

His voice softer, Michael Rougemont says: 'It's all right. I'm not going to tell them. Your sister, your husband, I'm not going to say anything.'

I do not reply.

'But why didn't you tell me? Why didn't you tell Kirsty? Why did you lie to us?'

I do not break my silence.

'What did you do here last weekend, Lucy?'

A slab of sunlight slants in through the windshield on to my lap. I watch the car's clock slowly change figures.

'Lucy, if you were here last weekend it won't take me long to find out what you did and where you went and who you saw. Save me a day and just tell me because I need to know.'

But when I shake my head and the silence has stretched on longer than any silence should, then Michael Rougemont opens the car door.

'Okay,' he says amiably. 'If you won't help me, I'd better get to work.'

As soon as I am back in Daddy's den I dial New York. I'm calling Mittex. Not only is Jay Kent in his office today but his secretary has clearly been told to put any call from me right through to him.

'Lucy! Good to hear from you!' he says and I am surprised by my own reaction, the way my heart thumps as though it just jumped out on me from a doorway.

'I tried to call you,' he tells me, 'but I got some woman I couldn't understand . . .'

'My Aunt Zina.'

'Does she speak English?'

I realize for the first time how heavily accented Aunt Zina's speech must be. I never noticed Mother's accent either and when kids at school told me my mother talked funny I was baffled.

I tell him: 'She couldn't understand you. She said you sounded like a machine-gun.'

Kent likes that and he laughs his machine-gun laugh. 'How are you, Lucy?'

'I'm okay. Have you started organizing those proposals for Gregory Hifeld?'

He groans. 'I thought you weren't working for a week or two.'

'What did you think of Gregory Hifeld?'

'Lucy, he didn't like me. But I admired him a lot. Unfortunately, he's retiring and you're offering us George.'

'But maybe as a pilot . . .'

More rapid gunfire as Kent laughs. 'You're smart, Lucy. It's one of the first things I noticed about you, it's one of the reasons I wanted you. I wanted that smartness. But I'm not sure even you can turn this deal around.'

I hear my own voice, strained, echoing back to me as though there's a large empty space out there. 'Thinking Toys is a good company, Kent. You need it, and the price is fair.'

'The old man isn't going to sell to us. He didn't like our attitude. He wants to play Santa to his little elves. He doesn't want mean ol' Mittex waving balance sheets around in Toyland. But I don't want to talk about any of this, Lucy. I want to talk about you. Have you found out what happened to your father?'

'Well, yes . . .' I pause. I consider not telling but Kent's waiting and finally I say: 'It was homicide.'

There is a silence.

'Homicide?' And for the first time his voice loses its certainty.

'That's what the police say.'

More silence. If Kent ever stopped to think about it, he assumed I came from a nice waspish community and a nice churchgoing family like his own. He didn't guess I had aunts who speak incomprehensible English or the kind of father who gets himself killed.

'I thought your dad was a prof . . .'

'He was.'

'But do you have any idea . . . have the police . . . ?'

'No, Kent, but this morning something happened.'

'To you?'

'To you and me.'

Another silence. He knows what's coming next but he's waiting for me to speak, hoping he's wrong.

'A detective told me that he's found out about last weekend.'

'What?'

'Last weekend. Someone knows.'

He is cautious. 'How much does he know?'

'At the moment, just that I was here.'

Kent's voice rises. 'Oh, he'll find out. These guys find things out.'

'He says that by the end of today he's going to know where I was and who I saw and what I did . . .'

'Oh for Chrissake, Lucy!' I hear his anger, his fear. 'Oh for Chrissake!' He is close to shouting. He is thinking about his mother and the church she is devoted to back in Virginia and the way he was brought up to behave and the way he did behave and it seems to Kent now that his connection with the strange, bleak Lucy Schaffer has led him into just the kind of mess his mother might have anticipated.

'What did you tell him?' he snaps.

'Nothing. When they interviewed me I said I was home all weekend.'

His volume rises again. 'You've lied to the police! You've made a false statement! Shit, Lucy.'

'I'm trying to keep you out of it, Kent, that's why.'

But he's shouting loudly now and doesn't hear. 'Lucy, they're going to get you and that means they'll find their way to me. Shit, Lucy, shit, this could blow everything.'

'But what can I do? Now I've lied I can't change my story.'

'Nothing.' He breathes heavily. 'You can't do anything. Just sit tight and don't say anything if you can help it. I have to go now.'

Kent puts down the phone. He puts it down so hard that it misses its cradle and I hear it bounce on the desk before he catches it and slams it down again. There is electronic groaning on the line.

When I put down the phone the house feels sticky and

silent. No one else is here today. Scott offered to help but I told him to stay on campus because everything in the den is under control. Larry and Jane have also gone to their offices. They have now removed any rocks or other items which look valuable and are close to completing arrangements for the funeral.

'You should be safe enough by yourself here in the daytime now we have the new keys,' Larry told me. 'Just be sure to lock the door.'

The key the locksmith gave me felt more youthful than Daddy's key, shinier and plumper. I followed Larry's advice but right from the moment I walked in I knew that the house was too hot to remain closed. The walls have started to inhale the day's heat with more stamina than they exhale it at night.

I fling open the sliding doors to the deck and a hot breeze, like breath, blows right in. Outside the sun is strong and frisky as a freshman and the leaves shake a welcome at me. My eye searches from habit for all the valley's familiar landmarks.

When we were kids, we used to flip through the railings on to the deck at one end, where the sloping ground and the deck almost meet. I recall the liberation of self-propulsion then the thud of wood underfoot when you made a perfect landing. Now that there is no one here to see me, I scramble down to the slope, reach for the railing and take my feet off the ground. Hanging, which used to be painless, seems to pull my arms from their sockets. I swing myself once, twice and then flip on to the deck with a practised movement. My body is hurled into its own trajectory, I feel the strength of its arc, and then I am landing squarely on both feet. Satisfaction. The whole manoeuvre has taken a couple of seconds and my body's memory of it was perfect. I wonder how it is possible to be unaware of remembering something so well.

I go back to the den and call Jim Finnigan.

'Lucy, oh gosh, Lucy, I was just thinking about you. How're things, how're you feeling?'

He is loud and fast, he is New York.

'It's good to hear you, Jim.'

'Life's pretty bad, huh? When's the funeral?'

'Not until Tuesday.'

Jim probably has his lowest desk drawer pulled out and his feet resting on it. Or they're on the garbage can, maybe inside the garbage can. The phone is wedged between his ear and his shoulder by rows of thick jowels.

'Well, don't hurry back.'

'Ahem, Jim. You just said the wrong thing. You're supposed to tell me you can't manage without me.'

'Well, I can. So take your time.'

'I was planning on returning by the end of next week.'

'That's fine, stay longer if you need to.'

'What about Hifeld–Mittex?'

'Not good. But don't worry about that. So stay where you are. I'm doing whatever needs to be done.' Despite his words I hear that his voice is bumping along the bottom of some riverbed now.

He says: 'Lucy, the police contacted me yesterday. About you.' Bump, scrape, the riverbed is rocky.

'What did they want?'

'Oh . . .' he exhales so loudly it's almost a sigh. 'Some guy's flying out here to talk to me.'

'A guy? What's his name?'

'Er . . .' The rustle of paper. 'Rougemont? Does that ring a bell?'

'He's coming to New York?'

'On the weekend. He'll be in the office on Monday. I have to produce a schedule of the hours you spent here in the ten days before your father's death. That kind of stuff.'

'Oh.'

Jim hesitates. His voice rasps a little. 'Lucy . . . was your father really killed?'

'The police think so.'

'That's terrible. Do you have any idea who would −?'

'There just isn't anyone, Jim. Daddy was a nice guy who never would have given anyone a reason to hurt him.'

'Do people always need reasons?'

'I guess not if they're crazy. Did Rougemont ask you anything else over the phone?'

'He wanted to know how you spent the weekend. You said you were visiting friends and I told him so. I hope that's okay.'

I don't like Jim's anxiety, the suggestion, half a suggestion, that I might be hiding things from the police.

'Sure, sure. I already told them too.'

'He also wants to talk to Fatima.'

'Uh-huh.'

'Lucy, he's asked for the tapes of your telephone calls for the last two weeks.'

I am silent, first with shock, then because I am thinking. Wondering what I said to Kent or he said to me over the company phone.

'Lucy?'

It is normal and accepted for the bank to record calls. I assume no one ever listens to them unless there's a contract dispute or a suspicion of espionage. I wonder who keeps the tapes and who decides if they should be heard.

'Hey, are you there?'

'What did you tell him, Jim?'

'I said ̦no because the tapes contain sensitive banking information. He persisted. I had to refer it up in the end.'

'How far up?'

'I have a feeling it may have got as far as Semper.'

'Semper! Oh, shit, Jim. This could bring my career to an abrupt halt.'

'Yeah. It's like . . .' Jim swallows. 'Well, it's like you're some kind of a suspect.' He adds hastily: 'I'm sure you're not. But it sort of looks that way when the police start asking questions and checking on your movements. It's probably not a big career booster.'

'Will Semper give them the tapes?'

'He shouldn't do that without telling you first. But if you have a lawyer who –'

'Jim, I don't need a lawyer, I haven't done anything wrong.'

'Okay, okay. Don't say more, since this call is being recorded.'

'There's nothing in the tape the police shouldn't hear,' I insist. 'It's just kind of a . . . an intrusion. A violation. That's all.'

'Yeah. This is awful, Lucy.' He swallows again. 'But at least you don't have to worry about Hifeld. Just leave Gregory to me. You forget about us and spend this sad time with your family.'

I want to shout: my job is my family. But I don't. I know it's true of most of us at the bank, even Jim, but it's something we prefer not to acknowledge out loud and on tape.

I try to call Jay Kent again but his secretary has obviously now been instructed to intercept me. Humiliated, I wrap myself in the smallprint of Daddy's life, his files, his letters, his financial statements, his Medicare records. Occasionally there is the flutter of drapes in the living-room, otherwise nothing breaks the house's thin membrane of silence.

I slide open the desk drawer and guiltily, as though it's a slab of chocolate, withdraw the newspaper cuttings. Wedding News is on the top. The groom is a doctor. The bridesmaids wore yellow.

After the car crash I was sent home swiftly from hospital. I spent the long summer months waiting for Robert to call. And even if he hadn't called, he could have written. He didn't. I hoped maybe his mother would contact me. But she didn't either. I could only find one explanation for this. Robert and his family must blame me for the crash. He was after all stretching one arm across to me when it should have been on the steering-wheel. Had I encouraged or, worse, demanded this near-fatal attention? His silence seemed to suggest that I had and in my heart I have always believed the accident to be at least partly and probably wholly my fault. At the end of the long summer, Robert's summer, we both went our different ways to different colleges. When, later, someone told me Robert kept his leg but had a terrible limp and wouldn't play sports again, I felt more remorse than compassion.

I am immersed in these thoughts when I become aware that I am not alone.

I know someone is here not because they make any noise but by a sensation of movement. The movement is at the door of the den and I don't see it, I feel it. The hairs on the back of my neck stand up and I leap to my feet. The doorway is empty and the door still but I perceive that a reorganization has taken place in the air's molecules. Someone stood there, or at least passed by, just a few seconds ago.

I get to the deck fast. My nerve ends are sizzling and my mouth is dry as I lean over the railings. The sun glares. Leaves shift uncomfortably in the breeze. Otherwise, the hillside is motionless. Beyond, the valley bakes like a hard, brown loaf. I wait, holding my loud breath. Then I go back inside the house and search every room downstairs and, although the door was locked, I go out to the porch. The barn, the car, the drive. Nothing moves. Nothing changes.

Back to the deck and this time, far to one side, beyond the house and almost at the dirt road, I see motion amidst the dappled shade of the trees. Probably a man, probably running. He must have crouched under the deck, right underneath my feet, with the old lumber and machines until I went back inside the house. Then he escaped. The shadow is at the edge of my vision and in a moment it is gone. I wait, my eyes fixed on the spot where he used to be, but I am staring at the stillness of an empty landscape.

I jump down from the deck and retrace the intruder's route. There are some large footsteps in the dirt which could be his, or they might belong to the police or to Larry. I skirt around the house and then walk right over to the dirt road. There's a gap in the foliage where he must have escaped.

I turn back to the house. I stop at the sunken garden, looking, listening. My heart still fills my ears with its thumping. The garden is sheltered by arching trees and half-blanketed by ivy. Nothing has been disturbed here for a while. And then, I miss a breath. Peeping between the shrubs is something alien. The colour is wrong, the angles are wrong. It shouldn't be there.

I brush aside the foliage and tread cautiously on the stone steps. I lift my hand as I descend and feel feathery leaves slip between my fingers. Propped against one wall, I find a gravestone. I am so astonished by this that the stone seems to leap at me, its words flying out in jumbled letters like an explosion. At first I take it for some very late, overblown monument to Mother's dog, who was buried around here. But when I have stared at the words long enough I read: 'Remember me. Remember death. Eric Schaffer.' I read them over and over until they echo inside my head. Remember me. Remember death.

The headstone is grey and its face is rough, rougher than

the stone I saw at Joe Zacarro's and, although the words are so similar, their style is less ornate. There is a gap at the bottom for dates. It sits, with an absurd suggestion of jauntiness, askew on the uneven rocks which line the sunken garden.

I walk carefully back to the steps. Daddy built this garden from the same round, smooth rocks he used for the drive. Beneath it is buried Nickel Dog, a brown mutt adored by Mother which Jane discovered poisoned one day, probably by someone intending to poison coyotes. If you could forget about the Nickel Dog's unhappy fate, then the sunken garden should have been a good place to do your homework but it never was because the sun, trapped like a bear here, was doubly aggressive. I don't remember ever sitting on the stone seats.

The old swimsuit Scott returned to me is in the car. I pick it up and am locking up the house, sliding shut the doors to the deck, when some instinct pulls me, like gravity, outside again to stare over the valley. The farm where I walked with Lindy. The tracks where the farmer drove us home in his pick-up with the dirt blowing a storm behind us. The place where Robert Joseph's car turned over. The long, grey, straight road which leads to the intersection and along which, tiny, silently, a toy tow truck is now travelling. It points right to the heart of the valley and then, with the flash of bouncing sun, it turns north. I watch it until it is out of sight. Then I leave the house for Joe Zacarro's.

22

Joe is out. There is no reply to my ring at the bell or my yell and the car with the padlocked trunk is missing. The pool is empty except for the plastic armchair, moored by the steps. I walk right over to his headstone. Remember death. Joe Zacarro did. Different script but probably chiselled by the same craftsman.

I change into my swimsuit and the pool unrolls before me, a flat, bright rectangle of water. I climb in to my waist and feel its cold embrace while the sun batters my face and shoulders with its heat. I walk further and the iciness moves up my body. I am breathless when it grasps me like a ring of metal around my heart. I lift my feet and roll forward and in that moment I have changed elements. Now my movements are water movements, my thoughts are fish thoughts. I no longer feel the cold.

I swim rapidly, cutting a line through the pool's calm surface, turning and cutting again, like the scissors of a busy seamstress. Up and down, up and down, the water streaming each side of my face, holding me, caressing me, a calm parent as I kick and twist in its arms. My senses dulled, my mind lulled by the rhythm of my swimming, I continue, I have no idea how long, until, abruptly, I stop, mid-pool.

I climb out. I have washed away hours and perhaps days. I wrap the towel around me and watch the drips from my body make strange, dark shapes on the tiles around the pool edge.

'You sure needed that,' says a voice. Under an umbrella,

in a swimsuit, sits Mr Zacarro. He pushes an iced coffee towards me. 'It took me a while to make this, I didn't think you'd still be swimming by the time I finished.'

I sip the coffee and enjoy its sweetness. Joe rests his short leg up on a chair. I tell him about the intruder at Daddy's house and he listens and thinks and finally says: 'You came right over here. You did good. You're safe at Joe's, you remember that.'

'But the intruder may still be around. He went through the hedge into the dirt road.'

Joe frowns. 'He ran away,' he reminds me. 'If he'd wanted to hurt you he could've done it when you were alone in the house.'

I nod. I'm pretty sure the intruder has already left in his tow truck.

'Okay,' says Joe seriously, 'let's get this straight. He used a key. Twice. Until you got the locks changed.'

'Last night the police hid a couple of officers in the yard in case he came back to try again. But he didn't.' Jane called me earlier with this news. She sounded disappointed.

'So he either knew you'd changed the locks, or guessed you would, or he'd found what he wanted. Except, today he walked right in from the deck, saw you and ran right out again.'

'I guess he ran when he saw me. I don't know why else he would run.'

'So he's not planning on introducing himself.'

'I think he wants something.'

'What?'

'Something in the den.'

'Well, what's in there?'

'Just Daddy's papers.'

Joe gets up and walks distractedly into the pool. There's a

huge crash and water explodes everywhere. It leaves dark patches on the paving and wet patches on my legs. I stretch them out into the sun to dry.

Joe swims a couple of strokes underwater with a natural, easy grace and then turns over on to his back as if that's natural too.

'Gotta get in the water if I want to think,' he explains as swimming-pool cascades down his face. He tilts back his head and, a lot further down the pool, his toes appear. He floats. He closes his eyes.

'I also have a theory . . .' I begin hesitantly. 'I think he drives a tow truck.'

Joe opens both eyes.

'This guy who keeps coming to the house? You seen him drive a tow truck?'

'No. I don't even know where he leaves it. But on the two occasions when I sensed he was around, I looked down into the valley, ten, maybe fifteen minutes later, and I saw a tow truck.'

'Doing what?'

'Driving east. Then it turns north at the intersection.'

Joe closes his eyes again.

'If you only saw it twice then it's probably a coincidence,' he says.

'Did Daddy know anyone with a tow truck?'

The water is almost calm now. The waves Joe created have just enough movement to turn his body through a few degrees.

'I'll have to think about that,' he says at last. 'I mean, if you drive a goddamn heap of garbage like Eric did, you're going to need a number to call when it breaks down on the freeway . . .'

'I've already looked in his address book but there's nothing obvious.'

'Hmmmmm,' he says. 'I gotta think.'

He doesn't move or speak for such a long time that I suspect he's been thinking so hard he's fallen asleep. I don't know anyone else who can fall asleep in water without some kind of flotation aid but probably Joe can. It's time to go, even though I haven't asked him the very question which brought me here. I am gathering up the iced coffee glasses, quietly, without clinking them, the way Jane and I used to wash the dishes when Mother was very sick, when Joe opens one eye.

'Hey, Lucy,' he says, 'don't go.'

'I thought you were asleep.'

'Nah, like I said, I was thinking.'

'There's something else I wanted to ask you.'

'Uh-huh.'

'I found Daddy's headstone.'

He opens both eyes and sits up in the water, shattering its calm, creating small waves all over the pool.

'You did? Down in that pit in your yard?'

'The sunken garden.'

'Fancy garbage name.' He pulls himself up and, as he scrambles into the floating armchair, curtains of water run down his skin.

'So you knew the headstone was there?' I ask.

His legs dangle beneath the surface looking paler than the rest of his brown body. He puts his head back and closes his eyes. 'Sure. Didn't Eric mention it in his will? You're supposed to tell in your will and then your relatives are real pleased you saved them the trouble and expense.'

'I don't think he mentioned it anywhere.'

'Well, you probably noticed it's sort of like mine. Adam Holler's too. That's because we all got our stones from the same place, me and Eric and Adam.'

'Were they on special offer? I mean, three for the price of two or something?'

Disconcertingly, Mr Zacarro flings back his head and roars with laughter and the armchair bobs around in the water.

'It wasn't a joke,' I tell him when he's through.

'Economics didn't come into it, Lucy. We all wanted our headstones that way so we figured we should get them carved ourselves to make sure.'

'Remember death? Isn't that kind of strange?'

'Not so. People have been saying that for centuries. I mean, it's a modern, industrialized nation sort of thing to ignore death and think it's never going to happen to you. But if you remember that you're going to die some day then you live your life in a different sort of a way. Not necessarily better, but probably better. Different, that's for sure. We believe that. We all agreed on it, me and Eric and Adam.'

I look at him uncertainly.

'Be a nice gal and get me a beer and have one yourself if you'd like.'

I trot over to the porch and get Joe a beer. It feels icy in my hand.

I say: 'I don't recall Daddy ever talking about his own death.'

'Didn't mean he wasn't aware of it.'

I swallow. 'Was he scared to die?' I ask.

Mr Zacarro sighs and I see the sigh slip along his whole body. 'Oh sure, he was scared as any of us. We don't know how death's going to come or how much it's going to hurt and that's frightening. The only thing we know for sure is that it will come.'

There is a new quality in his voice. It has thickened. I look at him quickly. 'Are you okay, Joe?'

'I got interviewed this morning,' he tells me. 'Nice gal from the police department, long dark hair.'

'Long?'

'Kept messing with it. Wanted to know if Eric had an enemy or any reason to be scared of someone. In other words, do I know who killed him?'

'What did you say?'

His face is big and sad. 'The very dumbfool idea made me laugh.'

'What else did she ask you?'

'Well . . .' he pauses. The surface of the pool still dances from the waves I made. He watches the moving pattern of sunlight and shadow but his face is untouched by its gaiety. His jaw lengthens suddenly, his mouth turns down and he rubs an eye as if an eyelash, at this very moment, fell right into it. 'It was just the damnedest thing,' he says.

I wait for him and finally he turns back to me and I see that both eyes are red and there was no eyelash. He swallows. In a voice that is creased and used as an old rag he says: 'She asked about Lindy.'

'Lindy!' I echo. And for a moment I feel angry with the detective, playing with her imaginary hair, smiling her cold-eyed smiles, stabbing at people's pasts with her pen, slamming all the soft places with her notebook.

Sobs shake Joe Zacarro's big, brown body. I see the muscles clench and the flesh shiver as pain twists inside him like a fish on a line.

His face and chest and belly are soon wet with tears. He leans over and scoops up some pool water then pulls it across his cheeks like a towel and drops more water on to his body.

I reach out for his arm and he immediately puts a hand over mine, both trapping and protecting it.

'She asked me how Lindy died. I told her they already got

a file marked Lindy Wardine Zacarro somewhere. The police came that night and asked a lot of questions. I told this dark-haired gal maybe they still have the file somewhere if she's interested and she said she'd go look for it. Then she asked me everything anyway. Everything I could remember about the day Lindy died. As if I ever could have forgotten one goddamn second of it.'

He looks up at me and his eyes are still red.

'I guess that's me finished for a few hours.' His chest heaves and he snatches at breaths when they come. He presses my hand tighter against him. 'Do you remember? Do you remember when my Lindy died?'

It was summer vacation and all the neighbourhood kids were playing hide-and-go-seek. There had been some kind of argument. I don't remember why or what it was about, a trivial, childish difference probably, but my friendship with Lindy had cooled. Despite this, we still sometimes joined in with the other kids on the hillside during vacations. When it was Lindy's turn to hide no one could find her. We looked and called and finally it felt late and we just drifted off home in our different directions. Mrs Zacarro hadn't been too worried at first: it was hot and the mothers mostly sat around fanning themselves. But when Davis and Carter got hungry and there was still no Lindy, Mrs Zacarro knew something wasn't right. She took the car and drove around the neighbourhood, looking, calling Lindy's name. She came to our house. She asked for Mother but Mother, who had been ill, was resting and Daddy was out. We could see that Mrs Zacarro was angry with Lindy but now her face was starting to hollow with worry. She didn't know that the whole time Lindy was right there in the trunk of the car and had scratched off her fingernails trying to get out. The police said that the temperature in the trunk was so high she would have died within a half hour. When I used to think how Lindy was lying dead without fingernails in the car her mother parked right by our barn, I'd feel nausea all over my body and salt in my mouth.

'I don't understand,' says Joe. 'Why was this woman asking about my little girl after all these years?' He scatters more water over himself.

I pause. 'I've been thinking about Lindy a lot since I came back here.'

His face breaks into an indulgent smile. 'Yeah, you two were big pals. Remember how you used to play with your little toy horses and plait each other's hair and stuff?'

'Joe, did Lindy ever get a real horse?'

'Slim! He was a beautiful chestnut, I bought him from a cowboy in the mountains and we kept him at Tannerman's down in the valley and Lindy thought he was just great. When she died . . . I couldn't look at Slim. I couldn't even think about him. I just left him over at Tannerman's and I guess they took care of him, I don't know, I never asked. I sure hope he wasn't neglected. Finally someone called and said they wanted to buy him and I said, have him, we don't ever want to see him again. I feel sort of bad about that now. None of it was Slim's fault. He must have wondered what the hell was going on.'

'I remember seeing Lindy ride that chestnut horse,' I say. I'm relieved that it's a real memory and not a memory of my own dreams or of Lindy's.

'Wait,' Joe instructs me. He gets up and limps slowly into the house and when he rolls back out he is carefully cradling something against his body. As he gets closer I see that he is carrying framed photos. Lindy, looking pretty with bobbed blonde hair, on the chestnut horse. A younger Lindy, fuller-faced, longer-haired, posing shyly in her Brownies uniform.

Lindy laughing at the camera in a manner which makes me draw back a little. I remember that laugh. It wasn't always kind.

'Cute, huh?' says Joe. 'I mean, wouldn't she have grown into a lovely young woman? Like you, Lucy, just beautiful like you.'

Lindy was my friend but there was some kind of an argument. After that she became an expert in playground politics. She was always surrounded by the other girls in the class while I recall myself alone, on the edge of groups but never part of them. Sometimes I had friends for a while. I dreaded the day they or their mothers would invite me home. The friendship would start to end right there because I never could invite them back.

Joe sets off on his laboured journey to return the photos leaving me sitting, thinking, in the shade of a big umbrella.

23

When I walk down Joe's drive I look for the sticky-leaved plant with the pink flowers. I'm going to brush right against it and fearlessly allow it to transport me back to my childhood with Lindy like some kind of time machine. But today I don't see it and nothing which touches my leg has the same viscosity.

Inside Daddy's yard I go right to the sunken garden and stare at the headstone. Remember me. Didn't Daddy know that he occupied a place in the lives of those around him as solid as this big slab of grey rock he chose for his headstone? Didn't he know that we'd always remember him? I run my hands over the stone's surface and, because it has retained the heat of the day, it feels good. The pads of my fingers trace the words. Remember death. Remember Eric Schaffer.

Now my fingerprints are all over Daddy's headstone. Everywhere you go, almost everywhere you breathe air, you leave your prints. Odourless, invisible, silent traces of yourself. So that, even when you've gone, a tiny part of you remains.

When Lindy died, a tiny part of her remained. It was my secret and I told no one, not even Jane, that I made-believe Lindy was still alive and still my friend. I'd tell her things. I'd sit on the porch swing with her. We'd discuss school and teachers and the other kids. Lindy never said a mean word to me. One day I thought that maybe I preferred this Lindy to the way she'd been when she was alive, fickle in friendship and unpredictable in response. I knew that was a bad thought and from then onwards I tried to banish the make-believe Lindy from the swing.

I hear a car. I turn back to the headstone. The air has the calm maturity of late afternoon now. The day has lost its heat like a fever which has passed.

'Hi, Lucy,' says a familiar voice and I don't jump. I don't turn around. Mostly I'm annoyed, maybe because, without really thinking about it, I've been waiting for him. He said I had given him a day's work. Now, at the end of the day, here he is.

'Hi, Mr Rougemont.'

He sounds friendly. 'I sure wish you'd call me Michael.'

I shrug. I hear him scrambling into the sunken garden, his big feet slipping a little on the tipsy steps, the flutter of soil or stone minutely displaced.

I remember how he appeared on the night of Daddy's death as a shadow, talking to Kirsty outside the kitchen. Even in the flesh he is the shadow of a man, impossibly thin and impossibly tall, taller than I remember. His long head is turned to Daddy's headstone.

'Looks recent,' he says. 'How long have you known about it?'

'Not long. A neighbour and friend of Daddy's, Joe Zacarro, has one too. So does another neighbour.'

'Well, isn't that interesting?'

I shrug. 'It's nice in an odd sort of way. I like feisty old men.'

Rougemont gives one of his Hallowe'en smiles.

'What is this place anyway?' he asks. He sits down on one of the cracked slabs of stone which Daddy set in the wall as seats. He stretches out one leg like a giant insect and looks curiously around him at the big rocks, bruising with his fingers a small plant which suddenly smells pungent as summer.

235

'The sunken garden. Daddy built it with leftover rocks from the drive as a nice, private place to sit. And Mother's dog is buried here somewhere.'

'The one in the picture on the bureau?'

I pause. A photograph of Mother and Aunt Zoya with a small brown dog has stood on the bureau since I was a child but it has never occurred to me that this might be the famous Nickel Dog.

I concede: 'Probably. He was called Nickel Dog because Daddy bought him for a nickel from some guy who didn't want him.'

'Did you like him a lot?'

'I was very small . . .' I close my eyes and for a moment sense something brown and yappy brushing past me, its coarse hair wiry. The sensation of wrapping my arms around a warm, yielding creature, which could have been my toy Hodges or Nickel Dog. 'Jane told me he used to jump on me and scare me but I'm not sure if I remember that. I'm not sure if I remember him at all. I mean, it could be that I just remember Jane talking about him.'

'Oh yes,' agrees the detective, 'oh yes, it's easy to confuse what actually happened with things you've been told and things you've dreamed. It's good, real good, that you recognize how unreliable memory is. But it seems to me that the sort of thing you could remember is Nickel Dog dying. I mean, feeling upset. Your mother's unhappiness. Someone, I guess your father, burying him.'

I try to remember the demise of Nickel Dog, Mother weeping, Daddy looking grim with a spade, Jane white-faced, but the dog's death is as elusive as his life.

He asks: 'Did you ever sit here when you were a kid?'

'Occasionally. But if I wanted to escape it was to the porch at the front of the house.' As soon as the words are out of my mouth I want to reach out and grab them back from him. Rougemont's body quivers a little as if he's going to pounce.

'What were you escaping from, Lucy?'

The air around here. When I came home from school and opened the door I could smell it. I could smell Mother's unhappiness, Daddy's absence, the house's loneliness and my own.

'Or,' he adds, 'should I ask, who were you escaping from?'

One of Rougemont's legs has been folded up and now he stretches it out along with the other as he waits for my reply.

'You're probably wondering what I found out today,' he says at last. 'About your weekend.'

I am silent. I fix my eyes on Daddy's headstone. It is a long time before he speaks again.

'It would sure make my life easier if you'd talk to me, Lucy.'

When I maintain my silence he says: 'I don't just mean I want you to talk about the weekend although I sure wish you'd clear that one up. No, I'd like to hear about all the sort of stuff you don't normally tell people because they're not interested. A lot of people just do not have any interest in anyone but themselves. Let's take, for example, Mr Jay Kent.'

I don't let myself react. Not stiffen or start or move any part of my body.

'Now, Mr Jay Kent is clearly one helluva businessman, I understand he's going to head up one of the country's biggest toy manufacturers in the summertime. But, no matter how intimate he gets with someone, I'm prepared to bet that he shows no interest in their past. Asks nothing about their childhood, reveals little about his own unless asked. But I'm different from Jay Kent, Lucy. I like to know about people and I'd especially like to know about you.'

I am watching him now, watching his lips stretch over the big teeth as he talks. I remain silent but a heat that comes from within, which I can't control, is spreading up my body and soon it will reach my face and he will see it.

'I spoke with him today,' continues Michael Rougemont. He looks up into the foliage above his head. 'Yes, I spoke with Mr Jay Kent not long ago.'

Evening in New York. Did Rougemont contact Kent at the office or at home where Kent was playing at being with his wife and wriggling baby? I catch my breath.

'He wasn't entirely surprised to hear from me although I wouldn't say he welcomed my call.'

I watch the way the mouth forms its words, the way the eyes are hollowed by years of late nights and early mornings and worrying and pain. Life itself seems to have accumulated around his eyes. I touch my own face. It feels soft but it burns.

'However, he wanted to be helpful. I'd even say he was anxious to help. Went off into a quiet room by himself where he could concentrate on my questions and answered them without the smallest hesitation. See, Lucy, I've asked a lot of people a lot of questions over a long time and I've noticed that very often they hesitate. They hesitate for different reasons: maybe because they're formulating a lie but, in my experience, more often because they want to check it's okay for them to tell the truth. They want to run through the truth in their minds and establish what the consequences might be, for themselves or others, of revealing that truth. Jay Kent had no such concern, Lucy. He had no concern for the consequences of his words. He just knew that if he answered my questions, he'd get me out of his life fast. So he didn't hesitate, not once.'

Rougemont looks at me closely, so closely that I turn

away. 'You're not in love with him, Lucy. Reassure me that you're not in love with him.'

I say nothing but I find myself giving the smallest of half-shrugs. Rougemont takes this to indicate my indifference to Jay Kent. He sits back, nodding.

'That's good, I'm pleased about that. I believe you already knew how little he cares for you. He's an acquisitive guy, in my opinion. You met him because you have a company that's looking for a buyer. Thinking Toys, I believe it's called. Thinking Toys is for sale, Lucy, but you aren't. You're not the kind of woman a Jay Kent sort of a guy can acquire.'

I look straight into his grey eyes. I say: 'Mr Rougemont, for someone who's supposed to ask questions, you sure answer a lot.'

He laughs now, guffawing like a donkey.

'Okay, Lucy, okay, I'll stop telling and start asking. I'll ask you about last Sunday. Mr Jay Kent was looking around stores with some untermensch from his empire. What did you do?'

When I am silent he delves into his bag. It's a large bag which he wore on his shoulder until he sat down, the kind of shapeless black bag people use for carrying a computer and a lot of documents and a mess of leads. When his hand re-emerges, it holds a shoe. He waves it at me.

'Wait, wait, just a minute. I can improve on that,' he says. He delves a little more. 'Yes . . . yes . . .' He produces another, its twin, although this second shoe has no heel.

'So, here's my question. Do you recognize the exhibit?'

I am still standing by Daddy's headstone. I reach out for its grey coolness. I look at the shoes. They are women's shoes in soft black leather. Expensive, medium heel, ruined by contact with the wrong sort of ground. Red-brown dirt has insinuated itself into the leather inside and out.

'Hmmmm . . .' says Rougemont, examining them like a

doctor. 'Hmmmm, they're kind of dirty. But, do you think they might just fit you?'

I shrug.

'Would you try one? Just to see if it fits?' When I remain silent he answers for me: 'Sure you will.'

He gets up and, when he's standing right by me, drops suddenly and surprisingly to a crouch. The headstone beneath my fingers supports my weight as he lifts my right leg a little. The place he touches me, around my ankle, feels warm. With great gentleness he pulls off the shoe I'm wearing and inserts my foot into the shoe in his hand.

'Aha,' he says. 'I'd call that a fit! Wouldn't you call that a fit, Lucy?'

I yield to his pantomime without participating in it.

'And hey, this shoe I took off . . .' He holds it up to eye level, twisting it to right and left. 'Hey, the heel is worn a little more on the right side than the left. That's because your weight isn't distributed quite evenly when you walk: sometimes we favour one side of the foot, often we favour one leg.'

Click clack, click clack.

'For example, this shoe I just tried . . .' He wedges it off me in one deft movement and replaces it with my own shoe. 'Yes, this other one is also worn in the same place but perhaps a little more, not much. So the owner of this shoe also favours the outside of her foot. What a coincidence! Unless . . .' He looks up into my face and rolls his eyes comically. He's playing the game show host again. 'Unless of course . . . these shoes all belong to you.'

He stands up so he's towering over me. I grip the headstone hard.

'Shame about this one,' he sighs, holding up the heel-less shoe. 'Big shame.'

He takes the dirty shoes and sits down. The air is stiffened by the chill of early evening now and his voice cuts through it with a new crispness.

'You're a snail, Lucy. You aren't too experienced at covering up your trail. It was so simple to follow that I began to wonder if you weren't just trying to keep me amused. Late Sunday morning you hired a car and drove out of the city and you came up here to see your father. I'm not sure where you left the car. Somewhere it wouldn't be seen. Somewhere which meant you had to walk over some pretty rough ground. You certainly didn't want anyone to know you were here. I don't know what you did but your shoes sure had a tough time. Walking through dirt. Maybe even running. When you got back to town they were ruined and you needed some new shoes. You bought a pair at the department store just about a block away from your hotel. Well, I told you it was an easy trail to follow. And I mean, it was a Sunday, the store wasn't busy, the assistant remembers you. You put the old shoes in the box she gave you and threw them away in the hotel. That is, to you they were old. To the room maid they were a pair of beautiful shoes with the kind of price tag she could never afford, and which, if she squished her toes up, almost fitted her. So she took them home, intending to clean them up a little, stretch them a little, get a new heel put on, have herself a nice pair of designer shoes. Luckily, she didn't do any of that yet.'

He watches me. His voice drones on, lower now because he knows how hard I'm listening.

'I could hand them right over to forensic and ask them to analyse whether the dirt inside them comes from this immediate area. I could do that. But I won't need to do that, Lucy, if you tell me what happened here last Sunday. I especially need to know what time you were here. I think it was early afternoon. Am I right?'

When I am silent he sighs theatrically.

'I'm a generous guy.' I steal a glance at his big face. Right now he doesn't look generous but his expression is not unkind. 'I'm a generous guy, Lucy, and I'm going to give you a few days because tomorrow I'm leaving town for a short while. And when I get back I'm going to ask you to tell me what you were doing here at your father's house right before he died.'

He gets up and puts the shoes carefully in his bag.

'I'll see you when I get back, Lucy,' he says softly. When I think he's gone I turn around and find that he is standing at the top of the stone steps.

'Goodbye,' he calls. He's still hoping that I'll tell him what he wants to know but I say nothing. I don't move until I have heard the hum of his car on the drive. I sit down on the cracked slab of the seat warmed by Rougemont and, leaves murmuring softly overhead, I remember Nickel Dog's death. I remember Mother's sadness distilled into a high-pitched and unnatural wail, Jane's pallor, her fingers dancing nervously, Daddy holding with both hands before him the stiff bundle that was Nickel Dog wrapped in a blanket. And then I was running, past the old tow truck, around the bushes, in and out of trees, the thick grass bouncing me onwards. I ran until I reached a den we had made in the far corner of the yard under an overhanging bush. An old rug, some soft toys, and there, in the den, a friend waiting for me. Lindy.

24

When I've finished telling Seymour and Katherine everything I know about Daddy's death they think for a long time.

'Someone sure went to a lot of trouble to make it seem like Eric killed himself,' says Seymour.

Katherine snorts. 'As if he ever would!'

'I mean, leaving his clothes on the beach and all that.'

'Must be someone who doesn't watch TV crime shows,' says Katherine. 'You only have to watch a couple to know that the police can tell if a body drowned or if it was dead before it went into the water.'

Seymour looks serious. 'That should lead us to the guy. Since now we can eliminate almost everyone in America.' And, despite the circumstances and our sadness, we smile at each other.

I look around the room. It is padded with books and piled high with magazines. A few shelves are crowded with small, carved figures from Africa and South America and there is a mask which might come from some Pacific island. Everywhere there are the faces of smiling grandchildren and the primitive, blotchy pictures they have painted. Seymour and Katherine have led a full life and it's here for all to see, pinned to the walls, tumbling from the shelves. I think of Daddy's house where so much is hidden: in the barn, in boxes, in closets and in bedrooms which no one uses.

Seymour pours pale, brown liquid from a tea pot into tea cups.

He explains: 'This is Lemon Rose Pouchong, the tea club

selection for March. We belong to this club in England. Every month they send us a different tea.'

'The woman from the police department liked it,' adds Katherine.

'An attractive girl,' says Seymour. He is a small, bald, wiry man who played baseball back in the days when he had a full head of hair. Once, he played against Joe diMaggio. It's a tale he has dined out on ever since: Daddy said he'd heard it at least fifty times and it was just a little bit different each time and Seymour said: 'Well, I wouldn't want to bore you, Eric.'

The tea is too hot to drink. I inhale its flowery aroma.

'I wish you'd eat a cookie,' says Katherine, pushing the plate towards me. 'I just want to give you things, Lucy, you look like you need someone to do that.'

Ever since Daddy died even complete strangers, at some animal level, have recognized my grief. The clerk at the airport said: 'I'm going to try to find you a good seat for your flight tonight . . .' and she clicked at her keyboard until she had upgraded me. At the gas station the attendant looked slyly at my face while processing my credit card. 'Ma'am, we have a new promotion of speciality china and I'd like you to take home a deluxe prize today.' At the Russian bookstore I pass between the parking lot and Aunt Zina's apartment I stopped to buy her a sumptuous edition of Pushkin to replace her torn and faded copy and the assistant suddenly produced from behind the counter a presentation pack containing an apron and a collection of carved wooden spoons. 'Take this, please. We have a special gift for distribution only to the discerning buyers of Pushkin,' she insisted.

I accept a cookie and ask Seymour: 'Did you tell the detective about the discrepancy in the oil well payments?'

He turns his brown, nut-shaped head towards Katherine for a moment and then back to me.

'Well, no, I didn't, Lucy. But Katherine and I think that maybe someone should.'

'Why?'

'First, let me explain what I found out, which isn't much. Simms-Roeder is still producing. Smart Eric tied the company up in a watertight royalty agreement which keeps them paying and, believe me, if they could get out of it, they would. You're right that the money didn't go directly to Eric. It gets paid into another account.'

'Where is that account? Do you have any details on it?'

'Only the name.'

'Which is?'

Seymour gets up and goes to the bureau. He pulls a piece of paper from beneath a child's coiled ceramic. He reads: 'The Marcello Trust.'

I stare at him. 'The what Trust?'

'Marcello.' He spells it for me then sits back down and hands me the paper.

'What is it?' I ask.

Seymour shrugs. 'I hoped you'd know. Because I surely don't.'

Katherine says: 'We think it sounds like some kind of charity. Did Eric make many charitable donations?'

I shake my head. 'He could be real generous, he liked to help people out, but he didn't do much organized giving. I mean, not to charities.'

'Didn't Eric have an accountant?' asks Katherine.

'Sure, I've spoken with him. He knows nothing about the oil well revenues. I'll ask him about the Marcello Trust, though.'

'Did Eric know anyone called Marcello?'

'I'll look in his address book. I'll look all over. Let's check the phone book right now . . .' I pause. I'm thinking.

'Have you heard the name before, Lucy?' asks Katherine. 'Is it sounding familiar now?'

I shrug.

'I think I heard it recently. But everything sounds familiar if you think about it long enough.'

Seymour shifts the books and newspapers on the table into new piles as he looks for the phone book.

'Recently?' Katherine is surprised. 'Not from way back?'

'No, recently . . .' I drink the flowery tea. I grope through my memory looking for the name, a first name or a surname, of Marcello.

In the phone book I find eight Marcellos scattered widely around the Bay Area. 'I'll call them, every one of them,' I say. Katherine and Seymour exchange glances.

'It's probably all straightforward and you'll find some obvious explanation which we should have thought of . . .' says Katherine and the way her voice rises a little indicates that they have some less obvious explanation to offer.

'Or,' finishes Seymour carefully, 'there's one other possibility.'

Katherine warns me: 'You won't like it, Lucy. But maybe you should discuss it with that detective.'

I wait. The tea feels hot and the china cup separating it from my hand absurdly fragile, as though I could crush the cup between my fingers and release the scalding liquid.

Seymour says: 'Have you thought about blackmail?'

I remember the boys on their skateboards in Lowis, how enthusiastically they embraced the notion of blackmail.

'Oh c'mon,' I say briskly. 'You've been watching too many of those TV crime shows.'

'Maybe, maybe,' admits Seymour, nodding his bald head. 'But, when the police were here asking us questions we learned something. We learned how little we know Eric. We

246

learned that we know nothing of his distant past, the family he came from, we don't even know who his other friends were and, of course, we've never met your mother. By the time we were through shrugging our shoulders, that gal from the police department must have been asking how Eric and I could really have been such buddies.'

'People can only be blackmailed if they have something terrible to hide,' I point out.

'Maybe he had,' says Katherine evenly.

I remember the white ring around Daddy's wrist.

'I mean,' she adds, 'maybe something happened way back that he was ashamed of.'

'Now,' says Seymour, the skin across his bullet head tightening as he makes a small grimace of pain. 'Please don't get upset or take offence, Lucy. We all did things when we were a lot younger that we wouldn't be proud to own up to now. It's precisely your father's high standards of morality which would make him a good target for blackmailers. If there was anything in his past which he was ashamed of.'

I say: 'There wouldn't be.' The tea feels cool in my hand now. I drink the flowery smell but taste only the astringency of lemon.

Katherine sounds anxious: 'It's not a nice thought, I know, Lucy, but there's a remote chance it may explain why someone killed your father.'

Seymour says: 'The police need to get to the bottom of this. You should tell them about the Marcello Trust.'

I reply without looking at them. 'If Daddy had a secret, I'd keep it. I certainly wouldn't have the police, or anyone else, investigate it.'

They exchange dismayed glances and then Katherine takes my hand and squeezes it hard. I look at their kind faces and, for a moment, wish they were my family. A happily married

247

couple with children and grandchildren, interesting lives behind them and a retirement packed with as much volunteer work and travel and friends as they want. This is normal. Not for the first time, I wish that my family could be normal too.

When I get up, saying that I'm going home to call all the Marcellos in the phone book, they first try to dissuade me and finally Seymour offers to help.

'Sit down, eat something for heaven's sake, and I'll take turns with you,' he says.

Katherine watches us curiously as we make the calls. All the Marcellos who answer say they know nothing about a trust in their name and have never heard of Eric Schaffer. One is suspicious, then angry, and finally threatens to call the police.

'So,' asks Seymour, 'now what are you going to do about this?'

'Later I'll call all the Marcellos who were out. Tomorrow I'll search the den, ask the bank, phone the accountant. I have to sort this out, Seymour.'

Katherine has been watching us in silence. Now she asks: 'Lucy, have you seen Scott since you've been back?'

'Oh yes. We're still friends.'

Seymour says: 'I sure like Scott. And Eric was very close to him. He needed a lot of support after you left.'

'Scott always needed a lot of support,' I point out. 'One reason I went was that I couldn't give him that support when Stevie died.'

Katherine says: 'Losing a child is the worst thing that can happen to you. Not many marriages can take that kind of strain.'

'Having a child put enough strain on our marriage.'

They protest. 'You were besotted with Stevie! Both of you. And so proud.'

'I loved him more than I've ever loved anyone, ever. But that doesn't mean I was a good mother.'

When I leave Seymour and Katherine's I drive to the cemetery where Stevie is buried. I am surprised by the human traffic here at the end of the day. People with flowers, small groups, women walking alone, an elderly couple hand in hand.

As I approach Stevie's grave, I see a figure standing motionless in the dusky light.

'Scott?'

He swings round. When he sees me his face lightens.

'Luce!'

'I meant to come with you but we just didn't get around to arranging it so . . .'

'I thought the flowers we left on Saturday must be looking pretty dry by now,' he says. 'I just stopped by to tidy up a bit.'

'How often do you come?'

'Once a week, sometimes more.'

We stand before the grave in silence and I look around. Most of the small headstones in the children's cemetery are carved joylessly with nursery images. A teddy bear, a puppy, the man in the moon. It is like a playground which the children have vacated. There is no shade. In summer the sun will bake Stevie's small rectangle of earth, in winter the rain will fall on it. I see that he is unprotected in death as he was in life.

Scott has been waiting for me to comment. Now he prompts me. 'Luce? Do you like it?'

Stevie's little headstone is without the starkness of the newer graves. It reveals only his name and dates.

'Yes,' I say. 'I'm glad you kept it simple and didn't put a teddy bear on it.'

I stare at the grave. I know Scott wants me to cry. I try to cry. I am unmoved. This unyielding monument to Stevie's existence has nothing to do with the kicking, squirming baby which I remember.

Scott says: 'Are you starting to get over Stevie? I am. It's not that I forget him or it doesn't hurt any more but for a long time the grief was sort of physical, like something heavy on my back, and that's all lifted now.'

I squeeze his arm.

'I'm not sure if I've laughed since Stevie died.'

'You mean, since he was born.'

I turn to look at him and he squares his shoulders defensively.

'It's a stage in the grieving process, Lucy. The stage when you become completely honest about the decedent. I've reached it. I admit that I loved him a lot but I didn't enjoy Stevie. Not at all. Right from the beginning it was a shock for both of us. Nothing prepared either of us for the sacrifices and the losses of having a child. That's when I lost you. When he was born.'

When I'm driving home I admit to myself that Stevie's six months was six months of madness. Nothing happened when it was supposed to, nothing got done unless I was far away from him in my office. I forgot things. I lost things. I shrunk the laundry. I burnt the toast. I arrived late. I arrived on the wrong day. And all the time Stevie voiced his objections. I rocked him and it made no difference. I shouted and it made no difference. I sang to him and it made no difference. Eventually I'd stand there while he just filled me up with his noise as though I was an empty beaker. And after he died, I slept for twenty-four hours.

It is late when I finally drive across the bridge and back into the city towards my Russian family. The lights, the smells, the city's constant and purposeful motion, all please me. It is so late that I decide to park right inside the lot and risk antagonism from that unpleasant person and bad neighbour Dimitri Sergeyevich. I have been leaving the car a couple of blocks away in the lot where Mother parked when she brought me, as a child, to visit with Grandma. A man with cross-eyes used to take our money. He exchanged a few routine pleasantries with Mother and this was always the first Russian of the day. I look for him each day but of course both he and the shack he used to sit in have gone now, replaced by a machine.

I drive slowly between intersections, the window down, remembering how I used to walk these streets holding Mother's hand, past the Russian stores and restaurants and the Cyrillic billboards. It is good to hide inside these memories. They are a soft, kind place and in them Mother is barely sick at all.

I held her hand and we walked down these streets and I trusted her. Of course, we never went inside any of the dark doorways or spoke to the groups of men who stood around on street corners speaking Russian. Occasionally a passer-by would say something to Mother but she would not reply.

'Did that man know you?' I asked once.

Mother grasped my hand tightly and marched on. 'No, he's just impertinent.'

'Did you understand him?'

'Of course I did! Only too well!'

'Then why didn't you say something back in Russian?'

'Because this isn't Russia! It's America! We don't speak Russian here.' There was a hysterical edge to her tone which meant it would soon be time to stop asking questions.

'How about the guy in the parking lot?' I inquired cautiously.

'He is too simple to learn English.'

'How about Grandma?'

'Grandma is too old.'

It was useless to point out that Aunt Zina and Sasha and all the aunts and cousins spoke Russian with each other all the time and that, although Sasha had been born here and went to an American school, he would never be so completely an American as Jane and I were.

On our monthly visit to Grandma's house, I watched Mother as first her language changed and then her mouth changed shape to accommodate the language and then gradually the whole of her face and body pupated into someone young and sweet-tempered. The woman who had married Daddy and named all the rock layers in the geology department cake.

Grandma would sometimes talk to me using her few words of heavily accented English but mostly she would smile and hold me and stroke me and coo over me as though I was some much admired, small, tame bird. The aunts spoke better English. Katya and Olya, who had been born after the family's arrival in the USA, could sound almost completely American and their language had all the colloquialisms and inconsistencies that Mother's correct English lacked. They would break off from their Russian conversation to ask me questions and, almost incessantly, they gave me food. I basked in their love and admiration and home-made candies. As I ate I listened to their lyrical language, not understanding a word but feeling an intimate part of their circle. When I left I felt satiated, perhaps with love, perhaps with candy.

'They're stifling, I hate it there,' Jane said. Mother seemed sympathetic to this view and Jane was seldom made to visit Grandma. This was not perceived as a slight: on the contrary, Grandma and the aunts asked constantly about Jane, reminding one another, in broken English for my benefit, of her beauty and cleverness.

And now, here I am again, not a child but a woman, driving not walking, alone and without Mother, passing the shops and billboards and bars of the Russian quarter again, making my way towards Grandma's apartment, although Grandma is long dead and Mother is incarcerated at Redbush clinic for her own safety and possibly others'.

The streets have changed little. Perhaps the shops are brighter, lit by some flickering, far-off reflection of the new Russia, but they are still un-American. There are no groups of men on the corners but when I stop at a light I can hear Russian spoken by a passing couple and the rise and fall of their voices sounds as though they are singing some long, sad song. When I get out of the car the very air of the dark streets, cool after a warm day and a hint of fog thickening the air, seems pregnant with melancholy.

I know now as I knew then that I am about to enter a place where I am loved, unconditionally and uncritically. I hear my feet on the asphalt. Their stride is even. The night lights, the salty air, they please me and make me feel guilty that I ever could have wanted to trade my own family for Seymour and Katherine.

Aunt Zina has already taken her Pushkin and gone to bed but in the kitchen I find a light on.

'Lucia!' His leather jacket slung over a chair, smelling strongly of smoke, sweat and liquor, Sasha is raiding the cookie jar. 'I just got home and thought you must already be asleep. Look, Mama left a meal here for you if you want it.'

'I ate with some friends of Daddy's.'

'What have you been doing today?'

I sink down into a chair near him. Suddenly my legs are weak with fatigue.

'A million things. Mostly Daddy's paperwork.'

'Ah, the good daughter. Analysing figures. Double-checking, cross-referencing. Drawing a neat line at the bottom of her father's page as she closes accounts and terminates pensions.'

'I also found his headstone.'

'Good gracious, wherever was it?'

'In the yard. It says Remember Death. His pals have similar stones too. They think you live your life differently if you remember that you could die any minute.'

'How many pals?'

'Just three of them.'

'The Remember Death club. I love it. Perhaps your father's death leaves a vacancy and they will allow me to join.'

Sasha passes me the cookie jar.

'Why so late? Have you been in a meeting?' I ask.

He smiles mysteriously. 'A most stimulating and fascinating meeting, to which Natasha's contribution was frankly sensational. Wait here, please.'

He disappears from the room and returns with whisky and two glasses.

'Oh no, Sash, it's too late for that and I'm tired.'

'The best talks are tired talks.' The bottle exclaims a little as he pulls the stopper from it. 'And is adding columns of figures so very exhausting for a banker?'

'Adding isn't. Thinking is.'

He fills one glass with ice and we listen to its protests as he pours whisky over it. Then he pushes the glass towards me and lifts his own.

'A toast to Lucia, a loving sister and beloved cousin.'

He touches my glass with his and the two emit a note of religious purity.

'And what have you been thinking about so hard, Lucia?'

'I think I know who killed Daddy.'

He rubs his hands and sits down across the table from me. I sip the whisky and feel its heat run through my body, even to my toes.

'Have you shared this information with anyone else? That charming detective who was supervising on Monday night, for example?'

'I can't tell her. I can't tell anyone.'

'Except for your adoring cousin. How flattering.'

'Sasha, I've lied to everyone. The police, Jane, Scott, even you.'

He raises his eyebrows. 'Sasha can be relied upon to keep your secrets, Lucia.'

'I've told everyone I haven't been to California for three years. But I have. I was here last weekend. Here in San Francisco.'

I didn't enjoy it. I didn't enjoy any of the weekend. From the moment the plane landed, no, from the moment it took off, I was watchful, anxious, that some relative or old schoolfriend might see me. And Kent was so on edge he didn't even sit next to me on the flight. Later, he looked my naked body up and down without warmth and with no indication of admiration and then he pulled me on to the bed. He was a talented and insistent lover. Sex with him was single-minded, pursued by both of us with an energy and determination that excluded love and even lust. Afterwards we lay still, our bodies touching without connecting. A deep loneliness fell across me like darkness. I looked at Kent and wondered if he felt it too but I knew that if he did he could only acknowledge its presence by further sexual adventure.

Whenever the phone rang, he answered it and I leapt up and into the bathroom and turned on the shower because it might have been Mrs Kent calling. Mrs Kent with the blade of a baby swishing and cooing in the background. When the call was over he would switch off the shower and say: 'You can come out now.' He wrapped me in one of the big, soft hotel towels and I mistook this manoeuvre for affection. Only now, sitting in Aunt Zina's apartment with its smells and dust, do I recognize that here I am loved. I am loved by Aunt Zina and Aunt Zoya and Sasha and Jane and Larry and Scott. I am wrapped up in their love like a bug in a curling leaf and I know I never should have chosen to mistake hotel laundry for affection.

Sasha raises his eyebrows.

'But why did you do this thing with this man?'

'I don't know, Sash.'

Once, when Kent had fallen asleep and my isolation threatened to engulf me, I went to the bathroom, picked up Kent's razor and drew it across my thigh. I watched a thin, red line open immediately behind it like the vapour trail which follows a jet. A moment later, the pain came. It was so intense that it absorbed my loneliness like a sponge.

'Do you care for him?'

'No. I couldn't come back here with him on the third anniversary of my baby's death if I did. And, I mean, it's an unprofessional relationship. It shouldn't have happened because we're negotiating a deal and my clients are called the Hifelds and their interests, not my sexual needs, are supposed to come first. That's why I was wrong. Kent was wrong because Mittex fosters a clean, family image and expects its executives to behave that way. Especially its soon-to-be chief executive. Kent's paranoid about someone finding out, first his wife, then his colleagues. End of marriage, end of job. That's why I told the police I was home all weekend.'

The whisky is heating my whole body now. It warms my

mouth, my head, my toes, my fingers. It insulates me from the night's falling temperature. 'But it wasn't the only reason.'

Late on Sunday morning Kent left to spend the day with a regional manager visiting stores. As soon as he had gone I hired a car and drove to the cemetery. I trod cautiously, scanning the faces of the living who haunted the place for any who might know me, barely noticing the mighty trees or the monuments. Then I reached Stevie's plain little grave. In life Stevie was surrounded by complication: the elaborate crib, the changing table, the ergonomic buggy, the breast pump, the bottle-warmer. Now I sobbed and sobbed at the stone's simplicity and its smooth perfection. There were small bouquets arranged lovingly around it. I sobbed as I placed one pink rose at the base of the stone, little more than a bud with a promise of beauty to follow. I sobbed as I walked back to the parking lot. I sobbed as I drove to Daddy's house.

I could have called him. I wish now I had called him and visited in the normal way, except nothing was normal that day. Daddy would have asked about Kent, expected to meet him, begged me to stay. He might have called Jane and Larry and Scott and invited them over. After three years my return would have been an event.

'Your reluctance to see Uncle Eric is understandable, Lucia. Please stop trying to justify it.'

'But, Sash, I had to see him. Whenever I spoke to him or to Jane I felt as though there was something they weren't telling me. Or maybe, I knew I wouldn't let them tell me, that I hadn't listened to them. Occasionally they'd mention his hip. Or Jane would say casually that he was getting forgetful. Or I'd think his voice was rasping or notice that his handwriting was sort of shaky. And then I wouldn't think about it any more because it was too painful, because Daddy was supposed to be a rock, not an old man. So when I drove out to the house on Sunday, I just wanted to look at him. I just wanted to reassure myself that he was still okay.'

'You planned to see him without him seeing you?'

'Does it sound crazy?'

'No.'

'I parked my car way down in the valley in case any neighbours were about and I walked up an old trail we used when we were kids, around people's lots, up through the Holler orchard. It was pretty damp and dirty and overgrown and by the time I decided to give up I was almost there so I carried right on. I sneaked around to the back of the house and flipped through the rails on to the deck just the way I used to flip through them when I was a kid.'

'Lucia, Lucia, you are so very smart that you take me aback. What seemed like the whim of a bereaved daughter on Monday night – to stare across the valley from her father's deck – was an act calculated to mislead the police fingerprint expert.'

I blush.

'You have impressed Sasha. While Sasha was steadfastly refusing to provide his fingerprints you were taking pains to litter the place with yours. But why, on visiting your father, did you choose to climb, flip, on to the deck?'

'Because I figured that early on Sunday afternoon Daddy might be in the living-room, reading or listening to music or something.'

'And was he?'

'He was in the living-room. But he wasn't alone. There was someone with him and they were having a fight. I mean, Daddy wasn't fighting. The other guy was. His voice was raised and he was standing right over Daddy in a threatening way.'

'Who was he?'

'I don't know. He was tall, a little younger than me, but not much. He had jeans, dark hair, a dark face because he didn't look like he'd shaved in a while.' Sasha smiles and runs a hand across his own stubbly chin. 'I didn't get much chance to look at him because this guy saw me within a few seconds. He leapt towards me, came right after me without one moment's hesitation. I jumped down from the deck and then ran around the barn. I could hear him looking for me. He was shouting. God, Sash, it was terrifying. I thought my heart was going to burst. I ran the heel off my shoe. He went around the other way and that meant I could slip along the bushes by the drive and down by the Holler orchard while he was still running around the sunken garden yelling for me as though he wanted to kill me. It wasn't until I got back to the car that I realized I wasn't a criminal and didn't have to behave like one. I mean, it's my father's house for heaven's sake. But I felt like a hunted animal.'

'And, your papa?'

Daddy, a moving figure half-glimpsed through the big sliding doors from the deck. The last Daddy before the cold, stitched effigy of him at the mortuary.

'I hardly saw him. Mostly he looked shocked.'

'Perhaps by the intrusion?'

'Or by this guy, yelling at him, standing right over him. Oh Sash, if I'd called him and visited in the usual way, I would have seen him before he died. I might have saved his life.'

Sasha reaches out and covers my hand with his.

'If your supposition is correct that this young man's anger threatened Uncle Eric's life. Is there no way of identifying him?'

'When I was running away through Daddy's yard I saw

259

something out of the corner of my eye parked right outside the barn. I didn't get a second look but I'm almost certain it was a tow truck, an old, chrome one. It must have been his. That didn't give me much to go on, until the woman detective arrived talking about a tow truck . . .'

I tell him about Officer Howie and he strokes his chin the way Larry strokes his beard. Then I tell him how I discovered the old tow truck at Big Brim, how its driver, a man, tall, dark-haired, knew himself to be followed, and escaped.

'He is at least running away from you now, rather than the other way around.'

'I think he ran away twice today. The second time was at the house. He sneaked in, saw me there and took off. A little later, I saw a tow truck driving away through the valley.'

'I wonder why he flees. Still, he cannot escape much longer. At Big Brim you took the number of the tow truck and a few letters of the garage's name? Fetch that, Lucia, and with the help of the Yellow Pages we shall see if the letters fit the names of any garages. It will be like a crossword puzzle and I may say, without false modesty, that I excel at crosswords.'

I stand up and my legs surprise me when they almost buckle under me.

'It's in the car.'

'Two blocks away!'

'Well, no. I was so tired that I parked downstairs tonight. I planned to leave in the morning before Dimitri Sergeyevich wakes up.'

'He never sleeps, that one. He maintains a twenty-four-hour vigil over his small domain. However, I will accompany you, we will collect our information swiftly and return before he has even found his slippers.'

We let ourselves out of the apartment and summon the

rumbling elevator. The coolness of the night air shocks me and I stumble a little when I first inhale it. Sasha steadies me.

'I wrote it on the back of the map the hirecar company supplies. It's just on the passenger seat,' I say, lifting the papers and files which I left there. But beneath them is no map. Sasha waits, stamping a little in the night's coolness the way he stamped on Monday outside Daddy's house. I search through the papers, assuming the map is entangled with them. But it is not. It is neither on, under or behind the seat and it is not in the glove compartment.

'Think, Lucia, think. Could you have left it at your father's house?'

'No, I haven't taken it out of the car . . .'

I sit sideways in the car, my feet hanging out. I remember parking right by the tow truck, walking all around it, writing down the number, examining the faded letters which remained on the door, copying them on to the back of the map. Then I thrust the map on to the passenger seat, ran across the road, and at last there were the sand dunes, strewn at the roadside with old, dry litter, and sand was trickling through the crevices in my toes and I was running hard uphill at the speed of a slow walk.

I close my eyes. There is a brief silence between throwing the map in the car and crossing the road and I try to fill it now with the click of a lock closing. I massage my memory, I pummel at it, I punch it, I kick it. But it cannot supply the click. I recall my return to the car, hot, dishevelled, breathless, staring up and down the blacktop as though it might give me some clue to the direction the tow truck turned. I search for, but cannot find, the click of the lock opening.

'Perhaps it was removed from your car outside your father's house? The tow truck driver was there today.'

'Maybe.'

'I expect it is upstairs in your purse,' Sasha suggests, leading me back into the building. 'In our house, most things which went missing could eventually be found in my wife's purse, even, on one occasion, the cat.'

In the kitchen, our glasses full again, we search my purse.

'No cat?' asks Sasha.

'No cat. That guy. The tow truck driver. He stole it. He saw it lying on the passenger seat and he stole it.'

'But –'

'It wasn't too difficult. Because I think I forgot to lock the car.'

'And did you park next to the tow truck?'

'Yes.'

'On the driver's side?'

'Yes.'

'So this man walked past your car and saw details about his truck prominently displayed inside it and the door unlocked. Naturally, he decided to confiscate them. Well, he obviously isn't stupid. Now, if you had the number of this truck then I would suggest that you handed it over at once to the police for tracing. But since you do not . . .'

'I couldn't hand it over without telling them about last weekend. Except now, one of them has found out.'

I tell Sasha about Rougemont. How he confronted me with my own shoes.

'You lied to them not just to protect Kent but to protect your family from the knowledge that you visited San Francisco without seeing them. Your untruth looks suspicious but, apart from allowing yourself to be seduced by an unfeeling brute, you have done nothing wrong.'

I look at him and he seems to be dancing. I realize that Sasha is still but my eyes are losing and regaining focus.

'Sasha, when someone dies, should you keep their secrets?'

'Most certainly every attempt should be made to maintain privacy. But this is seldom the case. Lucia, do you suspect that your papa had secrets?'

'The tow truck driver was sort of a secret. Daddy knew him but he didn't tell me about him. He didn't tell Jane.'

'You think he had some significance in Uncle Eric's life?'

'I don't know. But if I set the police on to him, Daddy's secrets could come spilling right out.'

Sasha sips his whisky and rolls it over his teeth with pleasure before swallowing it.

'So, you prefer to clarify the situation yourself. Well, Lucia, proceed if you must. But I advise you to proceed with caution.'

25

Jane calls me early on Saturday to say that the police want to see us at Daddy's house. My mouth is dry and my head parched and rattling like a bone which has been left to bleach in the sun.

'Kirsty wants to see all of us, Scott too.'

'But weren't we going there anyway?'

'They asked to meet us at ten.'

I sigh. 'Don't they even rest on the weekend?'

'God knows when Kirsty rests. She has small kids.'

'What about Rougemont?'

She pauses. 'I don't know about Rougemont. I get the feeling he lives alone. And apparently he's away so he won't be there today.'

When I go down to the car there is an altercation with Dimitri Sergeyevich in two languages although we each understand only one. His furious cadences ringing in my ears, I drive away. I stop before I reach the bridge to pick up another coffee.

When I arrive, Scott's car and Larry's are already there, side by side. Scott's car is nondescript because Scott doesn't much like cars or driving. Larry's is long and low and sleek. He not only likes cars but he enjoys buying them, poring over product details and accessories, comparing models, arguing with salesmen over the price. Daddy loved teasing Larry about his expensive cars. Once they pulled up alongside each other at stop lights and Daddy claims the Oldsmobile burned Larry right off.

Scott is pleased to see me. He has already thumbed through the letters I left on Daddy's desk for him to sign.

Jane puts an arm around me and kisses me lightly on the cheek. 'Sorry I couldn't get here yesterday. I hope everything was okay.'

If I tell her that there might have been an intruder who might have driven a tow truck then she'll get that thin, worried look. She'll ask questions and make calls and lift the whole situation right out of my hands. I say: 'Everything was fine.'

'What's cooking?' I ask Larry, sniffing the warm, spicy air, knowing that if someone's already been at work in the kitchen then it must be Larry.

'Paella,' says Larry modestly. 'This recipe is supposed to take twenty-four hours and I'm doing it in three so don't expect too much.'

But the paella will, of course, be good. Mostly Larry and Jane eat out with friends but, when they're at home, Larry usually cooks. He says it helps him to unwind. If Jane gets back late from the hospital there's invariably a fine meal waiting for her. She eats it by herself while Larry works or watches TV. Then she reads the newspaper. When she's had about an hour alone, Larry comes in and they talk. It's hard to imagine how their lives would have been if Jane had been able to have children, how she would have coped without that hour, whether it would have been hard to give up expensive vacations, a busy social life, scores of friends. Maybe they couldn't imagine it either because when children didn't happen they decided not to seek help and they didn't consider adoption. And when I saw Jane with Stevie, I understood that maybe she never was meant to be a mother. She loved him a lot but their relationship was limited by her professionalism.

'What's this?' asks Scott, picking up a yellowing newspaper cutting from the desk.

I try to pull it away from him. 'Nothing really, I found it in Daddy's drawer . . .'

But Scott has opened it out and is already reading: Wedding News. Marriage of Dr R. D. Joseph and Miss K. K. Sylvester.

Jane shoots me a rapid, penetrating look.

'Did you know?' she asks.

I shrug. 'No, but why should I care? I haven't spoken to him for years and years.'

By now Scott has recognized the groom's name as one he doesn't like. I see his jaw clench and his body stiffen.

Jane gestures at Wedding News. 'We thought it was better not to tell you,' she says, and while I'm still deciding whether my reply should be aggressive or defensive, Larry asks: 'Who is he?'

'Robert Joseph, Lucy's teenage heart-throb,' Jane explains.

'The one she always wished she'd married,' adds Scott bitterly. I made the mistake once of telling him how much Robert had meant to me. It was soon after I met Scott, when we both knew we were embarking on an important relationship and thought we should tell about all the other important relationships.

'I wish I could take up the space Robert Joseph takes up in your heart,' Scott said then. 'But I never will.'

'That's ridiculous!' I told him.

He made the same observation several more times, even after we married, and, although I always denied it, a small part of me agreed with him and Scott somehow knew that.

He has turned away from me now and is heading out of the den saying something about coffee. I want to ask Jane how old the newspaper cutting is and whether she has ever encountered Robert at the hospital, or if she heard his father died, but I cannot now betray an interest.

Larry has been watching us all keenly, stroking his beard, possibly enjoying himself. He seems about to comment when there is a voice at the door. Kirsty is here.

We lead her to the kitchen and she pauses for a moment. 'Wow, something smells good,' she says.

Larry is apologetic. 'It won't be ready until lunchtime. But if you're still here, then please join us.'

'I sure wish I could,' she says and she means it. She's thinking about the dried-up sandwich she's likely to eat for lunch. Probably she was home late last night, and probably she doesn't have a cooking husband like Larry, so it was another dried-up sandwich then too.

Kirsty is about to tell us why she's here when Larry says: 'Kirsty, there's something I'm still worried about . . .' and Kirsty looks at him evenly, without any sense of anticipation as though she's going to hear his worry but not share it.

Jane groans. 'Larry, you're wasting Kirsty's time.'

'No,' insists Larry, 'I think this is important. The guy I told you about. He was there again last night. I think he's hanging around outside our apartment. He could be following Jane.'

'He's probably hanging around because of Gerry downstairs,' says Jane. 'There are always guys hanging around because of Gerry.'

Gerry is absurdly attractive and has a complicated love life.

'What makes you think he's following Jane?' asks Kirsty.

'Last night she drove over to the Walrus House to check that everything's okay for Tuesday.' There is to be a buffet lunch at Daddy's home after the funeral and the Walrus House is catering it. Their food is good, although Jane worries it may be too adventurous for some of the guests. 'The guy disappeared when Jane left. Then, when Jane came back, he came back.'

'How late did he stay? All night?'

Larry's eyes flick from side to side. 'Well, I'm not sure what time he actually went. But of course he was gone in the morning.'

Kirsty pulls out her notebook and asks Larry to describe the man. Tall, dark-haired, generally unshaven.

'How old is he?' I ask.

Larry finds it difficult to judge the age of anyone under fifty.

'Thirty?' he suggests hopefully. 'Twenty-five?'

'Okay,' agrees Kirsty. 'We'll take a look.' Nothing in her tone indicates whether she shares Larry's concern.

'Don't waste too much valuable police time,' Jane tells her. 'I'm sure Larry's wrong about this and Gerry would never forgive us if we drove away an admirer.'

'He has plenty of other admirers,' says Larry.

Kirsty reaches into her bag and pulls out a small plastic sack, half-covered by labelling, which I read upside down: case number, officer in charge, date . . .

'You've found Daddy's keys!' Jane exclaims.

The woman nods. She pulls them out of the sack and lays them on the table.

'Take them. Tell me if you think they're all here.'

Jane picks up the ring. I recognize it as the kitschy key-ring I bought Daddy when he came to New York. It features a tiny Empire State Building. You can press the end and a light flashes at the top. It's a flashlight and key-ring in one and I am absurdly pleased to find that Daddy used it every day. I want to touch it but Jane has spread the keys out evenly on the table around the ring as though we're playing poker and she's showing us a royal flush.

'I don't recognize them all . . .' she says, 'but this is the door, car, barn, our apartment, maybe a suitcase key . . . did he have a key to your house, Scott?'

'Uh-huh, since I went to France last Christmas. It's right here . . .' Scott points at the key to the beach house. I didn't know he'd been to France. I guess he went with Brigitte.

Jane continues: 'Not sure about that one. Or that one, but that one must be the tractor. Well, as far as I know, nothing's missing.'

'Where did you find them?' Scott asks the detective.

'With the kids who took the Oldsmobile from the Big Brim parking lot on Monday morning.'

'Kids stole Eric's car?'

'Nice kids who live in Lowis and never stole a car before. One of them had a little brother who told.'

I remember the boy who sat astride his skateboard, wheeling himself backwards and forwards with his feet flat on the ground, the one who glared at me from under his crewcut.

'It wasn't too hard to extract the keys. They couldn't give us the note, though. They hadn't kept that.'

We look at her, waiting.

'Note?' says Jane at last. 'What note hadn't they kept?'

'I can show you. We actually have our own copy.'

She reaches into her notebook and pulls out a sheet of paper with a few lines printed on it. She reads: 'To my daughters . . .' I hear her voice as though I'm under anaesthetic and can feel no pain. 'To my daughters. I'd like you to remember me as a strong man, not old and shuffling and helpless. So I've chosen to leave you now and I hope you'll see that this is a brave act and an act of great love. Jane, Lucy, I love you both very much. If I've done my job properly then you should be fine without me. Lucy, when you feel very alone, I know Jane will be there for you. With much love, Daddy.'

I look around at the shocked, pale faces. I guess I must be shocked and pale too. Jane's fingers play some silent tune on the table top. Larry holds his beard tightly in one hand. Scott is motionless.

'We should have known about this letter before,' says Larry at last.

'The copy in the stolen car was lost and we've only just accessed it on Professor Schaffer's computer.' She looks at Jane. 'Thanks for all the passwords you suggested, none of them worked, but we finally got around it. This is what we found.' Kirsty looks from face to face. 'So, what's your reaction to this letter? Does it sound like the Professor Schaffer you knew?'

'Well . . . I guess so . . .' says Jane.

Larry nods gravely. Scott is silent.

I take the paper from her and study it.

'No,' I say.

The detective turns to me. 'You don't think he wrote it?'

'No.'

'What makes you so sure?' Kirsty watches me keenly.

'Well . . .' He would have written us separate letters. I would have received a note with my name on it which was only for me, signed: Daddy. 'Well, he just didn't.'

'Is it the words? The way he uses them?'

I study the letter.

'He didn't write it,' I say stubbornly. 'This isn't how he would have done it.'

She turns to Scott.

'What's your reaction?' she asks. She half smiles encouragement but he remains stony-faced.

'Lucy hadn't seen Eric in a long time,' he says. 'Maybe the Eric she left behind wouldn't have written this but the Eric he became – sort of older, worried, burdened – well, I mean, it's highly unlikely . . . but sometimes he didn't say a lot. You didn't know what he was thinking. Maybe this is what he was thinking in all those silences.'

I shake my head but Scott does not look at me and the woman turns to Larry.

'You have a certain professional insight here, I'd be grateful for your comments,' she tells him. He moistens his lips a little with his tongue.

'This letter has the kind of balance I'd expect from Eric. He's perceptive about each daughter. He correctly assumes that Lucy needs extra reassurance and he correctly assumes that Jane will be there to provide this. He anticipates their possible reactions – angry, hurt – and tries to deal with them. He doesn't dwell on the doubts or difficulties or fears he must have experienced facing death because the whole note is designed to alleviate his daughters' suffering. I'd say the letter is the selfless and well-reasoned work of a selfless, reasoning man and therefore I think it's genuine.'

'Thank you. Jane?'

Jane stares at the letter with red eyes. She opens her mouth to speak but instead she starts to cry. I watch, fascinated and shocked. I have seldom seen her cry and never like this. Her features are habitually still, even when she speaks, but now they are in motion. Her jaw pumps with a soundless rhythm, her eyes are red and her cheeks swell. When she throws her head back the tears run into her hair and ears. Sobs shake her entire body like electric shocks. I want to jump up and hug her but Larry has already put his arms around her.

The detective watches dispassionately.

'Are you crying,' she asks, when the sobs finally begin to subside, 'because you believe he really killed himself?'

Jane, her voice transformed into something strange and tremulous, says: 'Isn't this proof?'

'Oh no,' says the detective, looking sharply around at all of us. 'No, it isn't. I don't believe Professor Schaffer wrote this note or knew of its existence. It was the last document stored in his computer and it was dated 4.08 on Sunday afternoon. After analysing the keyboard, our forensic department said that whoever used the keyboard last, and it's reasonable to assume that it was last used at 4.08 on Sunday afternoon, wore ordinary domestic rubber gloves. We think it unlikely your father would have typed his suicide note wearing rubber gloves. So probably, although not necessarily, whoever killed Professor Schaffer was here, at this house, at 4.08 on Sunday afternoon.'

There is a silence. I feel the hairs on the back of my neck bristle as though someone's standing right behind me. Kirsty looks around at us to gauge our reactions. There is no reaction. No one moves.

'Did Eric know someone was here on Sunday?' asks Scott, his voice hollow, as though it's not his real voice but an echo.

Kirsty shrugs. 'We don't know what Professor Schaffer was doing Sunday afternoon.'

'Didn't anyone see anything on Sunday?' Scott persists. 'A neighbour, a friend . . . ?'

Kirsty looks at all of us but perhaps particularly at me when she says: 'If they did, no one's telling us about it.'

I look at my watch, involuntarily, to calculate what time I hid on the deck on Sunday. Kent left the hotel at eleven, I went to the cemetery, drove to the valley, walked up the hill . . . maybe one-thirty. Less than three hours before Daddy's killer. At four o'clock, the killer, displaying detailed knowledge of his victim's life and family, was right here in the den typing a fake suicide note. I dig my fingernails into my palm. My knuckles are drained of colour.

'Yes, Lucy?' The detective is looking right at me. I jump a little. 'Were you about to say something?'

I shake my head.

Kirsty continues: 'You've asked me a few times how Professor Schaffer died. Well, we have good although not conclusive evidence that he was electrocuted.'

'Oh!' says a woman, her voice half a breath, half an exclamation. Did the oh belong to Jane or me? I look at Jane and she is staring intently at the detective. Kirsty seems to be inside my head, saying over and over, he was electrocuted. We have good but not conclusive evidence that he was electrocuted.

'He was electrocuted,' repeats Larry, and the word seems to reverberate around the room now. Jim Bob Holler who lived next door was electrocuted. He was only fourteen. His father didn't wire the swimming-pool lights properly and he died when he dived into the pool.

'It was an accident,' I blurt out. Everyone turns to me in surprise.

'When Jim Bob Holler got electrocuted in the swimming-pool it was an accident,' I explain.

Kirsty regards me with interest. 'It's hard to see how Dr Schaffer's death could have been an accident.'

'How sure are you of this?' asks Jane.

'Professor Rossi and the ME, Dr Angela Ball, are both prepared to stake their reputations on it.'

Dr Ball. Fine perfume, jewellery which chatters softly like a whispering chorus as she moves among the dead.

'Tissue analysis of a small blister on your father's neck seems to indicate that it was the site of a massive electric shock. Professor Schaffer instantly had a heart attack.'

Kirsty reaches into her bag and produces a small black box. She lays it flat in the palm of her hand and holds it out to us.

'You've probably seen this kind of thing. Stun guns and tasers are widely marketed for self-defence purposes. You can buy them over the counter. This is a taser. You only have to touch someone with the probes and you can override their central nervous system. Their muscle tissues contract uncontrollably and for maybe thirty minutes they can see, hear and even feel but they're incapable of carrying out any controlled movements. Tasers have a one hundred per cent drop rate. Stun guns are similar but more primitive. They shoot up to five hundred thousand volts into the body, which leaves the victim weak, dazed and confused.'

We stare at the taser. It looks like a flashlight, or maybe an electric razor. Larry says, his voice stripped of its usual certainty: 'Which was used on Eric?'

'Probably a taser.'

'So,' says Larry, 'Eric was touched with one of these things and left in the water. Unable to save himself.'

Daddy, plummeting down the rocks at Seal Wash, feeling the spray, hearing the roar of the sea getting closer, the water closing over him, powerless to struggle or swim.

'No,' says Scott, 'that's what his killer intended. Eric would have drowned and his death would have looked like suicide. But the taser gave him a heart attack. Before he hit the water. That's how you know it's a homicide.'

Kirsty nods assent. She looks around each of us in turn.

'Do you have any questions?' she asks. She smiles, not a broad smile but a receptive one.

I don't know how my face got covered with my fingers. I have to move them now to ask: 'Does it hurt?'

Before Kirsty can speak, Jane says: 'Oh Lucy, probably electrocution isn't too painful. And you know, death, any death, is almost certainly a pleasant experience. Imagine slipping away into total relaxation.'

Larry says: 'You'd probably be too stunned to feel pain.'

'Maybe not,' Kirsty tells him. 'Certainly people report that tasers cause pain to the point of nausea.'

I close my eyes.

'Do you have any more questions?' Kirsty repeats.

We shake our heads. We don't have any more questions. I get up.

'I need some fresh air,' I say.

I go out to the deck but the air here is not fresh. It is stale and unmoving as though the valley just exhaled it. My eye follows the roads, the tracks, the orchards to find its usual landmarks but they bring no comfort.

26

When the detective has gone she leaves a silence in the house which is like a blanket. We work and eat and talk but the silence never fully goes away. It makes us edgy. We glance out of windows frequently, jump at small sounds and ask ourselves if that was really just the house creaking.

'Does anyone know anything about the Marcello Trust?' I ask at lunchtime. They shake their heads.

'Did Daddy know anyone called Marcello?'

Jane thinks and then shakes her head. 'Doesn't mean a thing to me.'

'Try his address book,' suggests Larry. Even he is subdued.

'I have. I've tried the bank, the accountant, the phone book, a list of charitable trusts, Daddy's files . . .'

'Sorry. Can't help,' says Jane. Larry passes around more paella. We all compliment him on it again. I drop a fork. Everyone jumps. Scott asks a few questions about rocks and I snap at him then feel bad when he explains that he and Larry are trying to concentrate Daddy's whole collection in just one place for the geologists Jane has invited from the university to inspect it.

All afternoon we work in different rooms. The front door is double-locked. Larry sorts out boxes upstairs and, if they have rocks in, he pulls them into the hallway for Scott to move to the barn. Jane won't let Larry lift rocks because he has back problems. She has started to sort through all the stuff in an upstairs bedroom near him.

When I'm tired of bending over files in the den I make everyone a cold drink.

I find Larry busy marking rock boxes with a red pen.

'Thanks, just leave it there,' he tells me.

I linger at the door.

'Why would someone be stalking Jane?' I ask him.

He looks up.

'You might be asking for a rational explanation for disturbed behaviour,' he tells me.

'Maybe it's some crazy patient from the hospital.'

'Maybe. I just know we can't take any chances right now, Lucy. I personally feel that the Schaffer family is under some kind of threat. Eric's dead, the house has been entered. All we can do is stay alert and that's why I want Kirsty to check this guy out.'

Jane has closed the door of her old bedroom. I pause outside, watching the ice circling in her drink. When we were kids I was only allowed into Jane's room if I knocked or if she asked me. I used to hang around outside hoping she'd invite me in. It was full of pretty things like a shell collection and a patchwork bed cover, and the shelves were stacked with books which had no pictures.

I knock. I don't open the door until I hear Jane's voice. She is standing among columns of fat cardboard boxes as though she's lost in a forest.

'I closed the door because of the dust,' she explains.

I squeeze in shyly. The bedcover's still here, paler than I remember it, and, just visible between some of the boxes, I see the shell collection.

'What have you found?' I ask, passing her the drink.

'Nothing but junk.'

'What sort of junk?'

'Oh, you know. Old High School yearbooks, diaries with

277

no entries past January six, dolls with broken arms, clothes you thought were so great you couldn't throw them away even though they were worn out, clothes you never wore at all, photos of people you don't even remember, a camera which I meant to get fixed but never did, a leash which must have belonged to Nickel Dog . . . junk.'

'Are you really throwing away your High School yearbooks?' She pulls a face.

'Yes.'

'What are you keeping?'

'Nothing.'

'But won't we want something to remind us? Just a few things? The Schaffer family won't be here any more. Nothing of ours will be here.'

Jane puts down the drink and begins to shuffle through the contents of the box right in front of her. She waves an old cut-out book that no one ever cut out. Pin the Clothes on the Doll.

'I don't need anything to remind me. There's already too much of it inside my head.'

I say: 'I know what you mean. Stuff from the past, people, things that happened, it all keeps sort of jumping out on me like some crazy dog. Like Nickel Dog.'

Jane giggles, a half giggle. She's often told me how Nickel Dog used to jump on me. 'He'd knock you right over but mostly he was being affectionate.'

'I think I remember when he died.'

'You do? I'm not sure how old you were.'

'What happened?'

'I just found him on the porch steps dead one evening and Daddy said he'd been poisoned. The Carmichaels around the hill were having big coyote problems and they'd put down some poison so we assumed . . .'

I speak quickly. 'I remember that, Jane. I remember Mother crying. Daddy had Nickel Dog all wrapped up in a blanket. He was carrying the body to the sunken garden. And I ran past the tow truck and down the yard to some den that I'd made with Lindy Zacarro. And Lindy was right there, too.'

Jane smiles apologetically.

'You've imagined that.'

'No, I see it so clearly!'

'Lucy, we didn't let you see the body, not even wrapped up in a blanket. And Daddy buried him when it was dark, after you were asleep.'

'But I remember! Daddy was carrying the blanket down the steps . . .'

'Sure you remember. You remember the way you imagined it.'

Rougemont said: it's easy to confuse what actually happened with things you've been told and things you've dreamed. It's good, real good, that you recognize how unreliable memory is.

I look past Jane out of the window. Once you had a clear view along the drive from Jane's room and mine but now the trees have grown so close that their thin fingers almost tap on the glass.

'I guess you're right,' I say. Nickel Dog's death was no memory but a tapestry I wove from recent events. It was a blooming of buried dog and crying mother from seeds dropped by Rougemont. It was an acknowledgement of the previously forgotten information that Daddy once owned a tow truck. It was a small dirge for my long ago friendship with Lindy Zacarro. It had the colour and texture of memory but it was impure. It was nothing more than a fabrication.

Scott is in the barn now. When I step off the porch and

279

out from under the trees the sun ambushes me. I push my way through its light and heat slowly, as though I'm walking through water.

The barn is big and red like barns in story-books. That pleased me when I was a kid although when the door opened it became a huge cavern which swallowed sound and was impenetrable to light, and that scared me.

Scott has bolted the small door from the inside. I bang with my foot.

'Who's there?' he yells. He sounds nervous. When he unlocks it I stare into the barn's great blackness.

'Bolt it behind you,' he instructs me. I can hear his words retreating with him into the body of the barn.

'Scott, where are you?'

'Right here!'

'I can't see a thing . . . why don't you turn the light on?'

'I have! It's just the sun outside's so bright you have to wait for your eyes to adjust.'

The tractor is the first thing to materialize. Daddy spent hours underneath it, smelling of oil, spanners clanging, until eventually there would be the sound of a loud, rumbling motor as though the whole barn was just about to drive away.

'Oh boy,' I say, shaking my head as gradually everything else appears. Outdoor stuff like sacks and machines and logs and lumber, Daddy stuff like tools and nails. Old bed frames, machines, or parts of machines, planks and squares of wood and wheels. Boxes, some labelled with rock names. Scott is surrounded by them. When I hand him the drink I see he is dusty and wet with sweat. He gulps it greedily.

'I can't believe you still get mad about Robert Joseph after all this time,' I say. He doesn't stop drinking but he grimaces at me over the top of the glass.

'I mean, you go off to France with Brigitte and you still get mad about some boyfriend who I haven't seen since I was eighteen. For heaven's sake.'

He puts down the empty glass and gasps for air. 'It was the strange way it ended with that Robert guy,' he says. 'Inconclusively. You never were able to slam the door shut on the way you felt about him.'

'I haven't thought about Robert for years and years.'

He shrugs and bends over a box. 'Then why did you fish out the report of his wedding?'

I pick up the glass and mutter something about sorting through Daddy's desk, finding all kinds of things. My words seem to get lost in the barn's vast, gloomy interior.

'Whenever we made love,' says Scott, 'it was like you weren't really there. Not all of you.'

I am surprised and hurt. I look at him and I can see him clearly now. His face is shining with sweat.

'But I thought you enjoyed it! I thought it was good!' I protest. 'I mean . . .' I add honestly. 'Before Stevie was born.' Afterwards, there was almost no sex.

Scott's voice softens a little. 'Luce, we had great sex but not the greatest. Because a small part of you just wasn't there.'

I think of lying in the downtown hotel with Kent, crying silently into the dark while he slept. I think of the line, smooth as red ink, which followed his razor across my thigh. When Kent and I had sex, neither of us was there.

I say: 'I don't know what you're talking about.'

'Sure you do, Luce. There was always something missing. And Robert Joseph had it. You gave it to him years ago and you never asked for it back. That's why I still get mad about him.'

Later, much later, when the square of sky over Daddy's

den has turned pink and then pale blue and then deepened to black, I stretch and yawn. The house is still because the others are all out in the barn now, organizing hundreds of rock boxes. They even had to move the tractor to make more space. It started first time, roaring lustily as Larry drove it outside and parked it by the barn and when he switched off it sounded reluctant, like a dog who really wanted to take a walk.

I straighten the desk. In one corner is Wedding News where it has lain haphazardly just as it was left this morning. I hope everyone has noticed that it has been untouched by me all day. Since they are outside, I take one last glance at it. The bride's antique lace. Robert's hand, just visible on her shoulder. And then, something from further down the page leaps out at me. Marcello. The name I have been looking for is right here. When Seymour first gave it to me there was a familiarity about it: I'd read it here, in the list of guests at Robert's wedding. B. Marcello.

Someone walks right past the open door of the den. I hope they didn't see me looking at Wedding News. I put it hastily away. I thumb through the phone book but none of the Marcellos is a B. A possibility occurs to me that makes my heart beat faster. I could drive down into the valley to the Joseph house. I could ask Mrs Joseph about B. Marcello. Maybe she'll even have heard of the Marcello Trust.

I go out to the deck. A big insect flies right past me on some private route home. I know it only from the displacement of the air, the buzz of its wings. I look across the long, dark ocean that is the valley. A couple of car lights. A few farmhouses.

A rustle close by makes me jump nervously. Then I see that Jane is already here, sitting on a wooden chair with her feet up on the railings.

'It sure is a warm night,' she says. 'I mean, it would be a warm night in the summertime. In March, it's ridiculous.'

I sit down next to her and we stare out into the darkness.

'I wish you could stay here a while after the funeral and help with everything,' she says.

'I can stay until the end of next week. But no longer, Jane. There's this deal and I'm losing it fast . . .'

'Sure,' she says quickly, quietly. 'Of course, Luce. It was selfish of me to ask. It's just I'm tired and when I'm tired I allow myself to get overwhelmed by all there is to do.'

Her voice is helpless, sad. 'No, I'm being selfish, not you,' I say. 'I'll try to come back real soon.'

'But what about your deal?'

I shrug. 'I've probably already lost it. And there'll be other deals.'

I see the lights of an airplane flashing. I cannot hear the drone of its engine as it begins its high journey across the valley.

'Do you remember the time Lindy Zacarro and I walked right out into the valley?' I ask Jane. 'Right to the Sturmer Orchards?'

'Boy, I was worried, you were gone so long.'

'I was real good friends with Lindy. Except at the end. I had some kind of argument with her and she died before we could make it up. So I always felt real guilty.'

'Why did you argue?'

'Can't remember.'

'Probably something to do with Mother,' says Jane. 'I mean, Lindy always wanted to play here.'

I nod. 'Mother made almost any friendship impossible because you never knew what she was going to do. Even when she was between breaks you never knew what she was going to do.'

There were times during vacations, and sometimes they lasted for a week or two before our participation collapsed and we were alone again, when we roamed the hillside with the other kids, building camps and declaring war. Lindy, Davis and Carter Zacarro. The Carmichaels. Phyllis Schneck. The Dimoto triplets. Jim Bob Holler and sometimes his big brother, the Spelmanns, Miranda and Michael. But we always had to pull out of the group as soon as they indicated they wanted to come to our house. Then once, they did. All of them, maybe twelve or thirteen kids. Mother produced a big jug of Kool-Aid and set out some cupcakes but the Kool-Aid was undiluted and the cupcakes were just dough. All the kids sat there without saying a word. Then when she left the room, they started laughing. I didn't know whether to laugh with them or maintain an embarrassed but loyal silence.

'And when she was just sinking down into psychosis again,' adds Jane, 'we knew exactly what she'd do. That time all the local kids came by and Mother was feeling real bad and we were sort of creeping around the hallways . . .'

'Oh, I remember creeping.' Don't wake Mother, don't annoy Mother, don't upset that delicate, intricate mechanism that is her mind because the smallest pressure can have the most terrifying, cataclysmic consequences.

'We'd kept everything quiet and then a bunch of kids appeared on the porch yelling and shouting for us. And they rang the doorbell. They rang it so loudly that the whole house sort of shook.'

'Like there was about to be an earthquake. In fact, there was. How did we handle it?'

'We had to lure the kids away down the drive on some ludicrous pretext. Mother was screaming and yelling and we just edged out as if it was perfectly normal. But of course they all knew. I don't recall them ever coming here again.'

My face feels hot. Acting normal. A desirable state and the opposite of acting Russian.

'Where was Daddy?'

'Out. At work. I don't know.'

We fall silent again. I wait for the night air to cool my hot cheeks.

Jane breaks the silence. 'Lucy . . .' she says quietly. 'I saw you reading that report of Robert Joseph's wedding just now in the den.'

'Jane, for Chrissake I was just looking at the names of the guests!' I say defensively. 'It so happens that one of them is Marcello and I've been looking for –'

'Luce, don't act Russian. Just tell me: have you read it over and over?'

The railings squeak a bit, or maybe it's the crickets. The night is so still that I can smell the sweetness in Jane's breath, the summery flowers of her perfume.

I sigh. 'Maybe. It was an important relationship for me because it was the first which Mother couldn't wreck. She was safely in the clinic by then and she was obviously going to stay there. And I guess . . .' I hesitate. 'I guess the first time you fall in love it means a lot. Actually, his whole family meant a lot.'

The Joseph oasis in the valley. Mrs Joseph, involved in her sons' lives without ever controlling them. Laughing at their jokes. Watching them play volleyball, enjoying their small successes. Mr Joseph was older and his body stiff but he was jovial, he joshed with his sons and admired their girlfriends. I liked the way he spoke with his wife too. One of them would talk and the other would listen respectfully and then they'd change roles. I used to think: that's how conversation should be between a husband and wife. No shouting. No indifference. No domination by either party. They took time to talk together although their home was always full of people. There was Ralph, Mrs Joseph's brother, who lived with the family and helped in the yard. No one raised an eyebrow or even commented on his behaviour. There were Mrs Joseph's friends. There were other kids, cousins, friends of cousins. It was hard to be alone there sometimes, despite the size of the place, but I liked that. I came from a house where it was hard to be anything but alone and the slam of the screen door always heralded the beginning or end of a spell of solitude.

After the Josephs rejected me, so emphatically, so long ago, could I really just drive down there, appear at the door, ask questions about B. Marcello and help myself to another slice of their tantalizing lives? The thought makes my heart thump again.

Jane points out: 'He wasn't so wonderful. He nearly killed you down in the valley.'

'I wasn't badly hurt.'

'You could have been, he was. And the car was such a mess, it really scared me.'

Jane, arriving soon after Mrs Joseph and her friend, minutes before the ambulances, her eyes gleaming as though she might cry any minute, surveying my body for damage with a doctor's cool professionalism although it was years before she qualified.

'You didn't show it.'

'I had to be calm so you wouldn't get frightened.'

I turn to her. I can see her eyes shining in the dark.

'I owe you so much, Jane. I have a lot to thank you for. I know we both want to leave most of the past behind but it's you I have to thank for the good things. Not just for taking care of me when I was sick or saving me in the swimming-pool. But all the other stuff. Helping me choose the right clothes. Say the right things. Get better grades. Act the right way. I don't think Mother brought me up at all. It was all you, and I'm . . .' Inexplicably and embarrassingly, my voice breaks for a moment. 'I'm grateful to you. And especially, most of all . . .' My voice cracks once more. 'When Stevie died. How you supported me.'

So now I've said it. Without any preparation, without knowing I was going to say it. For years I've been aware that I should express acknowledgement and appreciation, that Jane long ago was entitled to expect this and may have been waiting for it. But, for reasons I don't understand, I have withheld it from her until now.

Her reply is delayed and when I glance across at her, despite the darkness between us, I see that tears are leaking from her eyes. 'Oh, Lucy. Oh thank you. I mean . . . it sometimes seems like you don't remember.'

'I do remember,' I assure her. I can feel tears making a hot, wet, thin line down my own face. 'I know just how much I owe you. And I never thanked you. I just went away. Without saying a word.'

This is not the kind of conversation we have. Crying this way is not the kind of thing we do. We don't look at one another but throw our words, quietly, urgently, over the railings and into the valley and when we are silent we continue to stare out across its infinite darkness, sniffing occasionally.

When Scott and Larry appear, smelling of the barn, we struggle to make our voices normal, to tow the conversation back to a landscape we can navigate, but they detect that something significant has passed between us and look at us searchingly. I watch a pair of car lights, their beam straight as the road, move sluggishly through the darkness. Suddenly it seems essential that Jane and I shoulder our weighty burden of memories together. I think, for the first time, that maybe I'll move back to California.

27

On Sunday morning, I leave with Sasha and Aunts Zina and
Zoya for Redbush clinic. I am relieved that I won't be visiting
Mother alone but Aunt Zina explains: 'It's not good for
Tanya to have more than one visitor so we will wait while
you see her.'

'But what will you do?' I ask.

They shriek with laughter. 'Talk!' they cry.

Redbush is thirty minutes north of the city and in the car
the aunts, who have insisted I sit in the front seat, question
me about the progress we are making at Daddy's house.

'There's so much to do,' I groan.

They nod wisely. Aunt Zina leans towards me: 'Lucia,
there will be much to sort out. It takes a long time to do this
after a death but it is necessary and it will perhaps be helpful
to you in your grief.'

I think of the house, groaning with boxes, papers, drawers,
closets. 'It feels like a gross invasion of Daddy's privacy.'

'When someone dies,' says Sasha, 'it is hard to maintain
their privacy or their secrets. God, when Papa died I found
the exposure of his life to the entire family unbearable. But
from all this I came to know him better.'

'From all what?'

Sasha looks in the rearview mirror at his mother for
permission and somehow, with an eyelid or a nod, this is
given. 'When Mama and the sisters went through his
things . . .' another swift look at Aunt Zina '. . . and I still
think it should have been me who did that, they discovered

a number of magazines of a nature which no one would ever have dreamed might interest him. And he had debts, gambling debts, which was most astonishing in a man never known to take risks and always parsimonious with the family's money.'

'Uncle Pavel! Gambling debts!'

'Are you amazed?' cries Aunt Zina, flapping her arms in a gesture of disbelief. 'Everyone was amazed and most of all me. I simply thank God that Mama died a year before and so knew nothing of it.'

Sasha straightens his body and assumes an expression of camel-like disgust that is so reminiscent of Grandma that we both break into giggles. Sasha's is a strange, high-pitched squeak which makes me laugh still more. But Aunts Zoya and Zina are not amused.

'Shame on you for joking about your dear old baba. She was a good woman who suffered much.' Aunt Zoya looks significantly at me. 'You, of all people, should understand this.'

I say soberly: 'Of course. I know. Her baby died. On the train.'

'Her suffering was great,' confirms Aunt Zina. 'Whenever my Pavel was annoyed by her I reminded him of this suffering.'

Sasha raises his eyebrows at me. 'But do you see, Lucia? You have in these few minutes learned more about my father in death than you might if he were sitting in the car with us smoking his pipe. The same may be true for your own papa. You will come to know him in a different way now. Because we all have secrets, even perhaps you.'

Redbush has high walls and security cameras. It looks more like the spacious estate of some movie star than a clinic for mental illness and drink and drug rehabilitation. People on this latter programme are separated from patients like my mother and they are referred to by the uniformed staff as clients. It is possible to see them walking alone in the extensive grounds.

Patients on my mother's side of the complex do not walk alone. They are always accompanied, occasionally by another patient or a relative but usually by a member of staff. Doctors do not wear white coats so sometimes it is hard to tell them from patients. Once, when Scott and I visited Mother with Larry and Jane, Larry went right up to a dishevelled old man who always seemed to be around and grabbed him by the hand. I had taken the man to be a long-term patient but now it was revealed that he was a senior psychiatrist who had once worked with Larry.

Sasha pulls up to the security guard at the gate. Faces scan us from behind thick glass before anyone appears. The guard, who is uniformed to look like a police officer, asks for proof of everyone's identity and there is much clucking and clicking of purses in the back seat.

'Are you all visiting the patient?' he asks.

'No, just her daughter,' says Sasha, gesturing to me.

'Please get out of the car and come right around here,' instructs the man. He looks me up and down suspiciously. He examines my card, holding it up to the light as though it could be a forged $20 bill.

Finally he hands it back. 'I'm sorry. But we have to check. We got a celebrity, big-time, in rehab and women have been trying to get past me all day.'

We drive into the grounds. The grass is decorated with a pattern of perfect misty triangles. When the sun catches them they seem to throw out small rainbows.

'Ah, even the sprinklers are beautiful here,' sighs Aunt Zina, her eyes searching each face we pass. None looks like a big-time celebrity.

'Such a peaceful place,' Aunts Zoya and Zina agree. 'Look at the trees. Look at the flowers.'

I enter the low, red building with exactly the feelings of despair and helplessness I felt entering Redbush as a teenager. In those days, anything could happen. Mother might be all charm, welcoming me as an honoured visitor, asking me polite questions, looking with an exaggerated fascination at the photos I brought. Or she might sulk and refuse to talk to me. Or she might be zealous in her pursuit of some obscure principle, or angry with me, or conspiratorial in her hatred of a staff member or fellow patient. Gradually, as she aged, she mellowed into silence. Visits became more of a chore than an ordeal.

Sasha, as if detecting my mood, puts a plump, leathery arm around me.

'Don't worry, you won't have to stay in there long,' he says.

We are told to wait in the conservatory. The aunts speculate, in busy whispers, about who the big-time celebrity might be. I know what they are saying because, although they speak Russian, names I recognize jump out of their conversation.

I wander around the conservatory, picking up magazines and putting them down again. I look across the lawns for the celebrity. I am nervous. I make a mental list of topics I might talk about.

A man in a loose green uniform arrives. He looks at all of us and nods recognition to the aunts.

'We can't take so many,' he says, 'you know that.'

They explain, simultaneously, that only I am to see Mother today. The man looks confused until I step forward.

'Miss Schaffer? Hi, I'm Jonathan, Tanya's nurse.' His familiar use of my mother's first name, and not just her name but its diminutive, startles me and I am slow to respond when he extends his hand. He holds mine firmly in a grip

291

which must be useful for difficult patients. He says: 'Please come with me to your mother's room.'

I fall in behind him obediently but the nurse is friendly and hangs back so that we can speak.

'How long are you home from New York?' he asks. We pad past colourful, childish paintings along the hallway. The nurse's feet are almost noiseless. 'Your mother says you got a real good job there.'

'She said that?'

'Oh sure. She's proud of you. She talks about you a lot.'

'Mother does? She talks about me?'

'Why the surprise, Miss Schaffer?'

'I thought Mother didn't speak much any more.'

The nurse smiles as he holds a door open for me. 'There are days when she's real talkative.'

'Have the police been back to interview her yet?'

'They came just once.'

'When are they coming back?'

'Well, they did say they'd be back next week sometime with an interpreter because Tanya just gave them one big lot of Russian but I'm not sure they'll bother. I think they understood she wasn't going to be too much help.'

'When did Daddy last visit her?'

'Saturday.'

We are standing outside a door and the nurse clearly intends to open it but I obstruct him.

'Did he stay long? Did you see them together?'

'Oh, I don't know how long he was here, maybe a half hour. I saw him at the beginning when I escorted him in, like I'm escorting you now. And at the end.'

'Did he seem . . . just like normal?'

The nurse's face splits, revealing large teeth. 'Now normal is not a word we tend to use around here, Miss Schaffer.' His tone is teasing. 'But . . .' he says, 'Tanya was sort of upset afterwards. Not sort of. Very. She was very upset. I couldn't understand it because usually when your father goes she's quiet and contented.'

'Did she explain why?'

'Well, no, she didn't. She cried a lot. I would say, as you're asking me, that her mood has been melancholy since his visit. I mean, she seemed upset before your sister came to break the news of his death.'

'As if she guessed what was going to happen.'

'I have come to believe,' he says, 'that the human mind works on a lot of levels and we don't understand them all. When people don't function in the normal way we think they're handicapped. But at other levels, they may flourish.'

He reaches across me to open Mother's door. I swallow hard as her room is revealed. Smaller than I remember it but even more like an expensive hotel. The drapes are heavy, the door handles elaborate. At first I can't see Mother at all but the nurse leads me to a small bundle of humanity wrapped in a fluffy blue shawl which sits huddled on a chaise longue. An old woman I at first mistake for Grandma.

'Your daughter's here!' says the nurse jovially.

'Hi, Mother.' I want my words to slip along easily but I fail. I sound tense. I stoop to kiss her thin skin then sit down some feet away from her. The hunch of her shoulders, her smallness and frailty, the protuberance of her limbs, all this reminds me ludicrously of a balloon which has lain around the house long after the parade, slowly losing air.

Mother is looking out of the window and does not acknowledge my presence. I say: 'So, how are you?' but to my relief she does not respond. It's going to be just as Jane told me. I'll chat to her a bit and sit with her in companionable silence and then, duty done, I'll be free again.

The nurse has been busy in the adjacent bathroom, filling a vase for the small bunch of flowers I brought.

'These are beautiful!' he comments jovially, emerging with the vase. 'Anemones. Tatiana sure likes blue. Right, Tanya?'

Mother does not respond but the nurse continues just as though she has.

'Yup, sure you do. The last time Eric came, he brought some blue flowers, right?'

No response. The nurse keeps up his side of the conversation. 'That's right. I mean I only threw them out this morning. Say, Tanya, do you want your eyeglasses? So you can see your daughter and the beautiful flowers?'

But Mother gives no indication of any interest in flowers, daughter or eyeglasses.

'She really doesn't see well at all these days,' shrugs the nurse, holding out the glasses. 'Want them, Tanya?'

Mother ignores him and he puts them down on the table.

'She won't mind,' says the man to me, 'if you move closer. She may not see you too clearly way back there.'

I acknowledge his words but I do not move. I feel something like panic as he walks towards the door. 'I'll be back in around twenty minutes but if you want to leave before, or you need me for anything, you can just push that button.'

The button is red. It is hidden discreetly by the drapes. The door clicks shut behind him.

We sit in silence. I study Mother's white skin. Despite the impression of great age, she is unwrinkled. Her eyes are large and their blue is paler than I remember, as though they thin as her mind loses its substance.

I start to talk, awkwardly at first, my voice rusty and my speech hesitant. I tell a little about the funeral and the people who'll come, how Sasha and Aunt Zina will be taking Mother.

I try to speak to her as though she's a fully functioning adult but sometimes I hear false notes in my voice: a forced cheerfulness or a patronizing tone. Occasionally Mother's hands make tiny scratching movements and sometimes she blinks, otherwise she is still. I do not know if she is listening to me or if she can understand anything I say but gradually I find her silence liberating. I start to talk about Daddy, how I miss him, until I almost forget the still, silent woman. I say: 'This grief is different from when Stevie died. I mean, it's another shock but after the shock, then the grief is different.'

Suddenly, Mother's face turns to me. She is nothing more than a ghost now but I recognize, as if for the first time, that she is the ghost of a beautiful woman. I fall silent. She watches me, silent too, and I absorb her madness and her unhappiness.

We stare at one another for more than a minute, my Mother and I. It is hard, as it always was, to hold her gaze. I had a childhood horror of her stare and would hide my face behind my hand or stand on one leg and look at the ground to avoid it. Now, when I realize that she is opening her mouth to speak, my heart beats faster. Gradually, its movement unhurried, her face twists. I shrink back in recognition at this process. The first time I saw her face twist this way was in the desert on the sweltering silent blacktop, when I emerged, limping, from the canyon.

The room feels hot now and small balls of sweat seem to ricochet over my skin but I am unable to move. I watch as her face twists until it is inhabited by a cruel, monstrous creature and involuntarily I brace myself against the back of my chair, ready for the beast to strike.

She speaks in a whisper and she spits with venom. She says: 'Why did you do it?'

I notice, through my fear, that her accent is as thick and un-American as Aunt Zina's. I didn't notice it as a child and when I remember her I eliminate it.

She waits for a reply but I have none. My heart is pounding and sweat is speckling my face and body like glitter now. My hands hurt as they clasp the scrolling on the chair arms. She is not small, old and helpless but a deadly snake and I am a little girl who is terrified of her. She leans forward. She hisses: 'Why? Why did you hate him so much?'

Involuntarily I jump up. My fingers scratch at the folds of the drapes for the red button. When I find it and press it a light in the button flashes but there is a disconcerting silence. I hope it is working. I press it again.

I hardly dare look back at Mother and when I do so it is through half-closed eyes as though I am looking at the sun. She says something more, something incomprehensible in Russian. Then she turns to the window again and her face unwinds. By the time the nurse arrives she has almost resumed her earlier vacancy.

'Everything okay?' he asks, looking at me hard and then at Mother. Whatever residue of her anger remains, he knows her well enough to detect it.

'Oh Tanya, did you turn mean?' He is apologetic. 'Are you all right, Miss Schaffer? She was really looking forward to seeing you, I don't know why she had to turn mean.'

He walks towards me and gently takes my bare arm. He examines it lightly.

'Did she harm you?' he asks.

I shake my head but he continues to examine me for damage.

'You sure she didn't scratch you?'

I shake my head again. I cannot speak.

'Okay, Tanya, well, I guess your daughter has to go now.'

Mother ignores him and I do not say goodbye. As the nurse and I make our way silently back down the hallway he says: 'She couldn't do much damage but she does try to scratch sometimes. I have to keep her nails real short.'

We can hear the aunts, giggling and gabbling in Russian, their voices raised now and then lowered, as we approach down the hallway. Sasha looks at me closely. I do not look back.

'Sounds like you ladies are having a good day out,' says the nurse, smiling at them.

'Perhaps you think they don't see each other often,' says Sasha. 'They, believe it or not, live only one block apart.'

'Oh, but it's such a treat to go out together!' they protest loudly.

'Since you have known of this treat for days, why has it been necessary for you to speak for so many hours on the phone this week?'

Aunt Zoya's long, thin body wavers over Sasha. She says imperiously: 'Young man, would you attempt the Olympics without training for it?' The upright bodies of the two women collapse into hearty laughter. Sasha rolls his eyes at the nurse and me.

The two men try to stand at one side of the conservatory to arrange Mother's attendance at the funeral. They try to discuss whether the nurse should accompany Mother but Zina and Zoya refuse to be left out and interrupt constantly with comments and suggestions, transforming the men's hushed conversation into a noisy drama. How is it that Mother's elder sisters have such animation while her own house, apart from the sad, vicious ghost which occasionally rattles through its rooms, is empty? Finally they agree that Sasha can manage with only the help of his mother and aunt. Mother will be taken to the funeral and she will return immediately afterwards without eating at the house.

'Boy,' says the nurse, backing off with mock exhaustion, holding his hands up in mock defence. 'Boy, I'm sure glad I only have one of you sisters to take care of.'

Aunts Zina and Zoya yell with delighted laughter.

The nurse starts to go, then pauses. 'Are you sure you're okay?' he asks me quietly.

'I guess so.'

He looks at me curiously but walks on.

As we leave, the aunts cluster around me, so busy and noisy I feel surrounded by many people.

'How did you find our Tanya? Is she very much changed?'

'Well . . . I guess she's a bit smaller and older.' My voice sounds hollow.

'Despite the difference in colouring, you look a little like her,' says Aunt Zoya.

'It's true, it's true,' agrees Aunt Zina.

I say: 'I don't want to be like Mother.' And in that moment, as we cross the parking lot, I hear again the click clack of my own walk, with its threat of imbalance, an advancing imbalance which cannot be controlled. The aunts, perhaps alarmed by my tone, are busy assuring me that only in the matter of great beauty do I resemble Mother.

'And Jane too,' one adds.

'Absolutely,' confirms the other. 'Jane also has great beauty, so rare in both sisters of one family.'

But by the time we reach the car they have fallen silent and I am the subject of sidelong and significant glances from all three.

'Lucia . . .' begins Sasha. 'I fear that your reunion was not entirely a happy one.'

I look away from him across the green lawns. I am trying to dam my tears, dam them at a source somewhere lower than my eyes, somewhere almost as low as my belly.

'Oh my poor Lucia,' moans Aunt Zoya softly.
'Dear child,' mutters Aunt Zina. 'How you suffer.'
And at this kindness the dam breaks.

28

The four of us find a seat near the parking lot and sit in a row looking right ahead of us as though we're in a movie theatre. I sob between my aunts.

'Did she shout?' they ask.

'Did she scratch?'

Finally I say: 'She really seems to hate me.'

'No, no, she adores you.'

'She has certainly always adored you,' Aunt Zoya insists. 'Let me remind you that she could barely be parted from you when you were a child, even for a short time. And you, Lucia, were a most devoted daughter.'

'Consequently,' adds Aunt Zina, 'the change in her was harder for all concerned. Including Tanya. She has suffered much.'

'And,' says Aunt Zoya, 'you should always remember that your mother's illness is the result of circumstances and not something you pass to your daughter, you understand.'

'She's schizophrenic,' I point out. 'There's a strong genetic element.'

'Doctors can call it what they like, in our opinion it was entirely due to circumstances,' Aunt Zina insists.

And suddenly it is obvious to me that there were circumstances. All my life people have hinted that there were circumstances in Russia but their detail has been withheld and I have been expected simply to infer their emotional significance.

I ask: 'What circumstances?'

Sasha, at the end of the bench, rearranges his legs. He's seen the movie before and he knows it's a long one.

Aunt Zoya says: 'In Moscow we were a lucky family. Papa was in a trusted position with a large apartment and a large family. Both were a privilege. But it was impossible, even as children, not to know what was going on all around us. And Tanya had the misfortune to witness it with her own eyes. That's all. I don't think she was ever the same again.'

'What did Mother see?'

The aunts exchange glances. Aunt Zoya is silent and when Aunt Zina starts to speak she looks away.

'Her best friend out at the dacha was a girl, Rita, of similar age and in a similar position. Our fathers were friends. The girls were playing one day in the orchard or the forest, I don't remember where, but I know they had climbed a tree, when they heard men. They hid in their tree and watched. What they saw was nothing so unusual. But they would have done better to close their eyes.'

Aunt Zoya leans forward, hanging her head, and I look behind her to Sasha. He looks back at me, expressionless.

'What did they see, Aunt Zina?'

'They saw Rita's father beaten, beaten to his death.'

I gasp, not so much at the information, which is shocking enough, but at its leaden delivery. 'But . . . why?'

'Oh, how can I tell? I don't know the reason NKVD turned on Rita's father. That's what happens in a pack of wolves. That was life under Stalin. One minute you were popular and the next someone wanted your apartment and they informed against you, some manufactured charge, and you were dead. It occurred frequently, I'm not telling you anything remarkable. It's just Tanya had the misfortune to see this and it would have been better for her if she had not.'

'Who were the men?'

301

She looks across at her sister. 'Oh, I don't know. Thugs.'

'Unfortunately,' says Aunt Zoya, 'they were supervised by Papa.'

'Grandpa killed Rita's father?'

'Well of course he didn't get blood on his hands.'

'Grandpa killed his friend!'

Sasha raises his eyebrows at my indignation. He says: 'You weren't there, you didn't live in those times, you have no right to judge.'

Mother said: 'Why did you do it? Why did you hate him so much?' Maybe the words came out of her childhood.

'Even perhaps,' Aunt Zoya is adding, 'Rita's father had done the same himself to many. And for Papa it was the last time and probably the reason he left.'

'Unhappily,' says Aunt Zina, 'he and Mama paid a great price: the loss, in their escape, of their baby son.'

I nod. 'The baby on the train. Mother used to tell us that story in great detail but I've forgotten most of it now.'

'God, Lucy.' Sasha rolls his eyes. 'You should have lived with us and you wouldn't have been allowed to forget.'

Aunt Zina ignores him. 'It was terrible. He died in Mama's arms. The man took him away and Mama was always haunted by the possibility that the body was simply thrown off the train.'

'And,' says Aunt Zoya, 'she was probably right.'

Once more I look at Sasha who looks back at me unblinkingly.

'Did you catch the train right out of Moscow?' I ask.

'Certainly,' Aunt Zina nods. 'Certainly, it was a most bold exodus. Papa had been appointed head of a trade delegation to Latvia and it was supposed to be the train for Riga but somehow we boarded another.'

'Where did you go?'

'It was . . . complicated. A complicated and dangerous route.' They look at each other.

'But where did you sail from?'

They exchange a few words in Russian. 'Possibly Rotterdam,' says Aunt Zoya at last. 'We're not sure . . .'

She stands, slowly and stiffly.

'Enough!' Sasha jumps up. 'Lucia has suffered enough today without such a trip through Andreyev history.'

Aunt Zoya looks hurt. 'We tell you all this, my dearest Lucia, not to make you unhappy, or to shock you, but to give you some small understanding of your mother's pain. Some small explanation for her madness. Some small opportunity to forgive her.'

'And remember . . .' Aunt Zina says, 'Tanya also lost a son, a suffering which you will understand.'

I lean forward a little to look from face to face. I say: 'Do you realize that we all lost baby sons? Grandma, Mother and me?'

They look back at me. They seem to be waiting for me to say something more. When I am silent, Aunt Zina speaks at last.

'Well of course,' she says gently. 'Of course, Lucia. Didn't you know this before?'

We drive north from Redbush clinic. We are expected at the home of Aunt Olya, just twenty minutes away, for a barbecue lunch. Aunt Katya and her husband will be there too and various cousins.

'Are you ready for such an encounter or are you so melancholy, Lucia, that you would simply prefer to return home?'

I would simply prefer to return home but I know this answer would disappoint them so I insist on continuing. We drive in silence. Involuntarily, I scan every truck we pass and once, when there is a tow truck on the opposite side of the highway, I am almost jolted from my seat, causing Sasha to turn to me in alarm. But it is some other tow truck and now I realize that the car is not silent but that in the back seat is the constant murmur, like the to and fro of the ocean's waves, of my aunts speaking in Russian.

After about ten minutes the traffic slows and soon we are stationary.

'Construction?' suggests Aunt Zina.

'An accident?' suggests Aunt Zoya. We inch our way forward, the aunts' heads bobbing in the back seat as they speculate on the reason for the tailback.

Eventually we see flashing lights ahead. A police car, siren wailing, passes us.

'How terrible, how shocking,' cry the aunts.

When we reach the source of the delay it is clear that there has been a collision between a car and a truck. Both have swerved off the road in a last-minute attempt to avoid each other. Aunts Zina and Zoya revert in hushed tones to Russian, the language of tragedy.

'There is no reason at all,' points out Sasha as we finally accelerate away, 'for such a tailback. The damaged vehicles, the police and the ambulances are off the blacktop in the field and the highway is in no way blocked.'

'Ah, but everyone slows to look!' says Aunt Zoya. 'Despite one's great reluctance, one is compelled to look at this horrible sight.'

'We look,' explains Aunt Zina, 'thinking that the crushed car could have been ours. We remind ourselves of our vulnerability.'

'Of our mortality,' agrees Aunt Zoya.

'Even now,' adds Aunt Zina, 'the traffic flows evenly and drivers sit at their wheels with less speed and more concentration. For a while at least, each driver has been reminded of his own death, and considers the consequences for his loved ones of such a catastrophe.'

Joe Zacarro said: It's a modern, industrialized nation sort of thing to ignore death and think it's never going to happen to you. But if you remember that you're going to die some day then you live your life in a different sort of a way. Not necessarily better, but probably better. Different, that's for sure.

I turn to Sasha but have no time to speak because Aunt Zina is shrieking: 'Turn here, Sashinka, here!'

The family greets me with kindness and condolences. On their arrival in America, the Andreyevs hoped to have a son, as if they could simply replace the boy who died on the train with another. Instead they had Katya and finally Olya. Katya is married to a second-generation Russian from outside the tight community in town. Olya, like Mother, married an American. Both sisters dress American and talk American. They could be mistaken for the daughters of their elder sisters. Only when they speak Russian do they change: their facial muscles, their gait, even their hair seems to rearrange itself around their other language and culture. I think of Mother's place in this family. The middle sister, trapped between two worlds, rejecting the old but never fully embraced by the new.

Aunts Zina and Zoya exchanged ill-concealed looks of disgust when they learned that there are hot dogs for lunch but they eat the hotdogs anyway, at first gingerly, then hungrily.

'Did I cook them real well?' teases one of my young cousins, a teenager hardly known to me except by name.

'Oh, so you made them yourself?' demands Aunt Zina.

'Sure, on the barbecue.'

'No, no,' cries Aunt Zoya, 'did you grind the meat and add onion and spices?'

The girl shrugs with incomprehension. Her eye roves over the tidy yard with its basketball hoop on the garage and fat, contented dogs panting by the barbecue. To her two accented aunts she says awkwardly: 'We bought them at the supermarket this morning.'

'Then in our opinion . . .' says Aunt Zina.

'. . . You haven't cooked anything. Merely you have heated them,' finishes Aunt Zoya.

Aunt Katya, who is passing, pauses to put an arm around her niece.

'Just remember,' she tells the girl, 'that your older aunts are relics from another world. A world which isn't there any more. Treat them with all the respect you would show an exhibit in a museum. Like, for example . . .'

'A dinosaur bone,' suggests Sasha. 'Or why restrict ourselves simply to a bone? Imagine them as two living, breathing dinosaurs.'

He is admonished by his mother in Russian. The niece listens to them curiously then turns away.

'I fear,' says Sasha to me when desserts are produced from the freezer, 'that to such an all-American girl I must also seem like a relic from some other culture. The irony of my situation is that, when I travel to Moscow, that's exactly how I am regarded by my Russian friends there.'

I remember how Jane wounded him on the night of my arrival when, irritated by his refusal to supply his fingerprints, she briskly reminded him of his nationality.

I say anxiously: 'Oh, but you speak Russian and behave in a very Russian way.'

He rolls his blue eyes at me.

'I know so much about the Soviet life of our contemporaries that I feel I must have been there. In my dreams I revisit Young Pioneers camp, where I sport a red neckerchief and sing with enthusiasm Soviet songs while I help build camp-fires in the woods. These dreams are so real that my fingers can feel the cold iron of the camp cot. When I wake I have difficulty persuading myself that I have not been revisiting my own childhood but that of other people.'

I am silent, remembering my own confused memories, how a few days ago I even thought I'd made Lindy Zacarro's daydream real.

'In fact, while our Russian contemporaries chanted slogans in their neckerchiefs, I was playing basketball in the park and, for a brief and ill-advised period, discovering soul music. But only when I visit Moscow am I reminded that I wasn't there. I didn't experience it, I didn't even go until the iron curtain fell. And although my Russian friends love me, Sasha has not suffered enough to be truly one of them. For me, being Russian is an essential part of my identity. To them I am a fatcat, privileged American and an outsider.'

29

Monday is even hotter than yesterday. When I open Daddy's front door I feel the heat jostling its way past me like an angry crowd. The atmosphere has intensified the house's own smell of wood and oil. I drink two glasses of icy water before setting off through the yard for the Holler orchard.

Our lot used to be four acres until Daddy sold two to the Hollers. I remember playing around the foundations of their house and then watching the bricks grow higher each day. Finally, the family arrived. Daddy and Mr Holler were neighbourly but they weren't friends back then. The friendship must have come much later, when wives were dead or departed and the surviving children all grown.

Like many houses around here, this one is built into the hillside, so it looks two storeys high when you drive in and three if you turn back and stare at it from the valley. When I was a child it felt clean and modern. There was no splintery old porch and instead of dark corners there were light, bright rooms.

I ring the doorbell and, after a long wait, Adam Holler's voice is heard over the speaker. 'Who is it?'

'Lucy Schaffer.'

'Lucy.' It is a statement. There is no surprise. 'I'm finishing my exercises, it'll be a minute before I can get to the door.'

'Okay.'

I try to remember Mr Holler but can recall nothing more palpable than the sense of someone physically stiff and verbally correct. I know little about him except that he is a man who has had to live with the most hideous of mistakes, a guilt even his wife could not endure, because it was Adam Holler who had been installing the pool lights that day Jim Bob dived in and died.

Bolts draw back and keys turn and Mr Holler stares at me from behind dark glasses. The other man who remembers death.

'Good morning, Lucy,' he says. At once I recall his whiteness: despite the shades and his hat, long sleeves, long pants, socks and shoes, wherever his flesh is exposed it flashes with the supernatural paleness of water.

He holds out a dry-skinned hand to me. Shaking it is like scrunching old parchment.

'I'd like to offer you my sincere sympathy on the death of your father. He was a man loved by many. There are numerous people in this area who can recount small acts of kindness on his part. For myself, I can also say that I will miss his company sorely. He had a rare energy and originality of thought.'

Now I recall Mr Holler's formality of tone. It masks an awkwardness, maybe a shyness which I always knew was there, even as a kid, from his stiff movements.

I say: 'Joe's probably told you that the funeral's on Tuesday.'

He nods and gestures for me to come in. He bolts the door behind us.

'I'm kind of slow,' he apologizes, leading me through the hallway. 'Arthritis. In the back. And in most places now. I've had it for years.'

Arthritis. That was why the Hollers built their pool long before anyone else dreamed of breaking up the steep, rocky hillside into a square of expensive blue water. Because swimming was good for Mr Holler's arthritis.

As I follow him down the hallway I feel big, too big for this house now, as though I've grown so much I'll crack my head on the ceiling or bang my elbows into the doors.

'I turned on the air-conditioning yesterday,' says Mr Holler. Air-conditioning was one of the things that made the Holler house seem modern. It was always cool. 'It doesn't normally go on in March but this is remarkable weather for spring and they say it's going to get hotter. Sit down.'

I look around me. Jim Bob was two years older than me and his brother two years older than Jane. Jane and Ed weren't real friendly but there was a vacation when Jim Bob and I played together all the time when I was nine. The Hollers' swimming-pool was newly installed and we played in it every day. Then the new semester started and Jim Bob suddenly seemed a lot older than me and we hardly spoke to each other again.

The sitting-room hasn't changed. It still has a glass wall which looks out across the valley and a complex system of shutters so you can close off the view or any part of it when it gets to be too much. Jim Bob and I were fascinated by the shutter system. We broke it in places without telling anyone and no one seemed to find out. I wonder if it's ever been fixed.

'Sit down,' Adam Holler instructs me for a second time. But I am drawn to the window. One storey beneath it is the terrace. Beyond the terrace are steps which lead down to a glassy eye implanted on to the hillside. I stare into the blue iris of the pool.

'How are you coping, Lucy?' he asks but his voice is hard. I am remembering the summer I spent playing with Jim Bob. He was small for his age, his skin was brown and his blond hair crewcut. He was teaching himself how to dive. I just liked to jump in and make a splash and Mrs Holler, who watched over us, would shriek her complaints. But that summer Jim Bob started to dive, belly-flopping at first, then gaining in grace and confidence.

'So, watch this, Lucy, Lucy I can do it, watch.'

He ran up to the pool, paused, but barely, and then he was airborne, cutting through the nothingness in a perfect arc. A crash like shattering glass as his body sliced through the water, neat and swift as a lean, brown knife.

You can love when you're nine years old and I loved Jim Bob at that moment and I loved him when his head, drenched and dripping, bobbed to the surface and he looked right at me with wet, bright eyes asking for my approval.

I danced around at the edge of the pool clapping my hands. 'Fantabulous, Jim Bob!'

That's what we used to say, Jim Bob and I, because we were copying the kids in some TV show. Fantabulous. And is that how Jim Bob, years later, dived to his death? Fantabulously? With a grace and skill that were almost lyrical? I hope it was a good dive, his best dive.

'Why won't you sit down?' asks Adam Holler quietly and I hear a sort of fear in his voice. He knows I'm remembering Jim Bob. I'm remembering his great mistake.

I say: 'I haven't been here since I was a child.'

'Your whole family used to come over sometimes. We'd have half the neighbourhood here and Bunny cooked hamburgers.'

'The whole family?' I only remember swimming with Jim Bob day after day that long hot summer, until even Jane became sullen at my absences.

'Sure. All you Schaffers and the Zacs and the Dimotos . . .'

I try to remember the Schaffers, all four of us, at a pool party. The idea embarrasses me. Mother would certainly have felt awkward. Even when the clinic said she was well enough to be at home, she dealt badly with almost any social situation. She either tried too hard and laughed too much or she sat in still silence as though someone had glued her limbs together.

'You don't remember? You don't remember how you nearly drowned in our pool once? Snorkelling?'

'I remember that . . . but I thought it was at the public pool.'

'It was here. You were snorkelling down at the deep end and you got into trouble. I'm not sure what happened. Possibly your mask filled with water. Possibly you tried to follow the other kids who were swimming deep and you took water in through the snorkel. I don't know. No one noticed, not even the other kids in the pool, because you didn't struggle, you just dropped your head and went limp. You didn't fight it at all. Only your mother saw something was wrong and she dived right in with her clothes on and saved you.'

I stare at his black, beetle eyes. 'I remember nearly drowning, I remember being saved. But actually it was Jane who –'

'No. Tanya saved you.'

'But Mother never swam. She couldn't.'

'She dived in and pulled you right out. She laid you down by the side of the pool and that's when Jane helped. Probably a few other people too but especially Jane. She rolled you on to your side like a rug and then she pulled you back again and sort of pumped at you until you threw up. She was calm and she was efficient. I don't know how old she was, twelve maybe, but Bunny turned to your father and she said: Jane's going to be a doctor, you wait and see.'

'Mother never went in the water, ever, because she couldn't swim, Mr –'

He raises his voice. 'Lucy, I saw it with my own eyes.'

His eyes. I remember recoiling from their colourlessness when he removed his shades to swim. It seems to me that those eyes are unreliable witnesses.

'So, Lucy . . .' He's wondering why I'm here. 'Is there anything I can do for you? Do you need any help over there?'

I say slowly: 'I guess the police have questioned you, Mr Holler . . .'

'Sure. A woman. She was about your age.'

'Did she ask you when you last saw Daddy?'

'Of course.'

'What did you tell her?'

'Sunday night, over at Joe's.'

'Mr Holler, what did you do on Sunday night?'

He gestures and the gesture is too large and too careless for a man whose movements are habitually so controlled.

'Well now . . .' he says awkwardly. He's looking for that relaxed, throwaway style that Daddy used sometimes and Joe Zacarro has perfected. But he can't wear someone else's clothes. The words don't fit him. 'I mean . . .' he tries again. 'Well, what do old guys like us ever do?'

I look at his body, square as a box because his shoulders have been tense for years. In his own well-lit home he doesn't seem so pale. Behind him the walls are white, ahead of him sun floods through the bank of windows.

I say: 'Remember death? Is that what old guys like you do?'

He twitches suddenly, the escape of a small movement. Within an instant his body is contained again and he has resumed his usual stiff-backed position. He looks at me in silence. His mouth is shut tight, the way mine was when Rougemont confronted me with the truth, with my shoes.

I am still standing by the window. I feel the sun flooding

313

the room from behind me. Maybe Mr Holler can only see my silhouette, maybe I seem like a shadow, the way Rougemont always looks to me.

I say: 'On Sunday night you and Joe Zacarro and Daddy drove out to the coastal highway in an old tow truck. You dumped a wreck right at the roadside where it would remind drivers the next morning how precious their lives are. To themselves and to others. A man sees a wreck and imagines his kids fatherless. A wife imagines her husband a widower. Young folk imagine their parents bereaved. Everyone thinks of the unfinished business, of how it would be if their lives just stopped abruptly, before they've done what they want to do, achieved what they want to achieve, said the things they mean to say. And, for a while, not for long, they slow down, they drive carefully, they live life a little differently. All thanks to you and Joe and Daddy.'

He says nothing.

'I'll bet you do it often. I'll bet you dump wrecks all around the area. And I'm not criticizing you for that, Mr Holler. I admire you for reminding so many people to readjust their priorities. I think you and Joe should go right ahead with it even though Daddy's dead. I don't want to tell the police or have them stop you. I only want one thing.'

He looks at me. His shades are so dark that I can see the window reflected in them, and, beyond the window, the valley. The tiny dots of distant trees, the right angle of the roads, the red-brown of the fertile valley dirt, it's all there between my eyes and Mr Holler's.

I say: 'I want you to tell me who the other guy is. The one who owns the tow truck. I need to talk to him.'

Before he has time to think about it, his response jumps out of him.

'No, Lucy. No.'

'Someone has to talk to him. If not me, then the police. And I guess none of us wants that, Mr Holler.'

He rearranges his legs. He sits more upright. He grips the arms of his chair too tightly.

'Lucy, I'm going to give you some advice. Stay right out of this one. It doesn't concern you. If your father had wanted you to know he would have told you. Just . . .' He waves a hand dismissively. 'Just, wind up his affairs, sell his house, take the money and go back east. That's all you need to do, that's all Eric wanted you to do.'

My heart quickens. Anger shoots through me as though someone just injected it into a vein.

'Mr Holler, Daddy didn't die the way he should have, quietly, with his family gathered around his bed. And I want to know why. I'm not going back east just because you tell me I don't need to find out any more. I have good reason to connect the tow truck driver with Daddy's death. You can help me locate him.'

I raised my voice. I raised my voice to this pale and arthritic old man. If anyone was looking through the window at us now, what conclusion would they draw? I turn back to the valley, not the one reflected in his sunglasses, but the real one where the colours are brighter and the lines are sharper. My eye follows the old, practised route like a dog who knows which way to slink home. Past the car accident with Robert Joseph, past the farm I walked to with Lindy.

'No,' he says.

I stare at him.

'I'm not going to give you any information your father didn't want you to have.'

'Daddy didn't know that someone was going to kill him.'

'I don't betray confidences. Under any circumstances. If you want to proceed, it will have to be with police help, not mine. That's my decision and Joe Zacarro will support me.'

I feel a quickening of my heart, the tightening of my nerve endings. 'Listen Mr Holler —'

He holds up a white hand to silence me.

'I don't want to talk about this any more, Lucy.'

Leaning on a stick, he shows me out in silence. He is a man who has developed a whole style of still dignity to contain his humiliation. He killed his son by mistake. A hideous own goal. The smallest of errors, just the width of an electrical wire, with outsize consequences. He unbolts the door. I wish he would mention Jim Bob. Jim Bob's thin brown body with its blond crewcut seems to lie between us.

'Good bye, Lucy.' His voice is flat as the valley. 'Your father arranged things the way he wanted them. I hope you'll think hard about his wishes before you go any further.'

30

You wouldn't drive into the valley without air-conditioning in weather like this. That would be crazy. All the straight lines, when you're right down among them, turn out to be fuzzy with heat. It rises like a spirit from the asphalt, making the edge of the road look crooked and distorting the rows of trees so they seem to sway like a drunken chorus line.

It's a long way to the intersection. When you watch from the deck it seems to take cars small as insects just a few minutes to crawl there from the valley side. Now I'm down here it feels like driving across the bed of an ocean that goes on for ever.

Finally I reach it but, from inside the car, the intersection is an insignificant landmark. I swing south. When I get to Sunnyfruit Orchards I try to pinpoint exactly the place where Robert Joseph turned over his father's car. I choose one spot then another and then another amid the rows of fruit trees. Finally I admit that I don't know where the accident happened.

I hope the Joseph home will look the way it used to. In my memory it is a blur of green light and green shade. I grip the wheel hard, my body tense, as I cross the aqueduct and turn into the drive. Immediately I am surrounded by new shapes and colours and I experience again the pleasure I used to feel on leaving behind the sunbaked brown dirt and systematic planting outside and arriving in this other country. I was happy here. The sweep of the lawn lifts my heart because it used to lift my heart. I smile at the riot of flowers and shrubs because they used to make me smile. The shadow patterns beneath the big trees delight me because they used to delight me. I look for the hammock where Robert and I spent all that summer but one of the old trees which it swung from has gone, and the hammock too. I wonder if the tree fell down. I wonder how loud the crash was.

The big house, freshly painted, gleams where the sun slips through the trees. I park right outside. Nearby, a woman who has been bending over a flowerbed straightens to stare at me. She is wearing a broad-brimmed straw hat and it is impossible to see her face. My heart thumps. It could be the gardener or it could be Robert's wife or the wife of one of his brothers or maybe even Mrs Joseph. My heart booms in my ears like a big machine driving by.

I stand uncertainly near the car, looking at the house, the green, green yard and the woman, who is walking slowly towards me. The figure is close when I realize that this is a man wearing a long, faded, loose-fitting dress.

'Ralph!' I say. The thin, white face breaks into a smile. He was walking slowly because he was afraid of me. Now he speeds up and takes my outstretched hand. His touch is light. He looks at me with bright, blue eyes and an undiminished smile.

'Hi, Ralph. It's Lucy. Lucy Schaffer. I haven't seen you for a few years.'

'Hi, Lucy,' says Ralph happily.

Ralph is Mrs Joseph's brother. He isn't a transvestite but whatever brake stops most men from wearing a cool dress on a hot day isn't a brake Ralph knows how to apply. In a curious misdistribution, Mrs Joseph got all the genes for being quick, bright, clever and capable. Ralph never would have been able to hold down a job or graduate from high school and Mrs Joseph made sure he never had to. When she married Robert's father, Ralph came too. During my summer with Robert, Ralph was always there, usually in the yard, planting, pruning, watering.

Ralph wanted to see what Robert and I did in the hammock and behind the rose garden. As he knew, sex is what we did. I had no sexual experience at all and Robert had less than he admitted to. We were technically incompetent. Robert generally came before he wanted to, with a cry of 'Oh no!' It didn't matter. I laughed at his embarrassment, his apologies. I said: 'I like you to do that, it makes me feel irresistible.' He said: 'You are irresistible.' He didn't understand that the way he held me, his need to cradle me in his arms, his pleasure at my pleasure, his delight in my body, every inch of it even my elbows, the love in his touch, was more exciting than split-second timing. Or maybe he knew it. Maybe he knew that his love made me a different Lucy and his power frightened him and that's why he disappeared.

Jane knew. Jane understood how Robert liberated me from loneliness and I think she was glad for me. We didn't discuss it. She asked once if we took precautions. I was dreamy and secretive. I just said, yes.

Somehow, wherever we hid to make love, Ralph always managed to find us. We checked behind shrubs and trees first, we sent him on wild goose chases across the yard into the orchard, we turned on the TV for him but, when we looked up afterwards, there was Ralph watching us with unashamed curiosity, his gentle blue eyes wide.

'How are you, Ralph?' I ask now.

'Good,' he smiles vacantly. He doesn't recognize me.

'Is Mrs Joseph here?'

'No.'

'When is she back?'

'She's staying with Robert.'

319

Something inside my belly contracts with disappointment.

'Oh, that sure is a shame. I was hoping to contact an old friend of your family. Someone by the name of Marcello . . .'

'Barbara,' says Ralph. 'Barbara died.'

More disappointment. The Marcello Trust and Barbara Marcello must be no more than a coincidence. I'm ready to thank him and get back in my car when I remember Barbara.

'Oh, but I knew her! She was Mrs Joseph's friend! She was real nice.' The friend who was there the day the car crashed, who held my hand and talked to me softly until Jane arrived.

'Shelley loved Barbara,' agrees Ralph.

Barbara was often at the Joseph house. She was tall with long hair which she wore loose at a time when most mothers had short perms. She had one son, a lonely, demanding boy. He was about eleven and he'd get disproportionately upset when Robert and I made it clear that we were more interested in isolating ourselves than in playing football or watching TV with him. Eventually, though, we'd look forward to the kid's visits because, when we escaped from him, he'd persuade Ralph to play cards and that way they'd both leave us alone.

'She was an artist, right?' I persist. I don't remember ever seeing her pictures but her talent gave her a kind of mystique.

Ralph smiles. 'Cancer,' he says.

'I think she had a son . . . I can't remember his name . . .'

'Ricky. Ricky fixes beautiful cars,' Ralph informs me.

'Ricky, that was it.' Then, for a moment, everything halts. My heart stops beating, blood stops moving around my body. 'Ralph, did you say he fixes cars now?'

Ralph nods. 'Up in San Strana.'

I start to move. I move quickly. It is so imperative that I drive to San Strana right away that I don't even ask about

Robert. I thank him warmly, shaking his hand again, edging towards the car.

'Shelley's home tonight,' he says as I slip behind the wheel. 'Come see her soon, she'd like that.'

I slam the door and he shouts something after me. I don't hear so I wind down the window for him to repeat it.

'That stuff you used to do with Robert,' he informs me. 'He must have learned how to do it right because now he has three children.'

I smile wordlessly.

'Come back,' he instructs me. 'We've waited a long time for you, Lucy.'

He waves as I drive away.

Out in the hot valley where everything else moves slowly, I'm fast. I drive fast. My heart beats fast. In my search for the Marcello Trust, in my pursuit of the tow truck, it never once occurred to me that the two might be connected. The journey takes almost an hour but for all that time there is a tingling in my fingers. Anticipation. Only as I approach the San Strana valley do I remember how much I fear this man and his truck. He was a strange and lonely pre-adolescent who barely touched my life and who I never imagined would re-enter it. All I know about him now is that he is tall and dark-haired, he avoids all contact with my family, he can run fast, he wants something from our house and he was aggressive to Daddy.

It is easy to locate Ricky Marcello's garage. I ask for directions in one of the tourist shops in Cooper, San Strana's main town, and three people are all able to assure me that it is just a couple of miles away. First I'll reach a converted barn called the Marcello Gallery and a hundred yards past it is the garage.

'Ricky's pretty good but he only fixes cars when he wants to,' warns one man. 'So I sure hope you're not in a hurry.'

I drive out of town through the green, wooded valley. The great trees bow under the burden of their leaves as if they've spent the day absorbing their weight in sunlight. A river flows through this fertile valley and the habitations which cluster around it are old and shaded by trees which have none of the slender, fast-grown appearance of the trees around Daddy's house. The whole place is like the Joseph farmstead, as though someone picked up a piece of San Strana and transplanted it to the big, hot valley.

Soon I pass signs to the gallery and start to slow. I had intended to pull into the garage but when I see the tow truck standing outside it I lose courage and accelerate instead. After a few minutes I turn. Then I drive past the garage again, real slowly this time. It does have a sign but the sign is small and indifferent to the possibility of new business. COOPER ROAD GARAGE, E. MARCELLO. Ricky must be a pet name or a diminutive. I wonder what the E stands for.

There are no gas pumps, no bright red posters advertising tyres or screaming the virtues of high grade oil. The garage is just some old sheds, a tow truck and a small collection of cars, most of them, like the tow truck, antique. It is too picturesque to be a serious business.

I drive past it one more time before I turn again and pull off the road. Then I approach the garage quietly, on foot, like someone whose car broke down nearby.

The shed doors are all closed. I stand behind the tow truck and listen, barely breathing, wishing my heart would pump more quietly. I am a raw nerve, waiting for noises or smells to touch me. A clanging wrench. A whistling man. Hot oil. But I detect nothing. I stay in the shadow of the truck long after I have concluded that the place is empty.

I can see most of the cars from here. They are in different

states of repair. A couple are complete wrecks. An old blue car, cigar-shaped, has white paint all around one light like a bandage. There are two vintage sports cars which seem in good condition.

I'll have to leave my hiding place soon. Standing here in motionless silence, ready to run if I have to, makes my fingers and toes jangle. But I remember how, when Daddy worked under the tractor, you sometimes didn't know he was there. You could wait a long time for movement or noise. I listen, all my senses alert, my body tense, my ears buzzing.

A path leads behind the sheds. It is gravel. I walk noiselessly on the grass at its edge. Once I knock against an old oil drum and its clang brings me to a standstill. Then I edge around the buildings. Behind them is a small field. A well-trodden trail leads towards a house, barely visible through the trees. I calculate that the house must be a little way behind the barn which has been converted into a gallery.

I feel exposed in the field. The sun is a cruel spotlight. I cross quickly. There is a bridge over a creek and then I am relieved to be invisible among trees near the house. When I see movement on the verandah at the back of the house, I lie flat on the ground, watching. A woman, with a baby. The house is large and mellow with age and the verandah seems to connect it to the trees outside. I see the baby crawl on to the verandah and then the woman follows and picks it up. She holds it high over her head for a moment. In the distance I can hear the baby's whoop of delight. I think suddenly, bitterly, of Stevie, who was never delighted by anything. Then the woman puts the baby down and walks into the house. The baby follows her. They leave a void behind them. They are inside the house together and I am alone in the woods. What am I doing, lying here with grass tickling my face? Trespassing. Peeping at other people's families.

Following some lonely trail of my own. And it seems, lying belly-down in someone else's woods in someone else's valley, that all my life I've chosen a lonely trail.

I want to cry but instead I stand up and walk back through the trees, across the river, across the field. I don't even trouble to hide. No one knows or cares that I am here. I walk back between the sheds and slip around the tow truck and then, so suddenly that I don't have time to think or react, I feel an arm around my neck. Suddenly, my face is pressing against the unyielding chrome of the tow truck so my cheek feels as though it's in my mouth and the smell of oil fills my head. A voice is hissing right behind me: 'What the fuck do you think you're doing?'

I can't answer because the arm is jammed under my jaw. I move my eyes to the right and the left. I can't see my assailant but I can discern that he holds some kind of a weapon. Then he swings me round, and his body is all power and I know it is useless to fight and that I cannot escape from his grip. I look at the weapon. It is a small black box which I recognize at once. He holds it near me like a threat. When he touches a button it throws tiny ribbons of blue, hissing lightning into the air. I hear Kirsty's voice so clearly that she seems to be inside my head: 'You only have to touch someone with the probes and you can override their central nervous system.'

Slowly, my eyes meet Ricky Marcello's. I know his face at once. Hirsute now but with the same gaunt, searching look I remember from way back when I was big and he was small. If he has any affection for those years and my bit part in them, it doesn't show now.

'What the fuck are you doing here?' he demands again.

His mouth is curled down and his eyes have a dark asymmetry and I know from them that he is either very angry

324

or crazy or both. I smell his sweat. I smell his body. Oil, rags, coffee, a garage smell.

'I'm looking for you,' I tell him. My voice is small. It doesn't want to continue but I make the words come. 'I have questions for you. What do you want at my father's house? Was he paying you? Why? Why were you shouting at him right before he died? You were yelling and threatening him and then the very next day . . .'

His face is livid. He swings me around like a doll so my back is against him and his hand is across my mouth. He's squeezing my lips against my teeth, his thumb against my cheek, stretching the skin on my chin, pressing my nose so I can't breathe. I struggle for the first time, trying to prise his fingers away, fighting for air, but his fingers are clenched too hard against my face.

'I don't want you here,' he informs me. He's speaking right into my ear like a lover but he's hissing and there is hatred in his hot, damp breath. 'I don't want you here. I don't want to see your goddamn face around my house, my family, my truck, my barn.'

I pull my right knee up sharply and stamp my foot down hard, as hard as I can, on to his. I feel pain's impact run through his body. The hand over my face loosens and I gulp for air. Then his grip tightens and I know I've made him even madder.

The taser appears in front of my face, just a few inches away, so that both my eyes are filled by the fizzing, unnatural blue manifestation of its power. One touch and I will be frozen, unable to struggle. I lift my right knee again and then push my foot down hard, harder this time. I manage more of an angle, so that the heel of my shoe, solid although not high, cuts into him. I feel the soft crunch of bone beneath my sole. Probably I haven't broken his foot but I've hurt it and before he can absorb the pain I raise my knee again. I think of Daddy, killed by the taser, tumbling over the cliff at Seal Wash, and this time my foot stabs deeply into his and then I grind it still further. As he relieves the pain by swaying on to his left leg I force my body weight left. For a moment he topples. I struggle. If I'm going to escape it will have to be now. I fight his fingers, I kick backwards, I push my elbows into his ribs. But his grip hardens around my neck, across my mouth, my nose.

Gradually my legs weaken and then my arms. I stop fighting him. I stop fighting for oxygen. There is none. My body goes limp like paper and as it does so, amazingly, he releases me. I stumble forward, disbelieving, biting at the air as though it's solid.

'Get out now,' he yells at me.

I put my fingers to my mouth. It's bleeding. My cheeks feel raw as though they've been grated.

As I stagger away he shouts: 'Get away from here. And keep your goddamn accusations to yourself and your god-damn mouth shut so I don't have to shut it for good.'

I break into a run. I feel blood dripping off my face and on to my shirt. I don't look back.

When I get to the car I fall into it and drive away fast. Ricky Marcello is standing by the garage, hands on hips, watching me go.

It is late in the afternoon of a sweltering day. Nothing in the San Strana valley moves quickly, not the horses which swish their tails under trees, not the traffic. Progress is frustrating. I drive holding a Kleenex to my face, checking my rear view mirror nervously for the tow truck.

When I am almost out of the valley I swing into a dusty parking lot. There are a couple of fruit stalls which, despite the boards all around advertising their low prices, have now closed for the evening. I reverse between them. From this hidden place, I watch the road, waiting, hardly allowing myself to blink. When at last the traffic eases I steal glances at myself in the vanity mirror. I look shocked and white-faced and one lip is swollen. There is a pool of dried blood under my nose. I try to clean my face without taking my eyes from the road.

I'm waiting for the tow truck but when the blue car with the white bandage on its fender passes, my body responds instantly. I start the engine and edge out of the lot. I reach the road a second too late to pull out in front of a pick-up which shudders slowly up the hill. It is laden with oranges. Four cars trail behind it in low gear. I try to pass. There are bleating horns and round, angry mouths and I am forced to fall into line. By the time the road evens and I leave the pick-up behind, I know Ricky Marcello must be far ahead.

I slot into the southbound traffic on the freeway. Below me I glimpse the red bricks of Lowis. An image of a red-faced boy sitting on a skateboard appears in my mind then disappears as I accelerate fast, leaving Lowis behind. I scan the darkening road for the blue car. When I don't see it I accelerate still more, until I'm breaking the speed limit, diving recklessly in and out of traffic. Remember death. Joe Zacarro said: if you remember that you're going to die some day then you live your life in a different sort of way. I sigh and accelerate again.

I don't see the blue car until we are almost at the bridge and then it appears so suddenly that I have to brake and fall into a lane of slower traffic to remain invisible. It's hard to keep it in sight without being seen myself. Now that darkness is gathering fast over the city a lot of cars look blue and to watch it among all the other tail lights I must drive closer than is comfortable.

327

When it leaves the freeway I notice in time to follow. My heart beats faster. This is the exit closest to Jane and Larry's apartment. I keep my distance but from now on stop lights are a problem. Staying one intersection back would be hard enough in daylight and in the dark it's impossible. I am just a couple of cars behind Ricky Marcello.

Then I make a mistake and it's a bad one. I follow the wrong car. The blue car I tail moves fast, weaving in and out of the traffic, and I hurry to keep up. When I stop at a light I realize that the car with the white fender is right beside me. I don't look at it. I don't look at the driver. I try to be someone going home from work who has a passing interest in the stores across the street but all the time I feel the proximity of Ricky Marcello, sense that his face is turned to me and his angry eyes stare at me.

The light changes and all the cars move forward with the grace of synchronized swimmers. Ricky Marcello is right beside me. I try to fall back but he slows too. In my mirror I see cars bunching behind us. I still don't look at him as we cruise to the next light but as we go through it I realize that he has gone, peeled off into the right turn only lane. I dare to look. His car is disappearing at exactly ninety degrees to mine.

I try driving around the block. Then I do a figure of eight. Soon I am in despair at the impossibility of finding one pair of tail lights in a city full of lights. In the hope of meeting him at his destination, I head towards Jane and Larry's apartment. I don't drive right past it but I look up their street from the nearby intersection. He's there. I glimpse the blue car pulling in by a parking meter right across the road from the apartment. I was right. Ricky Marcello is watching Larry and Jane.

I double back further up the steep hill and park at what

feels like an acute angle. From here I have a view of the street to the apartment. I can't see the blue car but I will if it pulls out. The hill is well-lit and, if Ricky Marcello tries to cross the street, I'll see that too.

This is an old, quaint area of the city. The town houses are clustered densely on the hill and the white apartment is on a second storey. Someone is home because the lights are on. Probably Larry, polishing and practising the tribute he'll be reading at Daddy's funeral tomorrow. Possibly Jane too. She was at the hospital today but I guess that she'll be home early, confirming all the arrangements. There's a car down the street which could be hers. I don't want to get out to check.

For a long time nothing happens. The temperature drops and I feel stiff and dirty and cold but I try to stay alert so I can drive away fast if Ricky Marcello walks up the street and sees me here.

Someone appears at the window of the apartment. I tense. It is Larry, peering anxiously out to see whether he is observed tonight. Maybe Ricky Marcello drives a different car each time he visits because something in the relaxed way Larry pulls the drapes indicates that he doesn't know he is watched.

My shoulders and face start to throb. When people ask me how my face got bruised I'll have to say I walked into a door. I can't tell anyone about Ricky Marcello, not until I learn why he was one of Daddy's secrets.

Sitting in the car, waiting, not moving, my mind is briefly inhabited by the woman I saw from the woods, the woman who held the baby high above her head. She was busy in the house and she glanced out to where the baby was crawling on the verandah then swooped down on him and delighted him with her sudden attention. He whooped with joy. I seldom experienced pleasure in my child except when he was sleeping and I can't remember him ever expressing such joy.

Ricky Marcello must live in the house among the trees and the woman must be Ricky Marcello's wife. The baby is his baby. I'm gathering information about him, although I don't yet know if any of it is useful. I try to remember the young Ricky whom I knew at the Josephs'. I recall only a sort of kinetic energy, his frantic and often irritating pleas for attention. Whenever I was at the Josephs' my mind was focused on Robert. Ricky was no more than a fly who buzzed around him.

At last, when my whole body is exhausted by doing nothing, my arms and legs ache for lack of movement, my stomach gurgles hungrily and the inside of my head constantly replays my battle at the Marcello garage this afternoon, something happens. The lights are turned out in the apartment. Sensible Jane, sensible Larry. An early night before the funeral. I feel absurdly grateful to them when I see the blue car slide out from its parking bay. I fall in behind it. Now that traffic is scarce we slip through the night, Ricky Marcello and then me, without difficulty. I see him as far as the freeway then turn towards Aunt Zina's. I ask myself what he could accomplish by sitting outside the apartment all evening but I am too numb to attempt an answer to this question.

31

When I wake on the day of Daddy's funeral my body aches as though someone has been pinching me all over for many hours. The bed covers are mostly on the floor. I do not feel rested. I look back on the night as a marathon of anger and tears but I cannot recall my dreams in any detail. I get out of bed stiffly as though my body is made of metal. When I stare at myself, expressionless, in the mirror, I am surprised to see that my face is unmarked by yesterday's encounter with Ricky Marcello.

I wear my New York clothes. They will be too hot but they are sombre. When I slip them on my body is unyielding like iron. The suit seems to hang limply, without its usual fluidity. I am unable to eat any of the food Aunt Zina offers me and even the coffee tastes sour on my metallic tongue. I add sugar and it still tastes sour.

Sasha and Aunts Zina and Zoya have already left for Redbush when Scott picks me up.

'How are you, Luce?' he asks, scanning me anxiously. His face looks white. He has slept badly and now is worrying about the tribute he will be reading.

I say: 'I wish it was all over.'

As we climb into the car, Dimitri Sergeyevich, obviously pre-warned by Sasha, restricts his disapproval to an eye-browish glare.

We join Jane and Larry in the lobby of the chapel by the cemetery. Jane kisses me. She smells of flowers as usual and looks almost translucently beautiful, her eyes like big blue butterflies which have landed on her pale, pale face.

Mourners soon gather. I recognize only a few of them but others introduce themselves and all murmur sympathy and something nice about Daddy. I try to thank them but this new tongue, hard, shiny, won't say the right words.

'Honey,' says a large woman putting her hand on mine. 'Grief is cumulative. Each bereavement brings back all the other losses. The cycle never ends but it does get better.'

I nod and store her words away to think about later. I am made of metal and cannot absorb them now.

When Seymour and Katherine arrive they each lock me in a tight embrace.

'We've been so worried about you since we saw you, Lucy,' says Katherine.

I wonder what I said or did to worry them.

'I'll be fine,' I tell them smoothly. Seymour hugs me again but the warmth from his body does not penetrate my new hard surface.

I watch Joe Zacarro limp in. Adam Holler walks stiffly behind him. As soon as he sees me, water drips from Joe's eyes.

'Shit, Lucy,' he says, grasping my hand in both of his. 'When you get to the funeral and you know you're going to see a goddamn coffin then you really have to believe someone's dead. Except I can't. Eric was the fittest of any of us, he shouldn't have been the first to go. Lucy, this never should have happened, he never should have allowed it to happen.'

Whatever makes Joe think that Daddy allowed himself to be killed? But I can't ask him while he's crying. I watch him impassively. I know I should say something, reach out to him. Slowly, with an almost superhuman effort, I stretch my hand to his arm. He grabs it and smothers it with his own big, wet hand.

Mr Holler says: 'Lucy, your father was a damn intelligent man. Usually people with that kind of intelligence aren't people you can love. But he . . .' His voice cracks. His rigidity is threatened. He is a building which is about to fall. He leans against Joe and then straightens. I pull a Kleenex from the supply in my purse and he takes it gratefully.

'Didn't think I'd be needing any of these,' he sniffs. 'You never can tell what feelings are going to come sneaking up on you.'

Grief is cumulative. Each bereavement brings back all the other losses. He's crying for Daddy but also for the son who died, for the wife who left.

I am soon passing Kleenex to other mourners until, when I look around the lobby, it seems that everyone but me is pressing tissue to their face. I am the only person in the room whose entire body, including her tongue and heart, is made of metal.

Almost late, but not quite, are the Russians. They arrive in a cluster with Mother at its centre. Her arm is linked firmly through Sasha's. Although I have already resolved to avoid her, when she walks into the room I am drawn, as though powerless, to Mother's tiny, shuffling body. I am prepared for her smallness but in this big room it takes me by surprise.

Jane kisses her lightly and then melts back into the throng of people before Russian hands can pull her to them. The hands capture me and drag me right up to Mother.

'Tanechka, aren't you pleased to see your own Lucia?' cries Aunt Zina and, although she says it in Russian, her words, as sometimes so inexplicably happens, cut through linguistic barriers and I understand her with a crystalline precision. Suddenly and surprisingly, through wisps of blonde, white, hair, the vacant eyes focus on me. There is a fluttering movement and Mother's face widens, her eyes grow bigger, her confusion leaves her and she is complete. For a sudden, haunting moment her beauty returns. She holds out a hand to me and I clasp it. A tiny bird rests in my hand and I do not let it fly away. Then, as though there has been some silent communication between them, the whole group moves on. Aunt Zoya, her hair slipping from its clasp, catches me excitedly.

'How happy she is to know you are here,' she says.

Guests melt away before the wife of the decedent. Sasha leads her towards the doors of the hall and they are now thrown open. We all follow Mother, who walks slowly and with dignity, into the hall. Sasha turns just before they are through the doors and, glimpsing me through a sudden window in the crowd, throws me a conspiratorial wink.

At the sight of the casket there is universal grief. Jane trembles and her tears fall quietly, Larry closes his eyes and stands very straight, his mouth twitching, Scott sobs unreservedly. During the music I look around and try to recognize people but it's hard to recognize anyone when their faces are buried in Kleenex. Scott, as he predicted, is halted by tears during his reading.

'He took his big candle
And went into another room
I cannot find . . .'

Everyone seems to break down with him. I turn to see Joe Zacarro and Adam Holler with their stiff legs pointing in different directions, supporting each other, tears flowing freely. Seymour and Katherine hold hands, heads bowed.

Scott finds his voice again and somehow completes the poem.

At the back, right by the door, are Rougemont and Kirsty. They are dry-eyed. They are watching. My eyes meet Rougemont's.

After more music it is Larry's turn. He takes his place at the front of the room, near Daddy's coffin. He has prepared a series of cards to help him remember his speech but almost from the first he does not look at them. I imagine him practising in front of the bathroom mirror last night, or behind the closed drapes of the living-room.

'We've been telling each other what made Eric Schaffer special for us. I'd like to try explaining not how Eric was special, but why. Yes, I'm a psychiatrist, as most of you know, and my professional training is relevant to what I'm about to say. But don't worry, I'll waive my usual fee.'

There is a ripple of movement which could be amusement but Larry changes cards and carries right on.

'If we want to understand people then we usually start with their childhood. Not easy in Eric's case: he almost never spoke about his early years. We know he came from a small, homespun community in the mountains and that life there was devoted to the church. Not the strict orthodoxy of the Mormon church but some splinter group which, because of its isolation no doubt, had developed history, beliefs and rituals of its own.

'We don't know much about his family but we can guess that it was a loving one. As the youngest of eight children, Eric probably enjoyed extra attention from his mother as well as the love and interest of his elder siblings and, if his community was polygamous and his father had other wives, maybe there was also the affection of his extended family. How do I know this? Because Eric was a loving man. I'll bet everyone here was the recipient, in some way, of Eric's love. His wife and daughters of course, but many others, to a greater or lesser extent, benefited from his ability to give love and to receive it. He can only have learned that in his childhood.

'Second, Eric was a kind man. He empathized with the

suffering of others and that's because he had suffered himself. We don't know how. As a child. When he left his family behind as a teenager and faced the world alone. During his struggle up the academic ladder. He was a brilliant man but, after all, he had no formal education until the age of sixteen.

'We do know that his marriage brought him great happiness, but when his beautiful wife fell sick, he coped because he'd learned in his childhood how to endure suffering. When his son died, a tragedy he almost never referred to, he suffered but he coped. When his grandson died, he suffered but he coped. When his daughter moved across the continent, he suffered but he coped. Most of us in this room can recall some small, quiet act of kindness from Eric. These acts usually said: I understand your unhappiness because I first met unhappiness long, long ago. I want to help you cope as I learned to cope long, long ago.

'Third, he was ruthless. He had to be ruthless to leave that loving family behind and start again, in a world he didn't know, entirely alone. He maintained that ruthlessness in the best possible way. He was ruthless in his pursuit of the principles he held dear. He did what he believed to be right, whatever the cost to himself.

'Fourth, he gave rocks. If there's anyone here who hasn't been given a rock by Eric, please raise your hand. I thought so. Eric had a personal mission to redistribute the world's rocks. Or maybe he was trying to dismantle a mountain. For instance, the one he grew up on.

'Finally, Eric was an outsider. Life in an isolated, possibly polygamous, quasi-Mormon community at six thousand feet above sea level was probably a little different from the way you and I grew up. After that, Eric didn't fit in anywhere and he knew it. No wonder he was such a great head of department at the U. He managed his team lovingly without ever getting involved in the factionalism and petty politics of university life. He grew up on Mount Olympus and he could look down on all that stuff. He didn't join things. He had plenty of friends but he didn't generally operate in a group. And when he married, he married Tatiana, a lovely immigrant, another outsider.

'Did Eric like to be an outsider? Well, I think it made him lonely. I think he suffered from a deep, deep loneliness which, at some level, we all recognized. I never talked to him about it. I guess I never tried to help. I regret that now.

'A lot of people have asked me: why did Eric die the way he did? Nobody knows the answer to that yet. It seems incredible that such an unobtrusive, sweet-natured man could be a homicide victim, the target of a calculated attack. So I've been looking into homicide. I've found out a few facts. I've found that lonely outsiders feature prominently in homicide statistics. But, we're not here to talk about Eric's death and we shouldn't let the word homicide stand between us and the Eric we knew. Let's celebrate his life.'

Larry snaps his cards together and nods at the mourners and sits down to the opening bars of a Mozart piano concerto. For the first time I feel something breaking through my armour. It is not sadness but anger. Larry's wrong. He's wrong about Daddy's early years creating a deep well of loneliness. He suffered, he suffered so much that he attempted suicide. But his great loneliness came later. I know because in the picture of him on the beach with us, he's laughing. Really laughing, the way nobody can when deep down they're lonesome and unhappy. He stopped laughing, but it wasn't because of anything which happened in Utah years back. It was caused by events which happened right here.

When the ceremony is over, family members leave behind the coffin. First, the Russians, Mother so small that she is almost invisible at their centre. Then Scott and Larry and Jane and me. We are burying Daddy and the sky should be grey, the day gloomy. Instead I am dazzled by the intensity of the sunlight. It bounces off the headstones and monuments and it ricochets off the brass on Daddy's casket like the ball in a fast, hot game.

'Did you think Daddy was lonely?' I murmur to Scott. 'Did you think he was an outsider?'

He nods. He tries to speak but more tears are falling.

The earth which is to cover Daddy is without moisture. When the first handful lands on the coffin, a powder-fine cloud fills the grave like vapour. I anticipated that the sight of Daddy's grave and the coffin within it would make me weak with emotion. I expected to moisten the dirt with my tears. But, while everyone else is doubled with grief, their faces wet, my new metal heart feels nothing. Emotions slide right off its shining surface. I see the coffin buried low and it pleases me that Daddy is becoming a geological stratum, a small seam of humanity in the rocky earth.

Looking up from the grave I see Mother. A rose drops from her fingers and tears tiny as jewellery trickle from each eye. Like everyone else, she stares, motionless, down at Daddy's coffin. Behind her, at some distance, I sense movement. A bird, flying from headstone to headstone. I look for it and see that it is a man. I catch my breath. He is not too far away for me to see his face. Ricky Marcello and I stare directly into each other's eyes. I want to yell. I want to chase him and demand explanations. But the grief of everyone around roots me to Daddy's graveside and I can only watch as he withdraws rapidly behind a headstone like a snake disappearing into long grass. He moves fast, slipping between monuments and over graves. As he grows more distant my view of him is frequently and at last totally obscured.

As we start to walk silently back up to the chapel, I am still looking for him. In the road on the other side of the cemetery I see something which could be the flash of chrome moving through the bright sunlight. A faraway roar could be a tow truck or an airplane. Close by, I can hear mourners, slamming car doors, starting their engines, leaving for Daddy's house.

Michael Rougemont is standing right outside the chapel as though he's waiting for me.

'Did you see someone?' I ask.

He looks at me, the sun cruelly lighting his strange physiognomy, and nods.

When we arrive at Daddy's house the mourners form a long, whiskery line up the porch steps. They are used to wearing overalls for gentle yardwork these days and the suits they have dragged out of the closet smell of mothballs and no longer fit. Mother has been returned to Redbush now and Jane and I shake many hands and receive sympathy. Scott and Larry are both congratulated on their tributes, Scott with warmth, Larry with admiration. Scott reddens at their praise but Larry accepts it routinely. He directs diners to the caterers' table out on the deck. In the far corner of the porch, obscured by shadow and foliage, I am aware of the stillness of the two detectives.

Soon people are sitting on the porch, on the deck, and in all the ground floor rooms. Only the den has been closed to them. The house buzzes with the murmur of low voices exchanging information, discussing news, predicting the end of the heatwave. This is the first gathering I can recall here. All the time I grew up there was never a party and seldom visitors. Apart from Mother's shouts, this is the noisiest I have ever known the house.

When Jane is helping an elderly mourner to a seat and

Scott has gone to fetch him some food, Larry appears at my side.

I say: 'Larry, did you ever call the police about the guy hanging around outside the apartment?'

He looks at me in surprise. 'Once. But it took them so long to arrive that he'd already left. I haven't seen him for a night or two, maybe he's given up.'

'Maybe he's hiding. Sitting in a car.'

'Maybe,' agrees Larry. 'It's not a nice thought.'

'Close the drapes just as soon as it gets dark,' I advise. 'Or leave them open but turn out the living-room lights like you're not home.'

Larry doesn't take advice from me on anything, certainly not security matters. 'I want to discuss this with Kirsty.' He starts to edge in her direction.

'By the way,' I call after him. 'How do you know that Daddy came from a polygamous community?'

He pauses and shrugs.

'It's a safe bet.'

Then he sidles through the people towards the detectives. He engages them in intense conversation. Kirsty listens to Larry while Rougemont's eyes wander over the room. From time to time he catches my eye but I do not acknowledge him and when he gives me one of his meandering smiles I do not smile back. Later, he approaches me. He is looking even more like a shadow than usual in a dark suit and a dark tie.

'How are you feeling, Lucy?'

'Sort of peculiar,' I admit.

'Like, you're not feeling anything?' he asks. I nod and he nods too.

'Yes,' he says. 'Yes.'

There is a silence. I wonder if he is going to ask me more

about the weekend I spent in California. Instead he says: 'Jim Finnigan is a good guy and he likes you a lot but he doesn't know you real well. Same with everyone I met in New York.'

I stare at him.

'You went there to be some other person. That's the Lucy they know. But the whole time the old Lucy was waiting back here for you.' I think of my old self in ragged shorts or a blue sundress, hanging around at the airport for the slim, efficient Lucy to emerge from a plane. 'I sure wish you'd listen to her. Because that other Lucy, the old Lucy, the one you ran away from, she has all the answers.'

I regard him stonily. 'What are you talking about, Mr Rougemont? I'm an investment banker. I've taken two weeks' compassionate leave following my father's death, and on Saturday night I'm flying back to New York city to resume my job.'

'Uh-huh,' says Rougemont, and his mouth is pulled into a shape which could be a smile or a grimace. I turn away from him. Jim has already called to announce that the bank has released tapes of my telephone conversations to the police.

'Do you need a good lawyer, Lucy?' he asked. I detected a vacuum in his tone where there used to be warmth, as though I've been away a year instead of a week.

'Of course not, Jim. Is there any update on Hifeld?'

'Gregory Hifeld's decided not to sell the company and Jay Kent was downright rude when I tried to follow up with him. Says he won't be doing any deal which involves us again.'

'Oh boy.'

'Semper thinks your career doesn't look too promising right now,' Jim warned me. 'I did my best with him but a deal which turned so mean plus the police asking a lot

341

of personal questions about you … well, it's sort of an unfortunate combination.'

'Am I fired?'

Jim hesitated. Finally he said: 'You're not dead yet. But you're seriously ill. Sorry, Lucy. Things could have been different. They should have been different.'

When I see Adam Holler and Joe Zacarro standing alone, I go right up to them. I ask them: 'Well, are you two still going to Remember Death out on the highways? I mean, without Daddy?'

Mr Holler is stony but Joe's face breaks into a broad grin.

'Lucy, how the hell did you work out what we do?' he asks. 'You must be real clever like your daddy.'

'There are at least two detectives here, Joe,' says Adam Holler. 'If you must talk about this, would you do it quietly?'

'Sorry!' roars Joe. 'I'm going to tell you our plan, Lucy.' He leans closer but does not lower his voice. 'Your daddy always intended to do the bridge. Can you believe that? The bridge! Think of the big chaos, big tailbacks, we can create if we dump a wreck on the bridge. We figured it could be a sort of Eric Schaffer memorial dump.'

Adam Holler watches the room anxiously.

'Problem is,' Joe goes on, shifting his weight around uncomfortably, 'that they have cameras on the bridge. Now that should be a challenge. We're going to have to drive over it a few times and take a look at those cameras.'

'Shhhh,' hisses Adam Holler.

Joe breathes out loudly and plucks at his ill-fitting suit. 'We gotta be real clever or we're gonna get caught.'

'Maybe,' I suggest, 'I could join you.'

'Hey, Lucy, you gonna help us?' Joe roars.

'Sure. I like the idea of the Eric Schaffer memorial dump.'

Joe threatens to get even noisier with delight and Mr Holler drags him away.

Joni Rimbaldi, Daddy's former secretary who was due to have lunch with him right after his death, tells me how she was about to leave the house when Scott phoned to tell her Daddy was dead.

'And you know,' she says, 'when I opened the closet this morning, I didn't want to wear the nice navy blue dress I keep for serious occasions. I took out the clothes I was wearing for lunch that day and I knew I just had to wear them to the funeral instead. Isn't that kookie?'

She laughs but the laugh is anxious and I try to reassure her. Joni, with her cropped grey hair, is both sensible and predictable and I can see it frightens her a little when she does this kind of thing.

'Is the jacket too bright?' she asks.

'It's fine, Joni, you look good, Daddy would have thought so too.'

'I guess I'll need to change into something warmer this evening. We're flying out to Maine.'

'Why are you vacationing in Maine when you already live at the most beautiful place on earth?'

When she retired, Joni and her husband moved up to Tigertail Bay, a seal-infested beach which is annually voted one of the most spectacular in the area.

'My sister's sixtieth is tomorrow. We were due to fly out yesterday but I just couldn't miss Eric's funeral. It would be like standing him up for lunch.' And she gives a watery half smile.

When all the funeral guests are eating and there seems nothing left to say to anyone, a woman, tall, slim and white-haired, touches my arm.

'Lucy . . . I guess you don't remember me?'

I study the woman. Her white hair is pinned up loosely. Brown eyes, even features, a kind smile.

'Oh! Mrs Joseph!' I am a gauche teenager again. 'Oh, gee.' I feel my face go pink.

'My hair certainly wasn't white when you knew me,' she laughs. 'And I must have been ten pounds lighter.' Age has crept up on Mrs Joseph. Her husband is dead, her children are all grown, she has grandchildren. She acknowledges time's passage with a rueful laugh.

'It's so good to see you. I'm sorry I wasn't home yesterday when you called. I've hoped for years you'd come down to the valley and visit with us. We all missed you so much after that terrible crash. I hope you've forgiven Robert now.'

When I can't find any words, she rescues me.

'It took him a long time to get over you. But he's been married a while and I think pretty well married. They're in Virginia and their youngest child is eight months old. I've been staying with them. I just got back last night.'

We talk about how Robert became a doctor after spending so much time in hospital after the crash.

'I guess it didn't change your life, at least not dramatically,' she says.

'Oh, sure it did.' But I don't admit how, when the Joseph family shut me out, doors closed in my head and in my heart. I say: 'I wasn't too mobile for a while and it was the reading and thinking I did that summer which took me into banking.'

She describes how Mr Joseph died of a heart attack suddenly one morning out in the orchard twenty-four hours after Robert had left to return to the hospital in Baltimore where he was working. He might have saved his father if his vacation had been one day longer. Step is teaching at MIT and Morton, the eldest of the three Joseph brothers, is running the farm.

'But I should have told you how sorry I am about your father,' she says. 'I got to know him pretty well over the years and I was very fond of him.'

'You were?' I had assumed her presence here was no more than neighbourly.

'Lucy, are you going to visit with Ralph and me down in the valley real soon?'

'I'd like to,' I admit. 'I've wanted to for years. But I'm leaving for New York on Saturday.'

'What are you doing after the funeral?' she asks. 'Oh, but I guess you should be with your family.'

I want to be with Mrs Joseph and for an embarrassing, confusing moment, it seems to me that she is my family.

'I can drive over to the farm later,' I tell her.

32

When I cross the aqueduct and turn into the Josephs' lush oasis in the valley, it seems as familiar and welcoming as home. The evening sun creates pockets of shadow across the lawn and covers the big house in a light so subtle that it feels like a secret.

Ralph and Mrs Joseph hear my car and come outside. A couple of dogs stroll at their side, panting, tails wagging lazily. Mrs Joseph has changed into pale, loose clothes and swept her hair higher on to her head. Ralph is wearing overalls. He smiles while Mrs Joseph hugs me unreservedly. Then he evaporates into the yard.

'Did you eat today?' she asks as she leads me indoors.

'No.'

'Are you hungry now?'

I am astonished to find that I am hungry and that, when she places an interesting salad in front of me, I can eat all of it. The big dogs watch me, waiting for scraps of bread, thumping their tails on the ground occasionally.

'Good,' she says when she comes back into the room and sees my empty plate. She has been collecting pictures and she sits with them at my side.

'This is the first thing we should do,' she explains. 'I mean, deal with your curiosity about Robert.'

One at a time, with a brief commentary, she hands me photos of Robert, some from his wedding or earlier but most of them recent.

'He's just the same,' I say.

'Not exactly. His personality deepened and changed after the car crash and I think that soon showed in his face.'

'His wife's beautiful.'

'I think she looks a little like you. And, she's a banker too. Isn't that a coincidence? Or maybe not. Now here's a very old one of you with all the boys.'

Three boys aged from about five to fifteen. They all have the same black curly hair and they are sprawling across a couch and each other. In their midst is a girl, aged maybe ten. She's sprawling like one of the boys, grinning like one of the boys.

'But . . . what was I doing here?'

'Climbing trees, risking your life on the rope swing, building dens, all the things kids normally do.'

I look from the picture to Mrs Joseph and back to the picture. 'I didn't ever come here when I was a kid.'

'Sure you did. Your mother wasn't around and your father had to go away a lot so you used to stay here.'

'Often?'

'Some years it was often.'

'Years? This went on for years?'

'You don't remember. That's a shame, we had some good times.' Her voice is even. Maybe I detect disappointment because she'd like me to remember those good times.

'Oh Mrs Joseph, I had some great times here but I thought they were all in one summer, I mean, Robert's summer.'

'Robert was a pal to you long before he became a boyfriend. That's probably why, when you both jumped, it was in at the deep end. You'd done the shallow end stuff for years.'

I sigh. Now I understand why this house feels like a home. I've contracted my memories and feelings about the place into one short summer.

'But . . . where was Jane?'

Mrs Joseph is standing up now. 'Your father left her with the Carmichaels, I think. Or the Spelmanns. I'm not sure where she went. Lucy, I have another picture of you. I'll be right back.'

While she is out of the room I examine the photos more closely than seemed polite in front of Mrs Joseph. First, me and the Joseph boys, draped over the couch and each other. I seem relaxed and happy. I have a pigtail, which one of the boys, probably Step but maybe Robert, is holding up so it's vertical.

Then I pull out a recent snapshot of Robert. I take it to the window and twist it in the light. I see that time's truck has been kind to him. It has rearranged his face a little but the lines he has acquired give him a sort of cragginess.

When I look up, there is Ralph, standing by the kitchen window, grinning at me in his overalls like Rebecca of Sunnybrook Farm. I wonder if anyone here has any secrets that Ralph doesn't know.

'Hi, Ralph,' I say with resignation.

'Nice picture,' he smiles, and then melts back into the green yard.

'Recognize these two young folk?' asks Mrs Joseph, returning with a small photo in her hand. A young Robert, hair curling over his face. His arm is tight around a green-eyed, dark-haired girl who smiles not at the camera but at Robert. I stare at the girl as though I'm staring at my own ghost.

Mrs Joseph waits while I study the picture. When I am silent she asks: 'What's intriguing you?'

'Her smile. I mean, my smile.'

'It feels that you're looking at someone else?'

'Oh yes. I can't believe I ever was that girl.'

Mrs Joseph gently removes the picture and scrutinizes it herself.

'Why not, Lucy?' she asks, handing it back. 'It looks like you.'

'I can't believe I ever was that happy.'

She gets up.

'Oh, sure you were.' She pushes the icemaker and the noise it makes, gurgling and scrunching, sounds as though there's a crime going on inside.

I lift my feet to the rung of the chair and hug my knees. 'I was happy here. I liked this house so much. The way lots of people came in and out and it was always full of talk and laughter and dogs. I liked the way you and Mr Joseph spoke with each other, polite and intimate at the same time. It was so respectful. I never realized before that respect is an important part of love.'

She smiles. 'What did you think love was about? Control?'

I smile too. I feel strong now. Strong enough to ask: 'Did you blame me for the car crash?'

Mrs Joseph turns to me in surprise.

'Blame you? How could anyone blame you?'

'Robert was driving with his arm around me.'

'Then if I blamed anyone, and I don't think I did, I guess I would have blamed Robert.' She puts two iced drinks on the table and sits down behind one of them.

'I didn't ask him to drive that way,' I add. 'But maybe something I said, something I did, made him think he should. Then I would be technically responsible.'

She sips her drink in silence. And her silence compels me to continue.

'I mean . . . I thought that was why Robert didn't ever call me again. Why you didn't try to contact me after the crash. Because you blamed me.'

Mrs Joseph looks away from me as she thinks. She sips more water. Finally she says: 'It was all a very long time ago and probably it's fruitless to discuss it. But let me ask you something.'

I wait.

'Did you call Robert after the crash?'

'Well . . . no.'

'Did you call me?'

'No. I mean . . . you didn't phone and I thought you were mad at me and . . .'

'Maybe we thought you blamed us. When you didn't call.'

The sun is shining through the kitchen window right on my face, heating it.

'Oh no, no,' I stammer. 'Of course I didn't blame Robert or you or anyone.'

She looks at me closely. Her smile is understanding. I wonder what it is she understands: 'Someone has to pick up the phone, Lucy. That's all I have to say about this.' She drinks some more. 'I'm sure you're not still the kind of person who sits around waiting for others to call you. Your father was real proud of how well you've done in corporate finance.'

'Investment banking, actually, not that Daddy ever appreciated the difference.'

'Maybe he was too busy suffering to think about it,' she says, and she giggles the way I remember, like bubbles surfacing. 'I'm sorry, Lucy, but your brother-in-law's tribute to Eric really was too much, it's been irritating me all afternoon. I mean, we all suffer from some degree of loneliness, we all feel like outsiders sometimes. I'm not sure those feelings necessarily have anything to do with living in a polygamous community as a child.'

I take secret pleasure in hearing Mrs Joseph disagree with

Larry. His expertise is considered unassailable in our family. I say, with some enthusiasm: 'I didn't like that tribute either. It made me feel terrible, all that stuff about Daddy's loneliness. When I think of the pain I must have caused him and how I wasn't here to alleviate his loneliness . . .'

Mrs Joseph shakes her head. 'Personally I don't recall your father as a lonely man at all.'

I think of the tiny ring of white flesh around Daddy's wrist. Daddy, sixteen years old and recently arrived in a fish truck, lying in a hostel and hearing the indifferent snores of the other occupants. Listening to traffic noise or voices out on the street he was unused to. Kept awake by the smells and lights of the city because he had grown up knowing the deep silence of the mountains where the only light was moon light. Missing his family, everyone and everything he loved.

'But,' I say quietly: 'Daddy never laughed.' It's hard to admit that. It sounds like a criticism. Fathers are supposed to laugh.

'Oh, sure he did!' Mrs Joseph exclaims, opening her eyes wide.

'Not really. Not from his belly, not from his heart.'

'Sure he did! For heaven's sake, he's sat right where you're sitting now and laughed himself into helplessness.'

I look hard at her in disbelief but she's smiling privately. She's amused just thinking about it. 'It was Step who made him laugh so much. When Step was a little kid he was such a clown.'

'I've never known Daddy laugh himself into helplessness,' I say.

'Does it reassure you to know that he did?'

'I guess so.'

'Well, he laughed long and hard and often. And he had a good sense of humour and could make others laugh too.'

351

Daddy at the Joseph farmstead amid the noise, the people, the laughter. Sitting here in the kitchen, roaring like one of the family at Step's little kid antics. Knowing the Josephs well enough to leave me here while he went off on field trips.

Mrs Joseph can see me thinking all this. She's watching my thoughts like someone who's standing at the station and watching the train slowly approach. She's waiting at my destination.

I say: 'How come you knew Daddy so well? I'd like to ask you about that. And your friend, Barbara Marcello. Can you tell me whether Daddy had any connection with her or her son?'

'Did he tell you of any connection?'

'No.'

'Then it was either non-existent, insignificant or private.'

'Daddy paid money annually into something called the Marcello Trust. I'm sure it has something to do with Ricky Marcello. Ricky certainly knew Daddy. When I tried to ask him about it he got real mad. He attacked me.'

'Oh, I'm sorry to hear that. Did he hurt you?'

'Well, no actually. But he held me and threatened me.'

'I'm glad he didn't hurt you. Did you hurt him?'

I am too ashamed to admit how hard I tried to break Ricky's foot. When, at her request, I demonstrate my stamping action, I grind my heel daintily into his imaginary toes and act the whole manoeuvre without malice. Mrs Joseph laughs out loud, her sudden, bubbling giggle. She says: 'Lucy, it sounds like he came off worse in that encounter.'

'But I had to do something,' I protest. 'I really thought he was trying to kill me.'

'Sure you did. I can imagine Ricky's real scary when he wants to be. He's always had a terrible temper, you must remember that. Barbara used to worry about it but even she had to admit that he'd never hurt a fly. And he's been a kind friend to Ralph.'

She's not describing the Ricky Marcello I've been encountering lately.

'I mean,' she adds, 'he takes Ralph out driving in the automobiles which he fixes up in San Strana. And occasionally, he sits up in the tow truck with Ralph and lets him drive it around the farm. Now that's heroic. None of us ever lets Ralph drive anything.'

I shake my head. 'I think Ricky Marcello has another side to him which you don't know about, Mrs Joseph.'

'Probably. Most people have.'

'It's a mean side. Real mean. To be honest, I suspect that he was involved in Daddy's death.'

She pours some more water. A big slice of lemon from the jug falls into my drink and small drops of water explode on to the table.

'Now, Lucy,' she says. Her face has retained its strength and, when her brown eyes shine this way, her beauty. I wonder if her eyes are sparkling with amusement or curiosity. But when she speaks her voice cautions me. 'Lucy, what evidence do you have to say a thing like that?'

It is late when I return to Aunt Zina's apartment. Sasha is reading the newspaper, small glasses perched on his broad face. Aunt Zina, who learns a little Pushkin each day, has her nose buried in her battered and disintegrating old copy and not, disappointingly, in the pristine edition I gave her.

They are pleased by my arrival. They have been waiting for me, hoping to discuss the funeral, the tributes, the mourners.

I sink into Uncle Pavel's chair. He sat here daily smoking his pipe and the chair carries evidence of both activities.

'Thank you for bringing Mother. And thank you for

everything,' I say and they know from my tone that I am about to announce my departure. Their faces fall.

'I haven't booked my flight yet but I'm intending to leave on Saturday,' I tell them.

They urge me to stay longer.

'I really have to get back to work or I won't have a job,' I insist.

'Then,' says Aunt Zina, already on her feet and heading for the kitchen, 'take another. Here in California.'

I tell her I've eaten and beg her not to feed me but she reappears anyway with plates of home-made cookies. We discuss the funeral, agreeing that Mother behaved impeccably today and that she brought a dignity to the occasion which was reminiscent of Grandma. They tell me Larry has aged and Scott is handsome.

'And Jane,' adds Aunt Zina, 'still has great beauty. More so, perhaps, than ever.'

'Mama, she always did look like Greta Garbo,' insists Sasha, who spent more of his youth than Aunt Zina considered healthy watching old movies.

Aunt Zina shyly produces a small parcel, wrapped in tissue paper and tied with a ribbon, the sort of ribbon that was saved from a chocolate box years ago and has been used and re-used ever since. It is still pink in places. The rest has faded to colourlessness.

She says: 'I have undertaken a small work for you, Lucia. It will be completed by Saturday. I only hope I have been equal to my task.'

She hands me the package and I pull at the ribbon and it falls silently away. I peel the tissue paper. It crunches as softly as meringue. Inside are letters.

'These are the letters of a mother to a daughter. They were written from Grandma to your dear mama. When

Grandma died, your papa gave them to me, a thoughtful, generous gesture, so very typical of that good man. It is a humble project of mine to translate them for you. I hope you approve.'

I pull a thin, crisp sheet from its envelope. Across one side is bold Cyrillic script. Aunt Zina is milking these dry pages for something that a mother should give a daughter because, whatever it is, she knows my mother could not give it to me. The paper crackles a little between my fingers and the sound seems to resonate painfully in some soft place inside me. Nothing written here can replace a loving maternal touch.

'Thanks,' I say quietly. 'I appreciate that.'

'The translation will be completed before your departure,' she assures me. She gestures to her battered Pushkin. 'I began by translating a little of our greatest Russian poet for you but it soon became clear that my poor English is inadequate.'

Sasha has taken the bundle of letters and is surveying them through his tiny glasses.

'Is the content interesting?' he asks.

'The letters are full of maternal advice which is of the utmost relevance to a young woman.'

Sasha peels away an envelope at random and glances through the letter it contains. 'Mama, Lucia hardly needs to learn how much flour to put in a piroc,' he says.

'Oh, I'd like to learn to make piroc,' I assure them quickly.

'The advice takes many different forms,' Aunt Zina says. 'Grandma did not like to use the telephone and preferred to write and it is good that she did so.'

I peer at the impenetrable Cyrillic of another letter as though it's a code.

'Let's see,' Sasha says. 'This one is dated June first. My

dearest Tanechka . . . hmmmmm.' His eyes scan the page. 'Okay. My dearest little Tanya, there are no words to express my sadness, sadness for myself and for your family and for the poor darling little Nicolai . . .'

'Ah, I haven't yet translated that one. It is the last letter she wrote and it relates to the death of your brother, Lucia. After that Grandma went to stay with your family for a long time.'

'. . . But most of all my little one, for you. Only a mother who has lost a son can understand your grief and . . .' Sasha shrugs and pauses. 'Oh I don't know. Toska.'

'Unhappiness?' suggests Aunt Zina.

'Not strong enough. Anguish? You get the gist, Lucia.'

'Yup.' Inexplicably my throat is lumpen.

'Now you will watch other children, even trees, grow to maturity and as you watch them you will think with grief of the great man your Nicolai might have become . . . Good God, Lucia, what prose style the babushka had. Now, let's see . . . I will come and when you can talk you can tell me how this terrible . . . catastrophe, accident, occurred and when you have told me you can . . . tell me again. Because you see, when I lost my beloved Pasha I will never forget my horror. The expression on the face of the railway official who said the baby was dead and he must remove his body from my arms. I cannot now think of the emptiness of my hands when he had taken my son's perfect small body away. I wanted to walk up and down the train wailing and telling everyone of my loss and again on the boat and then the same when I arrived in this America. I wanted to tell everyone in America about my son and how he had died . . .'

Sasha breaks off and looks at me mischievously. 'To tell you the truth, Lucia, I think she did. We certainly had to hear about it often enough.'

'My mother suffered much at the loss of Tanya's son,' says Aunt Zina. 'She behaved as though her own son had died all over again. Frankly, we were glad when she left to join your family. There is no doubt that Tanya needed her.'

I say: 'I don't remember my brother. I don't recall anything about his death.'

Aunt Zina looks up and stares at me fiercely.

'Nothing?'

'No.'

'Come now, Lucia, you were small but so was I,' Sasha points out, 'and even I remember this cataclysmic event.'

Aunt Zina says: 'Sashinka, you and Lucia were both four. How can you remember more than she?'

'Everybody crying. Aunt Zoya sitting where you are sitting now and saying: "My poor dear Tanya," over and over. Grandma inconsolable. Lucy, I believe your brother gave me my first childish glimpse of death, no, perhaps not of death but grief.'

A terrible catastrophe, accident. Everywhere, toska. The whole family crying, Grandma overwhelmed by grief, rushing to Mother. The glassy surface of our lives shattered, maybe for ever, by the death of a baby boy.

I say, with a huskiness in my voice as though I just crawled up into some dusty attic: 'I don't even know his name.'

'Americans called him Nicky but we didn't,' says Aunt Zina. 'He was Kolya to us.'

'Kolya? Kolya.' I want to say it over and over. Its blush is familiar but its face is shy. 'Kolya,' I repeat, as though the name might lead me directly to the memory. But the face has turned away.

'Kolya is a common diminutive of Nicolai,' explains Sasha. 'Does the name Nicky, Kolya, sound at all familiar, Lucia?'

'I don't think so . . .' My throat clenches. It tries to censor

357

my words. I could never ask this question if Daddy were still alive or if Jane were in the room. I say: 'What exactly did happen when the baby died?'

Sasha and Aunt Zina exchange looks.

'Well,' says Sasha, 'have you discovered the interesting coincidence that father and son both died at the same place?'

'Yes. I took it as just another indication that Daddy's killer knew him well. If he knew the baby died there, he probably thought Big Brim was a credible place to stage a suicide.'

'Indeed,' nods Sasha.

'Although,' I add, 'it could just be an extraordinary coincidence.'

They exchange looks again.

'Coincidences do happen,' agrees Sasha.

'Oh yes, I have seen many coincidences,' Aunt Zina is quick to concur. 'Indeed, a long life teaches how common coincidence can be.'

There is silence. I persist: 'So . . . what exactly happened at Big Brim beach?'

'Tanya set the baby down too close to the water's edge, thinking perhaps that the light and movement might amuse him. She heard the crash . . .' Aunt Zina's arms are expressive. They are the whole Pacific Ocean. '. . . Of a large wave, a huge wave, a wave without precedent that day. When she turned, she saw her son dragged from the shore as the wave receded. She waded straight into the water but he was already in the deep and beyond her reach. He was soon pulled down beneath the surface.'

I stare at Aunt Zina. The great wave, the massive body of ocean water, the helplessness of a baby pushed this way and that and finally under the water.

'But she could have swum in . . .'

'Tanya was the weakest of swimmers,' states Aunt Zina.

I remember how Adam Holler said that Mother saved me in the pool. 'But she could –'

Sasha looks at me over his half-moon glasses and raises his eyebrows. Aunt Zina cuts through my protests. 'She would have been quite incapable of saving him.'

'So . . . she saw her baby die?'

'He returned to the surface several times but finally he disappeared for good.'

'She saw him die,' I repeat. 'After all those other things that she'd seen.'

Aunt Zina's head nods vigorously. 'Yes, yes, she saw him die.'

'The body,' adds Sasha, 'was never found.'

Aunt Zina asks: 'Is it any wonder that she went mad?'

As I lie in Grandma's bed, seeing the dust circling like a shoal of tiny silver fish each time the room is lit by headlights, sleep doesn't come. I think of a baby, tossed by the great ocean and finally swallowed by it and I think of Stevie, lying in his blue crib, and after a while the two babies are one.

33

The next morning I move fast through the city. It seems a long time since I used to walk to work like these people, my eyes fixed right in front of me, my mind fixed on the day ahead.

I enjoy the morning's early freshness. Soon the city will swell and bubble but right now it is possible to move quickly, unimpeded by heat. I feel alert. I notice hanging skirt hems and broken earrings and, above me, the depth of blue in the sky. The smell wafting from the breakfast diners is so intense it feels as though I'm actually eating. At a sidewalk café I note that each table is taken by a solitary diner. I watch a small group of white gulls swooping down to one man, who stamps his foot and waves his hand until the gulls soar away again, gliding first through the people then high above their heads. For a minute I feel some part of me is soaring over the sidewalk and the buildings as high as the birds. I can see myself far below, moving fast down the street, the diners reading their newspapers at the tables.

Finally I reach the library. It is huge like a cathedral. It feels cold and cool air seems to bounce from its walls. I ask an assistant for help and a few minutes later the newspapers I have requested appear on the desk in front of me.

I open the first and turn each page respectfully, with a big sweep of my arm. I had expected the tone and typography of my childhood years to be subdued, like an elderly relative. Now I am surprised at the robust headlines.

Initially I allow myself to be distracted by articles which

interest me, then I turn the pages faster and the news flashes by me like a time machine.

My grandmother's letter of condolence was dated June first. I don't expect to find a report of my brother's death until May thirty-first. June first is also a possibility. When I reach June second and there has been no mention of the accident, I lose hope. I give June third and fourth a cursory scan. Maybe the death on the coast of a small baby wasn't considered newsworthy. Then, on the front page of June fifth, I see it: Baby Drowned By Freak Wave.

I bend over the story. It says: 'Eight month old Nicholas Schaffer was swept out to sea at Big Brim beach yesterday by a freak wave.'

The death occurred at 10.10 a.m. Mrs Tatiana Schaffer had been playing with her two daughters, leaving her baby son at the shoreline, when a large wave carried him away. Mrs Schaffer was a non-swimmer. She had, nevertheless, assisted by others, attempted unsuccessfully to reach the child. Coastguards had later joined in the search for the body, which had still not been found. Dr Schaffer, a university lecturer, was absent at the time of the death fetching sweaters from the family's car across the dunes. No one else saw the wave carry the baby away, although there are quotes from someone who watched Mother's floundering, unsuccessful rescue attempt.

'Dr and Mrs Shaffer are being interviewed by police,' the article concludes. 'Detective Rougemont declined to comment on the case.'

In the next newspaper, I read: Police Warn Parents To Watch Out For Waves. The article repeats the story of Nicholas's death, stating the date again as June fourth.

'Police today warned parents that no child should be left unattended at the shoreline, however quiet the ocean seems. Nicholas's body still has not been recovered. Local fisherman

Kurt Langheim commented: "Big Brim's a death trap but the bodies are nearly always picked up down the coast at Retribution Bay. Maybe this one's just too small for that."

'The baby's father, Dr Eric Schaffer, is a college lecturer in geology and geophysics. Mrs Tatiana Schaffer was today still suffering from shock. Her husband confirmed that she is under sedation. The police issued a warning about beach safety but declined to make any other comment on the case.'

I walk back to my car and find the sun is already bouncing off the hood. The steering-wheel feels hot and hard like something baked in the oven.

When I bump up Daddy's drive I see Jane standing at the top. She is opening the barn door, reaching for the high bolts, her body elongated like an exclamation mark. I feel bad that she has been alone and vulnerable at the house and apologize for arriving so late.

She is forgiving. 'It's too hot to feel scared today,' she says. 'And the geologists from the U will be here any minute. I hope they're expecting this many rocks.'

Her hair shines metallically in the sun. The round rocks in the drive look like bubbles in the boiling cauldron of the day.

We walk inside the barn and linger at the door, seeing black, waiting for our eyes to accommodate the darkness.

I say: 'Jane. There's something I don't understand.'

She laughs. 'Only one thing?'

'Jane . . .' It is dark in the barn but not cool. My mouth feels salty dry. 'I've been learning about . . .' This is difficult. '. . . Our brother. His death.'

Jane swings around to me so that the ends of her hair bounce against her face.

'How come?'

'Well, Sasha translated this letter last night. From Grandma to mother, saying how sorry she was about the baby's death. And . . . it made me start asking questions.'

She raises her eyebrows.

'Like what?'

'It doesn't make sense, Jane. The story of how the baby died doesn't fit the facts.'

She studies me carefully in the diminishing darkness. The intense sunlight doesn't fall in here but I am aware of its heat, its light, right behind me.

'What facts?' she asks at last.

I start to tell her how Mother and Daddy took all three of us to Big Brim beach one day when there is the scrape of muffler on rock and the moan of an engine. The geologists have arrived.

'I'll get them started,' Jane says, 'then we should talk about this.' And suddenly it seems urgent that we discuss our brother, as though our great silence has collapsed beneath the weight of its accumulated years.

The geologists emerge slowly from their car in the sticky heat. One of them reminds me of Daddy, tall and kind-faced. The other is bearded and wants to tells us how much Daddy taught him and how Daddy loaned him the money for a field trip when he was an impoverished grad student.

'There is no charge for this evaluation,' he says, 'strictly no charge. I'm one of many people who has good reason to be grateful to Professor Schaffer and I want to pay my dues.'

I fetch them cold drinks while Jane leads them into the barn and explains how Larry and Scott have organized Daddy's vast and unruly rock collection. They're still talking when I take them their drinks. I wander around to the deck to wait for Jane, picking up a few napkins from yesterday's lunch which the caterers missed.

A heat haze still lingers over the valley. Soon the sun will burst through it like a fist. When the heat gets this intense it sits, lazy as a fat man, over the valley, and only a violent storm can drive it away.

Overhead the big, round leaves hang, limp as wet cloths, although they are dry. Below me the valley drops and stretches like the ocean although it is land, brown and parched.

Jane appears at my side.

'Okay, they're busy, they have a big jug of water, and they don't need us. Let's go, Lucy.'

I follow her back through the house and across the porch and the sound of the screen door banging and our feet clattering on the wood could be a sound from any time in our lives. We cross the yard and pick our way through the Holler orchard. Light and heat pour down on us, thick as water, so that walking feels like swimming.

'Where are we going?' I ask, although I am already consumed by the journey and don't much care.

'Down to the valley where no one can overhear us. Remember that old trail we used to take?'

I remember the trail because I walked up it the day before Daddy died. The heatwave has dried the dirt and made the bushes limp since then. In a couple of places I think I can see my own footsteps. Jane picks her way down the overgrown path, holding her arms clear of the leaves, her hips and long, slim legs swinging with the terrain. Small clouds of powdery red dirt circle every foot.

We skirt the trees in the Schneck orchard knowingly like animals. The dirt fills our shoes. We duck under low branches, and then cross the Spelmann lot, brown and uncared-for at these outer reaches. Back up around the houses we see flowers, unnaturally green lawns, hissing sprinklers.

Suddenly, we're at the bottom of the hill. We're in the

valley. It is still, eerily still, as though someone cast a spell on it. The earth is scorched. The sun dominates and there can be no refuge in sprinklers or pools or air-conditioning. It sears into the trees, the ground, the rocks, everything here must submit to its rule.

'Let's sit,' suggests Jane. There are rocks nestled into the base of the hillside. The rocks are hot but they are shaded from the sun's cruelty by a slanting tree which I think has always listed. We sit, taking a little relief from the light, smothered still by heat.

'Okay,' says Jane. 'I'm ready. Tell me the facts about Nicky's death.'

I am amazed to hear his name used with such casual familiarity. I thought Jane, like me, had forgotten all about him.

I sweat. I am breathless as though I am still walking through the swelling air. I tell her the story of that trip to Big Brim beach when I was four and she was seven. How Daddy went back for sweaters when the freak wave came and Mother was unable to save the baby.

She nods.

'That's it,' she says. 'That's pretty much how it was.'

'You remember?'

'Sure. It was a trauma I relived a thousand times. I remember every second of it.'

'But why did you tell the police you'd forgotten?'

'Because Nicky's death doesn't have anything to do with Daddy's. I was appalled they kept asking about it. I mean, it was a terrible, tragic thing to happen and it drove Mother literally insane. I know that in some families it's different but in our family we found the best way of coping with it was to grieve and then to put it right behind us. That's what Daddy did, that's what I did. And you just forgot about the whole thing. Until now. For some reason Daddy's death has made people talk about Nicky again. I couldn't believe it when Larry told everyone at the funeral about him.'

I swallow and taste the orchard inside my mouth.

'Tell me, Luce. What are these facts you've found that don't fit?'

'I guess it's nothing,' I say at last.

'Please tell me. Please, Luce.'

'I thought it looked like they staged Nicky's death,' I say and Jane stares at me, her mouth open a little.

'Staged it?' she asks softly. 'God, Luce, what do you mean?'

'This freak wave which is supposed to have snatched the baby away. It's hard to imagine there could be such a thing at Big Brim beach . . .' My words have been edging down a steep hill. Gradually, they gather a momentum of their own and start to tumble. 'I mean, that place is like a lagoon. There are almost no waves. It's not a safe beach but the danger comes from the undercurrents, not the waves. Then, this stuff about Mother not saving the baby because she couldn't swim. Well, she could. I know she never did but Mr Holler remembers her diving into their pool to save me once: you resuscitated me but she actually pulled me to safety. Why didn't she do the same for the baby? But the strangest thing of all is a letter Grandma wrote when Kolya, Nicky, died. In the letter she tries to comfort Mother. It's dated June first. But, according to the newspaper reports, Nicky didn't die until June fourth. So Grandma wrote a letter of condolence three days before the baby died. Isn't that bizarre?'

I am out of breath and out of words. Jane has been watching me, large-eyed, her hair sticking to the sides of her face, her body tilted gracefully forward on her rock.

'How could they have staged his death?' she asks.

'I don't know. But if the baby was already dead, I mean if

366

he'd died earlier in some other way, they could have pretended that he drowned at the beach to cover it up . . .'

She sighs.

'You shouldn't read too much into the date on Grandma's letter. She could easily have got the date wrong, so could the newspaper.'

'What about the wave? Do you remember the wave?'

'No,' she admits. 'I don't remember it. None of us saw it, although afterwards I sort of thought I remembered a crash.'

'What do you remember, Jane?'

She pulls her body back at an oblique angle and puts the soles of her feet up on her rock. Her body looks long and lean. It is unblemished by childbearing.

'Every detail,' she says at last. 'I remember the exact grade of grey in the sky. The colour of the ball we were playing with. The shirt I was wearing. Mother kicked the ball to you and then turned around and realized Nicky was gone. He'd been sitting on the sand in that dumpy, round-shouldered way small babies sit, and then he just wasn't there any more. She screamed and we ran up to her and we all stared at the sand as though, if we stared hard enough, he'd reappear. You dropped the beachball and the little waves sort of grabbed it and soon it was bouncing around in the water. When we looked in the water for Nicky we couldn't see him there either, just the beachball bobbing up and down. I mean, there was absolutely no sign of him. Mother started shrieking and flapping her arms like an enormous gull. She probably thought someone had taken him because she ran up and down the tideline but there was no one close enough to have done such a thing. Then I saw him. I mean, I saw his little blue hat. It wasn't far away and the beach there shelves gently so I waded in for it. Mother rushed into the water behind me, splashing and yelling, and grabbed the hat out of my

367

hand and then she went in still further until she was submerged waist deep and her skirt was sort of floating behind her on the surface of the water.'

There is a long silence. It sucks all the oxygen out of the air. I say: 'Didn't anyone help? Wasn't there anyone on the beach who could help?'

'There were a few people and yes, they did come to help. Not for a while, though. It turned out that they thought we were trying to get the beachball. And anyway, soon Daddy was back.'

'And did you see the baby at all?'

'A little way out, flung around by the movement of the water. He was face down as though he was swimming but I'm pretty sure he wasn't moving at all by then.'

'Why didn't Mother swim to him? Why didn't she try to get to him somehow? Anyhow?'

'Daddy did. He tried for ages but Nicky was right out of sight and Daddy had to give up when the currents nearly pulled him under. We all knew by then that it was way too late.'

'But why didn't Mother get in the water the moment she realized that Nicky had gone?' I demand loudly. The steep valley side throws my words back at me. Gone, gone, gone.

I see that Jane is crying silently.

'Luce, I've never told anyone this. I never even discussed it with Daddy, but I think he knew it too.'

I wait, while she fights with her tears.

'I suspect . . . I've always suspected . . . that Mother may have drowned her baby.'

The heat pins me to my rock. I can feel the small crags and craters digging into my skin but I am powerless to move. It has been here for hundreds, thousands, perhaps millions of years and it took many more millions to form. It was created by elements relentless as today's sun, expanding it, contracting it, washing against it, chipping it, sculpting it. A lizard peeks out from underneath the rock, moves a few feet and then stops. It is motionless in the dust as though the heat pins it, too, to the earth's surface. Its dry, scaly skin is timeless, its way of life is timeless, its primitive thoughts are timeless. In the intense heat I don't know where the lizard and the rock and Lucy end or begin. We are all made from the same elements, and so is the dirt that lines the valley floor.

'Nicky was a problem for Mother,' says Jane. Her voice is a monotone. 'You and I had been easy babies but Nicky cried and cried. He was so cute. I mean, when he was asleep or playing he was adorable. But mostly he was yelling. Mother couldn't stop him so she ended up by empathizing with him and crying a lot herself. She loved him so much but she couldn't cope and Daddy had to cook all the meals and take time off to help with the baby and the whole house was tense. Mother was highly voluble but, Luce, I've always hoped, I've preferred to believe, that she didn't plan on drowning her baby. That would have been real calculating. No, I prefer to think it was more like a split-second decision not to save him.'

I am crying too now. I can feel the tears making hot lines through my dusty face.

'Don't judge her too harshly, Lucy. I know you won't. I know you'll understand.'

'I won't judge her,' I sob. 'How can I?'

Jane gets up and walks across the soft dirt of the valley floor. She puts an arm around me. 'I guess you must know just how she felt. Because, although she was responsible for his death, she really loved that baby.'

I howl. Like an animal, like a wolf. The valley side echoes

my cry until Jane and I are surrounded by a whole pack of wolves.

I remember how, when I had Stevie, love seemed to spill out of me, slopping everywhere, in quantities not previously experienced. You share, said Aunt Zina, your mother's great capacity to love, and it seems to me now that my love for Stevie had all the unpredictability and force of some terrifying flash flood. But I was awash with a love to which Stevie seemed indifferent. He was dissatisfied with my inadequate attempts to feed him and nurture him and he showed his dissatisfaction continually. He cried and cried and, because he felt like a part of me, his wails seemed to express some great sadness inside me, some pain I didn't even know was there. He was expelling my misery for all the world to hear. And, when I pulled back the blanket and knew from his special stillness that he was dead, wasn't my first reaction, before the shock, before the suffering, simply relief that there was silence at last?

I say: 'It was my fault Stevie died, Jane. It was all my fault.'

When he was dead, when the police had gone and the woman in dark clothes had taken him away, I slept. I slept for twenty-four hours.

'Shhhhhhhh,' says Jane as I sob on to her shoulder. 'Shhhhhh. I know. Shhhhhhhh now.' She hushes me softly like a baby. 'It's all over now, Luce. Nicky's dead. Stevie's dead. We can put it all behind us.'

When I look up, I say: 'Mother got sick right after Nicky died. I understand now. Her grief was compounded by guilt.'

Jane nods. 'Probably we went to Arizona too soon after his death. I think it was only a week or two later.'

'What a terrible vacation for her.'

Jane takes my hand and holds it fiercely in hers. She says: 'Luce, do you ever think about death?'

'I think about it a lot.'

'Are you scared of it?'

I sniff. 'Yes.'

'Sometimes I think it must be sort of wonderful. All the dumb things you worry about, the headlong chase for happiness, the suffering even wealth can't prevent, the knowledge that the second half of your life can only be a decline ... I've watched people die and, no matter how much they dreaded death, they always seem to sink into it with a kind of relief. Like when you get into bed at the end of a real tiring day. When they finally slip away they look so grateful it's all over. I'm telling you this because I want you to know, it really wasn't so bad for Stevie. It wasn't so bad for Nicky.'

I feel grateful to her. Her kindness is like the sun. I thank her. I stand up. Rows of big fruit trees stretch away from us to the misty horizon. Each one is different. The branches fall differently. The trunks curve differently. Every bark has a different patina. The dirt beneath the trees is furrowed into deep, uncrossable waves and, like the sea, it is thick with life.

Knowing that, now Daddy is dead, we only have each other in the world and that we alone are guardians of our family's past, Jane and I lean on one another as we begin our ascent. The sun dries our faces as we stumble back up the trail, around houses, across overgrown lots, through the orchard. The effort of climbing erases all thought until we get to Daddy's yard and then I become aware that I am dirty all over. The clouds of earth have settled on me like a mass of butterflies. It is inside my shoes, it clings to my legs and I can taste it in my mouth.

'We should shower,' says Jane hoarsely.

I gesture for her to shower first and while she is gone I stand hanging over the deck, looking down on the place we just left. It looks different from up here. Its vastness is well ordered. The trees are identical, evenly spaced, symmetrically shaped and mirrored by short, neat, shadows. The dirt looks flat, its furrows uniform.

I retreat to the house. Upstairs I pass Daddy's bedroom, Jane's, my own, until I reach the pastel blue room at the end of the hallway which Kirsty said must have been my brother's. I sit down on a dusty box and try to remember. I try to remember anything about Nicky. His tears, his face asleep, his death at Big Brim beach. But there is nothing. Every time I reach out for him, I find Stevie's small, white body.

Outside, the sunken garden is so still it looks like a photograph of itself, so motionless it seems to be holding its breath.

I sit down by Daddy's headstone. I think of the terrible burden he carried, the terrible burden of his knowledge.

'Hi, Lucy.'

I turn and see the bony features of Michael Rougemont. His grey eyes survey me sadly. Followed by Kirsty, he steps down into the sunken garden and sits near me in dappled shade.

'You okay?' Rougemont asks. He surveys my tear-stained face, my dirt-red hair.

'You look like you've been mud wrestling,' says Kirsty.

'I just took a walk down to the valley.'

'Oh, you must like it down there,' says Rougemont. 'You went the day before your father died. I had Forensic analyse the dirt on those shoes and they said you'd been in the valley as well as this yard.'

I sigh. 'I parked in the valley, that's all.'

'Why did you come here that day?' asks Kirsty. I look at their faces. Rougemont's battered like Aunt Zina's copy of Pushkin. Kirsty's lit suddenly as a branch overhead bends aside for the sun. It filters the colour from her eyes and gives them a new penetration.

'I wanted to see Daddy. But the circumstances weren't right for a big reunion. I looked in through the sliding doors on the deck. He was in his chair. Then I went back down to the valley. Then I returned to town. I was probably here at about one-thirty.'

'Uh-huh,' says Rougemont. His head bounces. 'Thank you for telling us that, Lucy.'

I look at his strange face. The stretched mouth, the big nose. For the first time I recognize his sharp intelligence. When he investigated Nicky's death, did he suspect the truth?

I say: 'I'm sorry I lied to you.'

'When you lie,' Rougemont says, 'it's generally to protect someone else, not yourself.'

Kirsty nods: 'You have to stop taking responsibility for other people, Lucy. It could be dangerous.'

I look at her in confusion.

'Where were you on Monday night?' she asks. 'After dark?'

'Monday?' Sitting in the car watching Ricky Marcello watching Jane. 'Oh, I just sort of drove around. Then I went back to my aunt's.'

'Uh-huh,' says Rougemont.

'I didn't get out of the car. Not until I was back at Aunt Zina's,' I insist. It feels good to tell the truth, like putting your foot down when you're sea swimming and finding sand beneath it.

Kirsty says: 'You didn't get out of the car. But you didn't drive around too much.'

'Uh-huh,' says Rougemont. 'You were right outside your sister's apartment all evening.'

I blush. I am fighting tears, the tears of a small angry child who wants to stamp her foot and bang her fists. I haven't told them about Ricky Marcello because he was Daddy's secret but now it seems that they've known all along.

'Oh, don't misunderstand us,' adds Rougemont. 'We think it's real nice of you to be so concerned for your sister's safety. But we have some advice. Please take it, Lucy.'

'It's this,' says Kirsty, carrying right on as though Rougemont just threw her the ball. 'Leave the police work to us.'

'Okay?' Rougemont gives me a ghostly smile. 'We know what we're doing and it's important. As you probably already realize, there's more than one homicide involved. We're hoping that this case will help us close a few others which have been open for a while.'

My heart slips down inside me like alcohol. I want to ask him about the other homicides but my throat is too dry. I wish I could get up right now and go to the faucet and pour cold, clear water inside me.

'We'll do the police work,' continues Rougemont, 'and you go back to New York.'

Kirsty agrees with him. 'You'll be safer in New York where you're only responsible for yourself.'

They look at me. Covered in dirt and on the edge of tears. Their looks are kind.

'Lucy, Lucy,' says Rougemont. 'Stop taking so much on yourself. You've always done it, even when you were a little girl, back in the days you used to stare at me and point at my nose. You didn't spare my feelings much then, either.'

Beneath the dirt, I blush again.

'No matter what questions I asked you, mostly you'd cry. I never got anywhere with you. Your sister was different. She was barely seven but she described exactly what happened when your brother died, and she was precise too. Your mother was so emotional she was incoherent. Your father had a sort of grimness about him. I recognized his internal landscape at that time, only too well. God knows my own

374

was bleak enough. And then there was you, little Lucy. Four years old, scratching constantly at the poison ivy on your legs. You cried for your dead brother. You cried and cried and said over and over that it was all your fault. You seemed to be accepting responsibility for your whole family.'

I am silent.

'Don't you remember any of that?' Kirsty asks me. 'Not any of it?'

My head feels heavy, as though there is a thick crust around it. I say: 'I've tried. I've tried real hard. But it won't come back.'

When the police have left and Jane has volunteered to stay late with the geologists, I drive back to town. The air feels cooler and thinner now. Maybe the heatwave is ending at last. On the way I detour to the cemetery where Stevie is buried. I place some small, yellow flowers from Daddy's yard on the grave and when I stoop close to the tiny headstone I have to fight a foolish urge to cradle its cold stone in my arms.

A tune thumps through my head with sudden and un-expected insistence. I pause to listen. It is a song of nursery simplicity and someone is humming it. At first I catch stray notes, then whole bars, finally a voice I recognize at once as my mother's sings the whole song through. The words are incomprehensible, but involuntarily I lift my hands to form the fluttering bird which flies away in the last bar. The music sails through my head a few more times and then, as I walk down the hill, it sails right away. I try to capture its notes or phrases but, as suddenly as it arrived, it has departed.

34

When I get back to the apartment, Aunt Zina is out at Aunt Zoya's and Sasha is alone in the kitchen.

'Mama has left enough here for at least ten people,' he says, ladling food on to my plate. 'And I have already eaten half of it.'

'I'm not real hungry, thanks Sash.'

'In our family, as you very well know, Lucia, that is considered a pitifully inadequate excuse for refusing food.'

When I am silent he looks at me closely. I showered at Daddy's but had no change of clothes and the orchard's dirt still clings to them. 'Something's happened. What is it?'

I put my head in my hands.

'Lucia?'

I look at him. His kind, broad Russian face, his thinning hair, his blue eyes, full of concern. A good man.

I say: 'The police investigating Daddy's death say that there's more than one homicide involved.'

He passes me the plate of food and fills another for himself. He sits down and picks up his fork.

'That doesn't surprise me. Did the police reveal anything about the other deaths?'

'Just that they happened years back. Sasha, I think they mean Nicky. I think they mean Stevie.'

Sasha stares at me. 'Your brother? And your son?'

'It can't be a coincidence they've hauled in old Michael Rougemont. He investigated Nicky's drowning all those years ago. And they're using Kirsty because she was there after Stevie died.'

'Lucia, neither can be regarded as homicide.'

'I think they know the truth.'

'Which is?'

'That Mother was responsible for Nicky's death. And that I was responsible for Stevie's.'

Sasha puts down his fork and pushes his food away.

'Lucia, now what is this madness?'

I pause. 'The madness of motherhood.'

'Lucia.'

'Motherhood isn't the way it looks in TV commercials. It's an awful, awful mix of great love and hatred. The love I experienced for my son was beyond anything I've known or knew how to deal with. And in return he was demanding and selfish and unforgiving. Babies never take their mother's needs into account and everything she gives they seem to swallow up and then demand more. You can't control them and you can't control your life and sometimes you hate them for it.'

'And so you kill them? For heaven's sake, Lucia.'

'There were times when I wished Stevie dead. That's enough.'

'Your Stevie died tragically but not unnaturally. There are many SIDS deaths each year and his was one of them. No one is responsible. May I suggest that, until you can talk about him more easily and even tell the story of his death to a complete stranger on a park bench, you will not overcome your grief?'

'I don't want to sit in parks talking about Stevie!'

'We all need to tell stories. Stories frame events. Once we massage life's traumas into a narrative form they become less destructive. The fact of Nicky's death may provoke uncontrollable emotions but the story of how he drowned at Big Brim at least offers us a way of working through them.'

I consider this. 'Like the story of Grandma's baby on the train?'

'Precisely. That story has certainly played its part in the family's grieving process. Even though it is untrue.'

I stare at him. He picks up his fork again and scoops up a mouthful of food.

'If you're interested, I'll tell you what actually happened.'

I nod for him to continue and he finishes his mouthful and then reorganizes his broad body in the chair.

'First you should understand that one of the advantages of emigrating is that you can hope to be a reptile, a snake perhaps. You plan to shed your skin and leave it behind. Well, I happen to believe that you can never leave it completely behind, that it bobs up to the surface sooner or later like something from a shipwreck. However, many emigrants try. Maybe you know this. Maybe, when you exiled yourself to New York, you took advantage of your isolation in that big city to reinvent your past.'

'No.'

'Not at all?'

'I just sort of cancelled it.'

'You never even talked about it?'

I shake my head.

'That's one way. But when our family, Grandpa, Grandma and their daughters, came here, they chose to, shall we say, reinterpret their history.'

'You mean . . .'

'I mean not everything they have told you is true.'

'But, the apartment in Moscow, and the games they played and the story about their papa forgetting his hat. Did they invent that?'

'It's hard to tell how much is invented. The one about your mother witnessing an assassination in the forest is, curiously enough, probably true: the old man was certainly NKVD and he was ruthless enough to organize the murder of his best friend if he had to.'

'I can hardly remember him.'

'That's because you didn't live within reach of the flat of his hand. I remember, only too well, how that hand felt when applied swiftly to the back of my legs. Of course, he had been both a victim and instigator of violence. To him smacking a small child was nothing. No, the family's most magnificent multi-tiered, white-iced wedding cake of a lie is their best story. The Escape From Moscow.'

'Sasha. What are you saying?' I am almost speechless at this challenge to family mythology.

'The train ride ... it's all nonsense. Probably they've eventually come to believe it themselves, so much detail does it contain, some of which I hope you have been spared. Aunt Zoya never omits the man who reached into his pocket and withdrew a sandwich before the round eyes of the ravenous children. He ate it while they watched, every crumb. It was days before they ate again and then it was only a few spoon-fuls of kasha. I credit Aunt Zoya also with that last touch as she has always hated kasha.'

'But ...' I protest lamely. 'There was a train journey. We've always known about their train journey. Mother was telling us the story when we were still in diapers.'

'It was exactly that. A story.'

'But ... what about the baby? The baby boy who couldn't survive such conditions? And the railway official who took the body away and wouldn't look at Grandma when she asked him to ensure there was a burial?'

'No truth in it at all.'

I watch Sasha as he forks food into his mouth energetically.

'How do you know this?' I ask at last.

'You don't need to know a great deal about Europe in 1941 to know how improbable their pan-European train ride is. Papa confirmed to me shortly before his death that it was all a myth and I have every reason to believe him.'

'Oh, Sasha. Why would they construct such an elaborate lie?'

'For all the reasons I have explained. They needed a narrative to lend structure to life's chaos and, in their case, perhaps to cover the unpalatable truth.'

'Was there ever really a brother?'

'Oh yes. There was certainly a baby brother who died. And if you're hinting that the story was concocted around his death then you're absolutely right.'

I cup my hands and put my face inside them.

'So how did the baby really die?'

'I'll tell you if you want me to. But if you prefer, you know you can keep the train journey. Do you want to stay on the train or get off it, Lucia? This is the moment to decide.'

'Tell me.'

'Well, given your fondness for the idea, you'll be glad to know there actually was a train ride. But only from Moscow to Riga. Grandpa was indeed sent to Latvia to head a trade delegation and the family travelled there by train but it took perhaps only thirty hours, stopping often, and it was no great hardship. The travellers were Grandpa, Grandma and the three girls. No brother. In Stalin's Russia even a valued and vetted member of the NKVD could not be sent away without some kind of guarantee against defection. One family member had to be left behind. Grandpa invited Grandma to decide who this would be. It was an informed choice. She understood that he planned to flee from Riga and therefore that the child she left behind in Moscow, and the relatives taking care of that child (I believe her brother and his wife), would be removed to labour camps and almost certain death. What a terrible decision. We can imagine her long, sleepless nights as she tried to select which children should come to America and which one would go to its death. She finally elected to pawn her baby son for their freedom.'

'But what happened to him?'

'The brother's family and the baby all disappeared as anticipated. We don't know what happened to them. But we can guess all too easily.'

'So . . . Grandma effectively . . .' My throat is dry. My words scrape against it as I force them out. 'She effectively killed her son.'

Sasha looks at me and blinks.

'And the escape?' I ask.

'Soon after their arrival in Riga, one sunny Sunday, the girls were told they were going on a picnic. They thought the picnic hampers were heavy but they transported them anyway to the edge of the great river Daugava from where they planned to watch the boats as they ate. However, when they reached the river they were told to board a waiting fishing vessel quickly and quietly. Their father had bribed the fisherman to take them to Sweden. This manoeuvre was not without its dangers but once they were across the Baltic they knew they were free. They took a liner to America and I believe the ship was salubrious. Their escape involved little hardship. At least not to themselves.'

Sasha produces a cigarette, which he lights, something he is not supposed to do anywhere in the apartment but his own room. He smokes slowly for a moment.

'A story,' he concludes, 'that they were perhaps wise

to conceal. But please note that, despite the fact that our sweet-faced, white-haired old babushka effectively, as you suggested, murdered her son, her grief was no less, and may have been greater.'

I am silent. Finally I say: 'Grandma should have refused to defect. Right?'

'Not a good choice. If Grandpa was determined to go with or without his family, and I believe he was selfish enough to go alone, then all those who stayed behind would have been sent to a camp.'

'But what would have been the right thing to do?'

'The right thing to do. God, Lucia, can't you imagine a time and a country so confused that there is no right thing?'

I massage my temples. Finally I look up and say: 'So what would you have done?'

'Why, murdered one of the girls, of course,' he tells me. 'I'm surprised Grandpa did not insist on this because most men desire a child created in their own image. In Russia, as you know, fathers even assert their claims through patronymics: children take their father's first name as well as his last. Grandpa was Dimitri and I'm sure it was always a matter of regret for him that the price of his escape was his Dimitrich.'

Later, when I get up to go to bed, Sasha's short, leather-clad arms close tightly around me.

'Oh, Lucia,' he pleads. 'Stop, please stop, feeling responsible for your son's death and start telling stories about it. Because it really doesn't matter if they are true or false. If you tell them often enough you won't even remember and the trauma will become more manageable.'

The temperature is low now, lower than it has been for days. I take an extra blanket and fall asleep rapidly. As I do so I try to capture the tune which appeared in my head at Stevie's graveside. Just once I think I hear my mother's voice, clear, youthful, in the distance but before I can reach her she is gone.

35

The heatwave is certainly ending. Not only is the air cooler at Daddy's house but it is more energetic.

Jane is at the hospital today, the geologists are back and Larry is helping them out in the barn. I work in the den. I hope that, with concentration, I can complete my executor chores for Scott this morning and have him sign the last letters this afternoon.

I am interrupted only once, when Larry brings me coffee and one of the enormous peanut cookies he likes so much.

'I couldn't help it,' he says guiltily. 'I drove past the store on the way here and there was a parking place right outside. Who could resist that? It was meant to be.'

'Larry, did you need to take the route past the store?' I ask him. 'Is that the only way to get here?'

'Oh boy, you sound like me,' he says, backing out of the door.

I use Daddy's printer for the last batch of letters for Scott. Then I close every file and start to stack them in the empty boxes, probably once intended for rocks, which I found in the barn.

When I get to the oil royalties file I pause and open it. In Daddy's financial life at least, loose ends have now been tied and inconsistencies smoothed. Except for this one.

I review the oil file's long history. Daddy started by keeping his payments. Then, a few years later, just as the Simms-Roeder income started to soar, he stopped collecting. From that point on, I have failed to trace this income. All I know is that Daddy had it paid to the mysterious Marcello Trust. I try to calculate how old Ricky Marcello was when his family started to receive these payments. I was about seven. That means Ricky Marcello must have been a baby, or not quite born.

When I step on to the deck the view has a new clarity. There is no haze and no mist. There is even an intimation of the hills on the far side. The straight lines of the valley, its right angles and the regular spacing of its trees, order my thoughts. As I stare, the valley seems to get closer, bouncing up to me like a dog.

'Where are you going?' Larry asks when I tell him I have to go out right away. Larry and the geologists have rigged up a temporary lighting system as bright as the midsummer sun and the barn is blazing. The strong light illuminates all the corners and crevices which have remained dark for so long. The three men sweat in their small circle of summer beneath the lamps, Larry and the bearded geologist on boxes and taking notes, and the quiet geologist on the dusty floor, surrounded by loose rocks, wearing a magnifier across his face.

I answer Larry's question without precision.

'There's just one file I haven't been able to sort out,' I say. 'But I'm going to fix that now.'

When I get to the Joseph house, Ralph is in the yard as usual. The dogs wag their tails and Ralph greets me. He is wearing overalls again today, and he is shirtless. The skin on his back and shoulders is deep brown. His neck and face are an almost supernatural white beneath his big hat.

'Is Mrs Joseph home?'

'Sure. Morton just went.'

'I'm leaving California soon, I came to say goodbye.'

He does not move so I walk over to the house and ring

the bell and then Ralph joins me at the door. We stand there together like a pair of Mormon missionaries, waiting while Mrs Joseph unlocks it.

'Hi Lucy. Hi Ralph,' says Mrs Joseph as though she is equally pleased and surprised to see us both. I smell the house's own aroma. Old wooden house, loved, cared for, full of flowers.

The three of us go to the kitchen, the kitchen where Mrs Joseph and Barbara Marcello used to spend so much time. Robert and I could hear their voices when we passed, on our way up to the bedroom or out to the hammock. They talked quietly, intensely and then, without warning, the voices would rise to peals of laughter.

Now Barbara Marcello smiles down on us from high on the dresser, her long hair escaping from the scarf which secures it. She holds an arm over her forehead to shade her eyes and half-squints at the camera as though it is the sun. The picture suggests beauty and strength but the detail of her face is obscured by shadow.

'When did she die?' I ask, gesturing to the photo, as Mrs Joseph supplies us with cold drinks. She's cooking today and the baking trays which are spread across her work surface have been half filled by something which might be brownie mixture. The kitchen smells of chocolate.

'I guess it's two and a half, no, almost three years ago now,' says Mrs Joseph, pausing, as though in homage, at her friend's picture. 'Ovarian cancer. They thought they'd caught it in time. But they hadn't. It seemed terrible when it happened but it wasn't such an awful death and anyone over fifty is guaranteed to have seen a few of those, I certainly have. Barbara was calm about it and she worked hard on those closest to her to help them accept that she was leaving them. The end was peaceful. Of course, we all miss her. I miss her every day.'

An unobtrusive death. Barbara Marcello was an unobtrusive woman. Suddenly it seems in character that Daddy, with his energy and bluster, should have a death marked by flashing lights and police tape across the drive.

Mrs Joseph returns to her cooking.

'I'll fix some lunch when I'm through with this. I got behind with my schedule because I didn't want to bake during the heatwave.'

'Brownies,' explains Ralph.

'In a weak moment I told the Valley Easter Barn Dance Committee that I'd make a hundred and fifty brownies. I do them in batches and then freeze them.'

'For Russian Orphans,' Ralph adds.

'Not the brownies. The money we raise,' says Mrs Joseph.

Ralph takes his hat off. The hair beneath it is pure white. The contrast with his childlike face shocks me.

We sit in silence, sipping our drinks, while Mrs Joseph pours the brownie mixture from a big green bowl into the pans. When the bowl is empty she scrapes a spatula around it. The spatula leaves clean, green lines behind.

I say: 'Ricky isn't Ricky Marcello's real name. Do you know what his real name is?'

Ralph shrugs.

'I've always called him Ricky,' says Mrs Joseph.

'I saw on the sign outside the Marcello garage that it begins with an E. I think it's Eric.'

They both look busy, Mrs Joseph with the brownies, Ralph with his drink.

I say: 'Who is his father?'

Mrs Joseph puts down the bowl. Ralph puts on his hat, hastily, as though it looks like rain.

'I guess Barbara didn't make a habit of telling people,' says Mrs Joseph at last. She opens the oven and for a moment we all feel its hot breath. She slides the brownies inside and closes it rapidly. Then she takes off her oven mitt and sits down across the table from me. She looks open, receptive, but her brown eyes are concerned.

'Are you still worried by Ricky Marcello, Lucy? Please don't be.'

'Ricky's my friend,' Ralph assures me.

'I'm sure he doesn't want to hurt you,' adds Mrs Joseph.

I say: 'I think he's my brother.'

And when I hear the words, when I've slipped them on to the kitchen table with the same swift precision that Mrs Joseph slid the pans into the hot oven, I know they are true from the way the silent room receives them.

Mrs Joseph continues to look at me, her eyes perhaps a little wider than usual. She waits for me to speak.

'Men like children created in their own image. They want their children to take their name. If not their last, then their first name and sometimes both.'

'Now just because they have the same first name, you can't conclude that they're father and son,' says Mrs Joseph carefully.

'Oh, there's a lot of other evidence too which I didn't know or wouldn't see. Daddy stopped taking his oil well royalties and started paying them into the Marcello Trust just around the time Ricky was born. He taught Ricky to fix things and gave him the old tow truck. He came here with Barbara and when he was with her he was different, he was happy, he laughed, you said he laughed himself helpless. It was through Barbara he knew you, right? And when he used to leave me here . . . was he going on field trips? Or was he going to stay with Barbara and Ricky?'

Mrs Joseph sighs.

'Your face is red, Lucy. You look angry. You look hurt.'

I glare up at Barbara Marcello. Smiling. Half in shadow. 'I thought I liked her. She was nice to me,' I say bitterly. 'After the car crash, before Jane got there, she was so goddamn nice. I didn't know she'd stolen my father and given him to Ricky.'

I sense movement and see Ralph shrinking inside his hat. He looks so miserable that for a moment I feel bad.

He says: 'Aren't you pleased your father was happy?'

I want to cry with the pain but I'm too angry.

'Why did we have to get the lonely, sad Daddy? Why couldn't we have him happy too? It makes me feel I didn't know him at all.'

Mrs Joseph is compassionate. Her face droops as though she's about to cry for me. 'We never can know all of someone.'

'I didn't know he was a liar and a cheat. I thought he always tried to do the right thing. I respected him, I measured others by his standards.'

Ralph and Mrs Joseph are silent. I become aware of the trees shaking in the new breeze outside. Plants and shrubs tap on the window as though they're trying to clamber through it. One of them sends its heady scent into the kitchen and it seems to settle on our silence. Then, quietly, Mrs Joseph starts to talk.

'I don't know what a husband is entitled to expect in a wife. A companion, a mother, a helpmate, a rock, a lover, a wealth-creator, a cook, a homemaker, a decorator, a friend. Whatever your definition, through no fault of her own, your mother couldn't deliver. Your father met Barbara very soon after your mother got sick and very soon after that they had Ricky. The relationship continued until the end of Barbara's life. It was close and it was happy. They were like man and wife but most of the time they didn't live together and it worked for them.'

Far off, across the valley, a dog barks.

'But . . . he was our father! Jane's, mine!' I protest. 'How could he have another family at the same time?'

'He only saw them once a week, occasionally more. He'd have vacations with them when you were away at summer camp or staying here. Having them didn't make him love you any less. He was a big-hearted man.'

'He was a big cheat,' I mutter.

'He needed support and kindness. He was coping with your mother and bringing up two daughters alone.'

There's a sniff in my voice. 'But it was such a betrayal.'

'Because he didn't tell you?'

'He kept one whole part of his life secret.'

'I guess he didn't want your mother to know because it would have upset her so much. But when you were old enough not to tell her, I thought he could have explained it to you. I thought you'd understand and be pleased for him that he was happy. But he chose not to do that and I don't know why.'

'He came to stay with me in New York . . .'

'Right after she died. It was a good vacation for him, Lucy.'

'But she'd just died and he didn't tell me. He was grieving and he didn't show it, I didn't realize.'

Daddy in New York. A man staggering and smiling in the elevator.

'I guess he'd trained himself pretty well to hide his feelings. He was adamant, even when Barbara was dead, that the two sides of his life should never meet. And that was sort of hard on Ricky because he knew about you and Jane. It's been hard for him too, Lucy. But he promised his father that he would have no contact. No contact under any circumstances. I think that added to his feeling that you were Eric's first family and he and Barbara were way back in second place.'

I get up and stand at the window and turn my back on Ralph and Mrs Joseph so they won't see me cry.

'Did Ricky know?' I sob. 'When I met him here as a kid? Did Robert know?'

'No one knew except for me. And Ralph, of course.'

'I know everything,' says Ralph shamelessly. 'I eavesdrop. But I don't tell what I hear.'

'When did Ricky find out?'

'Oh . . .' Mrs Joseph thinks. 'Maybe he was eighteen or so. Barbara wanted him to understand and she thought she could trust him with the information. She told him on the condition that he had no contact with you.'

He kept the bargain. Nobody could have tried harder to repulse me than Ricky. I remember how he hissed at me by the tow truck. I say: 'I think he hates me.' Involuntarily I cover my ear.

'I don't agree. It did take him a long time to come to terms with the situation. He was always a difficult boy. Barbara had a lot of trouble with him when he was an adolescent. But he's married to a lovely girl called Martha now and they have the sweetest baby.'

'Baby Jordan,' Ralph tells me helpfully. He's happier now the room's emotional climate is more temperate but not happy enough to take off his hat.

'Martha converted the barn into a gallery and she's doing real well. Ricky has inherited his mother's land and some capital and he can always earn money fixing things because he has gifted hands. He paints well too. I like him now, very much. He's spent a lot of time here.'

Ricky Marcello. He stole my father and then he stole the Josephs. All the years I was exiled, he was feeding off their laughter and comradeship.

I haven't even turned around but Mrs Joseph seems to know from my back what I'm thinking.

'Don't be bitter, Lucy. Your father was always there for you when you needed him.'

Daddy, I thought you were the rock in my ocean but now I recall you as a series of absences. The father who wasn't here when kids called at the house and Mother was psychotic. The father who couldn't be found when Mrs Zacarro came looking for Lindy that evening. The father who took field trips. The father who betrayed us, not because he lied, but because he didn't tell the truth.

I feel an arm slip around me, tender but timid. It is Ralph. He has stood up and crossed the room without making a sound.

'Are you going to forgive him, Lucy?' he says.

I sniff. 'Maybe.'

I feel the arm disengage itself and when I next turn around, Ralph has gone. Mrs Joseph is alone at the table. She is watching me, straight-backed, sharp-eyed.

'There's no reason to be jealous of Ricky,' she says.

'How can I not be? When they were together they were like a real family. Two parents who loved each other and their son. I'm jealous of that.'

'You had a lot of love too. Your mother may not always have known how to express it or even show it but she loves you.'

If Jane is right that Mother killed her baby, the consequences of her actions now seem even more immense. In one exhausted, desperate moment she lost her baby, her mind and her husband.

'Poor Mother,' I say softly. 'Poor, poor Mother. It's taken years, but recently I've stopped feeling mad at her and started to understand her.'

Mrs Joseph beams at me. 'Really, Lucy? I'm proud of you for that.'

Ralph has reappeared outside the window, hovering across the lawn like a humming bird around some big flowers which seem to shout their magnificence.

Mrs Joseph asks: 'Will you go see her before you leave?'

'My last visit wasn't too successful.'

'Will you try again?'

So many visits have begun in hope and ended in disaster. I am cautious. 'Mother's completely unpredictable.'

'If you feel differently about her now,' Mrs Joseph says, 'maybe you should tell her so. Maybe she'll feel different too.'

A warmth spreads over me when I think of the tiny figure dropping a rose into Daddy's grave. She is a victim, a victim of circumstances and a victim of her own passionate nature. She lost Daddy years ago to Barbara but not all of him. He continued to visit her, to care for her needs, to support her and, who knows, maybe to love her. Now, apart from Jane and me, she is pitifully alone.

'Will you go?' asks Mrs Joseph.

I say: 'Yes.'

36

I plan to go to Redbush clinic at the end of the afternoon. Before that I'll go to the beach house and before that to the San Strana valley. I have a small gift for Ricky Marcello waiting back at Daddy's house.

The gift is lying right on the desk.

Larry appears at the door of the den. He looks hot and tired.

I tuck the file under my arm and pick up the folder of letters for Scott.

'I have to go out again.'

'Why?'

'The file that's been worrying me. I've found out where it belongs. Then I'm going to give some stuff to Scott. Then I'm going to say goodbye to Mother.'

'Well, I've made you a sandwich. French cheese in real French bread. Aren't you going to eat it before you go?' He looks grumpy at the prospect of the uneaten sandwich.

'Okay, thanks.'

I follow him into the kitchen. He slides the sandwich towards me and pours us water.

'It's too hot in that barn now we have the lights,' he complains. 'I don't know how those guys stand it, it's worse than the heatwave. They don't even eat any lunch. I guess they're a lot younger than me.'

I ask: 'Is that man still hanging around outside your apartment?'

'Yes. I wish I could get Kirsty more worked up about it.'

We eat silently. Whenever I'm alone with Larry I don't know what to say to him. We talk about the heatwave, how it is not only ending but forecasters are predicting rain tomorrow. Then we fall silent again.

'So where are you going with that file, Lucy?' he asks at last. 'Into town?'

'To the San Strana valley.'

He nods and tears at his sandwich. 'I haven't been out there in a few years. Last time was with you guys. We met you for lunch at some place by the river.'

By that time Stevie had been born. The white, wooden restaurant was the same, the river was the same, we ordered eggs Benedict, but it was different with a baby. Stevie's ceaseless demands and complaints turned the whole experience into an ordeal.

'Who are you seeing in San Strana?' he asks.

I hadn't planned on telling anyone but Jane about Ricky Marcello but I guess Larry has to know sooner or later. I say: 'My brother. My half-brother, to be precise.'

It's nice to shock Larry. He has trained himself to control his reactions but now he freezes, sandwich in his mouth, his eyes wide and I enjoy my brief power over him. As I tell him about Daddy's other life my words are punctuated by his incredulity.

'And we never guessed. We never even suspected . . . Have you ever seen the guy? Have you met him?'

I do not plan to reveal any of my recent encounters with Ricky, here or at San Strana or Big Brim or outside Larry's own apartment. Not until I understand them better. I say: 'I might have glimpsed him at the cemetery when we were burying Daddy.'

'That's sad,' says Larry. 'Real sad. He should have been a leading participant at his father's funeral, not skulking around in the graveyard trying to catch a glimpse of the coffin.'

For the first time it occurs to me that maybe Ricky hangs around Jane's apartment because he shares something of the Schaffers' loneliness. Suddenly he seems no longer like a large, dark, threatening man but an isolated figure, seeking sisters then running away from them whenever he gets too close.

I stand up to go. Larry says: 'I don't know how Jane is going to react to this news. I'd like to phone her and talk to her about it right now.' Maybe Larry is hungry for the same power he gave me a few minutes ago, the power to shock.

When I get to San Strana the garage looks closed again but the Marcello Gallery is open. I pull right in like a regular customer. There is parking in a large gravel lot near the barn. The lot is ringed by bright garden flowers. Beyond are the immense, scaly trunks of old trees. High in one is the remains of a treehouse.

The gallery has the large windows of a modern space but the rough timber and high roof of a barn. Inside, the sun fills it. There is a woman working at a desk in one corner. She brushes her long hair over her shoulder and smiles when I walk in.

'Hi,' she says. 'Feel free to wander around. Ask me about anything that interests you.'

I recognize her as the woman who picked up the baby and held it over her head. And sure enough there is movement at her feet and a baby, fat and dribbling, emerges from under the desk. He waves a brightly painted wooden toy. Probably it's one of Gregory Hifeld's.

'Oh, he won't bother you,' says the woman, following my stare. The baby smiles. He crawls towards me. I back off. I haven't held a baby for three years.

The paintings are mostly big and bright. There are a couple by Barbara Marcello. They contain a hundred shades of green. When the woman sees me studying them she approaches me. She is so tall she seems to sway a little when she walks.

'Are you familiar with the work of Barbara Marcello?' she asks.

'No. But these are nice.'

'This is where Barbara Marcello lived and worked all her life: her family farmed in the San Strana valley. Her son has quite a few of her pieces but the rest are out there and they're rising in value fast. I buy back when I can. I'm trying to turn this gallery into a showplace for her work, but . . .' She grimaces. 'They sell too quickly.'

Another picture attracts me. When I've looked at it for long enough I realize the attraction is recognition. It shows the view from Daddy's house. The valley, the orchards, the intersection.

I point to it and the woman says: 'That's by her son, Eric Marcello. You can see there's a similarity of style.'

'Is he here?' I ask.

She looks at me uncertainly.

'You want to meet Ricky?'

'I've already met him a few times.'

The baby approaches and tries to pull himself to his feet on the long skirt of his mother. She stoops and picks him up.

'What's your name?' she asks me as the baby curves against her, the way babies do, tucking its soft head into her shoulder and peering at me from behind the safety of her arm.

'Lucy Schaffer.'

Her face has the beauty of perfect symmetry but I see it harden against me now as though she just slammed a door.

She sighs. 'Why did you come here?'

'I have to talk to him.'

'No you don't.'

'There are a lot of questions. He can answer them.'

'You don't need them answered. Go back to New York and get on with your banking.'

'I can't do that. It's like there's a row of tin soldiers and when Daddy died, maybe before Daddy died, the first one fell over and now they're all falling and there's nothing anyone can do.'

The gallery door opens with a quaint squeak and Ricky walks in. When he sees me he glares and lingers in the doorway.

'I thought I recognized your car. Would you just get the hell out of here?' He is aggressive but his tone is milder today, maybe because he has noticed the baby clinging nervously to its mother.

I hold out a thick green file.

'I'm leaving California. I brought you something you wanted.'

He takes it gingerly.

'It's Daddy's oil royalties. That's what you were looking for, right? The first time the guys towing back the Oldsmobile disturbed you. The second time you couldn't find it. You figured that I had it with me but, the third time, when you tried to sneak into the den, I was sitting right there so you ran. You want it, so here it is.'

He glances down at the file but only for a moment. His stare is fixed on me.

I say: 'I know you're my brother.'

The silence which falls in the room is brief and penetrating.

Eventually Ricky looks at the woman for guidance but her face is still closed and she turns away from him. The baby holds out his hands and whines for his father. Ricky takes him, tenderly, into his arms. Satisfied, the baby smiles at me broadly.

'Listen,' says Ricky. 'Dad didn't want you here. He didn't ever bring you here. He didn't ever tell you about us. That's because he didn't want you to know. And he made me promise never to make contact. I like to keep my goddamn promises but God knows he didn't tell me what to do if you kept sneaking around here.'

'You kept your promise as well as you could,' I say. 'Now you have to let me in.'

He looks to the woman again but she has turned her back and walked right away from us, shaking her head a little. She sits down at the desk and tries to look busy.

A car pulls into the lot outside.

'You better come into the house,' he instructs me brusquely. 'This kind of thing has to be bad for business.'

When the barn door has closed behind us he says: 'Look, go away, for Chrissake.'

'Somehow,' I say, 'I never imagined a brother talking to me the way you do.'

He sighs and, with the baby still in his arms, walks back into the house. And, although he doesn't invite me in, he leaves the door open and I follow him.

I recognize the particular disorder of the kitchen right away. Baby mess. Drawers open and their contents pulled on to the floor, toys, food all around the high chair, bottles, crusts.

'Here, Jordan,' says Ricky, putting the baby down on the floor amid his toys. Jordan ignores the toys and starts to examine a pair of shoes. I peer at him jealously. Daddy's second grandson. I hope Daddy didn't love him more than he loved his first.

Ricky is busy in one corner. He still doesn't say anything. When he turns around I see he has made us both coffee. He pushes mine across the table to me and gestures for me to sit down.

'It's okay, it doesn't have arsenic in it,' he says. He sits back and almost smiles. 'The police interviewed me last week.'

'How did they know about you?'

'My fingerprints were all over Dad's house. And you have to give your prints to get your tow truck certificate. When that patrolman said he saw Dad in the tow truck he pretty well led them right to me.'

'They knew all about you?'

'Yup. And they knew I was there Sunday afternoon and that you were there too. I told them everything.'

I redden.

'So,' he says, stretching his long body. 'So, who told you about me? The Zac? Adam Holler never would.'

'I worked it out. You were right to go looking for that file, it was the only link between us. There was no reference to you anywhere in the house, no pictures, nothing, but the file showed that, around about the time you were born, Daddy stopped receiving his oil royalties. When I was tracing them, I found you.'

Expressionless, he reaches out for the file. He opens it.

'Simms-Roeder,' he mutters, pulling out one sheet at random. 'Simms-Roeder put me through college and a lot else besides.'

Jordan has crawled over to my feet now. I can feel his small hands on me. I move my legs back under my chair.

'You probably hated us,' I say. 'I mean, Jane and me.'

'Yes,' he agrees amicably. 'When I learned that you were Dad's first family and that he'd fitted us in around your glee club gatherings and your summer camp, yes, I guess I hated you for that.' He pauses. 'But, I had this terrific mother. I caused her a lot of worry and I feel bad about that now. But she was terrific and yours was locked-up crazy. So I think I didn't draw such a bad ticket in the big raffle.'

He is relaxed. His tone is lazy. His long legs rest on a chair. I am irritated that he has access to my family history without any of its burdens and I watch my coffee as though it might do something remarkable. When Ricky speaks again, his voice is kinder.

'I guess it was real tough on you having that kind of a mom. When did she go crazy?'

'Right after her baby died. I was four.'

Jordan crawls over to him and he bends down and gently hands the baby some keys. Jordan grabs them and puts as many into his mouth as he can. Ricky strokes his son's hair. Something in the gesture, an affection, a gentleness, touches me. He looks up, waiting for me to say more.

'I was in a canyon in Arizona. Daddy and Jane and I went into the canyon to look for rocks and as usual Daddy got way ahead. I fell and hurt my arm and Jane went on to get help and eventually I made my own way out and there they were, Mother and Daddy and Jane. They were standing on the blacktop and it was so gooey with the heat I thought it was going to evaporate, Mother and Daddy and Jane along with it. And Mother was yelling. Crazy yelling.'

I try to remember her words. I close my eyes and I'm stumbling towards the canyon's mouth, my arm throbbing, the heat clogging whatever mechanism makes you walk, whatever makes you think, and there's a voice, so loud and high-pitched that it seems to have been drawn from the fierceness of the sun. I look for her words. I try to intercept them, I reach for them but they wound me and then escape.

'You mean . . . that was it?' Ricky asks. 'Just that?'

I send myself back to Arizona one more time, the blacktop sizzles again, heat ricochets off the rocks once more but her words still evade me.

'I don't remember what she was saying. But the tone of her voice wasn't like any tone I'd heard before.'

Ricky rearranges himself a little. 'So, you went into this canyon and she was okay. And you came out and she was insane?'

'That's the way it seemed to me.'

'Something must have happened.'

'Her baby had died just a few weeks earlier. I guess her grief must have reached boiling point right out there in the sun.'

He shook his head. 'Sounds to me like something must have happened while you were in that canyon.'

He pushes some dirty plates out of the way so he can put his elbows on the table and cup his chin in one hand. He smiles suddenly, a lopsided smile that seems to appear right out of his fingers.

'Well, at least we both had a great dad.'

I look into Ricky's dark green eyes. They are the same colour as my own.

'Why were you shouting at him? That day I watched you from the deck?'

He sighs. 'I've regretted it every day since. I wasn't shouting, but I probably came on too strong. I was telling him it was time to leave that big mean old house up there on the hill and come live with us. He could have had one whole part of the house here to himself and I'd have known he was safe. But no. He was too goddamn stubborn.'

'Safe? Did you think he was in danger?'

'Yeah, from daughters who sneak around his house.'

I stumble through an unsatisfactory explanation. He listens and then says: 'That the last time you saw him?'

I nod sadly.

'I last saw him when they brought back the tow truck real late on Sunday night,' Ricky tells me. 'I know you know all about that. They didn't mean to disturb us but I heard them so I went out to see how they got along. They were all real agitated because they'd nearly been picked up by Highway Patrol.'

'How was Daddy?'

'Oh . . . very tired. He'd been driving the truck and had his licence checked and stuff. And . . . he was sort of sad.'

'Sad?'

Ricky speaks quietly now. 'Like he knew what might be coming. I mean, when I said good night, he walked up to me and . . .'

I stare at him. His voice has stopped as though it just ran right off the road. His face creases. He looks down at Jordan and suddenly sweeps the baby on to his lap, hugging him tightly, placing the baby between himself and his grief. The child curls against his father's body but he cannot hide his father's tears. Ricky is stubborn. He doesn't want to cry, he wants to get those words out. When they emerge, they are almost incomprehensible.

'He hugged me and he said goodbye. Not good night. Goodbye. Like I wouldn't see him again . . .'

Ricky is crying hard now and the baby doesn't like it. He wriggles to get away. I stand up and, reluctantly, offer my arms to the squirming Jordan. He reaches out for me and I lift him. A baby in my arms, fitting its body to mine, looking up into my eyes, stretching its fingers to my face. I feel an intense pleasure and an intense pain. I kneel down and put my other arm around Ricky. He is, after all, my brother.

'Oh no,' says a voice. Martha is frozen in the doorway.

'No,' she says. 'No, no, this is not allowed to happen.'

We all look at her and Jordan reaches for her. She walks right over and removes him firmly from my arm. I take a step back from Ricky. His face is dark, his chin is shadowed, his pupils are so dilated that his eyes look black and beneath them are the dark smudges I recognize as grief's thumbprints.

'It's okay,' he tells Martha. 'She already knew everything.'

'So what? C'mon Ricky, you gave your dad your word. No contact. Looks to me as though there's a whole lot of contact going on here.'

'Martha, she's my sister. Dad's dead now and –'

'You promised,' she says. 'He wouldn't have made you promise if he didn't have a good reason.' They stare at each other stormily.

Martha turns to me.

'Why?' she demands. 'Why do you have to keep coming here like this?'

'If you found you had a brother, wouldn't you want to know him?'

'You didn't need him before. You don't need him now.'

But, despite his hostility, despite everything, it seems to me that I've waited for Ricky all my life. The brother whom I loved was taken away from me as a tiny baby and now it feels that he's come back as this big, dark, angry stranger.

'You've made a mistake,' Martha says, returning to the gallery with Jordan under her arm. 'Your father didn't want his two families ever to know each other because he knew something bad would happen.'

'What can happen?' I ask her but she has swayed through the door and slammed it shut behind her.

'Why didn't Daddy want us to meet?' I ask Ricky. 'Why? Did he ever give you a reason?'

He shakes his head. 'Martha will come round, I guess. She can take a while to get used to things.'

I say: 'I have to go now. I have to meet Scott and then get to Mother's clinic. They don't allow late visitors.'

When we go outside, the house looks pretty. A house and a barn, Daddy's other house, his other barn, the warm, bright side of his life.

Standing by my car, Ricky asks: 'Well, are we going to meet again?'

I look at him. 'Do you want to?'

'Lucy, I'm kind of relieved. I think this may just be one of the good things to come out of Dad's death.'

And to my amazement he suddenly puts his long arms around me and hugs me to him, this stranger who is my brother.

37

A wind from the ocean is blowing Scott's hair around and he is looking out from the porch through binoculars.

'It could be a whale-watching boat,' he reports. 'The migration might have started.'

The sea wind feels so cold that Scott has given me an immense sweatshirt. Here on the coast, March is back. The heatwave felt like June but it was just a strange, stifling faux-summer and only the ocean wasn't fooled, retaining the icy depth of its colour throughout.

Apart from the funeral I haven't seen Scott much recently. I suspect that Brigitte must be home from France and I hope she doesn't arrive while I'm here.

I place the big folder right in front of him.

'Just look at that through your binoculars,' I say. He tries, comically, and then puts down the binoculars and picks up the folder.

'Is this executor stuff?'

'It's everything. Done. Finished. Phone calls made, death certificate duplicated and enclosed where necessary. All you have to do is sign the letters and put them in the envelopes and get them to a mailbox. They even have stamps on.'

'Oh Jeez, Luce . . .'

He flicks through the pages of neat figures, letters and envelopes.

'Luce, I don't know how to thank you . . .' He leans across the scaly wooden table and kisses me. Not a long kiss, but long enough to show that, at the very least, he's grateful.

'When's your flight?' he asks.

'Tomorrow, three o'clock.'

'Can I come to the airport?'

'Okay, but you may see me again soon anyway. I'm thinking of moving back to California.'

For a second, no, a fraction of a second, I detect something like shock on his face. I wonder if things have already progressed too far with Brigitte for Scott to feel the State of California is also big enough for me. Then he recovers and smiles and there is genuine pleasure in his smile. He reaches out for my hand.

'That's terrific,' he says. 'How come?'

'Now Daddy's dead, maybe Mother needs me,' I say. 'And my family's here. Stevie's buried here. There are a lot of reasons to come back.'

'Luce . . .'

The wind has blown some colour into his cheeks. Or maybe he's embarrassed. I wait for him to speak then realize he's waiting for me. He presses my hand tighter. Beyond us the ocean is noisy. The weather has provoked it. No longer a slumbering zoo animal, it is a wild creature again. The waves crash violently against the shore. Neither of us speaks. We watch in silence as a couple of surfers, inexperienced or maybe just intimidated, attempt and fail to ride the sea's magnificence.

When I stand up to go the wind almost buffets me back down.

'I have to get to Redbush now so I can say goodbye to Mother.'

He releases my hand. We walk to the steps together. He says: 'Lucy, the police don't seem to have any answers. I'm not sure we'll ever know what really happened to Eric. Can you live with that?'

Not knowing. I remember how, when Sasha and I arrived at Daddy's house that night, I relished my last few moments of not knowing.

I say: 'Sometimes it's better not to know. And in the last couple of weeks, so many other things have been resolved.'

He halts suddenly and, holding my shoulders, revolves my body so we're facing each other. He studies me.

'You look good, Luce. You look terrific. So alive.'

I smile at him. 'I'm just beginning to feel good, Scott.'

I kiss him and turn to go. I clatter down the steps on to the beach. As soon as my feet hit the sand they are silenced.

I drive up the coast towards Redbush. The first time I visited Mother at the clinic, there was almost no Redbush town. I remember it as a small, rural community but now it has expanded beyond recognition. The houses are large with big front yards and well-watered lawns. Many are no longer new: children who were born here may already be parents themselves and the houses already contain childhoods, histories and memories.

I know that, before the houses, there were other histories and memories. I try, unsuccessfully, to equate the mature trees with the trees which used to stand next to the small farms here. I trace the lines of asphalted roads, looking for the tracks I remember that led to isolated houses with rusty pick-up trucks parked by rusty tractors in dusty yards. Suddenly, I am overwhelmed by the way the past has been replaced, built over as if it never existed. The houses and people and horses on the hill here have gone but if I remember them (a group of sun-drenched kids drinking pink liquid under a tree watched by a wide, aproned woman. A man kicking, in frustration, a truck with a flat tyre. A low red house with a horse, the same colour red, prancing inside an adjacent corral, sometimes a saddle slung over the wooden fence, sometimes actually a rider, the horse doing some fancy dance beneath him) then how can they be completely gone?

So long as you remember the past, it must continue to exist somehow, even when it obviously and indisputably is not there any more. I remember the suntanned people and their houses, their orchards. How I always looked out for the red horse when we drove this way and how it nearly always pranced and shone in the sun but sometimes it just stood still and ate hay. My memories of this road have the intensity of the recent past so it's hard, almost impossible, to reconcile them with the houses and pools and lawns which have stood here for many years creating their own memories.

When I reach the clinic the guard examines my ID closely and then, still looking hard at me, calls through to the clinic. Finally he nods.

'Uh-huh. Go right over.'

Mother's big, smiling nurse is waiting for me in the conservatory. He says: 'I'm real glad you're back for another try. I didn't think you would be after the last time.'

The hallways are silent until, as we pass one door, I hear people laughing. Perhaps five, six voices, laughing together with spontaneous delight.

'That's the Alzheimer's group having big fun,' says the nurse.

'I didn't know it's big fun to have Alzheimer's.'

'Oh, believe me, it isn't. But that group has a wonderful facilitator. She says, hey, it's a second childhood, let's enjoy it as much as, more than, the first one. Her methods are controversial but people have come from all over the state to watch her at work and they're generally very impressed.'

'How about the patients?'

'They love her. They just want Alzheimer's group all day.'

'Would Mother benefit?'

We're passing through a door now. He pauses.

'Um . . . she doesn't have Alzheimer's, of course. And to be honest, I don't see her laughing with the rest of them. She gets sort of sad.'

Mother at the graveside, shedding small tears like jewels. Surrounded by people, but alone now without Daddy.

The nurse says: 'I'm sorry you saw her mean side last time. She can be that way with your sister. I couldn't believe she did it to you when she hadn't seen you in so long.'

'Jane says Mother mostly doesn't know her.'

The nurse throws back his head and laughs. 'Oh, she knows Jane, that's for sure.'

He stops at Mother's door. My heart begins to clatter. My hands feel clammy. When I walk into the room I search for Mother's tiny body amid the ornate drapery, the cushions, the plush chairs.

'Wait and I'll get her. Her class is just over.'

'What class?'

'Ceramics. It finished five minutes ago.'

There is a blue felt folder lying on the bed, worn at the corners from use. When the nurse leaves I glance out of the window to make sure no one in overalls is watching me. Then I open it. The folder is full of photographs. Baby Nicholas. Me. Daddy. Grandma, the aunts. Me again. Daddy and me. Another baby, probably Nicky again. Me, gazing rapturously at Nicky in his cradle. The house, looking curiously unclothed without foliage, Daddy standing outside it. Along with the photographs are postcards, with my writing on the back. Postcards with abstract blues, a brown dog, felt-booted peasants in old Russia. Every postcard I have ever sent Mother is here, dog-eared with use, but careful use, like the photos.

I reach the back of the folder and there is just one more

picture. A class picture, three rows of smiling kids. Cornington School, Second Grade, says the small blackboard the
teacher holds. I remember the picture being taken in the fall,
right after we started in second grade when we had barely
learned the teacher's name. First I see Lindy, blonde, pretty,
her head a little to one side and, right next to her, me. I am
looking at the camera, smiling a little and cradling one arm
against my body. It is encased in plaster. I look closer. I was
six, almost seven, when I went into second grade. But I know
I broke my arm years earlier, in the canyon in Arizona,
because we took that trip right after my brother died and I
was four then, I'm certain of that. I stare at the plaster arm
in the picture, trying to persuade myself it is a white sleeve
or white paper, or even a joke. But the way I cradle it,
protectively, is unmistakable.

I hear voices in the hallway. I rapidly replace the picture
and close the folder. My mind swoops and wheels like a
seagull. My brother died when I was four. I broke my arm
in a canyon two years, not two weeks, later. We didn't go
to Arizona right after my baby brother died. It was years
afterwards that I walked out of the canyon with my arm
throbbing in time with Mother's yells.

I recall Ricky's voice, his lazy drawl: 'Sounds to me like
something must have happened while you were in that
canyon.'

The door opens to reveal Mother, her arm in the nurse's.
Today she wears eyeglasses. Their frames are severe and they
make her seem less vacant.

I walk right over to her. I don't want to frighten her so I
say, very softly: 'Hi, Mother, it's Lucy.'

'Lucy.'

She reaches out and there is a small, warm tug at my hand.
Carefully, gently, she embraces me. I submit to her maternal

caress and the moment has a strange, isolated sweetness of its own.

'I guess I'll leave you two,' says the nurse. 'I'll leave you two right now.'

I hear the door thud shut softly behind him.

I say: 'Mother, I've remembered a song. A song you used to sing me when I was little . . .'

She waits. She looks apprehensive. I hope the song will be there when I need it. I reach inside my memory to that strange evasive place where music is stored. A few broken bars of the nursery song float out. I hum them and Mother's face breaks into a wide smile and for a moment her eyes shine. Then she picks up the tune from me and gradually, uncertain at first, she begins to sing. I close my eyes while, holding both my hands, she sings gently. When we reach the closing bars, we both make birds with our hands and they fly away. We look at each other smiling, delighted.

I say: 'Mother, I want to talk to you about my baby. About Stevie and how he died. Just lately I've started telling about it a little but I want to talk to you, because you'll understand better than anyone.'

We go over to the window and sit in the same chairs we sat in last time. Mother looks at me, waiting for me to speak, and I see her mind is fully engaged. There is clay in her hair, clinging white to some of the strands. There is more clay under her fingernails.

I tell her how Stevie used to cry and cry. 'Each yell seemed to eat a little bit of me away. His unhappiness was my unhappiness. The misery he was expressing was the misery inside me. I loved him so much, he'd turned me from a solid state to a liquid one, but his demands, his dissatisfaction, his crying made me some other woman and, God knows, that woman wanted to smother him often enough. I just wanted him to stop. When he died, it felt inevitable. I had silenced him so many times in my head that I knew it must be my fault.'

I am crying now and Mother reaches out and wraps my fingers in her two small hands. When I look up, I see that she is crying too.

She says: 'It was my fault.'

I stare at her. I assess her eyes for knowledge, for coherence. She looks right back at me, tears falling, no longer silently but accompanied by a high-pitched wail I remember in my dreams. 'She did it again! It's my fault she did it again!'

Her words slip between the crevices. I am alone in a sizzling landscape of towering red rocks and sun-baked earth. I am approaching the mouth of the canyon, my arm throbs in pain and I hear a shrieking which at first I think is some angry desert bird. Then I know it is a woman and I know the woman is my mother. I listen and her words bounce off rocks, reverberate through the canyon, scramble along dry riverbeds. 'It's my fault, she did it again! She did it again! Oh God, she did it again!'

I say: 'Who did it again? Who?'

I look at Mother now, her blue eyes, her pale skin, the clay in her hair. Mother holds my hand tightly, staring back at me, waiting for me to know.

We were in Arizona two years, not two weeks after Nicky died. Jane and I went into the canyon. And Jane came out alone. That's when Mother started to yell. That's when her misery took her through the membrane between unhappiness and psychosis. That's why they all stopped and stared when I appeared, but it was too late for Mother. She believed Jane had done it again.

'Jane,' I say. Softly. Then louder. 'Jane.'

And Mother's whole body twists with distress.

413

'Jane . . .' I say. 'Jane killed Nicky.' The words come out so easily, so naturally, I wonder how it is that they've been choking me since I was four years old.

38

I sit outside by the parking lot where I sat with Sasha and the aunts, staring out across the expanse of unnatural green lawn. The sprinklers create a uniform pattern right across to the wall on the other side. When the nurse came in and Mother couldn't stop crying he told me I should go. Mother clung to me tightly and then planted a small, sad kiss on my forehead. I promised her I would come back soon.

Scott's sweatshirt is so big I can put my knees up inside it and hug them to me, but the new coolness in the air cuts through my clothes as though I'm naked. The breeze blows clouds across the sky and when they cover the sun I feel the temperature dip. But I don't care. I don't care that I'm cold. I want to be colder still, until I'm completely anaesthetized. I'd prefer my brain not to function at all but it still thinks. It thinks as relentlessly as a machine.

The dead baby was wrapped in a blanket in Daddy's arms. Mother emitted high-pitched wails. Jane stood next to them, her face white. There was no remorse. Her fingers leapt over one another as though they had a life of their own. Daddy went to the porch. He was carrying the unmoving shape inside the blanket which was Nicky. He was going down the steps to bury him. He was going to the sunken garden.

Rougemont said, when we were standing right by the grave, that it's easy to confuse what actually happened with things you've been told. Maybe there never even was a Nickel Dog.

Mother and Daddy had decided not to tell anyone what

Jane had done. Their beautiful, clever daughter, it was almost impossible that she would kill her brother, inconceivable that she would commit such a crime again. They foolishly, lovingly, fatally, protected Jane.

Eight-month-old Nicholas Schaffer was swept out to sea at Big Brim beach yesterday by a freak wave. Dr and Mrs Schaffer are being interviewed by the police. Detective Rougemont declined to comment on the case.

It was a secret. Maybe Rougemont guessed but nobody else knew how Nicky really died. Except for Lindy Zacarro. When Daddy left the house carrying the small body in the blanket, I ran. I stumbled past the glimmering tow truck and through the yard, in and out of trees, by poison ivy, around pungent bushes, until I reached the den we'd made under some branches. Inside was a rug, a few toy horses, and Lindy.

With Lindy, it wasn't so easy to disguise the facts by creating family mythologies about dead dogs. No, Lindy knew, and it seems to me now that as we grew older her knowledge turned acidic inside her.

I think of her curled in the trunk of the car, her blonde hair wet with sweat, her fingernails scratched right off her hands. I twist my whole body to avoid the thought but now Mother is emerging, hands fluttering like trapped birds, a strange new energy in her walk, from the Zacarro house. There is horror on her face.

Faces around the blue crib, contorted with horror. Stevie's body, motionless. Jane's eyes burning in her face, her fingers dancing. Daddy's eyes, full, brimming, slowly sliding off me. Off me and on to Jane, at my side. Daddy stared right at her. He knew. She's done it again. She's done it again. His tears, his roar. 'The police! What do the police have to do with anything?'

I moan softly.

I can hardly breathe for pain. I can hardly breathe for wanting to feel Stevie's soft body push itself up against me again. I am hardly large enough to encompass the magnitude of my grief. My howl seems to rip the green lawn like thin paper. I hear someone saying Stevie's name over and over, crying it and then muttering it. That person is me. I am powerless to silence her. Tears without end, grief without limit.

It's my fault, she's done it again.

I leap up from the bench as though it's on fire. There's no one to hear me except a few people crossing the parking lot who expect this kind of behaviour in a clinic like Redbush, but one of them, a man, well-dressed, concerned, walks over to me.

'Are you okay?' he asks me uncertainly.

I realize I have been gasping for breath. I stare at him.

'Are you okay?' he repeats.

I run to my car. And then, I drive so fast I forget every stretch of road as soon as it's behind me. I break speed limits, weave through lanes of traffic, irritate truck drivers, honk my horn. Along the freeway, through Lowis, half-glimpsing half-imagined boys on skateboards. Past fruit stalls. Past farmsteads. Past horses with their tails turned to the wind.

The Marcello Gallery, the house, the flowers all slumber. Out of the wind, everything here is still. The big trees don't move. High in one of them I register the dark shape of a treehouse. Daddy built treehouses here with Ricky. When he was here he could throw back his head and laugh and laugh. It was his other place, far from the stark, blistering hillside which was my home. It was his cool, green, secret place, a fairytale place. Destroyed forever if you tell about it.

Inside the barn I see Martha look up from her desk in surprise as the gravel protests beneath my car tyres. I park right outside, blocking the drive, and jump out. There is a big fly sitting on the barn door in the sun. It's too sleepy or lazy to move when I fling open the door.

Martha isn't pleased to see me. She stands and puts her hands on her hips with a deliberate slowness, silently demanding an explanation.

'Where's Ricky?' I ask.

'Out.'

'Where?'

She starts her spiel about how Daddy didn't want us to have this kind of contact and I interrupt her.

'He was right, Martha, Daddy was right, I have to warn Ricky.'

She raises her eyebrows but her face does not soften.

'I think he's in danger. It's my fault. Please, please, where is he?'

She studies my face and sighs. At last she says: 'He's taken Jordan to Tigertail Bay.'

'Tigertail?'

'Whale-watching. A woman called Joni something called. She used to work for Eric.'

'Joni? Joni Rimbaldi called you guys?'

'You know her?'

'She was Daddy's secretary for years and years.'

'Ricky recognized her name. She said that Eric told her all about us. Apparently he gave her some kind of folder with Jordan's name on it.'

I remember Joni at Daddy's funeral, worrying that her jacket was too bright, surprised at herself for wearing it. Was Joni Rimbaldi nursing Daddy's secret all the time she spoke to me?

'She asked Ricky to go right over and collect the folder. She said to take Jordan because she lives by Tigertail and there's a load of whales around the bay. She's meeting them in a parking lot so they can watch.'

My heart thuds.

'Did Daddy ever say he told Joni? Did he ever say?'

The barn's high roof echoes. Before it has finished echoing I've remembered my conversation with Joni at the funeral. I've remembered that Joni's in Maine. She's not at Tigertail Bay. There are no whales.

Probably I don't even say goodbye or thanks to Martha, or maybe I yell these words mechanically behind me because I've been brought up that way. I'm back in my car within seconds and I'm reversing into the Cooper Road and then I'm driving again, driving with the breathlessness and energy of a runner. Behind me once more, shocked faces, angry gestures, honking horns.

It seems a long way to Tigertail and as I roar along the winding road to the coast I feel the exhaustion and relief of a hunter who nears his quarry. I can see the rocks of the bay long before I can see the ocean. Then the Pacific is suddenly revealed as though it just blinked open one icy eye.

I drive between the clifftop parking lots looking for the tow truck, the blue car with the white bandage, any car at all with Ricky and Jordan inside it. I drive from lot to lot. There are few cars today and mostly they are parked so their drivers can watch the sea without getting out into the wind. I see a couple of pick-ups but no tow truck. In one lot there is a lone ice-cream salesman. I drive right up to him and wind down the window.

'Did you see a tow truck here?' I ask.

He nods.

'Saw an old one pass a while back. Thirty minutes maybe.'

'Which way was it going?'

He can't remember. He changes his mind twice. I thank

him and resume my search. When I have passed the small town and the parking lots have become wild and empty I turn around and check them all again. No Ricky. No Jordan. No tow truck.

Defeated, I park facing the sea. No whales either, but I was already sure of that. I watch the restless water throwing itself against the rocks, flinging spray into the air, sparkling suddenly when the sun emerges from behind clouds, its colour deepening in the shade like a secret.

There is no beauty in the scene before me. The shifting ocean is no more than the massive expenditure of purposeless, fruitless energy. It seems now that my life could be described in the same way. Watching the water's ceaseless battle with the rocks, I am overcome by fatigue. I feel tears sting at my eyes. I realize I wasn't looking for Ricky or Jordan here, I was looking for Jane. It is her absence which now shows me where I must go and exactly what I must do but I am almost drained of energy, the energy for life.

Just as I am leaving, the detonation of a massive wave makes me pause and turn. I glimpse a figure made matchstick by the hugeness of the surroundings. It could be Rougemont. The figure slides behind a rock. I do not wait for its reappearance.

39

By the time I reach Daddy's house the sun is easing itself behind the hillside slowly, the way Daddy eased himself into his favourite chair after a long day. Night is already concentrating the air. The crickets are starting their chorus.

The big barn door swings open with a high-pitched squeak. I wait for my eyes to accustom themselves to the dark then flick the old metal light switch. Avoiding the geologists' lamps I select a pickaxe, a shovel, a bar. I carry them along the winding paths that lead to the sunken garden.

I crouch down at the heart of the garden to examine the rocks I must remove. First Daddy's headstone, which I walk slowly away on its corners. Remember death. Then I begin to work on the large rocks beneath it. They are set in dirt, not concrete, but they were set long ago and the dry earth fits snugly around them. I work at the gaps with my pickaxe. Soon I am wet with sweat. I take off Scott's sweatshirt and dig further until at last the pickaxe propels a hard, metallic finger beneath the largest rock. Gradually, I lever the big, round rocks from the bed where Daddy laid them all those years ago. They offer little resistance to the point of the pick. Behind them is left a small, perfect impression of their time there. When I lift them, they feel smooth and almost uniformly round. Their weight is pleasing. The smaller rocks fit comfortably into my cupped palms. I stack them under a eucalyptus where the long, thin shards of bark lie rotting. The bass kiss of stone on stone pleases me.

I begin to shovel aside the first layer of friable, sandy dirt.

The physical labour feels good. The rhythm of my shovel, its gentle acceptance by the soil, the stretch in my arms as they lift the weight, all this anaesthetizes me against the fear of what I know I must find here.

Beneath the layer of loose earth the dirt is impacted. I stand up and feel the freshness of the breeze cutting through my hot body. I raise the pickaxe high over my head, until my whole body is perfectly balanced, until it feels this heavy tool grew right out of me. As I sway forward I slide my palm down the handle. The point of the axe drops deep into the hard layer of dirt and small stones. I lever it up and the impacted earth is loosened.

I continue until I hit a rock instead of the dirt. The rock does not break but the shriek of metal on stone sounds angry and the sparks that fly frighten me. I shovel out the dirt I have loosened. Occasionally I pause and rest on the shovel but the breeze, cooling rapidly so long after the sun's retreat, soon slaps me into restarting.

I jump into the hole to clear more loose dirt and some jagged, rotten pieces of wood along with it. I have pulled most of the wood free when I realize that the wood is an indication I am about to find what I am looking for. Daddy would have covered the body with something, put it inside some kind of a box. Coffin should be the right word but for such a burial normal semantics do not apply.

Below me there is the sound of an engine and car lights pick their way slowly along the dirt road. I crouch, still and silent, until the car has passed. The tail-lights shine on the dust that follows them, turning it an unnatural red.

I use the pick more gently now and scrape with my hands as well as the shovel. I can see a lot in this pearly light but I use the soft touch of my fingerpads to help me see more. There is already dirt packed under the nails.

After a while there are more pieces of wood and then my shovel taps against something that does not sound like rock or wood or dirt. It had a soft resonance of its own.

I peer into the dark hole and crouch to inspect the mottled object. It looks like old, dirty china and, ridiculously, I want it to be a doll or a small bowl but I know from its particular roundness that it is a skull and the knowledge comes so rapidly that it is more instinct than thought.

I do not touch my find but gouge at the dirt around it, which trickles with a new liquidity between my fingers. Shovel. Dig. Now the digging is arrhythmic, fast, punctuated by my breath and the drum of my heartbeat. Nausea starts in my belly and then spreads to the rest of my body. Small balls of sweat catapult like shooting stars across my flesh. When I have uncovered about half of the skeleton I pause in the dim light to look at it.

The bones are not a dog's bones because there never was a dog. They are those of a tiny child. It lies preserved in small perfection. I know the human skeleton to be a complicated mechanism, but not here. Not in death. It is as simple and straightforward as a line of trees on the horizon.

For a few moments, I pretend this is not my brother. It is an ancient body. The sunken garden was situated over a prehistoric cemetery. I should report my find to the university who will send teams of archaeologists. They will divide the yard into small squares and work methodically in the dust all through the long, hot summer. They will label their finds neatly. Each bone will bear a number. The dead child will be dehumanized. Its suffering, and that of the people close to it, will be so distanced by time and scientific inquiry that I will be able to stand over the tiny skeleton with an archaeologist discussing it in tones leached of emotion.

It is my sobs that wash away the archaeologist. I can feel

their force but I can't hear them. The shovel handle is wet as I remove the rest of the dirt to see the child in its entirety. Then I reach down and gently brush the last, loose covering of earth from the bones with the same care that I would turn back a baby's blanket. I bend down to the carcase, so small that even now I want to believe it is nothing but a bird or a lamb. I blow the dusty soil from it.

A tiny ribcage, slender feet, the hands, curled slightly, the finger joints clogged with dirt. A boy, a small dead baby boy. I look away from the eyeless head, the two tiny teeth in the open mouth.

Wearily I stand up. Dirt stains my clothes like blood. It clings to my legs, it discolours my shoes. Once, the shovel bounced off a stone on to my shin and a viscous line of blood has dried from the wound down my leg. It begins to hurt now. I become aware of the weight of my tired limbs. I try to recreate the comforting university archaeologists with their jeans and clipboards but I cannot, because I know that the child was laid in its grave during my own lifetime by my own father and that it is my own brother. It is Nicky but it might be my Stevie or it might be the Russian baby who died when his fleeing family left him behind.

I stand perfectly still in the darkness and listen to the rustling of small animals and insects in the grass and the whispering leaves and, when I finally notice it, the high scream of the crickets. My neck aches. I arch it back until I can point my chin at the sky. A clear night. A blanket of stars, stretching to infinity. Some are larger and brighter but this does not mean they are nearer. The rules of perspective are dwarfed into meaninglessness by the magnitude of space.

I sit down on the edge of the sunken garden and listen to the approaching car. I hear it turn into the drive and park outside the barn. Nothing surprises me now, nothing frightens me. I wait quietly in the dark. I hear the car door. The front door. The slam of the screen door. Silence. The screen door again. Silence. Finally, footsteps.

I am a butterfly pinned to a card by the fierce beam of Jane's flashlight. It shines first on me and then on the pile of stones and then down into the hole I have dug and it ends on the tiny, birdlike skeleton that is lying there.

Her voice is strange. It is cold.

'Luce,' she says. 'Oh, Luce.' Her use of my name is eloquent. Sadness, disappointment.

I say: 'It's all been inevitable, ever since Daddy died. Everything that's happened has been like those little toy soldiers we used to play with, the sort you stand in a line. You push one and then they all fall down.'

'We never had any toy soldiers,' she says.

'Then maybe someone else did, I forget who.'

The flashlight is on me again. I am shivering. I want Jane to come out from behind her light.

'Okay, Luce,' she says, 'it's time to go.'

I stand up. I walk over to Jane. I am a dirty, shivering person with blood stains.

We pick our way along the narrow paths and when we reach the drive, instead of turning up to the house, Jane steers me down towards the dirt road.

'Where are we going, Jane?' I ask. My tone is conversational. The answer doesn't much interest me.

'Swimming.'

'That's nice.'

'At Joe Zacarro's.'

'I'm kind of dirty to swim in his pool,' I say, but Jane is reassuring. 'The chlorine will take care of that, Luce.'

I am weak now after my efforts in the child's grave and I stumble up the Zacarro drive, leaning heavily on Jane. When

I stagger a little against the foliage one of the plants releases the sickly-sweet odour I know as the smell of melancholy.

'Boy, that stuff's strong,' says Jane.

She pulls me through the side gate and I can see the pool, looking like a black rectangle of polished obsidian.

She sits me down at the edge of the water and shows me something, a small black box.

'Are you okay, Lucy?' she asks kindly.

'Yes. Thank you, Jane.'

'I hope this doesn't hurt too much. It wasn't clear from the literature.'

'I guess it's my turn.'

'It's been your turn a lot of times before but you always came bouching back.'

'Yes, when you pushed me in the canyon all I did was break an arm. And in the swimming-pool Mother jumped right in and saved me.'

'There were other times, too. But after Nicky went, Mother guarded you like a jewel. She hardly let you out of her sight.' Jane sighs and I feel her sadness. 'It hasn't been easy for me, Lucy, none of it. You already know this: I'm a very special person.'

'Oh yes,' I agree. 'You've always been very special to me.'

'Mother and Daddy knew that. They understood. They handled me with care. They worked hard to give me the right kind of encouragement, the right environment where I could flourish. Then it all changed when you came along. They were besotted with you.'

Jane's face curls in disgust. I've never seen her look this way.

'Then there was Nicky. It was too much. When he started sitting up and grabbing things and making sounds which would turn into words one day I knew it was time to stop.

I've never regretted it. I just regret what I found out today. That Daddy betrayed me. He went off and adored some baby in secret and now the baby's grown and has his own baby. I wish I could have dealt with them today.'

'You pretended to be Joni Rimbaldi,' I tell her tonelessly. 'But when you got to Tigertail you must have backed off.'

'Police in the parking lots. No uniforms but you can tell anyway.' She shrugs. 'I'll try some other time.'

I shiver.

'Are you cold, Luce?' she asks, looking right at me now, sounding concerned.

'Just a little.'

'I can help you with that.' She leans over and picks up the box.

'Lindy knew what happened to Nicky,' I whisper.

Jane smiles. 'She wasn't bright. I mean, it was almost too easy to tell her I knew this great hiding place.'

I am shaking now. My teeth are chattering.

'Jane . . . I wish you hadn't hurt Stevie.'

'Oh, but I didn't hurt him. I just helped him to go. He really didn't suffer. He hardly struggled.'

'Did Daddy struggle?'

'No, he sort of knew it had to happen and he sort of accepted it. I warned him that he was spending too much time with those ridiculous old men . . .'

'You mean Joe Zacarro? And Mr Holler?'

'He was talking to them too much. I didn't like to think what he might say. When people get older and closer to senility their tongues get as loose as their bladders. I warned Daddy and he didn't listen but he wasn't surprised when I said it was time for him to go. He didn't struggle. Like you. Maybe he knew how nice it would be. I hope it's nice for you, Lucy.'

427

She touches my neck with the box and pain explodes through my body like a bolt of lightning, a pain that blinds thought, a pain that cancels movement. There are sparks before my eyes, fire falls from my fingertips, my face is cracking from the power of the explosion within. I topple backwards but Jane catches me before my head hits the paving.

'We don't want any bruises.' She lays me flat at the poolside. I can't move. I can't speak. I can see Jane only through a veil of sparks. When the fireworks subside a little I see that the face isn't Jane's face. It belongs to someone else. Thinner, the eyes unnaturally bright, the mouth twisting itself into new lines.

'I've tried to make life better for you. I've tried to look after you. You're not a strong person. Like I said, you're ordinary. I know how hard it's been for you. Now I'm going to release you. I'm going to set you free from all the things which worry you and which give you bad dreams and which make your heart start to bang first thing in the morning before you're even awake enough to think about them. Those deals in New York which you kid yourself are so important. Hurtful, unkind words. Rejections. Disappointments. Wanting things desperately which you couldn't have. That crazy mother of ours, hissing and snarling and yelling. Scott's reproaches. Larry's put-downs. Clingy Russians. All the sadness, Luce. I mean, the losses, and there are so many. From when we're tiny, life just feels like a series of blows and pain and losses, isn't that right? It's thanks to me Stevie was spared all that. I'm sure that deep down you're grateful, Luce. You've been through it all once yourself, you didn't want to suffer again watching him go through it too. All the things you thought mattered so much, I'm going to release you from them now. I think it will feel real good.'

Above us I see the stars. Their timescale is beyond anything I can imagine. My short lifespan is insignificant in their universe, too small even to be measured.

'I'll be real sad when you're gone, the way I was real sad when Daddy went and Stevie and Nicky. But, Luce, I want you to know that, more than any of them, I love you.'

I'd like to thank her but my mouth won't open and anyway, my body is already plunging through the air. She has thrown me so forcefully that I feel my arms and legs scatter like a doll's. I hear an immense splash, foam flies up towards the stars and then I am enveloped by cold water. I sink down, down to the bottom of the pool, water fills my nose and my mouth and my ears and I wait to experience death.

I think of Scott standing with his hands in the pockets of his jeans, shoulders hunched, looking wistfully out to sea at Needle Bay. The sudden appearance of the first toothless grin on Stevie's soft face. Sasha, pouring a whisky and rocking with ridiculous high-pitched giggles as he talks about his colleagues. Aunt Zina twisting her wrist to right and left as blini batter slides over the hot pan. Daddy, rolling himself out from under the tractor, with a look of tranquil concentration, his hands blackened by oil. Jane, crying on the deck at night, her eyes two pinpoints of light. Larry, eating a peanut cookie and pointing apologetically to his paunch. Ricky, pulling Jordan's small body to him when he talked about Daddy. Mother's arms wrapping themselves tenderly around me. I feel a moment of loss, loss so acute it may even be mourning, and then the water is both inside and outside me and consciousness begins to ebb away. Yes, it is sad to leave but my body is submitting now to a pleasurable, almost supernatural, relaxation: life isn't being taken from me, I am giving it willingly, joyfully. Jane is right that death is sweet.

40

I am lying on a couch, wrapped in some kind of a robe, covered in a rough blanket that tickles my legs when I move. I don't move. I don't open my eyes. I listen to the voices. There are a few muttering softly nearby but outside the voices are loud, mostly male, and sometimes they call to each other. A woman seems to be speaking some other language on a crackling radio somewhere.

I open my eyes to admit a slither of light. The colours change constantly like some kind of Christmas display. Red, blue and then white. Once, I don't remember when, Daddy's house was lit this way, in red, blue and then white and it wasn't pretty, it was eerie and unpleasant.

I open my eyes a little more and I see Lindy Zacarro. I wonder for a moment if I'm dead after all but there is a frame around her face, and she is riding a horse that is first red, then blue, then white. So I am still at Joe's and his may be one of the loud voices outside.

'Lucy . . .' says someone, without expression. 'Lucy, you're opening your eyes.'

Adam Holler. I recognize the way he speaks, blanched of tone or passion, but he's invisible. If I moved my head I could probably see him but I don't want to move.

'Thanks, Mr Holler, I'd like to talk to her if she's receptive now,' says someone else. A woman, young, her voice even because she's spent years editing her emotions from it like a poker player. I don't know any poker players but I recognize this voice. I can't recall the name of its owner.

'It's Kirsty.' She moves into my line of vision and leans over me and her brown eyes search mine curiously. So the lights aren't Christmas, they're a police car. It must be standing on the asphalt right outside Joe's living-room.

Kirsty says: 'The paramedics are pretty sure they don't need to take you in to hospital. They're just waiting for a doctor to confirm that.'

I look at her without curiosity.

'Do you know what happened?' she asks.

I blink.

'Do you understand what happened?' she repeats, a little louder this time. She looks tired. Pieces of hair have levered themselves out of place.

I don't much want to speak but Jane brought me up to be polite so I make an enormous effort. This isn't easy. Something's been rearranging my lungs and clawing at the inside of my throat. I make an odd, strangled noise.

'Okay,' she says. 'I realize it's hard for you.'

I try again. I'm trying to tell her that Jane will be here soon but the words sound like a braying donkey. She furrows her brow with incomprehension and then I try once more and this time the strange, cracking noises that come from my throat approximate to words. She looks up and I know she is looking at someone. Adam Holler? Or is there a third, silent person in the room?

'I guess,' she says sadly, 'you don't recall why you're here.'

'Sure,' I say. She waits while I croak slowly: 'It was my turn to die. Jane was helping me.'

She glances again at the silent person.

I explain: 'Nicky, Lindy Zacarro, my Stevie, Daddy . . . of course it had to be my turn.'

'You knew?' says another voice. Reedy, unmistakable.

'Lucy, you knew about your sister all along? And you pretended you didn't?'

'No, Mr Rougemont.' I sort of wish he'd move closer so I can see him. I've never liked looking at him much but right now I want to see him. Obligingly, he moves into view and I feel a surprising rush of affection for the long, rambling mouth and immense nose, for this shadow of a man. I say: 'I finally worked it out, too late. Then I realized that I'd known it all along.'

'I guess I knew it all along too,' he says sadly, 'but we couldn't do a damn thing about it. Except keep watching her until she tried again.'

'Where is Jane?' I feel a sudden rush of concern for her.

Rougemont's voice sounds strained. 'They've taken her now, Lucy.'

I don't like the way he says that. I don't like the finality of it.

'Taken her where? Mr Rougemont, she's a very special person . . .'

His grey eyes study me but he does not reply. There is a voice at the door. Kirsty disappears and Rougemont straightens with difficulty. There is a whispered discussion in some other part of the room. I hear cars backing and turning in the drive. The coloured lights which have been shining through my eyelids disappear suddenly. A couple of shouts. The woman's voice on the radio. More voices, loud, female, excited, heavily accented. My Russian aunts, speaking simultaneously to a police officer and arguing among themselves. With them are Sasha and Scott, sounding reasonable but persistent. Joe Zacarro roars: 'It's my goddamn house for God's sake. It was my goddamn pool! I've been real co-operative with you guys, me 'n' Adam helped you stake out the whole goddamn street, and now you won't even let me into my own porch to get one of my own beers out of my own goddamn fridge. I mean, I'll only take a quick peek at her and say hi, that's all I'll do.' His voice is drowned by a crescendo of aunts.

I smile and close my eyes. I feel as though someone just threw an extra blanket over me.

When I next look around, Adam Holler is standing right by me. He leans as far towards me as his stiff back will allow. He is without dark glasses. He watches me with his colourless eyes.

'Lucy,' he whispers. There is a new urgency in his voice, a pain. 'Will you tell me how it felt?'

'What?'

'Dying. How did it feel to die?'

I whisper back. 'Did I die?'

'Sure. Joe and the police officer brought you back, don't you remember? You were dead, Lucy. The police went right after you into the water but Jane started to run and she was so fast and strong, they had to catch her then restrain her. So it must have taken longer than they thought to get you out. You were probably dead for a minute. How did it feel? Will you tell me?'

I sigh.

His pale skin pinkens a little.

He says: 'Lucy, do you remember Jim Bob?' The boy's name seems to leap out of him, a name thought of but perhaps unspoken for years.

I say: 'Sure I do.' Adam Holler's own goal seems doubly hideous now. A death, a child's death and an unnatural one right in the next house. But Jim Bob's was not a death caused by Jane but by someone who loved him and has suffered every day since.

'Oh, Mr Holler, you want to know what he felt when he died. Right?'

I see small prisms of light at the corner of his eyes and realize that these are colourless tears.

'I can put your mind at rest,' I tell him, with such enthusiasm that I almost sit up. 'You don't have to torture yourself over it any more. Jim Bob didn't suffer, not one bit.'

When I hear him shuffle out there is a voice I don't recognize too close to my ear.

'You did good there, Lucy, real good.'

I struggle to see its owner.

'Hi, sis,' says Ricky Marcello. 'I sneaked in through the kitchen.'

'You're sure good at sneaking,' I tell him petulantly.

'Runs in the family.' He smiles broadly.

'What are you doing here? Have you been helping the police? Working with them?'

Tigertail Bay. The crash of a wave as Rougemont flickers along the clifftop.

'Only today. There was a whole crowd of us hoping to watch whales with her.' His face falls. 'Maybe too many because she backed right off. Before today I thought I was on my own. I thought I was the only one worrying about you.'

Ricky's blue car, sliding down the freeway at nightfall, waiting outside Jane's apartment.

'You didn't even know me.'

'Not really true.'

'You hated me.'

'Not really true either. And . . .' Ricky gives his lopsided grin. Fleetingly, eerily, he looks like Daddy. 'And Dad loved you. So I knew I had to take care of you.'

'You were taking care of me?'

'Listen, you're my goddamn sister.'

The door opens and for a few moments the voices outside get louder.

'I'm going, I'm going,' says Ricky. 'I was just passin' through.'

The door closes again and someone says: 'Jeez, what a bunch. Are they press?'

'Relatives.'

'Well, they sure want to get in here.'

He introduces himself. He says he is a doctor and then asks me the name of the president of the United States.

I hear myself laugh at him, a strange, clear sound like water or a bell. I wonder when I last laughed. With Sasha, maybe, or Scott. I name the president and then tell the doctor: 'I'm thinking coherently. Probably more coherently than usual.'

Back at Aunt Zina's I sleep a lot. I am astonished at my ability to fall asleep as soon as I feel tired, sometimes right after I have woken or even while Aunt Zina is talking to me. The sleep is peaceful as pale light.

'What's the matter with me?' I say incredulously when I wake up again in one of Aunt Zina's armchairs and see her at my side, bent over Pushkin, her mouth moving a little as she memorizes the poetry.

'You are making up for lost sleep. Not the sleep of days or weeks but the sleep of years,' she tells me wisely.

I can drive but mostly Scott chauffeurs me. I know Brigitte is back and I expect him to say one day that he's busy and he can't come but he shows up frequently, his face anxious, watching me.

We visit Ricky in San Strana a couple of times. We sit on the porch drinking beers and trying to catch up on all the missing years. Sometimes we play with the baby. Scott likes Ricky and buys his painting of the view across the valley from Daddy's house.

Looking hard at it, I say: 'Okay. I guess I'm ready to go there now.'

We climb up the steps to the porch and unlock the door and I stand on the threshold sniffing the smell of the place, Daddy's smell, before I walk right in.

It is hot here. Although the faux summer is over the house retains its residue like someone anxious not to lose their suntan.

'What are you going to do about it all?' asks Scott, gesturing around him at the clutter. Nothing has gone. Larry and Jane started the upheaval but everything is still here.

'I'm going to sort it out. I'll clear it. Then I'll sell the house.'

'I thought you seemed a little offended that Jane and Larry were doing it so soon after Eric's death. And I got the distinct impression you didn't want to help.'

'I don't feel that way any more. Now I want to do it myself. I'm coming back to California so I can deal with it.'

He stares at me.

'You're really coming back? You've decided?'

'I'm not running away any more, Scott.'

We have a small ceremony for Nicky. His remains are buried near Stevie's. Joe Zacarro and Adam Holler ask to come and they lean on each other weeping. I understand that they are mourning at the graveside of this scarcely known, long-dead baby and crying for their own children as Scott and I cry for Stevie. Everyone has someone to cry for. Only Mother cries for Nicky. We stand looking down at his casket, our arms around one another, locked together in our grief.

'Does she understand, do you think?' Sasha asks me quietly as we walk back through the cemetery together.

'She understands too well and feels too much,' I say.

We drive Mother back to Redbush. When we have delivered her to her nurse, Sasha and I hover uncertainly in the parking lot. Despite the rain, the sprinklers are still switched on across the grounds. Without the sun they do not sparkle.

'Well?' he says. 'Have you changed your mind?'

'No, Sash.'

Jane is incarcerated at Redbush too. Larry negotiated to have her bailed here to the secure wing.

'The reunion cannot be a pleasant one, Larry has warned us of that,' says Sasha. Larry has looked old and tired since Jane's arrest and now he has announced his retirement.

'I must go in, she's all alone,' I insist.

'Scott has refused to visit her and he is right. She killed his son, she is not entitled to his compassion.'

'No one could forgive her for that,' I say carefully, feeling the rain dampen my hair, my eyelashes. 'But you know, Daddy and Mother never should have covered up the first death. By protecting her, they exposed the rest of us to risk.'

'If they were wrong, they have paid dearly for their mistake, your mother with her sanity and your father with his life.'

I turn towards the secure wing.

'I have to go,' I say. 'Jane needs me.'

Sasha lights a cigarette before he follows me. 'Lucia, must we really regard her needs as paramount?'

'She loved me and looked after me for years and years. Should I just forget that now?'

'Loved you and looked after you.' He snorts. 'She presented herself as your protector when she was actually your controller and everyone but you was aware of this. She constantly diagnosed bogus health complaints which enabled her to regulate your life, she isolated you from your friends, she attempted to kill you on a number of occasions while appearing to save you, and she created a version of your past, a series of fictions about your childhood, which disguised her own destructive role.'

He draws fiercely on his cigarette.

'But Sash, we all create fictions about our past for our own ends and a couple of days ago you were recommending that to me,' I remind him. 'After all, you've created a Russian past for yourself which involves red neckerchiefs and singing Young Pioneer songs around the campfire.'

'We structure our own past with narrative. We have no right to structure other people's.'

He waves his cigarette at me.

'Since you are determined to defend Jane, let us visit her. But we can expect little thanks for our trouble.'

Despite everyone's warnings, I imagine myself talking over recent events with Jane. I even believe she might attempt to offer some kind of explanation. I am convinced that at the very least she will be pleased to see me.

I am told that I may only speak to her through a grille. When it opens I peer anxiously through it like a visitor at the zoo searching for some particularly well-camouflaged reptile. Finally I locate her across the room. She sits, her body still, her face turned away, her hair like a curtain between us.

I call her name gently and she does not respond. I say: 'It's Lucy. Jane, it's Lucy.'

I know that this will make her turn and smile, that she will come right over to me when she hears my name and ask me how I am. My heart beats faster. But she does not look up or respond.

Sasha and I drive home in silence. When we are back in the kitchen and Aunt Zina is crashing pans around us, I ask: 'Sash, what did you mean when you said that everyone knew Jane tried to control me?'

'Exactly that. For example, your childhood visits to this apartment.'

Aunt Zina pauses. 'She visited us seldom and when she did so, she sulked jealously.'

'It was clear to Grandma, Mother and me that she disliked your forming any relationship over which she could not exercise direct influence,' says Sasha. 'I imagine that she usually tried to dissuade you from visiting? And often succeeded.'

When Mrs Joseph came to see me she told me that, after the crash in the valley, Robert had called me many times. She herself had both called and written. Jane had intercepted each time, informing the Josephs I didn't want to speak to them again.

'If you'd had the confidence to pick up the phone yourself,' Mrs Joseph said, 'she never could have controlled things so effectively.'

'But unconsciously, Lucia,' says Sasha, 'you knew about her. You escaped from her to New York into a manageable world of figures and when you returned you chose to stay with us. I believe you knew it all.'

Scott takes me to the airport.

He says: 'Am I allowed to ask exactly when you're coming back?'

'I just have to say goodbye to Jim and pack my apartment. I'll be home in a week.'

He smiles and picks me up as though I'm as small and weightless as a toy and then swings me around.

'Everything's lighter now,' he tells me.

I am walking away from him as he yells: 'Lucy, don't take three years about it this time. Or we'll come and get you. Me and your brother.'

As the plane nears New York I see Manhattan glittering in the distance. The cab driver informs me that the weather just changed. That heatwave they had in the west has worked its way right across the continent, he tells me, and arrived, weakened by travel, in New York city.

439

'It's great, it's summer!' he says.

'It's spring,' I remind him.

My key in the lock of the apartment, my bag over my shoulder, a stack of mail from the lobby under my arm. The lock feels surprised, a little stiffer than usual, but the door swings open easily enough. It's been waiting for me a long time.

Everything's exactly as I left it. A few clothes on the bed which I thought of taking and then didn't while Jim Finnigan sat in the living-room weeping and talking to me. The phone a little out of place: I used it to call Sasha that night, to hear Daddy's message. Daddy's rocks, handled by Jim, rearranged.

I sit down and enjoy the silence and stillness of my own place. Nothing moves. One hour slips into another and all four figures on the digital clock change simultaneously and silently to four different figures. Then the apartment is still again. I can hear the noise of the street outside, the airplanes overhead, distant music from my neighbours, but in here there is no noise unless I make it, no movement unless I create it.

Eventually I stretch and fetch the mail I carried up from the lobby. I start to sort through it. Junk in one pile, reading in another, bills in another. One letter arrests me. Handwritten envelope. Familiar writing, small, intelligent, tidy. My hand starts to shake. I fight for breath. Tears sting at my eyes.

I sit down and stare at the letter that was mailed to me in some other era and has waited for me to return from my long, long journey. I stare at it, bracing myself for the new reality it might contain. I prepare for another shift in my knowledge, after so many, and just when I thought I was home.

Slowly, reluctantly, I tear open the envelope. I unfold the letter.

My dear Lucy, I've tried calling, now I'm writing because it's clear to me that I won't be around so very much longer. I don't want to go, Lucy. I don't want to leave you. But when I do, please don't be too sad. Don't be too angry. Don't ask why unless you're ready for what you might find. Don't come back to California. Don't have any more children here, have them in some other part of the world, but for God's sake, have them, you were a good mother and don't let anyone tell you otherwise. Don't think too badly of your father, he loves you dearly. And don't you dare forget me. As long as you remember me, I'm still there. Daddy.